7 P's

II

A.G.R

A Story for Mates

II

Published by ZANI

For information contact:

info@zani.co.uk

Front Cover design by Neville Godwin

https://www.ngdagency.com/

Chapter One

Other Blokes' Efforts

June 2004 Knightsbridge London

The early morning silence of the plush London Street was broken as a black taxi cab slipped between the lines of parked cars and scented blossom trees before slowing when approaching its destination. To the vehicle's front, the road parted into a fork, creating a half-moon crescent which opened up onto an area where a grassed garden and seats for the local residents to sit made pretty use of the space. The vehicle, almost at a crawl, skirted the railing-fringed garden, finally coming to a halt close to its middle at the communal area's entrance. As its diesel engine noisily ticked over its passenger exited from the rear door, took his wallet from his inside jacket pocket and passed some money back through the window to pay the fare.

Smartly dressed in a dickey-bow and full evening wear, the gentleman, having collected his change, began to climb the several steps that led to one of the shiny black doors that lined the crescent. While searching for his keys he turned to take in the blossoms' aroma and admire the peace and tranquillity that was slowly returning as the taxi disappeared into the distance. Opening the door, he reached inside and switched on the light, which brought some momentary illumination to a portion of the street before he entered and the door shut solidly behind him, the last word being had by the large brass lion's head knocker that sounded once as the door closed.

Inside the house the entrance hall was large, with high ceilings ornately decorated with fine coving and a central rose encircling a droplet chandelier. The walls were panelled in beaded wood, and a dark-stained, highly polished matching staircase rose in the far left corner from a tiled, again highly polished floor of large black and white squares. The man was tired and ready for his bed but toyed in his mind between having a night-cap or a hot drink before retiring. The nightcap, as it so often did, won the vote, compelling him to cross the floor and climb the stairs where his study – and in it his drinks cabinet – were situated on the first floor. Before starting his assent he removed his jacket and casually dropped it onto the mule post at the base of the hand-rail, which he then clung to firmly to aid his weary climb. At the top of the stairs he pulled at his bow tie, allowing it to fall loosely around his neck before undoing his top shirt button and giving his throat a relieving finger massage. Next to be discarded were his black shiny shoes, which he removed, using his other foot as leverage on the back of the heel, something he never usually did without untying the laces, but the heavy evening of food and drink was catching up, throwing his normal tidier undressing routine out of the window. The man was a retired Colonel named De' William, and that evening he had attended the annual regimental dinner, which was usually an excuse to pull up a sandbag, swing a lamp and compete with his old comrades as to who could tell the tallest war story. As the drinks would get larger so would the stories, and the night inevitably ended with the traditional toasts to the regiment and the Queen, which all contributed to the reason why he could not be bothered to bend down and untie his laces.

Entering his study, he reached back to the wall to switch on the light but nothing happened. He looked up at the shade in the middle of the ceiling and operated the switch two to three more times consecutively, but still there was nothing. Presuming the bulb had gone, he made his way across the study, guided by the light from the landing to switch on the lamp that stood next to his rolltop bureau. He paused before doing so, suddenly realising that the landing wasn't the only light he was being guided by, his computer screen was on. Thinking back to when he last used it earlier in the day he was convinced that he could remember shutting it down, but then came a second mystery as his nose was grabbed by the sweet smell of cigar smoke. Slowly he removed his hand from the lamp switch, leaving the room in semi-darkness and began to sniff the air in an attempt to follow the tobacco trail. His search took him to his high-backed leather chair in the centre of the room and then down to the small table at its side. An ashtray sat on the table, containing the offending cigar butt and to the side, a brandy glass with the remnants of the drink in its base. It didn't take much working out for the Colonel to realise that he'd had an uninvited guest who had obviously made himself at home whilst hacking his computer. The question was, had that person left or was he/she or they still in the house. He turned back to his desk and opened the top drawer of a set of three that ran down the right side in search of his weapon. It wasn't there, which caused him to hasten his rummaging through some papers and other contents, before questioning where he had left it and opening the other two drawers beneath. It wasn't in those either. Expanding his search, he pushed back the rolltop on his bureau, but was saved the further trouble by his visitor's voice.

"You won't find it, Colonel."

Behind him, from a darkened corner of the room, a man made his presence known in a tone the Colonel seemed to recognise. Slowly he turned in the half light and attempted to make out his visitor's shadow hidden features. Quickly he put together the clues as to the intruder's identity. The cigar in the ashtray, the brandy glass on the table and, who did he know who would have the impudence and the audacity to break in to his house? The answer was simple, it was Eli.

"Sergeant Major Moon, I hope that isn't my finest reserve brandy that you have been helping yourself to."

The Colonel's response was calm in a stiff upper lip manner but he knew he was in trouble because Eli didn't make social calls.

"Walk backwards and switch on the lamp," instructed Eli, ignoring the Colonel's attempt to lighten the situation. "Any sudden movements and I'll shoot you with your own relic of a weapon. I presume it works, seeing as how you were looking for it in the drawer."

The Colonel did as he was instructed, throwing light

on the confrontation and bringing the two men face to face. Eli looked at the odd-shaped weapon in his hand that he had earlier retrieved from the top drawer of the desk and then around the room at the numerous curious items, ranging from swords and mounted animal heads to paintings of the Battle of Waterloo. A full set of armour stood in the corner and above it a shield, bearing the Colonel's own family coat of arms.

"You do like your memorabilia, De' William. How old is this, then?"

Eli glanced back at the weapon in his hand with a disapproving look.

"It's a Luger, a World War Two German officer's pistol, and yes it works."

"Well if you don't mind," said Eli, swapping the vintage piece from his right hand to his left and placing it in his overcoat pocket while removing his own weapon from the right, "I'll just stick with my trusty Browning." He weighed up his weapon as though admiring its balance. "The old British Army issue 9mm was always good enough for me."

"What do you want Moon, is there something we should be talking about?"

In an innocent sounding voice, the Colonel declared his ignorance as to the reason for his visitor's presence.

"I think you've talked enough, don't you?"

Eli looked across at the computer on the desk, letting him know that he was referring to its contents.

"So you've been reading my memoirs," he deduced. "How did you get in?"

"You should change your password more often Colonel; half of Hereford's been pissing themselves at your e-mails for years."

The Colonel looked back at the computer, wondering if Eli was bluffing.

"Which extract did you not agree with, Sgt Major? Let me know and I will see about amending it. Writing is a new thing to me so I would welcome any constructive criticism."

The Colonel, in his own smug manner, was fishing as to the extent of Eli's knowledge.

"If you're finding the road to becoming an author a

bit bumpy then maybe you should take up a different hobby to fill your retirement other than writing books. Especially tell-all books that put others in danger."

"Tell-all books," repeated De' William, dismissively.

Eli shook his head at his blatant disregard for the rules when working in secrecy. Basically, you keep your mouth shut.

"You took the Queen's Shilling and signed the Secrets Act just like the rest of us. What gives you the right to go spilling your guts and naming names? You must know that by writing this book you are putting good men at risk?"

"What about you, Moon?" rebutted the Colonel, as though Eli was throwing stones in a glass house. "It's common knowledge that you and your team have turned rogue to line your own pockets."

"Is that what this is all about, money? Perhaps you should downsize from this Knightsbridge address if you're getting a bit skint. My lads and I are guilty of securing our future with the odd tickle but we did it through taking the risks ourselves, not putting other men in danger by grassing them up. With the knowledge you have, you could have written a fictional book and kept things tight. But you're too scared that your writing ability may not be up to the creation of a good novel so you're going to reveal names and secrets to give your work the edge it needs to get published and make a few quid."

The Colonel gave a slight laugh, dismissing Eli's criticisms as over the top.

"You talk about what I'm doing as being like some sort of double agent during the Cold War. I'm no Burgess or McLean. Besides, what we did is over, it's history, nobody is carrying any grudges."

Eli shook his head again in disbelief at the Colonel's naive and ridiculous statement.

"What planet are you on, De' William? That just goes to show what a stupid old bastard you really are. We spent years infiltrating organisations and eliminating their key members, men who had friends and family. People don't forget things just because a few years have gone by and a peace agreement has been signed.

People hold grudges. It's called revenge, a vendetta, an eye for an eye and if you go printing names we will all be looking over our shoulders."

Eli began to pace a few steps either side of his position. He struggled in his mind to understand De' William's thinking. He had actually hoped that when he confronted him that he may see sense, and the error of his ways, but he was being his usual selfish disregarding self, showing no signs of changing anything. This was a man who had held a position of trust, a man that others should be able to depend on. For him to be dredging up the past just to make a few quid was a disgrace, and in Eli's mind, a massive betrayal.

"The problem with you, Colonel, is that you were never a trigger man. You never had to kill anybody so you're not one of the men who will have to watch his back. The stupidest thing, and the hardest to contemplate, is that you actually believe that the troubles in Northern Ireland are a thing of the past that can be spoken of without reprisal."

The pair went back a long way but they had

never seen eye to eye. Obviously while Eli was in the ranks and De' William had been a serving officer, opinions were never openly voiced. Luckily, though, De' William had never held the position of Colonel of the Regiment, which angered him greatly, being the one job he coveted the most. Instead he was skirted around and given a job behind a desk as staff in London. Unfortunately, it was that very appointment that had given him access to the privileged information that now made up the contents of his memoirs and was soon to be readily available at any good bookshop on the high street.

De' William never let go his longing for the top job; in fact, whenever the Regiment was put into action he would try in some unscrupulous way to put himself in charge. Eli never forgot that at the outbreak of the Falklands War, De' William had come up with the brilliant idea of sending B, Squadron into Argentina on a suicide mission. He thought it was a great idea to hit the jets delivering the exercette missiles whilst they were on the ground and it would have been if they knew which airfield to attack but they didn't because the Argentinians would split the returning planes to different landing sites. There were two reasons for this. One, because of security and to stop just that type of attack from happening and two, they didn't want their own pilots realising just how many of their planes weren't returning. It would have been bad for moral to know that their losses were so great when not a single RAF Harrier had been lost. The clue though to why De' Williams plan wasn't very popular is in the name, suicide mission, and it was exactly that being that there was no extraction plan and was refused to be undertaken by the commander of B, Squadron for just that reason. De' William, who didn't like his subordinate's disagreeing with him promptly had him sacked and in doing so ruined a good man's career and name but the commander was only protecting his men from an idiotic idea of a man sat behind a desk in London and, if the truth be known, there lay the problem with the whole Falklands Conflict. It was being run from Northwood by bigoted idiots and Politicians and not by the men on the ground. This was another idea that was strongly rumoured to be De' Williams so that he could have a hand in the decision making. The whole thing would have been over in weeks if it had been left up to the soldiers on the ground. Eli knew that if his Squadron had of been available it would have been them that De' William would have tried to send to their death. Whilst it would have been De' William's way of gaining more notoriety for the Regiment, he would have also been trying to eliminate his worst critics, namely the seasoned and outspoken veterans of the Regiment that D Squadron contained. Fortunately though Eli and his pals along with N Company Royal Marines and some S.B.S lads were already at sea on board H.M.S Antrim, heading for the island of South Georgia to take care of the one hundred or so Argentinian Marines that had landed there two weeks before their main army landed at Port Stanley. When De' William was finally forced to take early retirement, the contents of the black cloud he left under were never revealed and remained a mystery, but perhaps his memoirs would shed light on the answer?

"Its chiefs and Indians, Moon," continued De' William. "Somebody has to give the orders and somebody has to take them. It was you who had the problem, you who never liked following orders."

"Not the right orders, Colonel. No soldier has a problem following a right order. It's the ones given by some jumped-up, silver spooned Sandhurst prick still pissed up on last night's port and brandy from the officers' mess that we don't like to follow. If you had done my job you would realise what it's like to infiltrate and get up close to someone. To watch them everyday, learning their every move. Sometimes even getting to like them whilst all the while knowing full well that in the end you would probably have to kill them."

"That was the job, Moon."

"Correct Colonel, that 'was' the job, but not any-more. So it's Mr Moon to you."

Eli raised his weapon, fully intending to bring the meeting to an end. It sickened him being in De' William's presence and even more talking to him when it was obvious that he hadn't – and wasn't willing to be – changed.

"You're not out yet, Sgt Major. Even though I am retired you will still be court marshalled if you kill me."

"Well then, Colonel," Eli smiled; "I better make sure that I don't get caught." He raised his weapon to waist height as De' William, realising that the end was nigh, swallowed the spit in his mouth.

"Wait, I'll do you a deal."

The Colonel raised his hands, showing Eli his palms in an attempt to buy some time.

"You have nothing to deal with. Nothing that I want or need."

"I have the original manuscript. It's in safe keeping at my solicitor's office. If you kill me you won't be able to stop it from being published. In fact, me being murdered will create an even bigger selling point, it will fly off the shelves. But if you don't, then I will rewrite it and take out all the names. Better still, I won't publish at all. I will write a novel like you suggested."

De' William was negotiating for his life, literally.

"You're lying," replied Eli, in a knowing tone.

"No, I swear I will write a novel. A fictional rendition of my service that will harm nobody."

"You misunderstand me, Colonel. I mean you're lying about having a copy of the manuscript with your solicitor."

"You are bound to think that, Moon, but you can't be sure. You dare not take the chance on my work being published after my death."

The Colonel almost smiled, believing he had played his trump card, but he didn't expect Eli's answer.

"Yes I can, you see we've got your solicitor bent over." A smile formed on Eli's face as the one on the Colonel's fell away. "He's ex- military, but you already know that, that's why you engaged him, old school tie and all that bollocks. He was a Captain in the Horse Guards, but fortunately for us, he's not your usual Hooray Henry. When we explained to him the contents of the book that you were writing, the pledge he took in the army meant a bit more to him than it obviously does to you. It was either that or the twenty grand in the envelope we gave him, or maybe even the gun my man, Ringer, held to his head, who knows. Anyway, one of them convinced him to play ball and he's our man now. He rang us three days ago and told us that you had made an appointment at his office for ten o'clock Monday morning, reference the copyright of a book. More to the point, he's never mentioned having any other manuscripts of yours secured for safe keeping."

As Eli talked, the Colonel knew his fate was sealed but he wasn't going quietly. Something with Eli's story didn't sit quite right.

"So why not just kill me months ago and stop me writing the book in the first place? Why go to all this trouble now?"

The Colonel was searching for motives, and more time.

"Because until you wrote it we didn't know if you deserved killing. I couldn't bump you off just because I don't like you, although the thought crossed my mind frequently in the past. We knew you would be at the annual regimental dinner this evening, so your guaranteed absence provided us with the perfect opportunity to get in and hack your computer before confronting you with the evidence."

The Colonel wasn't convinced. He looked across at his desk to where his computer sat. The screen had been angled towards the wall, which was why he hadn't noticed its light straight away when he entered the room. He took a couple of steps towards it but was quickly stopped by Eli, who followed his movement with his weapon. The colonel was intrigued, believing that Eli's intervention had confirmed his doubts.

"You didn't hack into my computer, did you, Moon?" The Colonel's deduction was accompanied by a smug grin, believing that he had uncovered Eli's little ruse. "You were hoping that if I thought you had that I would come out with my password, believing you already had it." De William began to laugh. It wasn't going to help his situation but what did he have to lose. "I see now what you are really after, Moon. You're not just happy keeping the book from the public, you want to know its contents as well. That's why you got to my solicitor, and why you waited until tonight to come here. It wasn't just because you knew I would be out. You were hoping that the manuscript would be all printed out nice and neat in black and white, ready to go to the solicitors in the morning. Then you wouldn't need my password. Well, I'm sorry to disappoint you, Moon, but you really must keep up with the times. It's all done on disc now. I don't have to download it until five minutes before I go out of the door." Again the Colonel laughed, enjoying the moment that would probably be his last. "So it looks like my memoirs will die with me. It's a pity, all that information going to waste, but it would have been too much of an education for you, Moon. Sons of South London barrow boys should stay in their place anyway, scuttling around the markets and tipping your hat at the gentry that buy your peddled wares." The colonel shook his head in a dismissive manner, the same manner that had caused him to be so disliked within the Regiment, the same manner that was about to get him killed. "Do you know, Moon, I actually felt sorry for you when your wife and son were killed, but the truth is that they're better off dead. If they were alive today they would only be disappointed to see what you have become. You're just a rank and file cannon fodder soldier, with ideas above his station and no respect for your betters."

Eli knew the insults were the final rants of a desperate man, but the mention of his wife and son was a bit close to the bone and almost had his trigger finger twitching prematurely. He calmed himself with pleasant thoughts of the Colonel's impending demise while playing him at his own game.

"Your right, Colonel, I did need your password – but only to verify that I was doing the right thing before killing you. Not any more though, you've already confirmed that for me."

De' William, stared at Eli in a momentary silence while going over in his mind the words he had recently spoken, searching for his slip-up.

"When?" he asked, coming up blank.

"When you said that if I let you live you would change the names in your book. In other words the names are in there, which makes you a grassing selfish bastard and a dead man. As for the contents of your computer, it may take a while but we will get in. We've got this whizz-kid hacker in the city who can get into anything given a little time and money."

"He will never guess my password," answered the Colonel, in a last show of defiance.

"Yes he will, because we'll give him all the information we have on you. You're smart, so the password won't be something obvious like a birthday or the name of a childhood pet, but that could work for us. It will save us a lot of time not having to go through all the trivial crap in your life. And you've just told me that it 'is' a password, not a pass key, which will save us even more time. You really should learn to keep your north and south shut, Colonel, which ironically is what brought me here in the first place. But don't worry about that because I'm going to help you with that problem in a moment. In the end all that matters is that your book won't be published and eventually our man will get your password and the information contained within will be a bonus for us. But if he doesn't, if you are a bit smarter than I think, then we will simply destroy your computer and no one – including me – will read it. The main thing is that your rebellious ranting and grassing jottings will never do any harm to nobody. Not that all this will matter to you, because by that time you'll be worm food."

With no further talk, the Colonel was shunted backwards as a single round from Eli's weapon ripped into his chest and exited through his back, accompanied by a large amount of his lungs and other parts of his torso. The conversation was over, as, almost, was the Colonel's life. Eli approached, collecting a cushion from the leather chair as he did. Watching as the final movements of his foe's twitching body slowly became less violent, he wondered why he had ever let this less than adequate nemesis live so long.

"I should have done for you years ago, you mug," he muttered, voicing his regrets, knowing that this situation and many other problems that the Colonel had caused in the past could have been easily avoided by a more than overdue double tap to the head.

He moved closer to finish the job, almost close enough to give him a kiss goodbye, but it was just Eli's way of giving his work the personal touch, which it was going to get after the Colonel's mentioning of his family.

"Wanker," Eli whispered, just loud enough for it to be the last word that the Colonel, would ever hear then before the final glint fell from his eyes, Eli moved the muzzle of his weapon to his temple and placed the cushion over his face. The second shot was released, causing an immediate scatter of brains and other matter to be propelled towards the study door from beneath the cushion shield. Eli paused in his crouched position while placing two fingers on his victim's neck. Sure of his work after finding no pulse, he stood up and looked down on his kill as a halo of blood began to form around the head. Standing there in a momentary silence of contemplation, he searched his conscience for any regrets, but found none. In fact, he felt nothing at all. His thoughts were of nothing, because De' William meant nothing, not to him anyway. Any respect he may have ever felt in the past were only for his rank and uniform, but never for the man. Actions justified, and head back in check, he returned to business.

"Be lucky," he said in a sarcastic tone whilst raising his head to look at a picture on the wall above the body. The snapshot elaborately surrounded in a gilt frame showed the Colonel receiving his O.B.E from the Queen, a number of years earlier. "Other Blokes' Efforts," he added, giving his interpretation of the initials. He moved back from the body to open one of the drawers in the bureau in which he replaced the Colonel's gun before swapping his own weapon for his mobile. At the same time he picked up the brandy glass from the small table and finished off what remained of the smooth drink.

"Come in." were his only words on the phone before replacing it back in his pocket and making his way out of the room and down the stairs. He collected the Colonel's jacket from the mule post and carried it with him as he crossed the hall to open the front door. A wallet was the only contents of the jacket pockets, but it was exactly what he was looking for. As he searched through it he was joined by three other men who entered the house: Errol, Ringer, and Oneway.

"Where is he?" asked Errol, as Ringer closed the door behind them.

"First floor in the study," replied Eli, whilst sifting through the wallet on the off chance of finding some information.

"Did we get what we were after?" Oneway asked.

"No, the old bastard sussed me out, and there's nothing in here of any help either." Eli replaced the wallet in the jacket pocket and tossed the garment into the corner. "It changed nothing, though," he continued; "he admitted naming names so he got what he deserved." The other three knew exactly what he meant by that statement. "Now we need to move fast, and get everything out of here before daylight. Where did you leave the van?"

"Down the road, about five hundred yards away?" replied Errol.

"Good, we'll leave it until the last minute before we bring it to the front of the house. In the meantime we need to get everything by the door ready to load. Errol, you and Ringer take the study, that's all the computer equipment and any paperwork. There's a bin under the desk that's half full, bring that along with the ashtray and brandy glass from the little table, they've got my DNA on them. I also fired two shots; make sure you recover the spent rounds and empty cases. One of the cases will be by his body and the other will have landed near the computer in the corner. The rounds will be found in the back of the study door and in the midst of the blood spatter on the wall. Me and Oneway will check the rest of the house. Its three forty-five now and sun's up at five thirty, so we've got an hour and a half, tops."

Eli's men looked at him, understanding what was to be done.

"What should I do with this?" Ringer, the larger, muscular member of Eli's quartet held up a plastic bag containing a dead rodent.

"Is that the Jasper, the long tail I ordered?" Ringer nodded. "Good, make sure you stick it in the grass's mouth before we leave. Well come on then, chop fucking chop, we haven't got all night."

The team spent the next hour going through the house with a fine toothcomb, looking for anything and everything pertaining to the Colonel's memoirs and anything that might give them a clue to his password. When they left they simply brought the van to the front, slipped on some facial disguises and loaded it up before calmly driving away. Eli made no attempt to hide the killing; in fact it was just the opposite. The Colonel's body lay exactly where it fell to let everybody know he had been executed, which is precisely what the second shot through the temple represented, an execution, and the 'rat' in his mouth, the reason.

It was common knowledge that De' William, was writing a book so the absence of his computer and notes left the authorities investigating in no doubt as to the motive for his killing. For the next few weeks the papers were full of conspiracy theories surrounding his death. The tabloids went to town on his military career pushing the headline, *Slaying of a hero*, causing an out-raged demand for answers from an ill-informed public. When the theories started to get a little bit to close to the truth the Home Office were forced to release a few secrets of their own concerning the black cloud the Colonel retired under, to soil the whiter-than-white portrayal the papers were publishing. Once De' Williams' reputation had been tarnished enough for the public to lose interest, so did the tabloids and the whole thing was brushed under the carpet. To the people in the know, Eli was the prime suspect in the Colonel's demise, but when the time was right to question him he wasn't arrested, merely summoned to headquarters at Hereford to answer questions.

Chapter Two

Avon Calling

11th AUGUST 2004. STERLING LINES, HEREFORD.

"Don't take us for fools, Sgt Major Moon; we know you were behind the Colonel's death."

The man doing the accusing was a member of MI5, called Fletcher. Two other men accompanied him and they had positioned themselves strategically on each shoulder of their boss, staring at Eli in an attempt to make him uncomfortable whilst being questioned. The last man in the room was Moon's present commanding officer, Colonel Mike Roberts. He was there more in the capacity of mediator to make sure that Eli was treated fairly, but his presence would have probably been more justified protecting the MI5 men from their intended prey.

"I don't know what you mean. Sir," denied Eli, starting his defence. "It's no secret that Colonel De' William and I didn't see eye to eye, but I had no more reason than any other man in the Regiment to want him dead, in fact everybody that met him wished him harm. He was a proper Billy Hunt?"

Eli gave his reply in a text book manner, knowing that although the interview (to his knowledge) was not being taped, anything incriminating he did say 'would' be used against him. Fletcher, paused, not knowing the meaning of the final name, but not wanting to admit that he didn't.

"Come on Moon, admit it. You wanted the Colonel dead because the contents of the book he was writing implicated you and other members of your troop in certain undercover operations."

Eli looked shocked, like you could knock him out with a feather.

"I didn't think you could be implicated in anything

for following orders, but if the Colonel was writing a book, that's the first I've heard of it." His answer was given with as straight a face as he could muster.

"You know he was writing a book," replied Fletcher. "There's been talk of nothing else in the papers lately, other than the secrets he was going to reveal."

"Well, there you go," Eli responded, continuing his sarcastic tone. "I make a point never to read the papers. I prefer the information on which I base the decisions I make in my life to come from a more reliable source, i.e., me. Surely, though, it's illegal to write a book revealing secret information? Whatever the Colonel was going to say can't be common knowledge, otherwise nobody would buy the book. I'm surprised you and the 'Thomson Twins' stood behind you didn't do something about that. Perhaps if you had, then De' William would have behaved himself and nobody would have had any reason to kill him. With that in mind, in a way, I suppose you could say that it's your fault that he's dead." Eli gave the three men a smile and a wink before pulling a cigar from his pocket. "Do you mind, Sir?" he asked, seeking Colonel Roberts' permission.

"Carry on Sgt Major. In fact, I think I will join you."

"Would you care for one of these?" Eli offered, pulling out another cigar.

"No thank you Sgt Major, I'll stick to the cigarettes."

Colonel Roberts opened a wooden cigarette case at the edge of his desk and placed one in his mouth. Fletcher shook his head and let go a sigh, put out by the pair's lackadaisical attitude to his proceedings.

"Colonel," he announced, demanding attention. "We are conducting an investigation into a murder of a high-ranking retired officer. Not drinking Gin Slings at the Raffles Country Club in Singapore."

The Colonel, taking his cigarette from his mouth, turned his head to the MI5 man, not appreciating his tone.

"Mr Fletcher, you are in my office, on my bloody Army camp. If you want this done officially then arrest Sgt Major Moon and take him to the police station. If not, respect where you are and to whom you are talking to."

The CO was the law on the camp, not to mention Hereford itself. Fletcher didn't like his bollocking but it was much to the delight of Eli, who gripped the smoking cigar in his teeth and gave him a broad grin.

"So tell me, Mr Fletcher," Eli continued, "why your mob, who are supposed to take care of internal security and enforce the Official Secrets Act, didn't put a stop to De' Williams whistle-blowing antics."

"Because until the book was printed he hadn't broken the law, so we had no right to do anything about it."

"So you're telling me that 'after' he had published his book, you would have done something about it."

"Yes."

"What?"

"We would have got a gagging order from the courts and recalled the book."

"Yeah, right," Eli huffed in disbelief. "After two million people had read it, and the papers had turned it in to a ten-part series, publishing extracts every Sunday. Meanwhile, i and my team have got the families and accomplices of every man we were ever ordered to kill converging on our homes to put a bullet in our heads." Eli puffed on his cigar furiously. He hated talking to the public-school types that knew nothing of the real world, but always seemed to land the jobs giving orders to men that did. "What really takes the biscuit," he continued, "is that De' William banned everybody in the Regiment from writing a book, and then wrote one himself." Fletcher gave no immediate answer, perhaps through lack of intelligence, or knowledge, so Eli decided to twist the conversation a little. "So when do the rest of the men arrive?" he asked. "Or are they being interviewed on a different day?"

"The rest of what men?" asked Fletcher, puzzled by his question, and showing his youth.

"The rest of the Regiment of course. The other nine hundred and sixty members, which had as much to lose as me if the Colonel had published this book you're going on about."

Fletcher, with a smug dismissive smirk, gave a damning reply.

"You're the only person that we will be interviewing in

connection with the Colonel's death, Sgt Major Moon. We don't believe we need to look any further. In our opinion, it would be a waste of time, money and resources."

"That's nice," replied Eli, trying his best to sound hurt. "Talk about being innocent until proved guilty. You'll be getting Albert Pierrepoint in next, to weigh me for the drop."

Fletcher's blank stare made it obvious that he had never heard of the man, or his significance to what Eli, had said. The Colonel leant forward from his chair to deliver a short history lesson.

"Albert Pierrepoint was a hangman from Bradford. He was that good at his job that after the war they flew him in to Nuremberg to hang the Nazi war criminals ten at a time."

"Correct, Sir," confirmed Eli, with his finger pointing at his CO. "Don't they teach you kids anything these days?" he added, looking at the MI5 men. His tone didn't go down well.

"Unfortunately, they no longer allow hanging," replied Fletcher, with an air of disappointment. "But come on Sgt Major, we know it was you, 'it's always you.' We've got you down for several unsolved crimes over the last ten years including the disappearance of one of our top IRA informants, four years ago."

Eli puffed on his cigar whilst reflecting on a brief memory of Maguire's brains skidding across the Heathrow warehouse floor.

"An IRA, tout you say? I'm afraid I can't help you with that one, Mr Fletcher," he replied in complete denial. "But if you've got any evidence to link me with the Colonel's death, then I'll hold my hands up and you can slap the cuffs on. If not, then all I can say is that who ever did kill him did us all a favour, and I'd like to shake his hand. But it wasn't me, or any of my men, and I can prove that we were elsewhere at the time."

"Oh yes Sgt Major, and what time was that?" asked Fletcher, trying to catch him out.

"Anytime you want," he answered, with a cheeky wink and his formidable smile.

"I suppose it will be a case of the four of you being at one of your houses watching the football with no other witnesses?" presumed Fletcher, expecting the usual alibi.

"Actually, I think we were playing poker at Ringer's place. That lucky bastard Errol won nearly every hand. We played all night, and seeing as how all four of us were present – that's me, Ringer, Errol and Oneway – I don't think we need any other witnesses, but if you do, let me know, I'm sure I can rustle some up from somewhere."

"Playing poker, eh, Sgt Major? It's funny that whilst the four of you were playing poker that four disguised men were loading the Colonel's belongings from his house in Knightsbridge into a van that can't be traced."

Fletcher wasn't happy. Eli, was making a mockery of the proceedings and telling them nothing.

"Sounds like a bit of a coincidence, that one."

"I don't believe in coincidences, Sgt Major, and your smugness will betray you."

Eli gave Fletcher's warning a little thought, but he had answered enough questions and the MI5 man was starting to get up his nose a little bit.

"A man, Mr Fletcher, can only be betrayed by someone he trusts." Eli locked eyes with him to push his point. "I trust no one, therefore betrayal will not be my downfall. Now unless you have finger prints, DNA, or some photographic evidence linking me to the scene of the crime, or any other crime that you may wish to fit me up for, I think we're done here." Eli again finished with a smile and a puff of his cigar.

"Don't take the piss, Sgt Major. You might put on the pretence of a South London barrow boy, but we all know that's all it is, a pretence."

Eli laughed, and removed the cigar from his mouth.

"Do you know, that's the second time someone has called me a barrow boy in the last few weeks, and I don't believe in coincidences either. So I'll log that one on the old computer," he said, tapping his finger on his temple. "The thing is, my dad did start down the market. Worked all his life, and never asked anybody for anything. He put me in the Army at the age of seventeen because one of my mates nicked a car, and I wasn't even there. The day he died his shoes were polished and his trousers were pressed. He went out the same way he lived, with dignity, and I try every day to emulate him, and make sure that I never do anything that he wouldn't be proud of, so for anything I've done, I'll answer to him, and not you, Fletcher." Eli, strengthened the tone in his voice to bring an end to the proceedings.

"It doesn't work that way Sgt Major. Someone has to answer, and we think that it's going to be you, but we're willing to cut you a deal."

"A deal, this will be the second one of those in the last few weeks as well. Go on then Fletcher, what's MI5 offering?"

"Only what we have offered you before, a job with us. We have need of your talents, and your knowledge, I'll admit that. Come and work for us at intelligence, and we will close the book on Colonel De' Williams' death."

Eli gently brushed away some ash that had fallen on his trousers from his cigar, and calmly stood up. He grabbed the collars of his overcoat and adjusted them on his shoulders, before taking the cigar from his mouth and looking in to Fletcher s eyes.

"In two months I'll be out of this man's Army, to which I've given thirty years of my life, with the extra service I've put in. And I won't be swapping one uniform for another. In recent years I've lost a wife and son in a car crash, but I've still got a young daughter that needs her dad, and it's about time that she had one full-time, not just when I'm at home on leave. So the answer, once again, is no, gentlemen. I hope the refusal doesn't offend but, as I've told you before, I'm not interested."

Fletcher wasn't happy. Eli's refusal 'had' offended, as it had done in the past, and he was beginning to take the whole thing a little bit too personal.

"We will get you Moon, one way or the other. We know you killed the Colonel, and if you're not with us, then you're against us. You may be looking forward to your retirement with your daughter but you'll find out that no longer being a member of the Regiment will have its disadvantages."

Eli, didn't like threats, or anything else that hung over his shoulder. Normally he would have dealt with it there and then, but given the circumstances, and where they were, he decided to answer it with one of his own.

"It's Mr Moon, to you Fletcher, or for the next two months Sgt Major. And if that was a threat there's one thing you should know when delivering ultimatums in my direction. Kill me, if you cross me. At least then you've got a good chance of surviving. After that you've just got to avoid being strangled by Ringer, shot by Errol, or blown up by Oneway."

He left his glare fixed on Fletcher and his two silent sidekicks, driving home the warning and creating an uncomfortable silence. A cough from the Colonel broke the standoff. Eli, looked across to see him raising his eyebrows as if to say, 'that's enough.' He took that as an order and began to leave the room. When he reached the door he grabbed the handle but turned for one last word.

"Still, it does leave you chaps with a bit of a quandary," he said looking back.

"What's that?" asked Fletcher, still with a look as though he was holding all the cards. Eli, not for the first time, noticed his smugness, and also logged that to be dealt with later.

"Well it seems to me that whoever did kill the Colonel also took his memoirs, and his computer. That means that they have the power over some very privileged information, a lot deeper information than the names he was going to mention in his book."

"So what's your point, Sgt Major?" Fletcher asked, making his own point of stressing Eli's rank after what he had just said.

"My point is this. If I had killed De' William, which I didn't, I would have that information safely tucked away. I would also have made a few copies just in case one was found. And in the event of my untimely or suspicious death, they would be released to the press. Not the bits concerning me or any of my comrades in D Troop of course, just the juicy bits concerning the government, and even your lot, Fletcher, Box 500, and Six for that matter (MI5 and MI6). De' William was in the corridors of power at a very volatile time, there was a lot of information in that old bastard's head. He was party to a lot of decisions made at the highest level. Now if a man had power over that information he wouldn't have to worry about being betrayed, would he."

"Is that a threat, Sgt Major?"

"Of course not Mr Fletcher, I'm just speaking hypothetically. Like I said, I didn't kill him."

Fletcher knew that whilst he was admitting nothing, Eli was leaving him in no doubt as to the consequences should he be arrested, or worse.

"Will there be anything else, Sir?" Eli asked, turning to his commanding officer, seeking permission to be excused.

"No Sgt Major, that will be all for now. But you can always buy me a drink in the Club sometime, we could have a catch up."

"I would be honoured Sir. I wish the old Paladryn Club was still open at Bradbury Lines."

"So do I, Sgt Major. If I remember rightly, the last drink we had in there was the night before you set off for the Falkland Islands, on board the Antrim."

Eli, in remembrance, nodded to the memory before

leaving the room while resisting the temptation of bidding Fletcher farewell with his usual "be lucky" goodbye, but only out of respect for his Colonel. As the door closed behind him, Fletcher looked across at Colonel Roberts, shaking his head. The meeting had accomplished nothing except to confirm what they already knew. Eli wouldn't play ball, and he certainly wasn't interested in working for MI5.

"He's a loose cannon," said Fletcher, now stood upright and straightening his paperwork by tapping it on the desk.

"He was, and still is, our best man," replied Colonel Roberts. "I know he's not battle fit anymore, but you can't have the intelligence that comes with age and experience, and still have the fitness of a new recruit.

"That doesn't give him the right to go bumping off people that piss him off." Fletcher showed his anger by forcefully stuffing the paperwork he had just straightened in to his briefcase.

"Let's have it right, Fletcher. You're put out because Moon didn't accept your offer to work for MI5, not because he bumped somebody off, as you put it. Which, by the way is a charge for which you have shown no proof? And if he is such a loose cannon why are MI5 showing so much interest in him? Besides, if Moon did kill the Colonel, then he did us all a favour. The thought had defiantly crossed my mind in the past. That book was De' William's way of striking back at the establishment that forced him to take early retirement. It would have caused the government huge embarrassment; you know what we got up to when 'she' was in charge. If Moon does have the Colonel's memoirs then there's no safer place for them to be. They will never find their way into any book or the tabloids, that's for sure."

Nothing Colonel Roberts said was going to console Fletcher. He wasn't happy with Eli, his attitude, or his reluctance to join MI5.

"Still," answered Fletcher, knowing he had lost the battle on words but still having his sights on the war; "we can't have him, and those other three lunatics he runs about with, doing as they please. I don't understand why you all hold him in such high regard."

"Well you wouldn't, would you? You've never faced the enemy, or had to lead men into battle, most of who are scared out of their wits. Sgt Major Moon is a veteran of countless such engagements, and his intelligence work whilst working under cover is the stuff of legends. If you are looking for someone who has a bad word against him, then all I can say is that they won't be easy to find. From what I can gather, the only ones who did have something bad to say about him, are dead."

"That rather confirms my point, wouldn't you say, Colonel?"

"Whether it does or it doesn't, Moon does what he does, firstly for his daughter, and then for the rest of his family, the Regiment. They are all he cares about now. As for the other members of his team, they are all decorated soldiers, who to my knowledge, have done nothing wrong. Within a few months they will all be out of the Army, and sadly, somebody else's problem. It will be the end of an era and of D Troop, but until then, they are mine, so if you wish to question any of them again, you 'will' follow correct procedure, and do it through myself, and Regimental headquarters. But if you really want my advice, I would let it go. No one cares who killed the Colonel, and Moon is obviously not interested in a move to Whitehall."

The CO was a good man, a good officer, and leader of men, unlike the late Colonel De' William. Roberts protected the men under his command, but he was no fool, and he knew Eli was no angel.

"Regiment," Fletcher said with a dismissive shake of his head.

"Yes, Fletcher, the Regiment. I'll remind you once again to remember where you are, and to whom you are talking too."

Fletcher acknowledged his second bollocking.

"Yes, Sir, but I've been instructed from the top to get him on board whatever it takes," he added. "We have an urgent and pressing predicament that needs his type of, shall we say, approach. So I hope he hasn't bought his retirement rocking chair just yet."

Now it was the Colonel Robert's turn to shake his head.

"Be careful, Fletcher, when you're dealing with Moon. He's a quandary, an enigma and a puzzle all rolled in to one. You'll never know where you are with him, but he'll be zeroed in on your every move twenty-five hours a day."

"I think you mean twenty-four, Colonel," replied Fletcher smugly.

"Not when Moon's wearing the watch," added the Colonel, making his point. "He's the only man besides Sir Alex Ferguson that can add extra time."

Once Fletcher had worked out what the Colonel was getting at, he seemed a little put out that he obviously thought that he might not be up to the job of handling any confrontation with the Sgt Major.

"Thank you for your concern, Colonel, but we know what we are doing. After all, we are MI5, not a bunch of Boy Scouts."

For the first time, the other two men in the office made themselves known, as along with Fletcher, they gave a little chuckle at his answer. The Colonel, once again shook his head whilst extinguishing his cigarette and arriving at his own comparison.

"Compared to Moon, you and your men are like a bunch of Avon ladies Now if there's nothing else?"

The Colonel walked over to the door and opened it for the three men who were obviously leaving. Fletcher wasn't used to being shown the door and he didn't like it, but as the Colonel had already made quite clear, it was his office, his camp, and his rules.

"You seem to think a lot of Moon, Colonel," Fletcher said, pausing at the door with his shadows. "You talk about him like he's some sort of James Bond."

"Sgt Major Moon is far from James Bond, Mr Fletcher. He's more at home with a pint in his hand than a martini cocktail, shaken 'or' stirred. He and his men take care of problems that we would rather not know about and pretend do not exist. We sleep safely in our beds at night because of the risks they take. I'm just telling you to be careful when dealing with him. Whether or not you listen is up to you."

Dismissing Roberts' words with a smirk and a pinch of salt, the MI5 trio left without uttering another word. Their lack of respect was duly noted by the CO, and it would not be forgotten in a hurry.

Outside Regimental Headquarters, Errol sat in the Range Rover, waiting for Eli, who was now coming out of the front doors puffing on his cigar, with his mind going over the things that had been said. For a while, the reference to the killing of Maguire four years earlier had almost had him on his back foot, but only because it held fond memories of better times. Overall, though, he knew they had nothing on him except suspicion, otherwise he would have never been allowed to leave the building, especially after his refusal of Fletcher's proposal. He was almost flattered that MI5 showed so much interest in him. 'There's obviously life in the old dog yet' he thought to himself, but also he couldn't help thinking that there was more to it.

"How did it go?" Errol asked, as Eli climbed in to the vehicle beside him.

"No problems, the CO was in good form."

"Who was asking the questions?"

"Some Toby Jug (mug) from Box 500 (MI5) called Fletcher. He had a couple of bookends with him that didn't say much. They just kept looking at me in an attempt to put me off my stroke."

"And did they?"

Eli looked to his right and gave Errol a dirty look for his question.

"Just drive the motor and stop asking silly fucking questions." Errol smiled as they pulled away and Eli ejected his half-smoked cigar out of the window. "I'm going to have to give those up," he said, slightly out of breath after his short walk across the barracks.

"I wish you would, I wouldn't have to spend half as much money on that Lenor, stuff trying to get the smell out of my clothes."

Eli looked at Errol blankly. He didn't have a clue what Lenor was; his wife had always done his washing, and since she and his son were killed her sister had taken over looking after his remaining daughter and all the other household duties that came with it.

"Do I look like a barrow boy?" He asked out of the blue, feeling slightly paranoid after being tagged with the same name twice in as many weeks.

"A barrel, you look like a barrel, with all that weight you're putting on. I don't know about a barrow boy."

"Cheeky fucker," Eli replied whilst tapping his belly proudly. "I've got a fortune invested in this rifle," (rifle butt – gut). Still smiling, Errol stole a quick look at Eli's girth whist concentrating on steering the vehicle towards the camp gates.

"Next you'll be telling me it's your chest that's slipped."

Eli again looked to his right, giving Errol a dismissive glance for his added comment.

"People keep calling me barrow boy. What's that all about?"

"It's that 'Sarf' London accent of yours that's all. Why, who called you it?" Errol was enjoying Eli being called names, but thought it best to wipe the smirk from his face and concentrate on the road.

"Well, first it was De' William, at his house, and now that Fletcher, from Box 500 just said the same thing."

"Why didn't you shoot him?"

"Who?"

"Fletcher, or whatever his name is, the MI5 idiot."

"Shoot him, what are you talking about Errol? You can't go shooting somebody just because they call you a barrow boy."

"Why not, you shot De' William."

"Shut it, you soppy git."

"And you shot him before he gave us his password."

"He was getting on my nerves. Besides you said this fucking whizz-kid mate of yours can hack in to anything."

"He can, I'm just saying it would have been easier to get the password before you put two rounds into him, that's all."

"I tried but he cottoned on. He was a conniving old bastard, not a fucking imbecile. He wasn't in the Regiment because he was as thick as pig shit you know. Anyway, he started to wind me up, talking about my wife and son."

Errol paused before answering, dropping down a gear to slow the Range Rover as they approached the entrance.

"Oh well that's different then. You should have emptied the full magazine into the fucker."

They gave each other a smile as they passed through the camp gates and Eli gave a wave to the M O D (Ministry of Defence) personnel on sentry duty as he raised the barrier. Looking over his shoulder, Eli realised that there was something missing.

"Where's Pepsi and fucking Shirley?" He asked giving the missing pair one of his pet names.

"Ringer's catching up on a few parachute jumps and Oneway's gone fishing."

"Oh that's facking nice aint it. I'm in there getting grilled by Box Five and Oneway's out giving it the old J.R fucking Hartley!"

"He's not fly fishing. He's teaching some new lads how to set depth charges in the river. Anyway, I notice you never refuse the trout he brings back that float to the top after the explosions."

"I do like a bit of Lillian, (Lillian Gish-fish)" replied Eli, again rubbing his belly, "and jellied eels. Its ages since we last had a bit of pie, mash and licker. Here, speaking of fish, that reminds me. We need to nip down to Poole and have a word with SBS Harry."

"Why, what's he done?"

"Nothing yet, but he's going too. We need to get to Belfast next month un-noticed."

"So, what's he going to do, smuggle us all across in his wetsuit."

"No, smart arse, he's going to float us across in the dark on one of their landing craft. Then we can take the Rover with us. He can drop us at one of the quiet beaches in the south. Dingle beach, that will suit, then we can drive up to the north."

"So the job in Belfast is definitely still on then. You haven't changed your mind after what just happened?"

"Of course not," dismissed Eli. "Just because Box 500 are on our case doesn't change a thing. We've waited five years for this one, it's our retirement fund, Errol, my old China, the icing on the cake. But I'll feel a lot better doing it knowing we have the information from De' Williams computer as back-up. If anything goes wrong we'll need it to bargain our way out, so you better get on to that whizz-kid mate of yours and tell him to pull his fucking finger out."

"What about this Fletcher fella? He's going to have people keeping tabs on us."

"All the more reason to get Harry to drop us off under the cover of darkness. Nobody will be any the wiser."

"Are you sure he'll do it? He thinks you had him over the last time he did you a favour."

"He got paid, so it wasn't a favour. If Harry sold his services too cheap, that's his fucking problem."

Errol gave Eli another sideways look. No one ever got a good deal out of him. When it came to haggling he was like a Turkish carpet seller in an Istanbul market. A person would have more chance of finding eight draws with Littlewoods Pools than they would of getting one over on Eli before the handshake.

"So when do you want to go see him?"

"Now, of course, there's no time like the present."

"Now? I can't go to Dorset now," exclaimed Errol, letting go of the steering wheel to look at his watch. "I'm taking a bird out tonight."

"Well you'll just have to ring Battersea fucking Dogs Home and cancel, won't you. Come on, chop, fucking chop, it's a two-hour drive to Poole. If you put your foot down we can stop at a pub and I'll let you buy me a pint and a bit of grub."

"Why do I have to pay?"

"Because you were the one that mentioned fish, I'm Hank Marvin now. I could just do a nice bit of Lillian with jockeys whips and mushy farters!"

Errol let go a huge sigh and did a U-turn. He knew it was pointless arguing. Eli always got his own way when it was to do with business but he wasn't that bothered about missing his date. He wasn't far wrong with his Battersea joke either, the bird was a bit of an old yard dog.

What Eli wasn't saying though was that since the meeting he now felt a bit more urgency to get on with the preparations for what they were going to do in Ireland. He hadn't expected MI5 to be the ones asking the questions and their involvement didn't seem quite right.

Something didn't fit, and despite his shrug-off manner, it bothered him. The timing of the robbery, though, was beyond his control. They had waited five years so far, whilst keeping their ears to the ground, and from the information they had received, the time had finally arrived. To pull the job, though, they were going to need some specialist help, and that would mean calling on four Irish lads that owed Eli a very big favour!

Chapter Three

Slant-Eyed Surprise

Old Bobby Tomes sat on the bench outside O'Reilly's Bar, supping his nine-thirty hair of the dog from a can of super strength lager, whilst to the front of him a large beer wagon arrived, bringing the weekly beer delivery for the pub. As the vehicle reversed into position to deliver its cargo, the large metal doors in the floor that led to the cellar of O'Reilly's Bar were pushed open from the inside, from where Michael Flynn emerged.

A lot had changed in the four years since the lads and he had sailed out of Chelsea Harbour. The money they got away with wasn't a life changing amount, not split four ways anyway, so they had done what they always did, stuck together and pooled it to invest. O'Reilly's Bar had been their first purchase; it made sense, they spent most of their money in there anyway, at least now they were putting it in to their own till. The bar wasn't breaking any records but the books showed a healthy profit each week and they owned the premises outright, so in a few years it should sell on and give them a decent return. Their next purchases were the trucks and machinery they needed to start up their own building company. The work they had done while being in London had rekindled their tradesman inclinations, and since the agreement had been signed, Ireland was seeing a boom in the construction industry, both in the north and the south.

Belfast was going through a great change. Each year that passed without any trouble saw more and more investors coming forward. The large shopping chains were returning and the town was becoming as popular as Dublin for the stag and hen nights, if not more so because of the cheaper drinks. The IRA and other groups were effectively inactive, apart from the minority members that were never in it for the cause. They were now fronting the drugs, prostitution and money-lending activities that inevitably accompanied any large city, a part of life that the IRA didn't agree with and had always kept down. Then of course was the old favourite, 'the protection racket'. While the different groups were active, this went under the guise of fund raising and support. Now in a time of peace, it had become what it always was, the extraction of money through threats and menace. It was a simple and effective way of getting all the business owners in the area to pay a weekly toll to ensure that nothing untoward stopped them from trading, such as a broken leg or a petrol bomb through the window etc. For obvious reasons the lads didn't pay protection, either on the bar or any of the sites they worked. One up-and-coming uninformed gang who thought they were the new kids on the block did approach them once, but there was never a second time!

The lad's personal lives had seen dramatic changes also. Michael and Roisin had been married for a year, as he always said they would be as soon as young Peter had turned sixteen and found work, work that hadn't been too hard to find because he was set on as an apprentice bricklayer by the lads. Michael moved in with Roisin when they were married, but his mother was still at the flat with Peter. She was still as adamant as always that she was staying put, despite Michael's numerous attempts to talk her in to moving. It was important to her to stay near her old friends and the things she loved and now she was working cleaning the pub every morning, she could afford to do more of the thing she loved to do the most, PLAY BINGO!!

Dermot? Well he was doing fine, thankfully. The events of recent years had loosened him up a little, but it was the arrival of Greasy Deasy's baby that gave him a new lease in life. It wasn't his, nor was it Sean's or Danny's. The baby was born with jet black hair and slanted eyes. It turned out that Michael wasn't the only one that was partial to a meaty bone from the Chinese! As expected, Sean took the piss constantly but Dermot didn't care, he was happy and relieved. He had not only escaped life with a woman who had been around the town more times than a black taxi. He had also saved four hundred quid on a blood test.

He was enjoying life, being part owner in a bar and a building company, plus a few quid in his pocket made him a bit more of a catch for the ladies, which in turn gave him a bit more confidence. He was enjoying work also. His role as site foreman in London continued in their company now. He ran things efficiently and effectively, dealing with all the ordering and suppliers, which was a job that none of the others could be bothered doing anyway, and it gave him the feeling that he was still in charge, which is the way the others liked it when it came to passing the buck and looking for someone to blame.

Danny was the biggest shock, though. No sooner had he got back to Belfast and made sure everything was ok, than he had returned to Notting Hill to be with Barbara. The lease on the pub was immediately put up for sale and Danny stayed for the six months it took to find a buyer before the pair packed up and moved back to Belfast. For some reason, though, whilst being in London for that six months, Danny was never tempted to go to the local night club for a drink!!

Barbara was now managing O'Reilly's bar for the consortium that the lads had formed, and she and Danny had moved into the accommodation above. Meeting the rest of his family had been a bit tricky for Babs, she was only four years younger than Danny and Sean's parents, but everyone could see that the big man was happy, and gave the amalgamation their blessing.

Sean was still in charge of all plant on the sites but it was the new machine he had bought for the night time that you would never expect. He was now Belfast's answer to Fat Boy Slim, but not on the disco decks, as a karaoke presenter. D'artagnan Karaoke was his new company, and as it happens, he didn't have such a bad voice. He resembled an overweight Tom Jones, with the husky tones of Neil Diamond thrown in; all the fags he smoked probably had something to do with that, but he was busy with his bookings around the town and he always played O'Reilly's on Friday nights. There was a new look in his physical appearance also. Nothing too dramatic, he was never going to be in line for winning any slimming awards, or appearing in any before and after photos, but all the jigging about he was doing while singing his songs was better than any diet the doctors had ever put him on, and he hadn't had to stop drinking. *Result*!!

"How ye doing, Michael son, do you need a hand with any of those beer crates."

Old Bobby was doing his good deed for the day offering to help with the delivery, or help himself to some of it at least.

"No thanks Bobby, I want the booze to find its way to the customers, and not into your pocket."

Bobby didn't appreciate Michael's refusal, or the insinuation that he couldn't be trusted.

"Well hurry up then and open the fucking pub so a man can get a proper drink, ye wee bollocks."

"It's not even ten o'clock yet, Bobby. Go down to the off-licence and get another one of those tins you have there. Or maybe I should drag you down to Greasy Deasy's for another feed, you old fucker."

"Ah your beer's shite anyway, shove it up your arse."

Bobby was already up off the bench and putting some distance between himself and Michael, before delivering the insult. Michael smiled, he had no intentions of giving chase. If he caught him it would probably cost him a tenner anyway. He carried on checking off the delivery as it was lowered down the drop before going back inside the pub via the front door.

Michael's mum, Catherine, was inside humming a tune to herself whilst polishing the brass hand and foot rail that run the distance along the bar.

"Who was doing all that shouting," she asked, taking a break from her melody.

"Just Old Bobby, chancing his arm chasing an early drink."

"That, Robert Michael Tomes, he'll never change that

one. He's never cared about anything else except where his next drink was coming from, and that was when we were at school. I think the last job he had was the milk monitor, and then he stole all the gold tops."

"I didn't know you and Bobby went to school together? You never told me that before, Ma."

"There's a lot you don't know, although you and your mates walk around the town as though you invented everything, and there's nothing you have to learn."

Michael laughed at his mother's derogatory statement.

"Well, he always asks after you anyway, Ma. Maybe he's been carrying a schoolboy crush around with him all these years."

"He can keep his asking to himself, and anything else he's been carrying around with him. It's a good shave he needs. If he spent more time in the bathroom and less time in the pub he'd be better off. And a visit to the chapel once in a while wouldn't do him any harm either. Their would be a few Our Father's and Hail Mary's said if that one confessed all his sins."

Michael couldn't help but smile at the thought of old

Bobby, in the confessional box. It was a knocking bet that the priest would get nipped for a tenner.

"Catherine, Michael, come and have a cup of tea." Barbara came out of the kitchen, bringing the tray of refreshments in to the bar. It was ten o'clock and time for their usual morning cuppa. Normally it was just Babs and Catherine, but on Fridays one of the lads was always there to help take the delivery.

"Ah, that's grand," replied Catherine, ready for the break. She peeled off her yellow rubber gloves and joined Barbara at the table where they always sat. The front door opened and they both looked round to see who had entered. Michael checked to make sure it wasn't old Bobby chancing his arm again, but it was Roisin, followed by one of the draymen with the delivery note to sign.

"It's only me," she called, while holding the door for the drayman and giving her husband a peck on the cheek as they passed. "I had a customer cancel so I thought I'd come round and see if there was a spare cuppa on the go."

"I'll get another cup," replied Babs.

While signing the delivery note Michael looked over at the three women, who were already getting their fags out in preparation of a good gossip.

"Have mine," he shouted, not fancying a seat in the proceedings, "I've got to go back down the cellar and lock the drop doors." He didn't even get a reply, just a raised hand in acknowledgment from Babs before he disappeared through the door that led to the cellar.

The draymen for once had done their job correctly. All the bitter had been chocked on the gantries, the crates stacked, and the empty barrels removed. Michael, happy that everything was as it should be, turned on the hose pipe and swilled the cellar floor down. "Nice and clean," he thought before turning the tap off and climbing the few steps up the drop to close the doors. As he reached for the handles his head was now level with the pavement outside and he found himself staring at a pair of shiny black Brogue shoes. He raised his eyes following the line of the crease in the neatly pressed trousers that brought him to the base of a dark Crombie overcoat, and before he got any further up that garment a whiff of memory-filling cigar smoke wafted up his nostrils.

"Alright my son, how's your luck?"

The voice brought a million memories rushing back through his brain. Without looking any higher he knew exactly who it was standing above him, but he continued raising his head anyway just to confirm his fears. "Oh fuck," he muttered with a deflating exhale of breath as confirmation was well and truly jaw-droopingly made. It was Eli. Although they had parted on good terms it was a reunion he had hoped as each year passed would never happen.

"I bet you hoped you'd never clap your mince pies on me again, eh, my old China?"

Eli took the thoughts right out of Michael's head, who was too shocked to even say anything.

"Well are you going to invite me in, or are you coming out in to the street for a natter?"

Michael looked from side to side, up and down the

road, mainly to make sure that old Bobby wasn't still lurking about.

"You better come down," Michael eventually said, thinking that the cellar was probably the best place for a meeting rather than upstairs where the women were. He moved from the steps to make way for Eli's entrance then climbed back up to finally close the doors. Face to face after four years, Michael was understandably a bit lost for words, especially as Eli seemed to be supporting the same unnerving cheeky grin he was wearing when they had parted.

"Have you still got that old boat?" Eli asked, starting the conversation with a sarcastic tone.

"Is that piece of information supposed to shock me," replied Michael, "the fact that you knew about the boat?"

"Well does it?" enquired Eli.

"It did when Fatty found your tracker whilst having the hull cleaned, but I knew that only meant that you would definitely be turning up one day, and here you are. Although as the years passed I did start to wonder. We sold the boat soon after because we presumed you would have had it bugged, although we did give it a good search trying to find the listening devices, but found none."

"Because there were none," Eli, enlightened. "Just the tracker." His lips formed a smile around his cigar that puffed away in his mouth. "You've got to stay close to your target with a listening device and we didn't fancy following you four back to Belfast. With a tracker the satellite does all the work for you."

"I've still got the tracker if you want it back, minus the batteries of course, they went straight in the bin. Mind you, I did think about going down to the docks and attaching it to a ship bound for china."

Eli smiled thinking that he wouldn't have fell for that old chestnut.

"Nah," he replied with a shake of the head concerning the return. "You could use that old thing as a door stop. We use a bit of kit now that does the same job that's the size of a ten pence piece."

"Technology eh," replied Michael with a smirk but also thinking that it would be something else that would be used against him. "What did confuse me though, was why you let us get away with so much money. If you knew about the boat you must have seen me store it there. And then to top it off you chucked in another ten grand."

"Well you did get away with a bit more than I thought, so I didn't know everything. The main reason though was to make sure that you had enough money to survive on. You know what you're like, Michael. I didn't want you coming up with another one of your schemes because you were getting a bit short of cash. And I wanted you to think that you did get one over on us, just to keep your pecker up, so as to speak."

"So you were keeping us sweet until we were needed?"

"Are you complaining? You've done well, a nice bar and steady little building company. You know a lot of mugs would have gone out on the piss with all that money and squandered it on fast cars and slappers, but not you lads. I'm impressed."

"So what do you want, Eli? You haven't come all the

way to Belfast to pat me on the back and tell me how proud you are of us."

"In a way I have. You've proved to me that I made the right decision back in that warehouse four years ago. I knew I would need some Irish help one day and the way you lads have conducted yourselves these last few years confirms to me that you're the right men for the job, because that day has arrived."

Michael was a bit put back at the speed it was falling on his toes. Eli's arrival had caught him out, and with no time to prepare he was cautious with his response. Cautious, but curious.

"So what's on your mind? If I remember rightly four years ago you described it as a bit of private enterprise."

"You remember that, do you."

"I'm not likely to forget anything about that night in a hurry."

Eli puffed and smiled again while nodding in agreement. He had his own memories of that evening as equally life changing.

"Just a little job," he casually enlightened, "nothing

that will turn your hair grey, and nothing that between us we can't handle."

"And what if we don't want to get involved in your little job, what happens then. We can't give you your money back, it's all invested. You'd have to give us the same deal as the Yardie and become a partner in this pub and a building firm."

"I don't think so," Eli, returned with a huff. "I've still got blisters on my feet from the last time I wore a pair of daisy roots. And that was over four years ago on that building site when I nearly ran you over."

Another smile formed as Eli paused to take a few last smokes of his cigar before dropping the butt on to the wet cellar floor, extinguishing it beneath his right shoe. He placed his hands into his overcoat pockets and looked in to Michael's eyes as though about to deliver an ultimatum. Michael, was unsure what was coming next. The last time he saw Eli do that move he pulled out a 9mm hand gun and blew Maguire's knee to bits.

"If you and the lads don't want anything to do with what I propose then I'll walk away. There'll be no money returned or any partnerships taken. You'll be free to continue with your quaint little lives and go on about your business as if we had never met. You have my word."

Michael didn't expect that as an answer, but if there was anything he had learned about Eli in the short time he had spent in his company, it was that he was a fair man.

"Will you still go ahead with the job if we refuse?"

"Of course, we've waited over five years for this one. It won't be as easy but we'll find a way."

"So what makes us so important?" Michael asked, searching for information.

"We need your knowledge, your professionalism, and your accents."

"That means it's a local job."

"Stop digging," said Eli, recognising Michael's probing ways. "It means that there are four of us and we need the four of you. If you decide to get involved then I'll fill you in with the details. If after talking to Danny, Dermot and Sean, you decide to opt out, then you forget this conversation ever happened and I will walk away and never bother you again."

"Seems fair," accepted Michael.

"It is fair, but I meant what I said. If you decide not to throw in with us you forget everything. Remember, we know more about each other than most men know about their own wives."

"I understand," agreed Michael, knowing the importance of a tight lip. "I'll talk to the other three. How will I get in touch with you?"

"I'll see you all here, six o'clock Sunday morning, when it's nice and quiet and there's nobody about. We'll have the meeting in the tap room where you used to plan all your jobs. It will be like old times for you lads."

Michael shook his head, the extent of Eli's knowledge into their lives still made him a little uncomfortable.

"Was there anything we used to get up to that you didn't know about?" he asked curiously.

"Don't feel so violated. Remember, we had men on the inside supplying us with information and intelligence. Personally, though, these days I tend to guess and bluff it most of the time, just to give the impression that I do know most things."

Eli's reply was given with a shrug of his shoulders, as though it was said to make Michael feel better.

"Something tells me that you've never guessed at anything in your life," Michael responded, not falling for the casual explanation. Eli smiled at his answer. The persona he portrayed was that of a man that knew everything, but the truth was far different.

"You'd be surprised how much I do guess," he admitted. "The difference is that my guesses are educated, based upon the things I see around me."

"Ok, I believe you, so we'll see you at six Sunday morning. I'll open the front door five minutes before so you can walk straight in."

Eli acknowledged Michael's timings, turned and walked back to the drop. He climbed the first couple of steps and pushed open the doors but paused before continuing.

"Congratulations, by the way," he said looking back.

"For what?" Michael asked.

"For your marriage to Roisin."

"You're a bit late but thanks anyway."

"I don't know when you got married, or if you even were, it was just an educated guess." Eli was just having a bit of fun before he left.

"Based upon what?" asked Michael, curious as to his powers of deduction. "I don't wear a ring."

Turning a little on the steps, Eli thought he would humour Michael's interest and have a bit more fun.

"Well, first you left her behind to go to London. Then instead of lying low as you promised her you would, you robbed a drug dealer. This resulted in her hairdressers being burned out, and you and your mates nearly being killed in a Heathrow warehouse. I bet when you got back to Belfast with a few quid in your pocket you were so glad to be alive that you went straight out, bought a ring and proposed." Eli gave a little tilt of his head, looking for recognition from Michael that he was on the right track.

"See you Sunday morning," was his only riposte.

Eli, laughing and saying the words 'educated guess,'

climbed the rest of the way out of the cellar, leaving the doors open for Michael to close. When he climbed the steps behind him moments later to do just that, he had a quick scan of the street, where there was no sign of his Cockney visitor.

"Has somebody died, son?"

Michael raised his head a little more to find out who was talking. It was Old Bobby Tomes, back on his bench with another can in his hand.

"Died, Bobby? Why do you ask?"

"Because I just saw an undertaker climb out of your cellar not thirty seconds before you did." Michael laughed at Bobby, and what he thought he had seen.

"That wasn't an undertaker, Bobby."

"He was dressed like one."

"He's no undertaker, he was just dressed smart," Michael continued to laugh, while adding another thought. "Mind you, he does send them a lot of business!" Still laughing, he pulled shut the doors and secured the cellar before going back upstairs, where he found the gossiping threesome still at it. He slipped behind the bar to retrieve his jacket and his fags from the pocket.

"Roisin, give me a light, would ye?" he asked, approaching the group.

"The tea's cold now son, would you like me to make a fresh pot?"

"No thanks, Ma," he answered, whilst bending down to receive the light from Roisin. "I have to get back to work. I'll have a drink with the lads when I get there."

"Will I see you at home after work or are you having a drink with it being Friday?" enquired Roisin.

"I think you best meet me back here. I've a funny feeling that the me and the lads will be sinking a few later."

"Any special reason?" asked Babs.

"Just a bit of reminiscing about old times and friends. I think we're going to have a lot to talk about. Right, I'll see you later, ladies. The cellars done, Babs, and I swilled the floor down and locked the drop." Michael gave Roisin a kiss and left the bar. He was either eager to get to the site and inform the others of Eli's return or he was warning them. The unexpected reunion had pricked his curiosity and brought back feelings he hadn't felt since their return to Belfast. The problem was he didn't know if the feeling in his stomach was one of excitement or woe.

As he pulled on to the site he gave a couple of beeps of the horn to attract the attention of the others. He climbed out of his vehicle and beckoned them over to his position. From their different work areas around the site they each looked at him, unsure of whom he was after. Stretching out his arm he pointed at each one of them individually before bending it back at the elbow towards himself. Danny, Sean and Dermot stopped what they were doing and made their way towards him, as did young Peter, who jogged to get there first.

"Do you want me as well, Michael?"

"No Peewee, go back and clean out the mixer. We're going to have a half day today, seeing as how it's Friday."

"Ok but I want paying the full wage. I can't afford to be clocking off early like you lads."

"Just clean out the mixer Peewee, and less of the lip."

"Half day," said Dermot, over hearing his instructions as he approached. "We've got a delivery coming this afternoon."

"It's ok, Peewee can wait for the delivery. That way he can get paid for the full shift." Peewee turned to look at his brother with a complaint on his lips. "Just clean the mixer and tools," Michael added, cutting him short while pointing his finger back towards the work area. "And lock up after you've taken the delivery." Peter wasn't happy and kicked the dusty ground with anger as he walked away.

"What's going on Michael, has something happened?" Danny asked as he and Sean arrived.

"You could say that, big fella. We've had a visitor this morning at the pub." Sean jumped straight in, voicing a worry he had been carrying around all week.

"It wasn't the father of that girl from the Karaoke the other night was it, because if it was she swore to me she was eighteen?"

"No Fatty, it wasn't an irate parent." The three all looked at Michael, waiting for the news as to who their mysterious visitor was. His mannerisms and the tone of his voice told them that it wasn't good. "Who from your past would you least like to bump in to?" he asked, causing his three mates to ponder on their answer.

"Maguire," revealed Dermot.

"I wouldn't have thought he was our visitor," Interrupted Sean. "The last time we saw him he was being dragged out of the Irish Sea doing a Robert Maxwell impersonation."

"If you were asking me," said Danny, adding his input, "I wouldn't like to bump in to my old bookie, but from the look on your face I'd say you were talking about Eli." Michael said nothing at Danny's correct presumption.

"You mean SAS Eli from London," exclaimed Dermot. "Fuck me, it's been four years. What the fuck does he want after all this time?"

"His money's-worth I shouldn't wonder."

"You wonder correctly, big fella. He wants to see us all at six o'clock Sunday morning in the bar."

"Six o'clock," moaned Sean, who loved his bed almost as much as his fast food; "does he think that we we're all in the fucking army?"

"Did he tell you what it was about?"

"A job, that's all he revealed. But to be fair to the man he did say that if after we listen to him that we don't want any part of it he'll walk away."

"Well we can't," Dermot blurted. "I mean, we've got jobs to do and a company to run. We've built too much to throw it all away now, and I don't believe that he will let us just walk away."

The other three knew that Dermot for once had a right to be worried but they didn't really share his foreboding.

"I don't know, Dermot, you can only judge a man by the dealings you've had with him in the past but from what we know about Eli, I wouldn't say he was a liar or a man that couldn't be trusted."

"Michael's right," Danny, concurred. "Let's hear what he has to say. Besides, I'm a little bit curious, aren't you?"

"I don't know about that, I think ignorance could be the safer bet where that fella's concerned."

Dermot's usual line of thinking was predictable so it was left to Sean to add his take on the matter.

"Well, I'm happy to go with the flow as always," he revealed. "So if I don't get out of bed Sunday morning just vote me in, or out. Basically whatever you decide." Sean didn't give a crap either way. He knew his brother would back Michael in whatever he did, and he in turn he would follow the pair in whichever direction they led him, so the decision as he saw it was out of his hands. Michael, however, like Danny, was curious as to what their visitor had in store for them. The feeling in Michael's stomach had definitely turned into one of excitement, and the look on Danny's face revealed much the same. Michael believed he could trust Eli, and that he would keep his word about walking away if they weren't interested. But truth be known, Michael didn't want to say no to his proposal, he yearned for a bit of the old days. The buzz and excitement he got from illegal work, which he presumed it would be, was something he missed and needed. It wasn't that he was unhappy with anything; he loved Roisin, the bar and the building company, but a leopard can't change its spots. Plus what Eli had said about, "leaving them to their quaint little lives if they weren't interested," words he had obviously said knowing Michael, wouldn't like it, did exactly that. It bothered him that his life had got a bit too easy and monotonous. Both he, Danny, and even Dermot were all starting to catch Sean with a bit of a weight problem, and the simple fact of it was that it was too early for him to retire.

There was no more work done that day. Young Peter, like a good apprentice, albeit not a very happy one, cleaned the mixer, his tools and everybody else's. The conversation or debate on Eli's return continued back at the pub and for the rest of the afternoon. Sean was working that evening presenting the Karaoke, and by the time he got the show on the road, like the other three he was a bit worse for wear from the drink. As usual it was a busy Friday night and the atmosphere was a good one. Since buying the bar they had really put it on the map as one of the in-places to be in the town, plus Sean had a good following and plenty of regular singers.

As a group of young ladies who were out celebrating one of their divorces sang the words to Gloria Gaynor's, 'I Will Survive,' Sean, dressed in his usual performing attire of a bright Hawaiian shirt jumped around behind them, doing all the actions, which were super-enhanced by the ten pints of Guinness that had already passed his lips. Danny, who always stood at the end of the bar near the doors so he could keep an eye on the punters coming in, was joined in watching the points, and Sean's antics, by Dermot, and Michael.

"Would you look at that fucking idiot," Danny said, as his brother bounced around the stage. "I'm not surprised he's losing weight, he's doing the Jane Fonda workout four nights a week."

Danny's words sounded derogatory but the smile on his face as he watched his sibling said otherwise.

"Ye, but if he has a heart attack who's going to give him the kiss of life," joked Michael.

"Not me. If his heart stops I'll volunteer to punch him in the chest but I'm not putting my lips anywhere near his ugly bulldog chops."

"Where's your brotherly love, big fella?" asked Michael.

"I do love him, that's why I'd hold Dermot down and make him do it." Michael and Danny, laughed, but a slightly pissed Dermot had other things on his mind.

"Do we really want to risk all that we have by listening to whatever it is Eli has to say?

Danny and Michael gave each other a look combined with a sigh. The four had agreed before Sean went to work to leave the well-exhausted Eli subject alone for the night, but that was easier said than done for Dermot.

"I don't know what it is you want out of life, Dermot," Michael, answered. "But if I thought that this was it, this was as good as it was going to get, I wouldn't be happy. Ok, I'd live with it given no alternative, but I wouldn't be happy. Yeh, the bars great and the building company's booming, but it just doesn't float my boat. I need something that will put that tingle in my balls and the butterflies in my stomach."

"What about Roisin?" Dermot added whilst looking down the bar to where she was sat with Babs and Michael's mother.

"What about her?"

"Well how will she feel? She won't be happy if you get caught. She might not even be there when you get out."

Dermot's words caused a pause in the conversation. He had said too much, but luckily Michael knew it was the beer talking.

"Dermot, if we were caught years ago doing something political and I was jailed she would have waited. I don't see that there's any difference now but I'll not stop doing the things I've always done just because the woman I love might not wait for me if I get caught."

"What are you talking about?" interrupted Danny, "Roisin wouldn't go anywhere. Dermot, leave it alone now, we don't even know what the job is yet and we're too pissed to speculate."

Danny emphasised the word 'pissed' whilst looking into Dermot's eyes. "Three more pints here, please," he shouted at one of the bar staff, trying to change the subject, but Michael had one last thought on the matter.

"When I met Roisin she fell in love with what I was, and what I was then, I still am now. A bit older and a little bit wiser, but nothing else has changed. You see it's the bar and the building company that are out of character for me, Dermot, not robbery and the prospect of going to jail. At the end of the day, if you don't want to hear Eli's proposal or anything else he has to say, then don't turn up Sunday morning, it's as simple as that."

Michael's final words on the matter were a bit abrupt but Dermot had pushed the subject and got an answer.

"Here we go," said Danny, passing the fresh pints.

"No thanks," refused Dermot. "Give mine to Fatty, I've had enough."

He turned and headed towards the door with a little stagger and a big strop on.

"Dermot, come back and finish your drink," Michael called, not wanting to part on bad terms.

"Ah leave him," said Danny, "he's pissed. He'll be alright after a kebab and he's chucked his ring up on the kerb. Come on, let's go down and join the ladies. We can shout abuse at that fat fucking idiot brother of mine."

The pair joined the women and a great night was had. Danny even got up and sang a few songs, which resulted in Sean receiving a clip around the side of the head for pulling faces behind his back. When his ear stopped throbbing they joined each other in a drunken rendition of the Hollies hit 'He aint heavy he's my brother,' followed by Sean falling off the stage and landing on the two tables where the ladies from the divorce party were sat.

The next day, Sean and Michael joined Danny in the tap room for their usual Saturday afternoon drinking and gambling, but there was no sign of Dermot. They thought about ringing him, but after discussing it decided not to. If he had made his mind up not to come to Sunday's meeting they didn't want to put him under any pressure to do something he didn't want to do. But if that were true, this would be the first time they would have ever done anything as three and not four.

Chapter Four

Kitty Kat Killer

Dermot pressed his face against the glass of the shop window to get a better look inside the premises. He had already tried the door, which was locked, and seeing that there were no lights on confirmed it was shut. He looked at his watch, it was quarter to six. He hadn't used the shop for quite a while, a good six months in fact, but it was common knowledge that Abdul, the owner, always opened at five. Even on a Sunday morning if you couldn't sleep or started work early you could always get your fags, some milk and even the papers if they had been delivered, but not this morning, it seemed. He carried on walking, making his way to O'Reilly's and the meeting that had occupied his mind all weekend. He had never intended not turning up. The reservations he had voiced Friday night in his drunken state were just concerned jabbering from sozzled lips. He wasn't scared of what Eli may ask them to do, he was scared of losing what they already had. Unlike Michael, he was happy with the way things were. For the first time in his life for the past four years he was a part of something that he enjoyed doing and he was against anything that might endanger that. Dermot was no fool though; he was a worrier but not a fool. He knew that the last four years had only been possible because of what Eli had done for them back in that warehouse, and part of the deal was that in return, they owed him a favour.

When he arrived at the bar the other three were already there; well, Sean was there in body, but not so much in mind. He was slumped in the corner, drifting in and out of consciousness with what remained of a pint of Guinness in front of him. Danny and Michael were at the bar with a cup of tea, so Dermot, when seeing Michael, shrugged his shoulders with a sheepish smile.

"Sorry about Friday night," he said, getting his apologies out of the way.

"Don't worry about it," replied Michael. "I said too much myself, it wasn't all you."

"I can't remember what was said. I just remember waking up Saturday afternoon with that feeling in my stomach knowing that I had been a dickhead the night before."

"Well the important thing is that you're here now, where you belong. All the musketeers together, as Fatty would say." The three all smiled, putting Friday's crossed words behind them.

"What's up with him anyway?" Dermot asked, looking at the worse for wear mess in the corner, still wearing one of his brightly coloured Hawaiian shirts. "He looks like he hasn't been home all night."

"That's because he hasn't," answered Danny. "He came straight from the pub where he was doing the Karaoke last night, pulled himself a drink and fell asleep in that corner."

"Well I'm awake now, so you can stop talking about me and pull me a fresh pint." Hearing his brother's words, Sean was brought around from his slumber with a stretch and a yawn and a Guinness beermat still stuck to his face. "And I didn't come straight from the pub. I came from that divorcee's house who was in here on Friday night. I bumped into her again last night and she took me home to fill the gap that was left by her husband fucking off."

After his explanation he offered up his glass to be replenished.

"Ye can have a cup of tea or nothing," replied Danny. "Dermot, do you want one? I'll go in the kitchen and make a fresh pot."

"Cheers, two sugars," he answered, as Danny walked behind the bar towards the kitchen. "Was she a good looker?" Dermot added, looking back at Sean for an update on his previous evening's conquest. "I can't re-member anybody from Friday night."

"Don't be stupid," replied Sean. "How could she be a good looker, she took 'me' home."

He obviously, without anybody else's input was in no doubt of his own limitations.

"Obviously she was a right minger. Apparently her husband got his eyes tested at Spec Savers, went home with his new glasses, took one look at her and put in for a divorce." Sean couldn't resist the joke.

"You won't be seeing her again then."

"Yeh stupid, I'm going back tonight." Dermot shook his head, with Sean wondering what the problem was. "Dermot," he continued, "when will you realise that the only difference between having sex with a beautiful woman, or an ugly one, is whether or not you leave the light on. Besides, with having to come here so early this morning I never got chance to try her breakfast. If she can make a decent fry-up, she could turn out to be, Miss Fucking World."

"Have you heard this?"

"What's that," Michael answered, having not taken much notice of the conversation between the pair.

"Fatty's giving advice on women and sex."

"Well, I'd say he'd have more of an idea than I would.

I've been with Roisin, for that long that I can't remember having sex. We make love, so she tells me."

"What's the difference?"

"The difference, Dermot, is that when you're in love, you make love. It's never sex. Even when you get down and dirty, you're still making love, because you've got love in your heart."

"I don't see what the difference is."

"You will Dermot, hopefully you will my mate, one day."

Dermot returned a look that hoped that day would never come. He had been close to commitment once before but wasn't sure it was quite the direction for him.

"And this is the man that won't take advice from me," added Sean.

"What's the crack with Abduls anyway," Dermot continued, seeing a chance to divert the conversation. "I thought I would grab a paper on the way here but when I got there he was closed."

"Haven't you heard?"

Dermot shrugged his shoulders being avoid of any information, and asked.

"Heard what?"

Sean, solemnly lowered his gaze towards the beer stained table.

"His wife closed it as a mark of respect," he said, before finishing off the stale drink and giving Michael a sly wink.

"Respect. Respect for what?"

"Abdul, he died last week," Sean answered, while realising that he had an unwanted accessory stuck to his head. Pulling the beer mat from his face he flicked it across the room and looked back at Dermot for the question he knew was coming.

"Abdul? Dead? How?" Dermot was shocked, thinking how the shop-keeper was only in his fifties and always looked so well. He didn't even drink.

Sean added.

"Well his heart stopped, that's always a good sign, but the true cause was because he was eating Kitty Kat?"

There was a pause whilst Dermot registered what had been said.

"Abdul. Abdul from the corner shop was killed eating fucking Kitty Kat?" he repeated in disbelief.

"Ye, last week."

The question was confirmed as though it was a regular occurrence.

"It was in the local paper, I'm surprised you didn't read about it."

"Abdul was killed eating Kitty Kat?" repeated Dermot, once again, still finding it hard to believe.

"Yes," repeated Sean, in a stern voice, as though Dermot's reluctance to believe him was starting to piss him off. But his voice then changed as a smile formed on his face when about to deliver the punch line. "He didn't die of poisoning though. He broke his neck afterwards when trying to lick his arse."

Sean broke into a fit of laughter, accompanied by Michael.

"Ha fucking ha, very fucking funny, you fat fucker," Dermot cursed whilst joining the laughter, seeing the funny side.

"Fuck me Dermot, I can't believe you haven't heard that one before," said Michael.

"I was caught out, it was a bit quick for this time of a morning."

"Did I miss something?" asked Danny, returning with the tea to a room full of laughter.

"Just me falling for one of Fatty's jokes, I must be still half asleep. Here pass me one of them teas, quick."

Dermot reached over and took one of the steaming cups from the bar.

"It wasn't the one about Nelson Mandela, was it?" asked Danny, who'd heard them all before.

"No, it was the Kitty Kat Killer," answered Sean, still laughing and still pissed.

"Nelson Mandela?" said Dermot, curious.

"Don't ask," Danny quickly replied before Sean, could lead off again. "He's been using us all as guinea pigs for the crappy jokes he tells in his Karaoke act."

"My jokes aren't crappy, and neither is my act. I notice you don't complain on Fridays when I work for nothing."

Danny was about to explain that it would be cheaper to pay him than carry on giving him free beer for his services but was stopped as Eli walked in to the room.

"Morning chaps, how's your luck," he asked as he walked around the room shaking hands with the lads, first Dermot, then Michael, followed by Danny and finally Sean. "Nice shirt, Sean. Where did you leave your surfboard?" Sean smiled and gave Eli a wink followed by a hiccup.

"It's nice to see you fella."

"Thank you Sean, that means a lot. I didn't think my reappearance would be welcomed."

"It's not," he answered. "But for all the Guinness I have drunk, the songs I have sang and the women that I have pleasured over the last four years I have only you to thank."

Eli smiled, his appreciation broken by the big fella.

"I think our luck rather depends on what you have to say."

Danny got the conversation straight down to business, answering Eli's earlier question. There was a pause, a moment's thought, a puff on a cigar before enlightenment was given.

"Ok Danny, one million, how does that grab ye?"

Eli, taking a leaf out of Danny's book, cut straight to the chase but his words didn't make much sense to the lads, or perhaps they thought they hadn't heard correctly.

"One million what?" asked Dermot, before any of his mates could say it first.

"One million pounds That's each, should you decide to take me up on my offer."

"Who the fuck do we have to kill?" blurted Sean.

"Oy, Steve McGarrett," quipped Eli, having another go at his shirt. "Calm down, we're not going to kill anybody. At least that's not the plan, but as we all know from past experience, things don't always go the way they are planned."

"Well, you have our attention with the million wage packet, you sly fucker. So what's the job?"

Eli smiled at Michael. Mentioning the money first was a ploy and it had worked; he had their complete and undivided attention, even Dermot's.

"The job is this, we are going to rob a bank. Not just any high street bank, a main distribution bank holding an unusually large amount of money. And, at the same time we get a little bit of retribution."

"Retribution against who?" Michael asked.

"Against our old employers. My three and me, and you four are going to rob a bank in Belfast and stick it to our old employers."

"Well it's obvious who you mean when you say our old employers, and I can believe that the IRA would be holding money in a Belfast bank, but why the fuck would the British government, who I presume you mean when you say your old employers, have money there as well?"

Michael wasn't on his own when he failed to see the connection. Danny, Sean and Dermot, looked equally as blank faced.

"It's a backhander."

"A backhander from who. And for what?"

"From the British government to the IRA, or Sinn Fein, we all know it's the same thing. And it's for the signing of the Good Friday Agreement."

"Bollocks."

Eli turned to look at Dermot, in response to his dismissive curse.

"If I remember rightly, Dermot, you didn't believe me in London when I told you about Maguire, either."

"Come on Eli, we all know Dermot can be a bit of a sceptic, but this time he has got a point."

"Michael, I didn't come to Belfast to find you four after four years just to tell you porky pies and lead you down the garden path. Now I could talk for hours about conspiracy theories but this isn't one of them. What I've told you is the truth, but I can't prove it to you yet. Now I've told you what the job is, and what the wages are. And, should we get caught, I don't think I need to tell you what the drawbacks would be. Now, before we go any further, I need to know if you are in, or out."

"I believe him," said Sean, from his seat in the corner.

"Why, what do you know that we don't?" asked Dermot.

"After what we've been through in the past, I'm just more open-minded that's all. Also, why would he lie? Anyway that's my input, time for a drink and I don't mean tea."

Sean got up and made his way behind the bar, heading directly to the Guinness pump. As he did, Eli couldn't believe how much weight he had lost.

"Fuck me, Sean, what have you been doing, you're half the man you used to be."

"It's the new me," he answered with a self-admiring smile. "Faster, stronger, and although it wasn't thought possible, sexier and even better looking. My body is now a temple."

With a hiccup he gave Eli a huge grin as the Guinness fell from the pump in to his glass.

"Stop throwing flowers at yourself, ye fat fucker, and sit down."

"No bro, I told you already that you've got my vote. I'll go with the flow. Forget about me, Eli, I'm voting by whatjemecallit."

Eli, thought about it but soon figured it out.

"Proxy," he added, offering the correct term.

"That's him," replied Sean, diving in to the creamy, still settling pint.

"Right, come on let's have it, what's the crack?"

Michael was growing tired of the distractions and was eager to hear the details.

"I've told you, the job is robbing a bank in Belfast. The wages are one million each, and the money belongs to our old employers. Now, before you hear any more I want to know that you're in because anyone that's not needs to leave now and catch a severe case of fucking amnesia about what's been said already." Michael, Danny and Dermot looked at each other and then at Sean, who just shrugged his shoulders whilst drinking his pint.

"Fuck it, I'm in."

"Michael, you can't," interrupted Dermot. "If this money does belong to the IRA and we get caught stealing it we're fucked."

"Dermot, if the money that's in that bank 'does' belong to them and it is a payment from the Brits it means that we've been lied to. For how long I don't know, but it calls in to question all the reasons they gave us for calling the ceasefire and signing the agreement. They left us skint and we had to leave Belfast. If all that was for a united Ireland or just equal rights for the Catholics in the North then fair enough. But if it was all about backhanders and under the table deals then I feel just a little bit robbed and fucked off, don't you?"

Michael turned from Dermot and looked at Eli.

"Now tell me that in the four years you've been waiting for this robbery that you've come up with a decent plan, one that gives us a fighting chance of pulling it off because banks aren't easy things to rob, you know. You're talking time locks, cameras inside and out and at least two members of staff that hold the code to unlock the safe after the time lock is disengaged."

Eli smiled.

"You've obviously thought about robbing a bank before," he noticed, listening to Michael reel off the obstacles.

"It's been an ambition of mine since I was a boy," he admitted with a glint in his eye.

"Well what about the rest of you. Are you in, or are you out?"

"In," confirmed Danny, "and that applies for my brother too." Sean looked up from his pint.

"You see, Eli," he said, nodding and shrugging his shoulders whilst pointing at his sibling, proxy'. Everybody now turned to Dermot, looking for a unanimous show. Dermot, with a sigh, conceded that his path was set.

"Go on then, I might as well. They'd do me in anyway if you three got caught, just for being guilty by association."

"ALL FOR ONE, AND ONE FOR ALL," shouted Sean, raising his arm and holding his imaginary sword at Dermot's acceptance.

Eli jumped at his raised cry.

"All for what, you mad fucker?" he returned, looking confused.

"Take no heed of him. My brother's just a silly fat fucker that thinks he's D'artagnan."

Eli smiled at Danny, and then looked back at his brother, who gave him another wink. He liked Sean, but there again he liked all the lads, which is why he was there.

With the job now a goer and everybody in agreement, the four Irish made themselves comfortable to let Eli fill them in with the details.

"Let me take you back to London, to the time when all this started." Eli took a cigar from his pocket whilst starting his story. "Back then in Yardie Allan's warehouse I told you that the agreement was about to be signed. That was privileged information, but in the corridors that me and my lads walked, it was common knowledge. You see, there had to be peace otherwise we were going to end up like the Germans, fighting on too many fronts."

"Too many fronts? The British weren't involved in any other conflicts at the time."

"No Dermot, not at the time, but within two years we were going to the Gulf."

"How the fuck would you know that, you didn't even go in first. It was Saddam Hussein and the Iraqis that invaded Kuwait."

Eli shook his head. "Dermot, Dermot, Dermot, when will you learn that about the only thing you decide for yourself these days is how many sugars you're going to have in your fucking tea? The rest is preordained by a higher force such as large organisations and governments."

"So you're saying that the British army wouldn't have entered into the Gulf war if there hadn't been peace in Northern Ireland."

"It was a possibility, and one the Americans weren't willing to take. You see, the Yanks knew that we struggled to do both when the Falklands conflict was on. That's why the then President Clinton got involved to make sure the agreement was signed. But all he was doing was feathering the nest for Bush to take over, because even that was part of a bigger picture."

"I thought Clinton got involved because of pressure from Irish Americans and NORAID?" said Danny, joining the question time.

"That's what you and the rest of the taxpaying world were supposed to think," answered Eli. "These days, whatever is put in front of you and presented as the truth seldom is. The Yanks have been pulling strings in British politics for a lot longer than four years, believe me."

"So why was it so important to them that the British enter the Gulf War?"

"Because, when the Americans go to war on their own they look like bullies, and people think that they are doing it with an underlying agenda, such as stealing another country's oil. So, to keep them legal, so to speak. They needed a coalition force, and if the British weren't a part of it, nobody else would join. I know you lads don't like to hear it, but the British army - that's England, Northern Ireland, Scotland and Wales - is the best fighting army in the world. Don't get me wrong, the Americans are brave men with lots of armaments and weaponry but it doesn't always work. The Russians had already proved that in Afghanistan. To win a war such as that when you're working so close to civilians you need a bit of the old Dennis Healey."

The four Irish, looked slightly confused at the mention of the former Politician.

"Dennis, fucking, Healey?" repeated Sean. All I remember about him were his bushy fucking eye-brows."

Eli smiled.

"To be far they were in need of a bit of a grooming," he answered, making light of his comment. "And he was quite a mild mannered man which is why he came runner up so many times in his political career but behind the scenes in the sixties as secretary of state for defence he ran a secret war in Indonesia. It was a war that the British public never heard about and it was won by hearts and minds, and the British army working undercover. Our own RAF wanted to bomb the place and give it a bit of the old Yank treatment like in Vietnam but Healey refused and persevered. Evan Callaghan, the then Prime minister didn't know it was going on."

Sean, nodded his head, absorbing the information.

"He was born in Kent, but he was educated in Bradford at the Bradford Boys Grammer," Eli added.

Michael intervened.

"I thought we didn't have time for conspiracy theories? Can we not get back to the bank?"

He was still anxious to hear the details of the robbery.

"I'm sorry. I can't help myself sometimes sharing information. It's all relevant though but I will cut to the chase. As I said, the agreement had to be signed, Clinton was getting involved and our lot were over-stretched keeping tabs on anybody that they thought may try and put a stop to it, and because we were so overstretched my team was pulled off our assignment at the time and given the job of watching you lot when you left Belfast and headed for London. Before that we had been providing the close protection on the real discussions, where the deal was actually hammered out and only three parties were present: the British Government, Sinn Fein and the Americans."

"So a deal had already been done before Good Friday."

"Long before, Danny, and it would have been done years earlier had Sinn Fein not held the job up."

"Held it up, why."

"Because the British government wouldn't give them what they wanted for keeping their mouths shut."

"Their mouths shut about what? What could Sinn Fein have on the government?"

"Proof that they had refused the offer of peace when it was offered in the late seventies and early eighties."

Dermot frowned in disbelief.

"Fuck off, I'm not having that. You're telling us that the IRA and Sinn Fein offered peace talks to the British government."

"Dermot, you were getting your arses kicked. The Regiment were all over you. Not just in the bogs of Armagh but in the whole of the North, Belfast and Derry included. The IRA, the Official IRA and INLA were that busy killing and grassing each other up that our job was made easy. We had touts and supergrasses coming out of our ears. Virtually every weapon you were using we had Jarked."

"Jarked, what the fuck's that?" asked Michael.

"Fitted with trackers," replied Eli. Every time a weapon was moved from a hide we knew about it and where it had gone. We couldn't tell which person had used it, unless we had eyes on them, but it did tell us which ASU was responsible for which killings. Some of our touts were so deep they were killing other touts to climb further up the ladder. Do you know how much some of them got paid to collaborate against the cause, or how much of a blind eye was turned which meant that they could earn their money in other unscrupulous ways. We had one bastard, and I mean bastard who was allowed to commit numerous atrocities on your own community because he was giving us so much information. And to this day he, like many others is still a respected member of your community, and so called 'Hero of the Cause'."

"Why did you let him, if you knew what he was doing?"

Michael's gut churned when he heard anything like this, anything to do with collaboration and traitors who had betrayed, not exactly the Cause, but his community.

"We tried, lad," Eli, admitted with a sadness in his voice. "We radioed in one evening for permission to intercede but we were told to stand down. There wasn't a man on the ground that night that didn't want to kill that grassing bastard.

"Do you know his real name?" Michael asked with a stern look.

"I know his code name and his real name," confirmed Eli. "But that information is not for you, not right now anyway. I need your mind clear if we are going to be working together on this job."

"If we do this robbery for you, and live to see it through, will you give us his true identity?"

Eli could see that Michael wouldn't let it go.

"I will. But not as a bribe or coercion for your help. I will give you it because you, and every other person who lost loved ones in the Troubles, deserves to know who that bastard was, and still is."

"Then I will do this job for 'that' reason, and not for my childhood ambitions of robbing a bank."

The two nodded, joined by the rest of the lads.

"But remember this," Eli added, in a warning tone. "Your lot at the top know what he got up too. They know he was a collaborator and what he did, and he's still walking your streets. That means he's got a lot of shit, on a lot of people. Enough shit to keep himself alive."

"Well he has fuck all on any of us."

"Just tread lightly, that's all I'm saying."

"We will, but first things first. Why didn't the Government accept the offer of peace, and put an end to it all?"

Michael couldn't help thinking that if they had have done, that his father might still be alive.

"I think you should think back to who was in charge at the time. I know you were only young then, but you must remember the lady who held office. Now there was a woman that didn't shirk from a bit of confrontation. Her nickname for us was 'My Boys'. She could call the SAS into action quicker than Wyatt Earp could draw his six guns, which she did on numerous occasions. She out and out, categorically refused to negotiate. Not just with terrorists, but with everybody. She even sent us in to Peterhead jail to sort out our own British prisoners. I know they were hard men in that nick but they didn't deserve Special Forces gate-crashing their little riot. And what she did to the miners, in 84, was well out of order. Mind you, that was Scargill's fault for winding up the situation. Do you know that he once went for a circumcision operation, but the surgeon doing the procedure said that he couldn't do it because there was no end to that prick? That was a joke, by the way, boys."

Michael interceded once again.

"We've had enough jokes this morning, Eli, from your Hawaiian friend over there."

Sean, realising he was the man in question raised his hand.

"I'll tell you some more later. But I liked that one, Eli."

"Come on Eli, finish what you were saying." Michael was always eager for information.

"I will, but I do like a good joke so, save it for me, Sean." Sean again raised his hand. "Anyway, it was that principle of hers, of non-negotiation that scared the Americans, and threatened to put pay to their future plans."

"We were all about twelve back in those days," interrupted Sean. "We had two interests at that age. Throwing stones at you lot, and wanking. I couldn't even spell fucking politics, so enlighten us."

"The Yanks wanted an end to the troubles, and if possible, although a bit of a long shot, a united Ireland."

"Didn't we all."

"Yes, Danny, but the Americans wanted it for their own reasons, not because they were getting soft on their Irish ancestry. They wanted the British army freed up so they could take part in other engagements, and a united Ireland so it could become a part of the NATO forces. Once again they were trying to back themselves up with fighting men."

"So what happened back then that made a difference?"

"In 1979 Margaret Thatcher was odds-on to win the next general election. That alone was a scary thought, not only for the IRA but the Yanks too. Couple her impending rise to power with the then Shadow Northern Ireland Secretary, Airey Neave, putting into action their much-publicised Northern Ireland Policy, and that meant double trouble. Together they would have brought all the terrorist organisations to their knees, with no negotiations.

"So you're saying the Yanks killed Airey Neave."

"It's not a fresh claim Danny. It's a well-voiced theory that they may have had a hand in it, and that MI6 may have been involved. Also, it was no coincidence that Neave was murdered in March, only two months before she was elected."

"Piss off, the I.N.L.A, killed Neave."

"Ye'h right, Dermot," replied Eli, with a chuckle. "Tell me then, what's your opinion of the INLA?"

Dermot paused for a little thought, but not for long.

"They're a bunch of mad fucking dogs," he replied, with agreeing nods from his mates.

"Exactly. Now would you say that they had the means and the intelligence to be able to break in to the highly secure Palace of Westminster, and plant a bomb underneath a car?"

"They might have attached it outside and it didn't go off till later," said Sean with his own thought.

"No, they couldn't," added Dermot, quashing his theory when remembering details of the I.E.D (Improvised Explosive Device) that had been used. "I read about it a few years back. The bomb was a mercury tilt switch. It would have gone off when entering the underground car park when it went down the ramp."

"Which means it had to be planted inside," interrupted Michael, catching on and finishing Dermot's surmise.

"Correct gentlemen, which all means that somebody had to get past some of the highest security in England, with a mercury tilt switch bomb under their arm. Then make their way down two floors to the underground car park where they set about the lengthy process of attaching the device to the vehicle. And all of this while under the watchful eye of the surveillance cameras. Now with all that explained to you, do you still think that the I.N.L.A or even the I.R.A planted that bomb?" After a short contemplation, all the lads together shook their heads. "That is, of course, assuming that they actually got the right target," continued Eli. "The car that the bomb was attached to was a communal vehicle, used by not only Neave, but the lady herself before she was elected. They could have been trying to cut the head off, and inadvertently got her right arm."

"So you're saying that whoever killed him, could have easily been going after her."

"I can't prove it, nor would I swear to it. But it's a possibility."

"But why would INLA claim responsibility if they didn't do it."

"Because somebody high up obviously told them to. The I.N.L.A weren't bothered, it put them on the map with a big feather in their cap."

"So why didn't the IRA accept responsibility. It would have been a good feather for them as well."

"Well that's the part that makes me think that it really was her they were going after. The patsies to take the blame would have had to be sorted out before hand, so they could claim responsibility straight away. That's why it couldn't be the I.R.A."

"Why not?"

"Because the I.R.A and their political wing Sinn Fein were going to go on to lead the Catholic people in the

Northern Irish Council. The Yanks knew that because they were going to help put them there. If it were known that they had killed a woman, and the future prime minister, they would never have gained acceptance."

"I bet the I.N.L.A didn't know that when they agreed to hold their hands up."

"I think you might be right, Sean. They are obviously upset about something, that's why they are still causing problems now. Maybe they finally realised that they were played by the CIA. Anyway, what happened, happened, and the rest is history. But personally, I believe that if they hadn't, killed Neave, that she would have negotiated, because she also had a hidden agenda. She wanted our troops free to retake the Falklands."

Blank looks once again filled the room, especially from Dermot.

"Hang on Eli, we were talking about 1979. The Falklands didn't start until '82. And to say retake, implies that she knew somebody was going to invade."

"Sugar in your tea, remember Dermot. I'll explain later, but for now, don't interrupt. Anyway, after they killed Neave, she must have realised that she may have been the real target, because she was un-moveable. But her refusal to accept the olive branch in the '80s from Sinn Fein came back to bite the government on their arse. If it came out now that she could have possibly negotiated a peace and put an end to the troubles in Northern Ireland back then and saved God knows how many lives, it would cause great embarrassment to the government, and leave them open to thousands of lawsuits. The only reason that the agreement came about at all is because MI6 were having secret talks with Sinn Fein, behind her back, promoted by the CIA of course. If she had found out about that she would have disbanded them, and MI5, in a second. That's how powerful she was and how sternly she stood against negotiating with terrorists. So just imagine her with Neave at her side as the Northern Ireland Secretary. Your lot wouldn't have stood a chance against them. We knew it, the I.R.A knew it, and the Americans definitely knew it."

"Freedom fighters," Michael corrected. "To you we were terrorists, but to us, we were freedom fighters.

Ask yourself, Eli, if you would have been any different than if the French were walking your streets. The Saxons and Bodicea they all fought against invaders, you're no different from us."

Eli gave an agreeing nod. He sympathised with the plight of the Catholic Irish people, more than the lads realised.

"So what did Sinn Fein want in return for keeping their mouths shut?" continued Michael. "Something for the greater good of the Catholic Irish people that our children could grow up and appreciate, I hope."

"Only if they don't spend it all at once, money," answered Eli. "Or you might want to call it redundancy pay, seeing as how it would be given in return for the laying down of arms. The problem the government had, though, was how to pay the money without it being noticed, and the easiest way to do that is in the form of compensation. So in a few years from then, once the I.R.A had proved it was sticking to the agreement and Sinn Fein was keeping everybody else under control the government would allow themselves to be sued.

"For what? You can't just make something up and drag a Government to the European Court of Human Rights."

"They'll come up with something, Danny, my guess is they'll start with 'Bloody Sunday.' There's going to be a lot of soldiers who served their country well, sold down the river with that one, especially seeing as how the first shot in that bloody exchange was fired by an I.R.A member who now holds a top post in your political organisation. But that's where we'll differ in opinion, and not what concerns us right now."

"They're not our political organisation," corrected Danny, sternly. "I think we've been at loggerheads with that lot for nearly as long as you have, Eli."

"You can say that again," agreed Sean.

"What we did, we did for Ireland. Not for no pocket-lining fuckers, or so we thought."

"Well, what we're interested in now, Danny Boy, is all the money that the I.R.A has laundered through dummy companies, and is now hidden in false bank accounts around the country. That's what we're going to take, or at least a small part of it."

"How, if it's scattered between so many banks, we can't rob them all."

"We won't have to. As I've said, a portion of the money has been conveniently transferred over the last few years – so as not to cause suspicion – into a Belfast bank. It's this bank that the I.R.A will rob and get away with in excess of twenty million."

"Hang on," interrupted Sean, who'd been listening to Eli's story up to this point without any queries. "If it's the IRA's money, why are they robbing it? Why not just draw it out."

"They couldn't draw it out before the agreement was signed because the Government knew about it. The I.R.A knew the government knew about it, so in the banks it stayed, gathering interest. Money of that magnitude when it is withdrawn has to be transferred not collected over the counter and when doing so you would be creating a paper trail to another account which then, along with the account holder also comes under investigation so nobody wants to put their name to it. So, now they have signed and stuck to the agreement, they can't draw it out because one, it would be illegal and against the terms and conditions of the agreement to use funds that were collected in the time of the troubles. And two, the money in this bank is just a small portion of the actual amount and its withdrawal would show up like a force ten earthquake on the Rictor scale; and three, a robbery is the only way of taking money from a bank without having to sign any paperwork and letting anybody know where it's gone, or who took it."

"So if the I.R.A is going to rob this bank and steal their own money, where do we come in?"

"We're going to rob it before they do."

Michael, stepped in once again, this time answering Sean's question in the place of Eli. Eli looked across at him, smiling and taking a large puff of his cigar. He knew it wouldn't take Michael long to catch on, and now they were singing from the same hymn sheet things would go a lot smoother. But you could always count on Dermot to throw a spanner in the works.

"You said there's in excess of twenty million in that bank," he said, going back to the amounts earlier mentioned.

"That's right, there could be even more. Anything from twenty to thirty million. We won't know until after the robbery."

"So how come we are only getting one million each. Do you expect us to take all the risks and get paid a pittance whilst you walk away with twenty million plus."

Eli, didn't answer the derogatory question straight away. He took a last smoke of his cigar before extinguishing it in the ashtray on the bar.

"Sean, give me a large cognac, will you?" he asked.

Nothing was said whilst the brandy was served, it was obvious to everybody in the room that Dermot's statement hadn't gone down well. Eli placed his nose in the large tumbler, breathing in the vapours of his favourite tipple, before gently sending the drink down his throat and answering.

"Dermot, I would never go in to business, or pull a job, with anyone that I didn't trust. You obviously don't trust me, so forget what I said earlier about it being your last chance to leave. I'm offering you another chance now. If you think that I'm the type of man that would take the lion's share, you should walk out of that door. The warning remains the same, though: keep your mouth shut about what's been said."

Dermot's usual moaning and snide remarks were accepted by his friends, but Eli was a different breed. He was a soldier through and through and loyalty, watching your mates' back, and trust, were attributes he lived his life by – that, and his seven P's of course.

"I'm staying," mumbled Dermot.

"What was that?" asked Eli, "I could hardly hear you. However, i didn't have any problem hearing you when you were questioning my integrity a moment ago."

"I said I'm staying," Dermot, repeated loudly, wishing he'd engaged his brain before putting his mouth into gear and making the statement in the first place. He looked across at Sean, who was smiling and making a wanking gesture with his hand, obviously enjoying Dermot's bollocking. Dermot mouthed the words 'Fuck You' back, like two kids in a classroom.

"Right then, just so there's no misunderstanding..." Eli looked at Dermot, embarrassing him some more.

"I'm going to explain to you how the money will be split once the robbery is complete and we know how much we have. Now there's four of you, and four of us. That's me obviously, black Errol, who you met in the warehouse, and the other two lads I didn't introduce you to back then, Oneway and Ringer."

"Oneway and Ringer, what sort of names are they?" asked Sean, knowing his nickname was self-explanatory but his question was much to the annoyance of Michael.

"Can ye stop asking fucking silly questions and let the man get on with the story? Does it matter what they are called. In another hour my mother's going to come threw that door to do the cleaning. Then we'll have to explain what the fuck we're doing here, and who the fuck Eli is."

"Ask them when you meet them, Sean?" continued Eli. "But Michael's right, we do need to get on. So getting back to the money, there are eight of us, which accounts for eight million, leaving anything from twelve to sixteen, maybe even twenty left over. This money will be left aside for pay-offs, because as you four well know from past experience that when you steal a lot of money, the people that owned it will come looking it and there's no point stealing it if you don't live to enjoy it. Plus we may leave little bits dotted around the country that can be easily found so we can send the police on plenty of wild goose chases. Anything that's left over when we know we're in the clear will be split 'equally', again"; Eli looked at Dermot before finishing his sentence, "eight ways."

Dermot sheepishly drank what remained of his tea, thankful for the shifting of Eli's gaze by Michael's next question.

"Why now, it's been four years? Why now, and why do you need us?"

Eli let go a little sigh. He didn't think he would have to explain things as much as he had done. He thought that by this point the Irish lads would have been well up for a bit of skulduggery and robbery.

"It's taken so long because of the Omagh bombing in 98, killing twenty-nine innocent people, which was an attempt by the Real IRA to disrupt the agreement.

The government wouldn't give the go-ahead for any of the terms agreed until after all the Republican organisations adhered to the truce, namely the IRA, INLA (Irish National Liberation Army) and the R.IRA (Real Irish Republican Army). You see, the INLA. weren't the only ones that didn't like the fact that Sinn Fein was taking all the credit and being put forward as the public voice. Even after the forming of the British-Irish council in 99, they still argued and made public threats against each other. Its only now, after the last few years of reasonably acceptable and agreeable behaviour, that the go-ahead has been given. Now as I said to you earlier, money has been filtered into this bank from various accounts for years, but the reason they're going to give for the bank holding so much money at the time of the robbery is that it was going to be used to fill the ATM machines over the busy Christmas shopping period."

"Well, it's only about a month until Christmas now, how long have we got?" asked Danny.

"It's the seventeenth of November today," Eli continued, whilst looking at the date on his watch. The IRA plans to commit the robbery four days before Christmas, on Tuesday the twenty-first of December. We are going to rob it the day before on the twentieth, which gives us just over four weeks to prepare and come up with a plan."

"I thought you had a plan."

"No, 'you' thought I had a plan, Michael. I've got all the details and timings of the robbery plus a few other tricks up my sleeve. I need you to fill in all the blanks and then I'll come up with plan that will fit in with that information. We know the IRA plan to take the bank manager and his family hostage the night before to force him to follow their instructions the next day. We're going to do the same, except a day earlier, and before any of you get squeamish about a bit of kidnapping, let me tell you that it is an unavoidable part of the plan. Are there any problems with that?" Eli, looked around the room and saw no complaints. "Right, I want us all to meet again on Tuesday at your site. I'll be wearing a suit and a hard hat so if anybody asks, you can say that I'm your architect. Between now and then I want you to get your heads together and voice any concerns you have so you can tell me about them then. I'll bring with me all the paperwork and details I have to set the ball rolling. Remember, this isn't as hard as it sounds, it's all arranged and ready to go. All we're going to do is jump the queue and get there first."

"Tuesday then, what time at the site," asked Michael.

"Ten o'clock." The four Irish nodded in agreement of the time and everybody stood up preparing to leave. "Before we go, how's about another brandy, it's cold out there." Eli pushed his glass towards Sean, who was now topped up from the night before.

"Aye, set them up, whisky for me."

"And me."

"And me." Dermot and Michael both agreed with Danny in his choice of drink. Sean charged the glasses and placed them on the bar.

"Well, I'll stick with the black stuff," he said, topping up his own pint and raising his glass. "This deserves a toast. What shall we drink to?"

"Trust," proposed Eli, looking again at Dermot, milking his embarrassment a bit more.

"Give it a rest will ye, I apologise, alright."

Dermot's expressions of regret brought a smile to the group whilst Sean, in his usual forgiving manner, gestured with another wanking movement.

"Alright," continued Eli, "apology accepted. Why don't you give us a toast?"

"Aye, go on Dermot, offer one up," said Danny, egging him on. Dermot thought for a moment before raising his glass.

"Here's to trust, new partnerships, and Abdul, God rest his soul. May he never again get a fur ball stuck in his throat?"

The four Irish broke in to laughter, leaving Eli wondering what he had missed.

"Who the fuck is Abdul?" he asked, sounding a bit like a Smokie and Chubby Brown song.

"Sorry, it's just one of my brother's jokes, and no, before you ask, it's not worth hearing."

"Tell us the other one you mentioned, the one about Nelson Mandela," asked Dermot.

"For fuck's sake, don't encourage him," complained Danny.

"Go on let him tell it," said Eli. "I told you, I like a good joke. I can repeat it to Errol, later. He's a big fan of old Nelson."

"Ok," said Sean, straightening himself up while adjusting the collars on his Hawaiian shirt, "but it's not a joke, this actually happened to my mate Patrick when he passed his Class One HGV licence. The first job he was given was to deliver a load of cars to Johannesburg in South Africa. Anyway, it took about a week for Paddy to get there and when he arrived at the address he thought it said on the delivery note he knocked on the door. A big black lady answered, and Patrick, reading the name from the note, asked if Mr Nelson Mandela was in. The lady, informed Patrick, that she was Winnie, Mr Mandela's wife, and asked what he wanted. Paddy turned, pointing at his truck full of cars and said they were for Mr Mandela. Winnie said that Nelson hadn't ordered any cars, but Paddy insisted he talk to Mr Mandela, after the long distance he had driven. Mr Mandela came to the door and confirmed what his wife had said and that he hadn't ordered any cars, but Paddy, reading from the delivery note in his hand, was quite adamant that he had. Mr Mandela, growing angry, grabbed the note from Paddy and read it for himself.

"You fucking Irish idiot," Nelson said, throwing the note back at Paddy. "It not say Nelson Mandela, it say Nissan, main dealer."

Danny and Michael had heard the joke many times before but still laughed with Eli and Dermot, who were pissing themselves. As Sean, also giggling, stopped to take a breath, he slurred a request, believing one good turn deserved another.

"Ok, I've told you my joke, now I want to hear some more of Eli's conspiracy theories."

"What do you want to know?" he asked, still chuckling and knocking back his brandy.

"Who killed JFK," he asked, not really expecting an answer to the half-a-century-old puzzle.

"Well it wasn't Oswald, that's for sure; he was as big a patsy as the I.N.L.A. Kennedy was a man of vision and peace, something that the warmongering American Generals didn't agree with. They thought he was a traitor and a Communist because of the way he handled the 'Bay of Pigs' crisis and they were still high from dropping the two bombs on Japan, which was done for no other reason than retaliation for Pearl Harbour. Then you had Bell helicopters and other military machine manufacturer's that were set to make a billion out of the Vietnam War, which Kennedy was against, and determined to pull out of. Linden Johnson, however, the vice president, wasn't so inclined and made it clear that if he was in charge that the war in Asia would go ahead. The rest is history. Kennedy got shot, Johnson took over as president and the Americans got what they wanted, a war. But a lot of people made a lot of money. I can't tell you who pulled the trigger, or should I say triggers, because there was more than one shooter. But if you want to know who was behind it, they are your men."

"Fuck me, it's a deep world we live in. It kind of gives you a feeling of insecurity."

They were unusual words from Danny, who seldom used the word insecure to describe himself.

"That's secret organisations for you, Danny. The

CIA, MI5 and MI6 are just a bunch of sneaky bastards that make the rules up as they go along, but they do slip up now and then."

"Like when."

"Like when they did kill JFK for instance. The cover story they put out to convince the world that the President was shot by Oswald went out a bit premature. They forgot about the time difference and released the story in New Zealand before Oswald had even been charged."

"It could have just been some reporter who was quick off the mark," observed Danny. "They did capture him being arrested live on TV."

"It could have been," agreed Eli, with a slight tongue in cheek. "In fact, that is how they explained it away. But it was the depth of the article that tells you it was a cover story. They knew everything about Oswald, from the fact that he lived in Russia, to biographical data, and it was accompanied by a studio picture. Two hours before, this was an unknown twenty-four-year-old man. Where did they get it from?"

The Irish lads stopped to think about what he had said, but all that was long before their time.

"What about Lady Diana," Dermot asked. "Don't tell us you know who killed her because I would lose all respect for you if you did."

"No Dermot," Eli admitted with a shake of his head. "I don't know who killed her, but I do think she was assassinated."

"That's a bit of a bold statement, considering it's the most debated question of the century."

"Not really, Michael."

"Well if you don't know who did it, how can you say for sure that it happened?"

"The clue to the answer is not how, when, or if she was. It's where. It's the location of her death that gives it away, that and the ensuing actions of the authorities immediately afterwards."

"It occurred in a tunnel in Paris, there's nothing damming about that."

Dermot failed to see the significance that the location may have. Eli pushed his empty glass back towards

Sean, asking for it to be filled again. He had met Lady Diana, Princess of Wales, several times, for one reason or another, and had always found her to be exactly as she was portrayed, a beautiful and kind person, although somewhat naive. Not in life, but definitely in the workings of the Royal family that she was pushed into.

"Do you know what Google Earth is, Dermot?" he asked, picking up his replenished glass and taking a large drink.

"Ye," he answered with a shrug of his shoulders, "it's that aerial view thing you can get on the internet. Why?"

"Do you know how those pictures are taken?"

Dermot again shrugged his shoulders. If this was a quiz it was well beneath his intelligence.

"By satellite, obviously."

"Quite a few satellites actually, and not just the ones that help you get a better signal on your mobile phone. These are military satellites. Satellites that photograph every square inch of the earth, every second, of every day. Then, after a few years have passed, the images are sold on to make a few quid to help pay for more satellites to be built. By this time, of course, all the things they don't want you to see have been blanked out so you can't go looking at any places of strategic importance such as military bases, the Pentagon or Buck Palace, for instance. But the intelligence services don't want you to know this, so they set up a dummy company and sell it through them."

"So you're saying Google Earth is a subsidiary company of some military organisation."

"No I'm not saying that, of course they aren't but what I am saying is that somebody buys those images from military intelligence, and as we all know they end up on Google Earth, or similar companies.

"What's all that got to do with Lady Diana?" asked Sean, as confused as the other three.

"What I'm saying to you lads is that if you're going to arrange the death of someone as important as a member of the royal family you have to make sure that you do it indoors, or in a tunnel where the satellite can't see you."

"So the fact that she was killed in a tunnel tells you that she was murdered," concluded Dermot.

"It does. That and the statement she made before her death."

"What statement was that?" asked Danny.

"A very naive one, made by a young lady that didn't realise she was signing her own death warrant when she made it. It was those words that killed her as sure as she'd put a gun to her own head and pulled the trigger. She said that when she got back from Europe that she was going to reveal a big surprise that would rock the Monarchy to its core. Now bearing in mind who her partner was at the time, this sent alarm bells ringing through the corridors of Whitehall."

"What was she going to say?" asked Dermot, enthralled in Eli's story, as were the others, who listened with as much interest.

"Take your pick; it could have been one of many. One, she was either converting to Islam because she was going to marry Dodi Fayed, which would have meant that the future King of England would have a

Muslim mother and stepfather. Or two, she was already pregnant, in which case the future King of England was going to be a half-brother to a Muslim brother or sister. Intelligence already knew that they had bought an engagement ring. Either way they could not allow her to return from Europe, sad but true. And worse still was that she was illegally embalmed within hours of her death, obviously to remove any traces of a foetus, if there ever was one."

There was a short spell of remembrance before Dermot spoke.

"I'm sorry Eli, to slander the English, but of all the fucking strokes the British Government has pulled that one takes the biscuit."

"Don't blame the Government, Dermot. They won't have known anything about it, especially Blair, he was too busy trying to become Prime Minister of Europe to be bothered about anything that was going on in England. Although to be fair he did speak up well for her afterwards and at the funeral. Decisions of that magnitude are made in far higher circles. You're talking MI6, or as

Mohamed Al Fayed believes, Prince Philip. And speaking of Mohamed Al Fayed, let's not forget his little hand in the game. He used Diana as a pawn, as a means for his own ends, just as much as all the others did. He invited her to spend time on his boat and as soon as she accepted he rang his son who was in America and ordered him to leave the woman he was with, a woman he was engaged to by the way, and join them, with the sole purpose of sweeping Diana off her feet. That was his way of getting back at the Royal Family for not giving him a British passport, which was also the reason he removed the Queen's crest from his Harrods store. He now has to live with the fact that the games he played killed Diana, and sadly for him, his son. But, it isn't over yet because those two young princes she left behind are going to grow up one day and when they are grown men and able to think for themselves they are going to realise that somebody killed there mother and, that the decision to kill her was sanctioned by someone, or maybe two or three members of the royal family. Their family, and those two lads are going to want answers.

Probably the youngest one because by that time he will have also started to ask questions as to whether or not Charles is really his father and, if he believes like most people that he is not, then he will also realise that he has no real Royal bloodline. That will cause a big rift in the Royal Family in years to come and a split that we haven't seen since Edward married Wallace Simpson."

Sean was about to dive in with the next obvious question but Michael had had enough of the conspiracy theories, and was doing a bit of clock watching moved things along.

"Right, that's enough Eli, you'll be giving them nightmares, and it's nearly time for Ma to arrive."

"Ok, me old china, but they did ask." Eli finished the last of his brandy and prepared to leave. Michael gave a little ironic laugh, still thinking of what he had said earlier. "What's so funny?" asked Eli.

"I was just thinking back four years, to the morning Maguire called at our flat. Ma told me that day that the different organisations would be carving themselves pieces of the pie, and I didn't believe her."

Eli gave an ironic smile. "Well, when she's finished doing the cleaning here, ask her if she wants a job with me. She sounds a lot smarter, and more open minded than 'Disbelieving Dermot' over there."

Dermot looked around the room, wondering what he had done to deserve being labelled with yet another derogatory tag.

"She is," answered Michael. "But in Dermot's defence, some things are a little bit too much to take in before eight in the morning, just like Fatty's jokes. You'll be telling us next that Bush blew up the Twin Towers himself." Eli gave another grin as he answered Michael.

"Well he wasn't flying either of the planes, if that's what you mean!"

Chapter Five

The Clown's Pocket

Tuesday, mid-morning. Eli did indeed look the part of an architect when he turned up on site dressed in a grey suit and tie. Carrying a brown leather briefcase, his disguise was finished off with a white hard hat, making his whole appearance look totally official. As he closed his car door and turned towards the site office he was confronted by Michael's younger brother Peter. For a moment, nothing was said as the pair eyeballed each other as though weighing up the opposition. Peter was now your typical gangly sixteen-year-old. Everything he wore looked like it was waiting for him to grow into it. The boots on his feet were like barge boats protruding from the base of his jeans, which hung off his skinny backside and spindly legs. His sweatshirt was in need of a pair of shoulders, and the safety hat on his head made his whole appearance look top heavy, but his gob was one thing that didn't need any growth.

"Who the fuck are you?" he demanded, sounding like ten men. Eli continued to look the skinny teenager up and down, admiring his spunk. He thought he knew who he was, but decided to play him at his own game.

"What the fuck's it got to do with you, ye gobby little mug. I'm after the organ grinder, not his fucking monkey."

Young Peter was a bit shocked by Eli's accent and his return, but he wasn't going to back down.

"Are you from London, one of them Cockney fellas?"

"That's right," answered Eli, keeping up the exchange with a bit of cheeky banter, "I'm a Cockney geezer, what of it."

"Nothing," answered Peter, with the signs of a smile growing on his face. "I was just wondering what your village is doing for a fucking idiot while your over here."

Eli was being beaten to the punch, and although he didn't like it, he did appreciate the young boy's spirit.

"You want to wind your neck in, you little mug. And curb that North and South before I land my boot up your Harris."

"Peewee, leave him alone," Michael shouted from the site office door.

"You said not to let any building inspectors in," he shouted back, defending his actions.

"He's not a building inspector, he's an architect. Now fuck off and load those bricks on to the scaffold like I told you to do, ten minutes ago." Peter set off to do his job but not before he gave El, one last piece of abuse.

"Jellied eel eating, Cockney fucker," he muttered, turning away. Eli, amused by the lip, walked towards the cabin.

"I like him," he said, shaking Michael's hand. "How old is he."

"Sixteen, and a gobby wee shite."

"Sixteen. He's more like sixty, the little fucker. He reminds me of a Millwall fan." Eli climbed the few steps and entered the office, still smiling at young Peter's cheek. "I am right in presuming that he's your little brother."

"He's not so little anymore. Especially his gob."

"You can say that again," added Eli with an agreeing grin.

Inside the rest of the team were sat drinking tea and looking exactly like what they were these days, hard-working, dusty navvies.

"What's in the briefcase," Sean asked as Eli placed it on the desk and began to open it.

"Funny you should ask that, you impatient fucker, because it's a list of requirements we need, and most of them are going to have to be obtained by you."

"It's a big case for a little list," Sean returned when seeing the A4 sheet being pulled from the case.

"The paper would have fit in my pocket, but I thought the brief case went with my disguise. I've never been an architect before." Eli smiled, whilst performing a little twirl to show off his suit. "What do you think?" he asked, adding a little catwalk to the show.

"Very convincing," added Sean sarcastically. "After the robbery, if I need a solicitor I'll know who to call. You could do that job as well in the same get-up."

"No, I wear my pinstripe suit when I'm a solicitor." Eli passed Sean one of the sheets of paper as the pair shared a smile.

"Old Bobby, had you down as an undertaker last week, I hope we don't need one of them," commented Michael, remembering what Bobby had said after Eli left the cellar.

"Who the fuck's old Bobby when he's at home."

"You don't want to know. If I introduced you it would probably cost you a tenner," replied Michael as he moved around to the other side of the desk and sat down.

"Any problems since our last little meeting?" Eli asked.

"We need to have a word before we go any further. We've been doing some talking since Sunday and there are a few things, well more conditions really, that we want you to be aware of." Michael, as usual, put himself forward as the spokesman for the lads.

"Fair enough," Eli replied, looking at the four of them. "If there's something you want to say, let's have it."

"Don't worry, we're not pulling out," Michael reassured. "We'd just like you to take some things in to consideration when planning the job."

"I'm all ears, my old China. What's on your mind?"

"The first thing is a condition; we won't kill. What we did before in the name of the cause was something we believed in. We will not kill anyone now for profit. The plan to rob the bank has to be one where weapons aren't needed."

Eli, as usual when having a conversation or doing any thinking, lit a cigar. He sucked on it several times, making sure it was well lit while the lads waited for his reaction.

"Look lads, there's no guarantees when you pull something like this, you all know that. When you robbed the Yardie's place in London, even though you went tooled up you didn't expect to kill anyone, but you did. All I can tell you is that if someone is killed, it won't have been part of the plan."

The four Irish were happy with his reply. He was right though, there were no guarantees, but at least now he was aware of the way they felt.

"The second thing which you should be aware of," Michael continued, "is how hard it's going to be for us four to pull a bank robbery in Belfast. We'll be shitting well and truly on our own doorsteps, and we aren't exactly the least inconspicuous and unrecognisable bunch in town."

Michael looked back at Sean as though trying to prove a point.

"What are you looking at me for? I'm not the only one that stands out in a crowd. What about fucking Sasquatch over there. He's not exactly Mr fucking Average is he."

Danny, ignoring what he presumed was an insult, calmly drank his tea, but he did have something to add to the conversation.

"Michael's right, Eli, the streets surrounding that bank are full of cameras. In fact, there's not an inch of the city that isn't wired these days. Even with masks on we'd be recognised in a breath once the video was shown on the news. And if we are wearing masks going in to the bank the police will be on us in a breath, we won't have time to steal fuck all."

"I blame that fucking Crime Stoppers," added Sean, still in a rant. "It's turned every fucker in to a grass."

Eli, paused for a second, slightly put off his stroke, either by Sean's statement or just Sean.

"Lads, I knew that your notoriety would be a problem four years ago when you left Chelsea Harbour, so I have had plenty of time to think about it. In fact, Dermot, the items on your list are to help deal with that very problem."

Eli pulled another sheet from his case and slid it along the desk top towards Dermot, who trapped it under his hand. Sean, scrutinising his list, had already found something to question.

"Why do we need so many vehicles? Four vans and three cars, and why does one of the vans have to be white?"

"We're not going through the plan today, Sean. You've got your list, now can you get the items on it?

Obviously there's nothing listed there we don't need. I'm not trying to give you any extra exercise."

"I presume I'm stealing and not buying them."

"Of course, and the white vehicle wants to be a Mercedes sprinter with both a rear and side door. Now you're in charge of transport, so do you foresee any problems?"

"None."

"Good, what about you Dermot, do you foresee any problems?" Dermot raised his hand so as not to be interrupted from reading the list.

"You've got down here that you want me to make nine mortar tubes out of oxyacetylene bottles, but it doesn't mention anything about the explosives for the charge."

"Don't worry about that, we'll supply the explosives and the projectiles they're going to shoot. If you were to obtain them you would have to go to your old suppliers and that would draw attention and leave a trace to follow after the robbery."

"Wow, wow, wow, hang on a minute, Eli," Michael,

interrupted. "Mortars and explosives, I thought we were robbing a bank, not storming the fucking Bastille. Where does that lot fit in to the plan?"

"In the part that stops you lot from being recognised. The reservations you've already voiced were obvious ones. Trust me, Michael, I've had a long time to think about this and I knew from the beginning that pulling a job with you lads in your own backyard without getting your ugly mugs and distinctive shapes caught on camera wasn't going to be easy. I had to come up with somewhat of an elaborate smoke screen to prevent it. Now it's a bit over the top, and when I explain it to you you're going to think I'm off my fucking nut, but it will work, and without anybody getting killed. Just make sure that the Sprinter you steal is white, the reason for this will become apparent later."

"Come on Eli, tell us the crack, you've got us all thinking now."

"Not yet, Danny, we'll meet again in a week or so when we have everything and go over the plan then. Now all we need in the mean time are the items Dermot and Sean are going to supply, and the information you and Michael will acquire concerning the bank manager. We need to know where he lives, and what time he leaves home and arrives at work. Also what type of car he drives, who he lives with, is he married, and if so, does he have any kids? Oh, and does he have a dog?"

"I understand what you want," confirmed Michael. "If we're going to take the manager and his family hostage we need to know his routine and everything else about him. Leave it to Danny and me. Tomorrow we'll go to that bank and make an appointment, I think it's about time we shifted our account."

"Don't forget that when the police do their follow-up investigation they'll go over all the bank's video tapes for the previous few weeks, if not months. They'll be looking for anything suspicious or out of the ordinary, so make sure your business there looks legitimate and can be backed up. The same goes for you, lads," Eli continued, whilst looking at Dermot and Sean. "The vehicles and the mortar tubes will be left behind, so don't let any part of them be traceable to us. From this point on you don't touch anything to do with the robbery without wearing gloves."

"Eli, you've given us our jobs, now let me and Danny take care of the manager, and Dermot and Sean take care of their end."

Michael wasn't used to being told how to suck eggs.

"Sorry, old habits," replied Eli, realising that he was treating the lads like a bunch of raw recruits. "Right Dermot, Sean, on the bottom of your lists there is an address of a farm just outside town. Take all the items there as you acquire them. Errol will be there permanently to let you in, so don't worry about turning up in the middle of the night with any of those vehicles. Have you got that, Sean?"

"I understand."

"From now on the farm will be our base and all planning and preparations will be done there. We'll meet in one week at six o'clock in the evening, by which time we should have everything we need to go through the plan. Don't worry if you don't have all your items or information. We still have three weeks, so the important thing is not to rush, and not to make any mistakes." Everybody nodded in agreement with what Eli had said. "Oh, and one last thing, don't be folding those lists up and putting them in some pocket where the police can find them later. Bring them with you to the meeting. I'll take them back and burn them."

"So you don't trust us to burn them ourselves," questioned Dermot. "We're not kids, Eli, if you tell us to destroy the lists when we've done, then that's exactly what we'll do." Eli held his hands up, he just couldn't help himself.

"Sorry again. It's not that I don't trust you, it's just that I have a problem with not taking care of everything myself."

"We know someone else like that," added Dermot, looking across at Michael. Sean and Danny nodded in agreement.

"I'm not like that," answered Michael, defending himself. "The only reason I take care of everything is because you three don't want the responsibility."

The others looked at him blankly, as if to say "ye'h right".

"What, you think I'm a bit of a control freak?" Another shrug of the shoulders was countered by Michael's furthered defence. "Look, Danny, you'll do anything I'll do, because you're my best mate and you won't leave my side. Am I correct?"

"Ye."

"And the feeling's mutual, big fella, as I would do for you. And you, Fatty, you'll do whatever ye brother does so long as there's some money and a plate of food at the end of it."

"Ye."

"And you, Dermot. You don't like to be in charge of anything, just so you can disagree and throw a spanner in the works to any ideas that anybody else comes up with."

"No," he returned dismissively, followed immediately by an agreed contradiction by Danny and Sean.

"Ye," they both spouted, confirming Michael's analogy.

"So I only do the job," Michael concluded, "because you three don't want too."

"Bollocks," shouted Sean. "It doesn't matter how you explain it away. You and Eli are like two peas in a fucking pod. You get off on giving orders and being in charge."

Eli and Michael looked at each other, but instead of offering an argument they just shrugged their shoulders and accepted Sean's analogy. How could they disagree, just the same as the other three couldn't disagree with what Michael had said? They both loved the planning, and the challenge. They were robbing the bank because it was there, and because they could.

"Right chaps," interceded Eli, breaking up the little lover's tiff, with a chuckle in his voice. "There's nothing else for us to discuss today, we all have our jobs. All eight of us will meet again next Tuesday at the farm and go through the plan as best we can with the information we have. Now, have any of you got anything for me, or are we all happy?" Again, Eli showed signs of a little smirk as he looked around at the quartet. Nobody replied with any queries. "Good. Then I'll see you next week." He picked up his case but stopped before he got to the door, with an inquisitive look on his face. "I forgot to ask you the other day, Dermot. Whatever became of that old bird from the café, the one that you knocked up?"

Dermot cringed at his question, knowing it would open up the flood gates for a piss take. Sean, not one to miss out on an opportunity to have a go at Dermot, waded in, feet first.

"Well," he began, as Dermot sank his face in to his hands. "It came as a bit of a surprise who the father was when the baby arrived, or should I say suplize, seeing as how it popped out looking more like Bruce Lee, than our own little Dermot Barry, here."

Eli looked at Dermot with a curious smirk before looking back at Sean for an explanation. Sean was only too happy to oblige, spilling the beans in his own delectable manner.

"It turned out that the new born belonged to the Chinese fella that owns the Flying Wok takeaway around the corner from O'Reilly's Bar. Apparently, she ordered a number sixty nine, and nine months later got the delivery."

"No, you're 'avin a laugh ain't ye."

Eli looked back at Dermot. Dermot just shook his head with a here-we-go-again look on his face, confirming Sean's rendition of the birth. He had heard every joke there was about Chinese people, and a thousand more that Sean had made up himself, hoping to get a rise.

"She's had another since then," continued Sean, with more information. Eli raised his eyes in acceptance of more enlightenment. "That's eight she has now. It must be like a clown's pocket down below. I'm surprised Dermot ever touched the sides."

Eli had heard some crude barrack room talk in his life but Sean didn't care what he said. After getting the picture of the 'baggy' clown's pocket and other things out of his mind, he offered Dermot some consolation.

"Well, I should count your blessings if I were you, Dermot. "It could have been a lot worse. When she went out for a takeaway that night the Chinese could have been closed and she might have ended up with a curry. Nine months later it could have been Ghandi popping out, and not Bruce lee!"

Another shake of Dermot's head followed, but he wasn't going to be as he informed them of the pro's of the situation.

"Aye, but I get a right discount on my 'chicken fried rice,' and I still get an oil change from old Greasy Deasy, when Jackie Chan's at the casino on Tuesday nights. In-fact, I'm getting the same as I did before, plus a meal, and there's no fucking maintenance."

Dermot, with a smug smile on his face, raised his arms high, saluting a good result.

Eli smiled.

"Fuck me, Sean, it sounds like Dermot's finally got one over on you."

Sean had never thought about it that way, but conceded the point with a nod of the head and a pout of the lips.

"And," added Dermot. "Whilst we are on the subject of women. I am taking a bird out this week called Mary Cahill, but before I do I want to know that neither of you Keenan brothers has had any carnal knowledge of her. Just so we can avoid any repeats of any previous situations."

"Carnal knowledge," repeated Sean. "You mean have I or Danny, slipped her one. And what is it with you and women called Mary. Haven't you learnt your lesson?"

"It's not easy in Belfast finding a woman that isn't called Catherine or Mary," explained Dermot. "Unless you start dating the Protestant girls but then they are all Debbie's or Sharon's."

"I bet the girls around here have the same problem," added Eli as about to leave. "They probably struggle finding a man that isn't called Patrick or Michael."

Michael gave Eli a look as he exited the office, leaving the rest of the lads with a huge smile, and returned to his vehicle. He opened the door and threw his briefcase on to the passenger seat whilst noticing young Peter still loading the bricks on to the scaffold. He put two fingers into his mouth and whistled to catch his attention. Peter turned to see him raising the same two fingers, before getting into his car, smiling at having the last word.

"Cockney fucker," young Peter, snarled.

Chapter Six

Mr Keenan and Mr Flynn

Roisin came out of the bathroom brushing her hair and entered the bedroom, where Michael lay on his back in bed. She was wearing one of his shirts which hung seductively from her breasts and barely covered the crotch line where her long and just shaved silky legs began. Her shape was picked out through the flimsy cotton garment by the light of the lamp making the view - even to a man that saw it every night - arousing. Michael, who wouldn't normally have been disinterested, didn't even look at his wife. He just lay with his hands clasped behind his head and his mind elsewhere deep in thought. Roisin placed the brush on the dressing table and walked to her side of the bed, pulled back the quilt and slid in next to him.

"What's up with you, you've been quiet all night. You're not ill, are ye?"

"I've a lot on my mind, that's all babes."

"Is it the building site? It can't be the bar, Babs said it's going great and turning over a good profit."

"No the job's fine, and so is the bar."

"Well come on then, tell me what's wrong," she asked, as she rolled towards him, kissing his chest and sliding her hand under the covers. "There's nothing wrong with this fella down here, it must be all in your head," she joked, giving his manhood a yank while biting his nipple.

"Behave yourself, woman, you're going to do me an injury." Michael brought his hands down to protect himself and tickled Roisin at the same time. Giggling, they fell into an embrace and kissed.

"Seriously, tell me what's on your mind." Roisin continued her questioning, knowing something was wrong.

She raised her hand and ran her fingers through his hair before sliding them down his face and back on to his chest. Michael returned his hands behind his head and settled into his original position. Refocusing his gaze back to the ceiling, he was trying to make a decision as to whether or not he should come clean with her about the robbery. He wasn't going to ask if he should do it or not, that decision had already been made. It was more to make sure that she knew what to do if things went wrong and they were caught. For this reason he had to tell her, and the other reason was because she was his wife everything that he was doing that would affect them both.

"Do you remember when the lads and I were in London?" he started to explain.

"A few years ago, of course I do. I'm still paying the extra insurance premium on my shop."

Michael laughed, while kissing her on the forehead for what he had put her through.

"I'm still waiting for those golf clubs," he said with a smile to accompany his sarcasm. "Anyway, I never filled you in with the details, but there was a fella back then that saved our lives. He even let us get away with the money we came back to Belfast with that bought the pub and set up the business."

"What do you mean, let you get away with? You told me you were paid good bonuses and that you had all made money on the horses backing one of Danny's tips."

"Yeh right, I'm surprised you believed that one."

"I didn't, especially the part about making money from one of Danny's tips."

They both chuckled at Danny's lack of equine knowledge.

"Well, obviously there was more to it, and this fella called Eli is the reason me and the lads are here today."

"Eli, that's a weird name, but it sounds like you have a lot to thank him for, and so have I for saving my man."

Again she kissed his chest lovingly.

"He didn't exactly do it for nothing, though. He said he would need us in the future to pull a job."

"What sort of job?"

Michael didn't answer straight away but there was no easy way of saying it.

"A bank robbery."

"Jesus Michael, a bank robbery. Who robs banks these days? I mean fair enough, a post office or a building society but not a bank, this isn't America. Who do you think you are, Jesse James?" Roisin was shocked but didn't create too much, believing Michael, was talking about something that wasn't going to happen. "Bank robbery," she continued, "let's hope this Eli fella never turns up."

Michael again wasn't exactly quick in his response. Still focusing on the ceiling, his quietness began to set off alarm bells in Roisin's head.

"Oh, My, God," she cried, climbing on to her knees as the penny dropped. "He's here, isn't he?"

She was now running her fingers through her own hair, spoiling all the earlier brushing.

"He turned up last week," confirmed Michael, "and he's here to collect." Now it was Roisin's turn to stay quiet, but not for long.

"Well, I hope he doesn't think that you're doing it for nothing. How much is he paying you?"

"Is that all you're bothered about. Are you not going to tell me not to do it?"

"Michael Flynn, you wouldn't have bothered telling me if you hadn't already made up your mind to do the robbery. Besides, I've never stood in your way, and I'll not start now. So what concerns me is how much are you getting paid. And is it enough to make the risk worth taking?"

Michael was now smiling at the ceiling, thinking of the money involved. Roisin, seeing his smirk, decided to give him something to smile about. She reached back under the quilt and took another hand full of his manhood, this time also sinking her nails in to his ball sack.

"Aahh, fucking hell woman, watch what you're doing with those nails, will ye. A few inches higher and you could have turned me in to a Jew boy.

"How much Michael," she repeated whilst tightening her grip.

"Alright, alright, calm down," she loosened her hold at his submission. "A million quid," he casually admitted. It took a second for what Michael had said to sink in, but soon a picture of a big one and six little zeroes following it danced through her head.

"A million fucking quid," she repeated at the top of her voice.

"Yeh, each," he added, beaming.

"Fuck me, do you need me to do anything?"

"Yeh, stop swearing and make me a cup of tea. One bank robber in the family is quite enough."

"A million quid."

"Seriously, Roisin, I'm only telling you about it in case we get caught. If we end up in jail you're going to have to hold everything, and everyone together. Especially Babs, she doesn't know anything about Danny's past, and I'm not sure that she could handle losing him."

"Leave all that to me. You just concentrate on not getting caught and bringing me home that million quid. Just think, we can buy a villa abroad."

"Don't go counting any chickens, just yet. But if we

did buy a villa it wouldn't be near that Marbella place, and all those fucking plastic gangsters. It would be up by Benidorm, where the proper people go."

"I don't care where it is so long as it's warm. It will be a great place to bring up the kids."

"Kids, what kids?" asked Michael, slightly alarmed at Roisin's indication that there were to be more than one. Roisin, with a big raunchy smile, began to seductively, one by one, unbutton the shirt she was wearing.

"Oh, not tonight babe's, sure haven't I just explained to you all the shit I have going on in my head. What about that cup of tea I asked for?"

Roisin's, raunchy and seductive grin said it all.

"There's plenty of time for tea later. Right now it's the time on my body clock that matters." She reached over to switch off the light, before returning her hand back down to his crotch. "The clock's ticking, and I'm ovulating," she informed him with a whisper in the dark. "Just stay laid back and I'll do the work." She removed her shirt on to the floor and threw back the covers before climbing on to the saddle.

"Oh, go on then," Michael sighed. "But only the once this time!!"

The next morning, Danny and Michael, made their way into Belfast City centre to begin their reconnaissance. After parking the car they walked the short distance to Donegal Square, where the bank was situated. In all their lives and visits to the centre, never before had they paid so much attention to their surroundings whilst being conscious that all the time, like everybody else on the street, they were being filmed.

"Who's doing the talking, me or you?"

"You do the spouting," answered Danny, "I'll follow your lead,"

Michael acknowledged as the pair entered the bank doors. They stopped in the middle of the room to read the different signs on the desks and above the teller windows, looking for the one they wanted.

"Can I help you Sirs, you look a bit lost?" One of the staff, a young lady, came over to help after noticing the pair's look of confusion.

"You can indeed," answered Michael, leaning forward to read her name tag. "Debbie is it, or do you prefer Debra?"

"Debs actually, but Debbie is fine for work."

"Ok, Debbie, nice to meet you." Michael gave the assistant a firm handshake before going into his role. "My partner and I are unhappy with our present bank so we are looking to take our business elsewhere. A few of our friends have accounts here and told us that your benefits and rates were competitive so you came highly recommended."

"It's good to know that we are doing our job properly."

"You are indeed, Debbie, and obviously the service is second to none, because no sooner are we through the doors than here you are offering to help us." The young lady smiled at Michael's words of flattery. "Would it be possible for you to look in the manager's diary and make us an appointment, unless he's available right now of course?"

"Actually, Sir, if you would like to take a seat over here at my desk, I am able to help you."

The woman turned and pointed the way to her desk in the corner with the words 'new accounts' written above it. The pair looked across, knowing it wasn't what they wanted.

"No disrespect, Debra, but we really wanted to see the manager. You see we have two large and growing accounts. One from a busy bar we own in the city and the other is for our construction company, which we use for the tendering of a lot of customers' money." Michael could see the young lady was about to reassure him of her abilities and continued to press the fact. "I'm afraid out of duty to our customers that we wouldn't feel comfortable trusting and discussing our business with anyone else other than the manager."

"It's got to be the manager," confirmed Danny, leaning over Michael's shoulder and adding a bit of weight to their request.

"Ok," she agreed. "If you would like to take a seat I will go talk to him."

"Thank you," added Danny, "It's much appreciated."

The lads remained standing to get a good look at who

she was going to see. They watched her go across the bank and in to a glass panelled office, which afforded them a perfect view through its windows of the man she was talking to. The pair moved a little bit closer to get an even better look at him, etching his face into their minds.

"If that's your man, there's no need to have the meeting. I won't forget his face," said Danny, out of the corner of his mouth.

"Neither will I," agreed Michael, joining the ventriloquist act. They continued to watch, even acknowledging as the manager looked at them through his window as Debbie indicated towards the two new prospective customers. She came back out of the office, bringing with her the manager's diary.

"I'm sorry, the manager is busy today, but there is an opening at ten in the morning," she informed them with the book open at the following day's date, ready to pen in the appointment.

"Was that the manager you were talking to?" asked Michael, fishing for the information they needed. "I'm sure I know him from somewhere."

"Yes that's right, Mr Wilson," she confirmed.

"Ah no, that's not the name I was thinking of, but his face does look familiar. He doesn't live up by me in Portrush, does he?"

"No, I don't think so. I think Mr Wilson lives in Downpatrick."

"Well it can't be him then, but they do say everybody has a double." Michael gave a little smile to the woman to accompany his bullshit. "Listen, we were talking whilst you were in the office with Mrrrr..."

"Wilson," added Debbie, completing the manager's name that Michael had forgotten.

"Mr Wilson, thank you. Do you happen to have any appointments available for the twenty-first of December to see Mr Wilson, because we can definitely make it that day?"

She flicked through the pages to find the appropriate date to check the availability.

"Yes there is an opening; at eleven o'clock, if that will do?"

"That would be grand," confirmed Michael, accompanied by an agreeing nod from Danny.

"And your name is," she asked with her pen on the page.

"Its Mr Flynn, and Mr Keenan." Danny, looked at Michael, confused as to why he had given her their real names.

"Right, Mr Keenan."

"No, I'm Mr Flynn, the big good-looking fella behind me here is Mr Keenan."

The girl looked up at Danny, who gave her a wink and a cheesy grin.

"Right, Mr Flynn, your appointment is confirmed for Tuesday the twenty-first of December at eleven in the morning. We look forward to seeing you then, when I am sure we can improve on the deal and service your present bank is offering."

"I'm sure you will, Debbie, you've already upstaged them in the looks department."

She blushed and then smiled. Then blushed again because the lads knew that she had enjoyed the compliment. The pair left the bank with all the information they needed.

Back on the street facing Donegal Square, Michael began to take note of his surroundings, wondering how Eli was planning to overcome the numerous cameras and how they were going to make their get-away in such heavy traffic.

"What the fuck was all that about?" Danny asked, breaking his friend from his thoughts.

"All what? We got what we needed, didn't we?"

"Yeh, and she got more than she needed. You gave her our names, made an appointment, and nearly charmed the fucking knickers off he arse."

"Danny," Michael stopped what he was about to say. Looking at the people on the street, he realised they were having the conversation in the wrong place. "Come on let's get back to the car."

A few moments later, climbing into the car, Michael pulled the pay and display sticker from the window screen, rolled it up and threw it in to his door compartment. He made himself comfortable and fastened his seat belt before starting to explain his actions to Danny.

"I gave her our names because like Eli said, the police will go over the CCTV footage of the weeks leading up to the robbery. How would it look if some smart guard (copper) noticed us then crossed-referenced it with the manager's diary and realised that we had given a pair of false ID's."

"So that's why you made the appointment for the day after we rob the place, to keep everything looking legit?"

"Correct, the appointment will never happen because the bank will be closed, but if we are picked up by the police we can say we turned up for the meeting but it was cancelled because some thieving fuckers had robbed the bank the day before. All they will know is that we turned up at the bank looking to transfer our account."

"Sorry," apologised Danny. "I must have been having a Dermot moment, but that doesn't explain you going all charm school on the lady."

"I thought we had upset her when we went over her head and asked to see the manager. It was just my way of cheering her up, that's all."

"You soft fucker."

"No Danny, I wasn't being soft. I just like to think that if I can go through life bringing a smile to the faces of the people I meet, that the world would be a happier place," Michael joked with a smile.

"Yeh, and then a few weeks later you can go back and rob them all. That would make your world a lot happier."

The two laughed as Michael started the engine.

"Where to now?" asked Danny.

"Let's go get a breakfast; at the same time we can have a look through the phone book and see how many Mr Wilson's there are in Downpatrick. Then we can come back here at three-thirty and follow our new friend, the bank manager, home to confirm the address."

Danny pulled on his seat belt but there were still a few things he and Michael hadn't discussed.

"I know we've come too far with this to back out," he said pushing the clip in to its housing, "but do you have any reservation about pulling this job?"

Michael turned to his big mate with a 'you're kidding aren't you' look on his face.

"Fuck me Danny, of course I have. The jokes I make are only to cover up my fears. Inside I'm shitting a brick."

"You seem your usual calm self to me."

"It's a facade."

"A what."

"A façade, a disguise, a front. Listen fella, we're about to steal a lot of money, which if what we are led to believe is true, belongs to the IRA. Couple that with the fact that our partners in this crime are not only former members of the British Army, but also the SAS Regiment, and it amounts to an unthinkable situation should we be caught. A situation that will make the problems we had in London look like a minor hiccup. We'll end up getting shot twice, once for thieving and the other for collaborating. The only good thing in my mind that I can think of is that this time, it wasn't my fucking idea."

"So that would be a yes then," concluded Danny.

"A resounding one, so much so that last night I told Roisin what we were getting up to."

"You told Roisin?"

"I did indeed."

Danny paused, unsure if Michael had done the wrong or the right thing.

"Did she rare up on ye?"

"Not really." He almost sounded disappointed. "She guessed that I had already agreed to take part in the robbery though. I swear that woman knows what I'm doing before I've even thought of it myself. And once I mentioned the million quid, well, she'd all but bought a fucking villa in Spain before she had even thought about how many years I would have to spend in jail."

Danny laughed.

"Fuck me, you can't have it both ways. Last Friday when we were all pissed you said you would do the job whether Roisin liked it or not. Now you're complaining because she hasn't tried to talk you out of it."

"I'm not complaining, I just don't like the fact that she can predict my movements."

"She has the measure of you that's for sure. At least she's stood by you. I don't know if Babs would react the same way. Do you think I should do the same as you and tell her the crack?"

"There's no need. If anything goes wrong, Roisin will take care of her and bring her up to speed with whatever the situation may be. She told me that last night."

Danny was happy with 'that' plan.

"Suits me," he agreed. "I'll settle for the quiet life any day."

"That's right, Big Fella, you sit back and relax. I wouldn't want anything playing on your mind and putting you off your betting."

Danny smiled at Michael's sarcastic gripe.

"I'm glad somebody's fucking happy," Michael continued, his moan extending to a disgruntled look as he drove away. Danny just continued to laugh. In all their years of friendship he had never been able to get under his mate's collar but Roisin obviously had the knack.

Chapter Seven

Sterling Lines, Hereford

"You're here again, Mr Fletcher, and once again without an appointment. And you've brought your entourage for company, how lovely."

Colonel Roberts didn't like surprises; who does? But he especially didn't like surprises from MI5.

"We like to catch people off guard, Colonel, that way we tend to get more of the truth. And my men go everywhere with me."

"Really? It must get cosy in the toilet." A smirk followed the Colonel's statement, which none of his visitors appreciated. "And if I told my men on the gate to refuse you entrance, you wouldn't be sat here now, so don't accuse me of being unprepared, or of being a liar. Now what is it this time?"

Fletcher, whose manner seemed to grow less polite with every visit, made no apologies. "Your man, Moon. He's dropped off the radar."

"Sgt Major Moon, you mean. And what of it."

"Where is he?"

"You mean, where is he, SIR? I'm getting sick and tired of your lack of respect, MR FLETCHER."

The Colonel gritted his teeth whilst pronouncing Fletcher's name.

"Where is he, Colonel? We have his house and usual haunts under surveillance, along with all the hovels his three sidekicks frequent and we are coming up blank at all addresses. Now, is he on the missing list under your orders, or is he simply missing?"

The Colonel lit a cigarette whilst leaning back in his chair. He didn't like lying, especially after recently denying being one, but if it was a choice between his Sgt Major and Fletcher, Eli, was always going to get his loyalty.

"Sgt Major Moon is on leave prior to his retirement from the Army. If I need him, I have a pager number. And no, before you ask, I will not give it to you. The fact that he is not at home, or anywhere else you may be watching, is not an offence. However, if you have charges to bring against him, and my superiors request it, I will summon him. If I am ordered."

"No," Fletcher admitted, now with his own teeth gritted. "There are no charges, as yet."

"Then why are you here?"

"I am here to reiterate our previous offer. We have need of Moon's expertise."

"Yes you said. When your offer was recently refused, in front of me in this very office. I don't think that Sgt Major Moon is the type to rethink things."

"He might."

"Why would he."

"He might," Fletcher paused. "He might if you asked him too."

The Colonel grinned. He took a drag of his cigarette and released a little laugh with the smoke. "Moon has you sussed. Don't you realise that he will not work with you because of you underhand ways, and here you are trying to coerce me into doing your bidding."

"I haven't offered you anything."

"No, but you will, when I don't play ball."

"You mean 'if' you don't play ball."

"No, I don't. You see, my principles are just as stern as Moon's, so it will always be a 'no' if you want to save yourself a lot of time."

"Come now, Colonel, everybody has a price, or yearns for something they don't possess."

Again the Colonel smoked his cigarette and smiled.

"You don't know much about soldiers and loyalty, do you, Fletcher? What I yearn for is to die with the respect of my comrades and friends. Something that can only be earned by myself in life, and not something that can ever be given."

It took a while for Fletcher to realise that he was being insulted, but eventually he got the message.

"Your refusal to co-operate with our agency's enquiries will not go unreported."

Colonel Roberts shook his head.

"Once again, Mr Fletcher, you have outstayed your welcome. Now if there is nothing else, leave, and take those two bullet stops with you."

Fletcher turned and looked at his sidekicks, feeling a little protective of his own men.

"They are highly trained MI5 agents. You SAS seem to think that you own the rights to being awarded the name of Special Forces."

The Colonel grinned.

"The only time those two would be highly trained is if you took them for a jog over a hill. Now get them, and yourself, out of my office."

The meeting was over.

Chapter Eight

Oneway and Ringer

A week soon passed, bringing around the time for the meeting at the farm to further discuss the plan. The route there was now becoming second nature to Sean, after he and Dermot had been regular visitors that week, delivering the items from their lists as they acquired them. Each meeting brought fresh anticipation and excitement, this one especially being that it would be the first time that they would be meeting the other members of Eli's group since their brief encounter on that unforgettable night in the Heathrow warehouse four years earlier.

"Watch the fucking road, will ye," Dermot shouted from the back seat at Sean, who was spending more time playing with the cigarette lighter than he was looking at what was in front of him.

"Shut the fuck up, you moaning little tosspot. Or would you rather get out and walk?"

Sean's retaliation was delivered in his usual coarse manner.

"You've already got a fag lit in your mouth. Why are ye fucking about with the lighter? As if there isn't enough smoke in here already without you lighting another."

"If the smoke bothers you then open a fucking window."

"It's fucking freezing outside and there's ice on the road, which is exactly why you should be concentrating on your driving."

"Lads, lads, will you give it a fucking rest," Michael shouted, growing tired of the bickering. "You've been having this same fucking argument since we were twelve years old. Either find something new to argue about or shut the fuck up."

"Ooooo, easy, Tiger. Who stole the sugar out of your tea," commented Sean on Michael's rant.

"Michael's a bit sensitive lately," said Danny, adding a bit of a piss-take. "He thinks he's become predictable, and that Roisin doesn't care about him any more."

"Predictable, where?" Sean jumped in, seeing an opportunity for a piss-take of his own. "Not between the sheets, I hope. A beautiful woman like Roisin needs a bit of variety. You can't just be jumping on top all the time, or diving in dry. Ye have to start with a bit of tender caressing as you make your way down to the fury cup for a bit of yodelling in the valleys. YODELLAHEEDEE," sang Sean, in a high-pitched voice.

"Button it, fat boy, and watch the road before I tenderly caress your jaw. It's got nothing to do with what myself and Roisin get up to in the bedroom. I just thought she would be more worried about the robbery, and less about how she was going to spend the money, that's all."

"You told Roisin, about the robbery?"

"Yes, Sean, she's my wife. Remember that the next time you're switching yourself on thinking about me going yodelling in her valleys. I thought I'd better fill her in with what's going on just in case we get caught, rather than trying to explain it later through an inch-thick glass window in the jail."

"You didn't tell your Ma as well, did ye?"

"Leave it out, Dermot. If we get caught, the window in the visiting room of Crumlin Road jail will be the only thing that protects me from her. I won't be telling Ma anything she doesn't need to know. I don't want anything putting her off her bingo."

They travelled a few more miles down the country lanes and Sean started to take more care on the slippery road as the light began to fade. The farm was secluded enough so as to be out of sight of any nosey neighbours, but close enough to Belfast city centre to make it workable as a base.

"How much further is this place?" enquired Danny. "I don't even know where we are."

"We're here now," replied Sean, as he slowed and swung the front of the vehicle out to make the turn in to the farm entrance.

"How the fuck did they find this place?" continued Danny. "In all the years I've lived here, I've never been down this road before."

"We're talking about Eli. He and his team probably know Ireland like the back of their hands, and a lot better than what we do," replied Dermot. "I'm ashamed to say it, but we probably know our way around the bars in Belfast better than we do the countryside that surrounds it."

At the entrance, Errol was waiting with the keys, ready to let them in. As he pulled open the gate and Sean drove the car inside, Errol was joined by Oneway, and Ringer.

"Alright Sean, Dermot," Errol said as they all climbed out of the car. The three had already become acquainted and friendly through the week, during their many visits. "Lads," Errol continued, "this is Oneway and Ringer. Oneway and Ringer, meet Michael Flynn, Dermot Barry and Sean and Danny Keenan."

"Just call me Fatty, everybody else does," said Sean, breaking the ice. Everybody shook hands as Errol locked the gates before Ringer and Oneway led the way to the house.

"It gives you a kind of open book feeling when someone you haven't really met before introduces you like he's known you all your life," whispered Danny in Michael's ear as they followed on behind.

"I know what you mean; I think it's safe to say that these three fellas know just as much about us as Eli does. But all that's in the past, Danny boy, let's just concentrate on the job in hand and the million quid."

Danny patted him on the back, showing his agreement. Dermot, being the last of the four, was hanging back, wanting some information from Errol.

"Why do they call him Oneway?" he asked. Errol gave a cheeky smile. Whatever the reason, his answer probably wasn't going to be the truth.

"His father was a Yorkshireman and his mother was Scottish, tightness runs deep in his family. If you are ever unfortunate enough to go out for a drink with him you'll be buying his drinks all night, and he'll never buy you one back, hence the name – Oneway."

Dermot, looked at the man's back as he neared the farmhouse door. He seemed average in every way, even the way he walked told you nothing about him. How tight can a man be, Dermot thought to himself, being of a careful nature himself when it came to spending money.

"What about Ringer, is that a pun on his name?"

"No, he got that name because he likes to work with his hands."

"Oh, right," Dermot winced, rubbing his neck.

Inside the farmhouse Eli was waiting in the large kitchen, which had been turned into a makeshift command centre. In the middle of the room was an old table, which he stood over while studying some photographs. A large wall in the kitchen had been painted white and upon it a map of Belfast City centre had been crudely sketched – specifically showing the area around Donegal Square and the Northern Bank.

"Come in, gentlemen, and take a seat," Eli invited as everybody entered. The group did so in chairs that were all facing the wall containing the large map.

"Have any of you had any problems this week?" he asked, directing his question to the Irish lads."

"I'm one vehicle short," stated Sean. "The white Mercedes Sprinter you requested. I've got my eye on one but it won't be safe to take it until the weekend. I hope that doesn't upset any plans, but you said not to take any chances."

"No, Sean, you've done well son. The Sprinter is to be used as the getaway vehicle and as such doesn't need any adjustments as part of the plan. The important thing when you do take it is that it's reliable and white, so take your time. I see you have been busy as well, Dermot, you've got everything on your list."

Dermot smiled at Eli's praise. He turned and looked at Sean, giving him the wanker movement with his hand, returning the insult from the Sunday morning meeting at the pub.

"What about you, Michael?" Eli continued. "How did

you and Danny get on?" Michael stood up and tossed a brown A4 envelope onto the table.

"Everything we need is in there. We followed the manager to and from work three times last week, and he never deviated from his route once. He's the first to arrive at the bank every morning, shortly after seven, when he's soon joined by the under-manager. We also noticed that when they meet on the steps of the bank that he always looks up at the camera covering the door and waves, obviously letting security know that they are ok. He's married with no children and no dog but he and his wife do live with an older couple in a large detached house in Downpatrick, probably her parents and not his, because when we fished some letters out of their mail box, there were two surnames. We also took a leaf out of your book after you going on about satellites last week and went to an internet café and downloaded some aerial photos of his house and the surrounding area, it's all in the envelope.

"Excellent," said Eli, very happy with what the lads had accomplished. "I'll study all the information this week, and at the same time my lads will put his house under surveillance to suss out our best form of entry. Tonight, though, I want us to go over the part of the plan which we do know about, and that's the robbery itself. We will start with you, Dermot, and the preparations you need to make in the next two weeks." Dermot sat up, paying attention as Eli started to get down to the fine details and his involvement. "Outside in the barn are the three transits that Sean this week has so skilfully acquired. Using the gas bottles you fetched, I want you to build six mortar tubes in the back of each vehicle." Eli passed Dermot a sheet of paper displaying some drawings. "I want you to build each set of tubes to the specifications shown here."

Dermot quickly studied the plans but he was already familiar with the design. Mortars were something he had used in the past; they had been a favourite weapon used in the attacking of security bases in the time of the Troubles.

"Why are the tubes in each vehicle set at different angles?" he queried.

"Because we have no way of knowing what the wind direction will be," Eli explained, "or its strength on the morning of the robbery. If the angle of the mortar tubes is different in each vehicle we can move their position on the road to where they will give us the most cover."

Eli's explanation slightly baffled the Irish lads. Michael, still concerned about the use of mortars, questioned the plan thus far.

"How will mortars give us cover, and cover from what? It's not as though we're going to be under attack from anyone."

Eli cracked a slight smile, knowing what they were thinking.

"Cover from the surveillance cameras on the street," he answered. "You need your identities hidden. This is how we are going to do it."

"How, by blowing up the cameras with mortars? They're not exactly selective with their targets either, and there will be people on the street. Remember what we said about not killing anyone?"

"We're not going to be blowing up the cameras," Eli

enlightened, now with a little laugh. "We won't be firing explosives from the mortars; we're going to be firing flour."

"Flour!" said all four Irish together, wondering if they had heard correctly.

"Flour," repeated Sean. "Flour, as in, bake a fucking cake flour," he added, always with food on his mind.

"Not exactly Sean, this is flour as in, eat your fucking Ruby Murray. Chapatti flour to be exact. Oneway has brought nearly a ton of the stuff back from Bradford. It will be packed in pillowcase size bundles, which will be fired two at a time and simultaneously from the mortar tubes in each of the three vehicles up in to the air. When the six packages are at the correct height and directly above the street in front of the bank a secondary charge inside each of the parcels will explode scattering the flour and creating a total white out." Eli took a breather from explaining the usage of the Chapatti flour to look at the reactions on the Irish faces. Whilst taking another smoke of his cigar he gave a tilt of his head, inviting any comebacks. After a reasonable amount of time and receiving no comment beyond four gob-smacked looks, he continued to explain. "The reason that we are using Chapatti flour is because it is heavier than the normal stuff. Hopefully it won't blow around as much in the wind, giving us more control over where it falls. It also burns your mince pies, as you will know if you've been for an Indian and forgot to wash your hands, then woke up the next morning still pissed and rubbed your eyes."

"I do that all the time," interrupted Sean. "It's lucky it doesn't burn your knackers as well."

Everybody in the room got the unpleasant picture of Sean waking up in the morning scratching his nuts.

"Thanks for that Sean. I'm sure it's bearing on the plan will be invaluable," said Eli, before continuing. "Anyway, if you don't like the idea, blame Dermot. I stole it from his plan to use cement in the same way to cover your getaway from the Yardie's night club four years ago."

"It'll work," agreed Dermot. "The same as it would have worked with the cement."

"And," continued Eli, "its incapacitating effects are short-lived. Unlike cement, which can blind you permanently." Everybody in the room nodded their heads, agreeing with the use of the flour. "Now, you may have read in the papers, or in Sean's case, seen on the news over the past few months that a lot of important people, such as politicians and the like, have been receiving suspicious packages through the post containing small amounts of 'Anthrax'. And that certain terrorist groups are making threats to commit a chemical attack on the British public."

"And?" said Danny, wondering what the connection was. Eli said nothing to explain, which in a way said everything.

"Don't tell us that was you lot."

"I'm afraid it was a necessary ploy, Dermot. It's what's called a long con. You see we've been setting our stall up, providing ourselves with a cover that will buy us more time. Don't worry though, the Anthrax we sent wasn't pure, and wouldn't kill anyone. It would just give them a nasty rash, that's all."

"Have you got any with you now?" asked Danny with a smile on his lips. "We could put some in my brother's underpants. That would give him something to scratch in the morning."

Sean took a few puffs on his tab, ignoring Danny's jibe.

"The week before the robbery," Eli continued, "we will send out a few more of those same packages to some important people around Belfast, which will hopefully, when it's reported in the news, create an air of paranoia. The desired result, if it works, is that it will raise not only the police's awareness of a potential attack, but also that of the public, so on the day of the robbery when the flower bombs explode it will be mistaken for exactly that.

"So you are hoping that the police and the public will mistake the flour for Anthrax."

"That's the plan, Sean. The noise from the explosions will make everyone on the street dive for cover while getting flashbacks of the Troubles. By the time they start to get up, the flour will be falling, hindering their vision and making them believe that they are under another type of attack from a chemical weapon."

"That's a nasty trick to play."

"Yes Michael, it is, but it is only a trick. The good people of Belfast have been living with scary threats from one organisation or another for nearly a hundred years. Believe me, they will get over it." Michael didn't like to think of anyone being scared, Catholic or Protestant. "Anyway, this will keep everybody out of our way, and also stop anyone getting our descriptions. The only harm that should befall any member of the public is a pair of sore yocks and a chesty cough. Now, as the first blanket of flour starts to fall to the height of the cameras, six more tubes will blow, sending up six more packages to replenish the cover. This process will be repeated for a third time, using the last six bundles when they're needed."

"I presume that you're making the detonations by remote control," interrupted Dermot. "Because there's no way I can set timers accurately enough to ensure that the cover of flour is kept even. Like you said, there are too many factors involved with the wind and the weather, it could even be raining, which would bring the flour back down to earth twice as fast."

"Correct, Dermot." Eli gave the little fella a wink, appreciating his grasp of the situation. "All the scenarios you just described will be taken into consideration on the morning of the robbery and will have a direct influence as to how long we actually spend inside the bank. Obviously the less cover we have, the less time we have inside, bearing in mind that the cover of the flour will also be used to make our getaway. All the detonations will be controlled by Errol, who will be on the other side of the street in the offices we have rented. From his position on the top floor he has access to the roof, where he will control the cover and use a strong pair of binoculars to keep an eye on the progress of the local police. He will also guide us out of the city when we make our getaway, hopefully in the opposite direction of the said constabulary."

"What about the police, Eli? Belfast is full of them. They could be on us within minutes."

"The police cover at that time in the morning is minimal because all the burglars are in bed after a hard night's work, and the shoplifters don't start until about lunch time. But just to make sure they are kept busy, we're going to create a diversion on the other side of the city. In the barn there are three cars that Sean has also supplied. We're going to fill two with explosives and the third with bricks. At the far west side of the city we're going to detonate the two cars containing the explosives in an area where nobody will get hurt; there's a perfect spot next to the wasteland between the Fall's Road and the Ballymagarry Estate. We'll do this thirty minutes before we enter the bank. This will drag every available police officer towards that area of the city and away from us. The third car with the boot full of bricks we will leave at the junction of the Fall's Road and Grosvenor Road. We'll rig a smoke device to go off inside the vehicle so that the police notice it. Once they check the number plate and realise that it is stolen, combined with the boot being weighted down, they will have to believe it contains a large bomb that has failed to detonate and evacuate the area, dragging in more police. This will also close off their route back to the bank once we begin the robbery. Any police that do approach our position will be hindered by the flour, the same as everyone else."

"I like it," said Michael, giving the plan his approval "I like it a lot. You've thought about the safety of the public and I think it will work."

"What about us and the flour, what will protect us from it?" asked Danny.

"Paint sprayers' masks, the ones with the air filter canister on the side and goggles. We will also be wearing the white sprayer's suits, the ones with the hoods. We should be virtually invisible in the flour."

Eli's plan was receiving more encouraging and agreeable nods from the Irish lads, who couldn't help but appreciate the flamboyancy, but simplicity of it all.

"Getting back to the mortars, Eli, I need to know what size charges to set. Not the ones inside the flour – they just need to split the package, sending the flour all over the sky. But I do need to know how high you want them to be when they explode."

"Don't worry about the delay, Dermot, Errol will also detonate the flour bombs by remote. We tested one of the bombs last year using a 50lb package with a quarter pound explosive charge, which sent it 160 feet in the air. If you stick to those amounts it should give us the height and cover we need. Like you said, just keep the charge inside the packs sufficient enough to give a good spread."

"What about getting inside the bank? So far you've only covered the outside."

"I'm coming to that, Danny, I just wanted to make sure you were all happy with the crazy part of the plan before going any further."

"I don't think its crazy," said Michael. "I think it's a good use of materials. I'm surprised that they've never used it in any wars."

"They did in the past, but you've got to remember that sometimes flour is a precious commodity when you're feeding an army on the march. The French had their own take on it, though. During the peninsular war against the Duke of Wellington they would save all the shells from the oysters they ate and burn them. The residue that was left behind was lime. They would wait until the British were attacking downwind and throw the lime powder in to the air to blind them."

"Froggy bastards," said Dermot, at Eli's history lesson.

"What bothers me is why those French ate all those oysters with no women around," added Sean, extracting a smile from the group.

"As I said, Danny," resumed Eli, "I don't want to go over that part of the plan concerning the manager's house until our next meeting, when I have had time to study the information you and Michael gathered. To make it easy now, though, let's just say that everything has gone to plan with the manager, and we are making our way to the bank early Monday morning. The three Transits containing the mortar tubes will be driven by Michael, Ringer and me." Eli moved away from the table and across to the wall supporting the roughly-drawn map of the streets surrounding the bank. "Ringer and I will arrive first, virtually seconds before Michael and

Sean in their vehicles. Ringer will park his Transit approximately one hundred metres above the bank doors on Donegal Square West." Eli took a marker and drew a blue square on the map where Ringer was to park and wrote his name next to it. "Don't forget that from his position overlooking the bank and the streets that surround it, Errol will be directing all this. Depending on the weather or anything unexpected cropping up, he might move you to a more suitable position." Ringer raised his thumb to show his understanding. "Now, at the same time I'll arrive from the direction of Bedford Street and park up at the junction with Donegal Square, blocking off that approach." Eli again drew a square to represent his vehicle, this time with a red marker. "Michael, you will be the final one into position, arriving behind Sean in the Sprinter, from the May Street end of the road. When Sean turns right to enter Donegal Square West, you'll stay at the junction, angling your vehicle slightly towards the bank in front of you." Eli took a green marker this time and drew a square to represent Michael's van. "Sean, will then drive the hundred yards or so to the bank, do a U- turn so he's facing the wrong way down Donegal Square West and park his vehicle directly in front of the bank doors. As each one of us gets in to position we'll turn on our hazard lights, showing Errol that we are ready. When all four of our hazards are flashing he'll blow the first mortars. I want all this to happen in the space of thirty seconds, giving the public no time to react."

"Hang on a minute, Eli," interrupted Dermot, finding a disturbing flaw in the plan; "you never said anything about you, Ringer and Michael, getting out of the vans before the first mortars are fired."

"That's because were not. We won't get out of the vehicles until after the secondary explosions and flour begins to fall on the window screens, letting us know that the cameras have been blinded. Just make sure that the charges are set correctly. As an added safeguard you could always weld some plate metal between the cab and the back where the mortars will be."

"I don't know about that," replied Dermot, unsure of that part of the plan; "one of you could get killed."

"That's why I will be driving one of the vans," answered Eli. "I wouldn't ask anyone to do something that I wouldn't do myself. The strength of the bottles will take most of the blast, that's why we're using them. The rest of the force should be spent in pushing the bombs upwards towards their height objective."

"Don't worry," said Michael, moving across and patting Dermot on the back. "He knows his job, I'm happy to be driving one of the other vehicles, there'll be no mistakes from Dermot."

Ringer, who as a rule didn't say much, didn't speak at all. He simply looked Dermot in the eyes and winked, showing his confidence in the Irishman's pyrotechnic abilities. Dermot acknowledged the encouragement but couldn't help thinking that if anything did go wrong, Ringer's hands could easily end up around 'his' neck.

"So the first six mortars have been fired," Eli continued, bringing them all back on track. "The secondary explosions have occurred and chapatti flour is starting to fall on the windows of the vehicles, giving me,

Michael and Ringer, our cue to get out and walk towards the bank. And remember before you get out of your vans to make sure that the hoods of your suits are up and that your goggles and face masks are on. When we reach the Sprinter we open the side door and let out Oneway and Danny, who will be dressed in the same gear before entering the bank. Sean, you stay near the front of the van in the same outfit. Keep the engine running and stop anyone from trying to take cover near the bank doors and getting in our way. It's important that the line between the van and the doors is kept clear so we can load the bags quickly."

"I get it," answered Sean, aware of his position in the plan.

"What about my job?" Dermot interrupted, this time feeling a bit left out. "I must be doing something else other than preparing the mortars."

"Of course you are, my little doubting china plate. Who do you think is opening the bank doors to let us in?" Eli gave his usual smile and puff of his cigar when informing him of his new and vital role.

"I thought the manager was," he answered, wishing he had never asked.

"We can't trust him," dismissed Eli, "even if we have got his family. It would mean giving him too much time by himself. He will already be suspicious because we turned up a day early. Even with his family being held hostage we can't depend on him to go through with it if he susses out we're pulling a fast one. He could well be more scared of losing the IRA's money than he is of losing his wife. He also might not even like his with and see it as a good way of becoming a single man instead of going through a costly divorce. Ye never know."

"So I'm to enter the bank with the manager and let you in when the time comes." Dermot received a confirming look from Eli. "What about the cameras? There won't be any chapatti flour covering my entry." Once again, Dermot was finding flaws with Eli's plan, or so he thought.

"You'll be in disguise."

"Come on Eli, this robbery and any footage is going to be shown on every news channel in Ireland. It's going to get more air time than a Claims Direct advert. A false moustache and a pair of dodgy black glasses aren't going to hide my identity." Dermot's continuing worries drew another smile and cigar puff from Eli.

"I was thinking of something a bit more elaborate, something in keeping with the time of year. A nice little red number with white trims finished off with some sexy black boots should do it."

Dermot knew exactly what he was hinting at. Eli chuckled, unable to hide his pleasure.

"Your going to dress me up as Father Christmas, aren't ye?"

"Correct."

The rest of the room now joined Eli with his smirks.

"I'm going to look like a right twat."

"Dermot, you little sceptic, does it matter?" Eli couldn't help continuing his laughter at the look on Dermot's face. "The main thing is you'll be an unrecognisable twat. It will be six days before Christmas, so nobody is going to look twice at a man in a Santa Claus suit. Plus it gives the manager a legitimate reason to explain why there will be an extra man entering the bank that morning. And the pay's good, you'll be on a million quid for an hour's work."

"He's got a point," agreed Michael. "You couldn't wish for a better disguise. The public will be more likely to mistake you for Fatty."

"That's a point, why doesn't Sean do it, and I'll drive the getaway van. He'd be a natural and you wouldn't need any fucking padding."

"No Dermot, it has to be you. Look, when you're inside the bank you're going to produce your gun just to make sure the under-manager does as he is told. Once the time lock has disengaged on the vault and they have both entered their pass codes you can tie him up and sit him in the corner out of everybody's way. For the next twenty minutes until we arrive at the door you and the manager will start to bag the money and stack it near the doors, ready to be thrown in the van. You will have to move fast and it will be hard work; the more you do in that time the less we will have to do once the flour bombs have gone up."

"Is that why you're not using me, because you think I'm not fit enough to do the work?" asked Sean. "I'd like to see that skinny little runt on the stage four nights a week presenting the Karaoke, like what I do."

Sean wasn't happy, he didn't like anyone thinking that Dermot could do anything better than him. Dermot raised his middle finger in reply.

"It's got nothing to do with your fitness, Sean," Eli reassured. "But Dermot was right, you don't need any packing, whereas we do. We're going to need a lot of good strong bags to load the money into, and a lot of those bags will be smuggled in to the bank by Dermot as the packing under his suit. These are the bags that he will fill with the manager before we arrive. Besides, you're the driver, things will go a lot smoother if everyone sticks to what they do best."

"Tell him the truth, he's a fat pie-eating fucker and we don't want his big lardy arse slowing us down."

Dermot continued to wind Sean up, scoring some points in the continuous slanderous battle that went on between them.

"Shut ye gob you skinny fucking geek, before I put my equally fat fist in your teeth."

"Fuck me, are they always like this?" asked Eli.

"Always," answered Danny and Michael together.

"Lads, put your handbags away and pay attention, or I'll shoot you both in the head." Eli pulled his 9mm out and pointed it in their general direction. Sean and Dermot, both looked shocked by his statement. "Just kidding," he added to their relief. "But now I think I have your attention we can continue without the petty bickering." The pair took their bollocking, but still passed each other a last dirty look.

"Once inside the bank, each man's job will be this. Oneway, you will stay on the steps between the doors and the vehicle to back Sean up, keeping the area clear of any pedestrians who may be staggering about, struggling to see in the flour. Just in case there are any have-a-go heroes who haven't been incapacitated you will both be carrying a can of pepper spray. Give them a squirt of that and it should make them the same as everybody else on the street. It's ok to use pepper spray innit, you're not going to count it as a weapon, are you?" Eli asked, sarcastically looking at Michael.

"Pepper spray is fine, but what about the gun Dermot will be carrying?"

"Fake, it's only to make sure the under-manager plays ball, plus I don't want to send Dermot up against two of them without a little persuader. Hopefully, though, the manager will behave himself and do his job. Remember, if he's in on it, he thinks that we are the IRA and he won't let anything endanger his family."

"Yes, but how long is he going to believe that, he's bound to catch on eventually."

"Michael, the only man to speak to him all night before the robbery is you. It will be your job to ascertain if he is in on it or not. If he isn't then just keep him scared, but if you thin k he is then simply tell him that we have come a day earlier because we didn't trust him, but the deal he had hasn't changed. If he does as he's told his family will be returned safely. Keep a pillow case over his head and ask him the same questions over and over and over again, writing each answer down but never answer any questions he asks."

"What questions should I ask him?"

"Ask him about his routine and what his pass and alarm codes are. What is the under-managers name, where does he live and the details of his family? Things that Dermot can use to make him play ball inside the bank, but never, ever, answer any of his questions. A wrong answer from you is the only way he can become suspicious. In fact, if he does ask any questions, hit him around the head with the fake gun and shove the barrel in his face so he can feel it through the pillow case but make sure you hit him on the back of the head, we don't want any bruises on his face that may be noticed by the security when he looks into the camera outside the bank that morning. Dermot, the same goes for you when you're travelling to the bank in his car. Ask him where he normally parks. Tell him not to forget to wave at the camera so he knows that you know his routine and continuously remind him that his family will be ok if he does as he's told. Don't give him any time to think, and again don't answer any questions. If his head is battered enough, and he's tired from being kept up all night he'll do everything you ask, and he'll make sure his companion does too. Understood?"

Dermot acknowledged that he understood what he had to do.

"Once the rest of us have joined you inside the bank, Dermot, your job will be to stay in the vault and continue bagging the money with the manager. Michael, Ringer, Danny and me will carry the bags from the vault across the bank and out of the doors in to the van. Are there any questions so far, is everybody happy with what they are doing?"

"What about communication?" asked Danny. "With masks on stopping us speaking and hoods up over our ears it's going to be a bit hard?"

"Good point, Danny, I was going to come to it at the end but now is as good a time as any. We will all be wearing ear and mouth pieces to receive and send instructions to and from Errol, but I don't want none of you to speak unless it is vitally important. So no idle chit chat, lads. We'll all be able to hear Errol's instructions, and when we are leaving, after I have checked that we are all accounted for, I will tell him. Now, as with the bombs, Errol will be running the show on the robbery. He will be watching the approaching roads and the progress of police and anything else that might worry him. He'll give us an ongoing commentary of what's happening outside so that in all our heads we have a picture of what stage we are at. The main thing is that we make our getaway whilst still under cover of the falling flour, so when Errol gives us the command to leave the bank, we do so immediately. I don't care how much money is left. We stop what we are doing and vacate, is that understood."

Eli, looked at everyone in the room including his own men making sure that they agreed with, and understood his instructions. After each of them acknowledged that they did he moved on to the final part of the plan.

"Ok, things to do before we leave. Michael, and Danny, you will help Dermot, to lock the manager and his assistant in the vault, Dermot don't forget to throw that snide shooter in with them before you close the door."

"Why are we going to so much trouble to make sure the police know we weren't armed?"

Sean, didn't see the point. He knew the difference in jail time they would receive if they were caught doing an armed robbery as opposed to an unarmed robbery could be as much as eight years, but it was all irrelevant in his mind because if they were caught the IRA would know what they had done so an extra eight years wouldn't matter because they would be dead.

"I know you think that getting caught will be the end of us, Sean, as do the rest of you Irish lads, but I wouldn't take that chance with your lives, nor with Ringer's, Errol's and Oneway's, without having a back-up plan. If we are caught, we hold our hands up, plead guilty and do the time, which will be five years if we are unarmed. Think of it as a few million press-ups, it will do wonders for your diet, Sean. As for the other problem of our old employers doing us in, me and the lads think we've got the answer to that, courtesy of a recently demised Colonel and the information contained in his computer."

"Well if we've got a get out of jail free card why do any time at all if we get caught."

"We will have to do a token stretch, Sean, the public needs to see that a bit of justice has been done. Besides, we'll only do three with time off for good behaviour, but let's hope it doesn't come to that, and if we stick to the plan it won't, so let's continue. Now whilst you three are taking care of the manager and his mate, Ringer and me will check the floor of the bank to make sure we haven't left any clues before going outside to the vehicle and retrieving a holdall from the back that will contain CS and smoke canisters. We will ignite and throw these about the street to replenish our cover and further hinder any approaching police. I should think the first on the scene will only be the local beat coppers, but we still need to make sure they are incapacitated. Hopefully between the flour the smoke and the CS they should be well fucked and unable to give us any problems. Once you three have finished in the bank lock the doors behind you. Then after a quick head count to make sure that we are all on board, we will depart as per Errol's instructions and directions. I'll get in the front with Sean as an extra pair of eyes and to convey Errol's instructions, and the rest of you will climb in the back. Make sure that all doors are closed and windows up, the masks we will be wearing will only give protection against paint spray and flour, they won't afford us any protection against the effects of CS gas." Eli, coming to the end of his explanation of the robbery, walked away from the map on the wall and returned to the table. "Well, that's it for now, gentlemen. We'll meet again in one week, by which time we will fill in the blanks of the plan concerning the manager's house. Think about what we've said tonight and pick the bones out of it. If you come up with anything that I may have missed or indeed any points that might improve the plan and our chances, bring it up at next week's meeting. So far, though, what do you think?"

"It sounds good," confirmed Michael. "Obviously the use of the flour is a bit fucking outrageous but if you lads say it will work, then we'll believe ye. As for the rest of the plan, I for one can't fault it. But I'm sure me and the lads will give it plenty of scrutinising over the coming week."

"Good, then the only thing left to cover is Sean, with the van."

"I'll have it here by Sunday night," he confirmed.

"Also, Dermot is going to have to spend most of this week here at the farm, constructing the mortars and preparing the vehicles, so you'll have to cover for him at work."

"That's no problem," said Sean "he does fuck all any-way. Young Peter can do his job, or if he's busy, we can always train a monkey."

Dermot's middle finger once again rose from his up-turned fist, directed at Sean.

"Oh, and Dermot, you can't keep the Santa Claus Suit, Errol's using it to do the children's hospital Christmas Eve." The four Irish looked at Eli, wondering if it was another one of his piss-takes. "What?" he said totally serious, "the hospitals in Brixton. You can't send a white Santa around there. He wouldn't have his sack long if you did."

The Irish still didn't know if he was joking about Errol, but it was obvious that the meeting had come to an end. Michael, however, had a bit more business he wanted to discuss with Eli, in private.

"You three get yourselves off," he said to the others. "I'm going to hang back for a while. There's something else I want to discuss with Eli. I'll catch up with you at work in the morning."

Danny, Dermot and Sean asked no questions, they just said their goodbyes to everybody else and made their way out of the room and back to the car. Eli wondered what was so important that it couldn't be said in front of anyone else, but gave the nod to his lads to leave himself and Michael alone. When the room had cleared Eli made himself comfortable to listen to whatever it was Michael, had to say.

"What's on your mind? If I had a wife as beautiful as yours at home I wouldn't want to stick around here looking at my ugly mug."

Michael smiled. He had left London with a deep admiration for Eli, and in the past week that feeling had returned.

"I'm in need of a bit more education from you. You know everything about me and the lads, Eli. You even told me things about my father that I never knew, but I know fuck all about you."

"And you think that puts you at a disadvantage." Eli thought he could sense Michael's unease of their situation, but wondered as to its extent and source. "Tell me, Michael, do you really trust me, or in the back of your mind, am I still the sneaky beaky SAS man that was your enemy."

"You've got me wrong Eli. If what went on in London, and now this robbery, is part of some elaborate plan or confidence trick, then you've got me flummoxed. It would be easier to keep up with an episode of 'Twin fucking Peaks'. I just thought it was time we sat down and had a drink together and put our cards on the table." Michael reached in to the bag from where he had taken the envelope earlier and pulled out a bottle of Bushmills

Malt and a couple of glasses. "I know you prefer a drop of the old Courvoisier, but when in Rome, do as the Irish do." Michael chinked the two glasses together, bringing a look of regret to Eli's face for his blinkered sight when jumping on the defensive. The look soon changed to one of 'why not' and a smile of acceptance to the offer. It had been a long time since he had relaxed, and he couldn't remember the last time he was drunk.

"I'm sorry," he apologised. "I didn't mean to offend, whiskey sounds good to me." Michael poured the drinks and passed one over. Eli raised the glass studying the clear golden liquid in an appreciative manner. "Do you know that Bushmills is the oldest distillery in the world?"

"I do," replied Michael.

"Of course you do, you're an Irishman, why shouldn't you know your country's history?" Eli was a mine of information which he loved to share. A lot of it you could describe as useless, the type of stuff you heard at pub quizzes, but when he learned of something that was historical or useful in life, he had a way of logging it in his head, usually by repeating it two or three times before storing it in his memory alongside a picture as a reference. He also loved to talk to the old folk. To hear about their experiences and the lives they had lived, and if he watched the television, which he very seldom did, it was always the National Geographic channel or a David Attenborough programme.

The pair knocked back their drinks and Eli immediately pushed his glass forward for a refill.

"That's an odd statement for you to make," Michael said, topping up. "You always refer to me and the lads as Irishmen, when technically we're British."

"You're Irish, Michael, born of an Irish man, your father Finbar Flynn, and, by all accounts, a good Irish mother, although I've never met the lady." Michael tilted his glass in acknowledgement of the praise of his parents. "It's not your fault that your country was divided around 80 years ago." Eli, breaking from the conversation, sipped from his glass before continuing. "When Michael Collins gave the English the north he was out of his depth. He wasn't a politician that was De' lavera's game, but he was too busy in America enjoying the flag waving and the hype. Collins was a soldier like your father. He was at home fighting at the GPO in Dublin and calling the men to arms. He shouldn't have been negotiating the future of the Irish people, especially against the English. They were masters at splitting countries and dropping bits where they didn't belong for their own interest."

"Be careful Eli, you're beginning to sound like a sympathiser."

"I suppose I am a bit. At least, I do believe in the reunification of the whole of Ireland.

"Amen, to that."

"As I believe that all countries that were once conquered or invaded should be given the choice of independence. I get sick of the English people getting the blame for things that happened, 100 or 200 years ago, when none of us were even born. The old English style brigadiers and generals that once ran the Army in the times of the British Empire are long gone. I didn't invade Ireland and steal the crops, leaving the Irish people to starve in the potato blight. Nor did I become a plantation owner in America and keep slaves, but we keep getting it rammed down our throats as though we are racist. It's time to put the past in the past. Everybody has lost family and friends but there needs to be an end to all the bickering and sueing."

The glasses were filled again as the two men began to relax in each other's company. Michael had wanted this conversation for a while. They were getting in too deep together to remain distant accomplices. He had noticed on their first Sunday morning meeting that Eli had relaxed a little whilst enjoying a brandy, so he had brought the malt along as an icebreaker in an attempt to learn more about the secretive Londoner. In the short periods of time they had spent together it was obvious that there was another person conveniently hidden behind the Cockney geezer attitude that he portrayed. The information and knowledge he possessed showed through his busy eyes, even though Eli attempted to hide it behind a cheeky smile and a twinkly gaze. But the knack he had for seeing both sides of an argument and a situation from every angle was uncanny.

"How old were you when you joined the army?" asked Michael.

Eli thought for a moment, once again staring in to his drink as he drifted back to his youth to answer the question.

"I was seventeen when I went through training. A lot of my mates were getting into trouble with the law, so my dad got me out of bed one morning and took me down to join up."

"Was he a strict man?"

"He was firm, but fair."

"Looking back now, are ye glad your father did it?"

"Yeah. At first I rebelled, I went 'AWOL' every month. I don't think I ever returned from leave on time. I was always shagging some bird or nicking something with my cousins to make a few quid. The guard house was my second home, and Colchester Military Prison was like a health farm I visited for a few months at a time. I soon grew up, though, and knuckled down. I had too; in them days you couldn't muck about like the kids do now. You'd end up with a size ten up yer 'arris and a left hook on your Vera Lynn. I took the selection for the regiment and to every body's amazement, I passed. Then along came the Falklands, and as they say it was time to put away childish things."

"Weren't you scared, even as a member of the S.A.S? It must still be a daunting feeling to go into battle?"

"The old April was twitching a little bit, but it wasn't the first time I had been in a firefight. When I finished my training they said I was too young at seventeen to join my regiment, who were in Hong Kong. So they sent me to another regiment, the PWO – Prince of Wales's own Regiment of Yorkshire, that is – who a month later were sent to Aden. So at seventeen I was too young for the cushy posting of Hong Kong, but not too young to fight the rebels in Aden. Within two weeks I was on my way to do my first Sanger guard on one of the rooftops when I spotted an Arab sniper who had a few members of a Scottish regiment pinned down. I got down on one knee, took aim and dropped him. I knew at that moment, because I never hesitated to pull the trigger that a soldier's life was for me. As for the Falklands, all those feelings went as soon as we landed on terra firma. We got down there first on board H.M.S Antrim and re-took South Georgia which was pretty easy once we had taken out their submarine with the attack helicopter we had on board. Then the same night our Squadron along with a company of marines and some S.B.S lads continued to the main Island. We had a bit of luck on the way though. We bumped into a small fishing boat which turned out to be one of the locals who told us that four jets had landed on Pebble Island the night before. Our gaffer made a command decision and re-directed us to take out the jets because being in such near proximity they would be posing a direct threat to our task force which we knew would soon be on its way. We were in luck again when we got there because accompanying the jets were another plane and a helicopter. Needless to say that none of the machines or the men that flew them were in a working order the next morning. This action turned out to be a decisive move but it wasn't appreciated by the powers above who wanted all decisions to be made by them. The problem with that though was that they were sat in an office in Northwood, London. It was a situation that nearly cost us the conflict, decisions were taking far too long. One of our submarines had the General Belgrano in its sights for a week while the Politicians were trying to make up their minds to sink it or not and in all that time it could have struck out at us whenever it wanted. It was a pathetic situation."

"How did you get to the Falkland Islands so quick and so far ahead of the Task Force if you yourselves sailed across?,"

"We had already set off before the Argentineans invaded. In fact it was because the icebreaker HMS Endurance left in the first place that they did invade. The Argentinians had always threatened to do so if there was no Royal Navy presence, so when Endurance, our last ship pulled out on the pretence that it was going to investigate what was happening on South Georgia which turned out to be some Argentine scrap men dismantling the old whaling station, or so we were supposed to be-lieve because whilst the endurance was watching over one hundred marines landed and as I say when we got there a submarine had also joined the party."

"Forgive me for being the proverbial Irishman but if the government knew the Argentineans would invade, why did they pull the ship out?"

Michael was once again confused at one of Eli's stories. He was only twelve at the time of the Falklands, but like all young lads of that age he remembered it well.

"It was a very shrewd move by the lady in charge, and she did it for two reasons. One, to stop the Argies invading Chile, whose president, Pinochet, was a personal friend of hers. By leaving the door open on the Falklands she hoped they would take the bait and attack there first, which they did. If they'd stuck to their original plan and invaded Chile first, our retaking of the islands after they'd invaded would have been a lot harder to do. We may have even failed because we'd have been up against their front-line troops and not a force made up of mostly conscripts. All their best soldiers were guarding their border with Chile because Pinochet, probably following orders from Thatcher, had moved his forces to the border with Argentina to make them think that they were going to turn the tables and invade them. One minute the Argies thought they had the upper hand when taking the Falklands, and the next they found themselves defending two fronts. She played a blinder. The second reason was that she also needed to get re-elected. Before the Falklands she was odds on to lose the next election, but after the Conflict she was a hero, and sailed through into another term. She played her trump card at exactly the right time, killing two birds with one stone, and it worked. The Argie's though had exactly the same idea. Their military leaders had taken over the country five months earlier and since then it had been nothing but turmoil and riots. They were hoping that by flexing their military might that it may bring the country together and as I say they had set their sights on their neighbour Chilli as the proverbial lamb for the slaughter. All thatcher did was dangle a carrot over the Falklands to divert their attention. In the long run, outside Thatcher's own reasons, the politics of it all boils down to one thing anyway: oil."

Michael added his thoughts.

"It certainly seems to be the motivating factor for most conflicts these days, and I don't suppose it's any coincidence that America seems to be involved in most of those conflicts."

Eli smiled at Michael's observation.

"I think you're finally beginning to catch on and understand how and why things really work. You were lucky enough, Michael, to fight for something you believed in, but the same can't be said for our soldiers these days. But that's the thing about the British soldier. They follow orders because they think if they don't they may let both their mates down and their regiment."

"You followed orders, Eli. Don't tell me you believed in everything you fought for."

In answer Eli, quoted some lines of poetry.

"Theirs is not to make reply, theirs is not to reason why, theirs is but to do and die. Alfred Lord Tennyson, every soldier knows that quotation."

"So a soldier is just supposed to do as he's told, even when he knows it could get him killed."

"Well he does have one thing to protect himself. Well, two actually."

"And what are they?"

"His seven P's, as you know, and his mates of course. Never forget your seven P's Flynny, lad."

Eli raised his glass and gave Michael a wink, which brought a smile to the Irishman's face.

"Those seven P's Eli; they don't make you bulletproof."

"I don't know about that, I'm still here, and it's only because I was better prepared than the other geezers that had aspirations of doing me in. Anyway, I won't be fighting for America's black gold anymore. They can oil that big machine of a country without my help in the future. But it's not always the Yanks that start it. When Thatcher pulled that ship out, she knew the Argies would invade, and she knew that British soldiers would die in the conflict to retake the islands."

"It's a bit like living inside 'Dune'."

"Dune, what fucking Dune."

For once Michael had Eli confused.

"Dune. It's a book by Frank Herbert. 'He who controls

the spice controls the universe,' except in our instance it's, 'he who controls the oil, controls the world.'"

"Well I've never read this geezer Herbert's book, but it sounds like he and Bush may have swopped a few ideas!"

Two more drinks were poured as Michael's questions continued.

"What about Errol, how did your two paths cross?"

"Errol didn't do much undercover work in Ireland for obvious reasons. I knew of him from the Regiment of course, there aren't many black lads, as you can imagine. He had a reputation for bravery and often worked alone, which always takes a lot of balls and earned him a lot of respect. Me, Ringer and Oneway back in the early eighties were part of a team following a terrorist cell through Africa that eventually took us to Morocco. Errol was our contact there. He was in deep cover as a Lucky Lucky Man type character – you know the ones that try to sell you crappy sun glasses and snide gold whilst you're having a few drinks with your mates on holiday? They're like the Chinese, they get everywhere."

"Dermot will vouch for that," joked Michael. "But the same can be said for the Irish," he added. There are more of us out of the country than there are in it."

Eli nodded, thinking that it was probably true.

"Anyway, after we made contact with Errol, we set up surveillance on the suspected terrorists, watching their movements and taking note of the people they met. After two weeks we had to pull back or it would have brought suspicion on our cover as British lager louts, nobody goes on holiday to Morocco for more than a fortnight. Errol carried on keeping tabs on his own whilst we pulled back and took up position in the desert outside the city. It was obvious from their movements that they were close to doing something big. We'd seen all the tell-tale signs before but we didn't know what, and worse, we didn't know when. Errol put himself in immediate danger by trying to infiltrate the terrorist cell because he believed that their target could have been somewhere in Morocco itself, which was packed with European tourists. It was an unselfish act and he did it without a second's thought for himself. He knew that they would suspect him, in fact he gave them reason to, in the hope that they would want to know more about him and torture him for information."

"Fuck me, is he fucking crazy?" asked Michael, almost cringing at the story.

"No, Errol's not crazy. Just very brave. He was counting on the fact that they wouldn't interrogate him inside the city but would move him to somewhere safer and, perhaps to their superiors. His whole plan depended on us seeing them leave the city and following. Obviously we did and they led us to a training camp about fifty miles into the desert. We laid down an assault, killing most of the terrorists and capturing four of their key members. We also found paperwork leading to the apprehension of ten more terrorist cells in as many countries."

"He sounds like a bit of a lad, and a lucky one."

"He wasn't that lucky. When we rescued him all his fingers were broken, his legs and arms the same and his balls had been crushed under the butt of a rifle."

Another cringe showed on Michael's face as he

grabbed his own ball's as though comforting them. A tingling feeling ran through him as it does any man when hearing about that sort of targeted pain.

"Fucking poor bastard. But to look at him you wouldn't think butter would melt in his mouth."

"That's why he's so good at his job. He also speaks five languages, as well as Cockney rhyming slang. To this day I've never heard him slate anyone or eat pork."

"Ye mean he's a Muslim?"

Michael was shocked, he'd never heard of a Muslim in the British army. Eli nodded and finished his drink.

"He's old school, he gives you less trouble than the Jehovah's Witnesses that walk down your garden path of a Sunday morning. He doesn't believe that a person should be killed just because they are an infidel and they don't worship his God. He kills people that need killing. People that break the laws of man, and by man I mean the innocent man. He's a bit of a defender of the common person and he's often been my conscience, keeping me on the straight and narrow. It was his idea to do the robbery in the way we are doing it. He won't kill for personal gain either, and he made that plain long before you and the lads said it."

"He ain't got a problem with stealing, though?"

"Not a bit. He loves a good deal and a haggle. And he's partial to a drop of Guinness, that's his other vice."

"It's obvious that you think a lot about him."

"I feel about him the same as you feel about your mates. Errol, Ringer and Oneway are like my brothers. There's no place in my head for the thought that I can't trust them. My back is always covered, as theirs is by me. All I have to do is concentrate on the job in hand whilst they patrol my perimeter, keeping us all safe. It's a nice feeling but I don't have to tell you that, you know exactly what I mean."

"Ye, although my plans don't always go as well as yours. I'm lucky those three stick by me."

"Ask them if they would change anything, I bet they wouldn't. Think of how boring their lives would be without you. They would all be working nine to five now down the local mill or the shipyard, if they were lucky enough to have a job. They might have even been on the old rock'n'roll, like three million others in the country, and not about to pull Ireland's biggest robbery."

"Don't say it like that," joked Michael. "It fills me with excitement, but at the same time I want to go to the toilet."

Eli laughed whilst offering his glass for another refill.

"You're not on your own. I feel the same way, but it's a good thing to be scared. It keeps you on your toes."

Once again the two enjoyed a laugh together, realising their similarities as their glasses were replenished.

"Errol seems to have recovered well, did the ordeal not have any lasting effects?"

"Physically he'll never have any kids, but mentally he's recovered, or at least he never indicates that he hasn't. He doesn't take many things personal, or to heart. The men responsible for his torture are all dead now. The pain he suffered saved perhaps thousands of lives and that means a lot to him. He weighs that off against what happened to him and in his mind the result was a good one. He never worked in that area again though, he stuck with our team after he recovered, working in London as part of Fourteen Troop, following your lot around. He excelled at that as well, no one ever suspects that the black fella behind them is an undercover soldier. A mugger, drug dealer or a rapper maybe, but not a soldier."

"What about Oneway and Ringer, do they have similar backgrounds?" Michael suddenly realised that his inquisitive questions may be a bit much. "I hope you don't mind me asking. Tell me to mind my own business if I'm going too far, it was you I wanted to get to know."

"It's ok. You've a right to know what type of people you are getting involved with. Oneway has done as much as me, if not more. He could be telling me what to do but he prefers to stay what we call a grunt. He gets his orders, carries them out, and if something's wrong with the plan it's not fault. He also has a problem with officers. There's been a few that have been mysteriously killed in battle whilst he was in their region. Basically, besides being the tightest Yorkshireman in the world, he doesn't give a fuck and it's always a good idea to stay in his good books."

"I'll remember that," said Michael, heeding the warning and once again topping up the glasses.

"Does he like curries?"

"Curries? Why d'you ask?"

"It's just that you mentioned Bradford earlier, where Oneway had got the flour from. My dad used to go to Leeds, years ago to see some mates. And he always made sure that his visit coincided with St Patrick's Day, but he wouldn't spend the 17th in Leeds, he always went to Bradford. He said that the celebrations there were better than anywhere, and after a rake of Guinness, you couldn't beat a proper Bradford curry."

"He was right. I've been to Bradford for Paddy's Day, they don't do the marching bands like New York but every pub in the town is packed."

"What were ye doing there?" asked Michael, curious.

"Following Finbar," replied Eli, with a smile. "Only joking. I was on the piss with Oneway. It cost me a fucking fortune."

Michael smiled.

"I'll go there myself one day," he added. Hoping

that after what they were about to undertake that they would still be free men and able to do so.

"We'll go together, Next Paddy's Day."

"It's a date," confirmed Michael, leaning forward to clink his glass with Eli to seal the arrangement. "Ringer," he continued and getting back on track. What's his story? He's not much of a talker."

"Don't worry about Ringer, he likes you four and always has done. He was at my side all those years ago when we watched you hold up your mother at Finbar's, I mean your father's funeral." Michael smiled whilst tipping his glass. He knew no offence was meant. "He doesn't talk," continued Eli, "because he's used to working alone; he's the closest thing you'll ever meet to a Ninja. I don't mean with all that dressed in black Kung Fu and Samurai sword shit. I'm talking about being an assassin. His speciality was to take out people who were hard to get to under a heavily armed guard. Places where to use a noisy weapon like a gun or go in team handed would bring down that guard upon you. Sometimes his orders were to make the killings look like an accident or suicide, so he would use chemicals that simulate a heart attack or tablets for an overdose. If they were up high enough they would suddenly develop a bout of depression and throw themselves out of a window, but most of the time he would simply sever their spinal cord with a knife or break their neck with his bare hands, hence his name, Ringer. There's many a dictator and war lord that have fallen fowl of Ringer's blade and grip. Sadly he's the only one of my team that I worry about. He'll never let us down, but he has got a bit of a death wish."

"I hope I'm not around the day he decides to check out," said Michael.

"I hope I am," answered Eli, "maybe I'll be able to stop him." The pair paused for thought, both hoping that it wouldn't be coming soon. "This is a good malt." Eli, appreciating the fine blend, swirled it around his glass before hanging his nose over the brim and taking a deep whiff. "Do you want to hear something that will shock you?" he said in a slightly cheeky tone. Michael, who was performing the same routine with his drink, had to laugh thinking that every time Eli opened his mouth, he was shocked.

"Eli, the amount of things you tell me I'm beginning to think I've been walking around with my eyes shut for the past thirty-five years. I'm shocked if a day goes by when I see you that I don't hear something that will curl my toes, but go on, shock me some more."

"I'm half Irish. Don't get me wrong, my father was a cockney geezer and a true cockney at that, but my mother's family were from southern Ireland, a place called Mountmellick in County Laois."

"You're fucking joking." He was right; Michael was shocked. "It's pronounced Leesh by the way, and I know the place well. My father used to take me there when I was a kid."

"I know how it's pronounced to you, but to me it's pronounced how its spelt, Laois. That's not all of it though. Do you want to know what my mother's maiden name was before she became a Moon?"

Michael waited for more revelations as Eli sipped his tipple.

"Keenan."

"Fuck off. You're taking the piss. You do know that Danny and Sean were originally from Wicklow, that's the next county on the coast." Eli nodded and took another drink. Michael started to snigger before breaking into laughter. The ironic situation tickled him to the point he nearly spilt his whisky. "Fuck me. Eli the SAS man is a half-Irish Catholic boy and could be related to the Keenan brothers. I'm going to have some fucking fun with that one.

Eli even laughed himself.

"It doesn't stop there," he continued with his revelations. "My mother's family weren't always Catholics. Before that our ancestors were called Dunn, and they were Quakers. And on my grandfather's side I'm descended from Irish Jews called Moss. They went of to America years ago after making money out of money lending and took it all with them. None of it mattered to my father though, he was never interested in religion. It didn't put food on the table or buy him a pint so he left all that to my mother, who put me, and my brothers and sisters through a Catholic education. I never got too involved in all the praying business but it did give me an open mind when I first served in Northern Ireland."

Michael listened to the rest of Eli's story whilst still smiling broadly at his earlier revelations.

"Do you ever go back there to visit your roots?"

"I've been back a few times, I took my mother there on holiday once. She dragged me around all the sights, including the Quaker museum and we revisited the old house in upper Mountmellick."

"What about your family, are your parents still alive? Were you ever married?"

"I was." Eli's reply was delivered with a softness entering his voice. "A wife and two kids, the ideal nuclear family."

"Was?" said Michael, speaking of the past. "What happened, didn't she like the hours of your job?"

Once again Eli's glass was tilted on his lips, followed by his cigar.

"She was killed, my wife. In a car crash, along with my eldest child."

Michael could have cut his own tongue from his head. He immediately thought when Eli said 'was' that he was divorced.

"I'm sorry, I didn't mean to bring up any bad memories."

"Don't worry, you didn't. I like to speak about them. It helps me to realise how lucky I was, and how good I once had it. And how lucky I still am, because my daughter survived the crash. I thank God every day for that, so I suppose some of my religious upbringing rubbed off. The truth is is that there was nothing anyone could have done to stop it. Even if I'd been there, and not in some foreign land, nothing would have changed. She always did the school run herself."

"Still, Eli, I'm sorry." Eli nodded as his eyes slightly welled with the memories.

"Your daughter? What's she called."

Eli sat up, revived at the new subject. "Kitty," he answered proudly. "Kitty Keenan Moon in full, after my Irish grandmother."

"Kitty, that's a nice name. It has a bit of a gypsy ring to it." Eli, laughed.

"Cheeky fucker. I admit to being half Irish, and Catholic. But there are no wheels on my fucking house."

Michael grinned at Eli's little joke, hoping that he hadn't upset him, or put his foot in it.

"Where's Kitty now, who looks after her when you're away? Or is she old enough to look after herself?"

"No, she's only twelve, nearly thirteen, and although she thinks she's an adult, she's still my little girl. The wife's sister looks after her when I'm away. She's been an absolute diamond. She moved into our house soon after the funeral, I don't know how I'd have coped without her. I was caught between comforting my child who'd lost her mother and brother, whilst grieving myself and wondering which direction to go in next. Trying to get a young girl back into a routine of going to school and playing out with her friends as though nothing ever happened is the hardest thing I've ever had to do. All the training I've had never prepared me for anything like that, how could it? There are no seven P's for that situation, believe me."

Michael could see Eli was getting a bit deep, so he quickly tried to change the conversation.

"Do you miss the army?"

"I'm not actually out yet, but I will be soon. They've asked me to sign on again, even though I've already done extended service, but when my time's up I'm off. What I said earlier about fighting for Bush's gold was the truth. The money from this robbery will ensure that my daughter and me can afford to do and go wherever we please. I haven't seen a uniform for almost two years anyway. I've been mostly on compassionate leave since the accident."

"Ye mean your wife and son were killed in the time since I last saw you in London."

"Just over two years ago."

"You've had a busy few years, then?"

"Busier than you think. I've attempted to take care of all business and tie off all loose ends. After this robbery I intend to drop off the face of the earth, but I can't do that without covering my back and the backs of my mates."

"Is the leverage you spoke of earlier going to help you do that, the 'get out of jail free card' as Fatty put it."

"Hopefully. That's the plan, anyway."

Michael and Eli looked at each other, both well aware from past experience that things have a habit of not going as they are planned. Finishing what remained of their drinks, they both looked at the bottle, which now sat empty on the table.

"It looks like we've polished it off?"

"That's the way it should be," answered Michael. "The old fella used to say, 'A man that puts the cork back in the bottle either can't drink or has no friends to drink it with.'"

"Your father was a wise man, I would like to think that 'we' just shared that bottle as friends."

"So would I, that's why I brought it. I feel a lot better now doing what we are doing, knowing a bit more about you and the other three fellas. But still I'm sorry to hear about your wife and son."

"Don't be, Michael. I had it good for a while, better than most men ever have it, and I've still got it with my daughter now." Eli stood up and placed his glass on the table. He picked up the empty whisky bottle by the neck and studied its label. "You should have brought another, you've got me in the mood."

"We'll do it again after the robbery."

"I' look forward to it. With a nice brandy next time, though. Not that I have any complaints about the Bushmills of course."

He placed the bottle back on the table as the pair shared a moment in silence, appreciating each other's character and the past that had formed it. They weren't exactly kissing and cuddling but they had bonded and sealed a friendship over a bottle of whiskey that would never be broken.

"It's time I was away, Eli, unless you have a bottle of something else hidden around here."

"Unfortunately not."

"In that case, then, do you think one of the lads could give me a lift back in to town?"

"Errol!" Eli shouted, as though beckoning a taxi. Within moments Errol, entered the room with a mobile phone to his ear, raising his head as if to ask 'what do you want'. "Michael needs a lift home, can you get one of the lads to run him into town."

"No problems," answered Errol, with the phone now pressed to his chest so the person on the other end couldn't hear; "but you need a lift back to London as well."

"Why?" asked Eli, wondering what was wrong. "Who's on the dog?"

"Joe 90," answered Errol.

"Who the fuck is Joe Ninety when he's at home?"

"Joe Ninety, the blonde computer geek with the glasses. You know the one that's hacking a certain computer for us. Fuck me, Eli, how many have you had."

"About a half of a bottle, but I'm with you now. Are we in, or are you sobering me up for fuck all."

"We're in," replied Errol with a happy grin, "but he wants one of us to get back there and pick up the equipment asap. The information he's seen has shook him up a bit."

"Ask him what the Colonel's password was," asked

Eli, eager to know. Errol put the phone back to his ear and relayed the question.

"He says it was Copenhagen."

Eli smiled, putting together a lot of memories from that night in the Colonel's study and matching them with the password.

"What's the significance?" asked Errol, with the phone back to his chest.

"The Colonel fancied himself as a bit of a historian," he explained. "And his favourite subject was Sir Arthur Wellesley."

"Go on, enlighten me," prompted Errol.

"Sir Arthur Wellesley, my uninformed China plate, was better known as the Duke of Wellington, who at the battle of Waterloo rode his trusty horse in a charge against the French. That horse was called Copenhagen." Errol said the name at the same time as Eli, realising where the story was going. "The statue of him sat on that horse now stands in Aldershot," Eli continued. "It used to stand in Hyde Park, but Queen Victoria had it removed because it spoilt her view."

"Never mind Queen Victoria. What should I tell Joe 90, he sounds a bit out of his depth?"

"Tell the soppy mare welcome to the real world and to stay where he is until I arrive tomorrow. Then let Ringer know that we'll be driving back to London to-night. We'll drop Michael off and catch the midnight ferry."

Errol, returned to the other room to continue his conversation and relay the instructions.

"I presume that's our get out of jail free card," said Michael, quickly catching onto the conversation.

"I hope so Flynny lad. I hope so!"

Chapter Nine

A Walk in the Park

The week whilst Eli and Ringer were back in London, Dermot was a regular visitor at the farm, working alongside Errol and Oneway, preparing the vehicles. The mounting of the mortars was a precise job. The angles had to be correct to ensure the projectiles went where they were supposed to and the chassis of the vehicles had to be strengthened to withstand the pressure of each blast. The roofs of the vans had to be cut off and replaced with cardboard and papier mache, so that when the mortars were fired the flower bombs could leave the vehicles unhindered. Finally, all three Transits were re-sprayed so that the doctoring of the roofs would go un-noticed during their early morning drive from the farm to the bank. Errol and Oneway were impressed with Dermot's knowledge, even though they understood that it was originally learnt to use against them. But all that was behind them now, now they were joined in one cause, their own. If anything, Dermot was the one with the complex. For a man that spent most of his life in a worried and paranoid state he couldn't have been put in a worse situation. Spending a week alone on a secluded farm with two members of the SAS had to rank right up there with one of his all-time most worrying situations. By the end of the first day, though, the unease had passed and they spent the rest of the week spilling the beans on the other members of their groups. The topic of the Troubles never arose.

In London, Eli and Ringer had met with the computer whizz kid, Joe Ninety. The look on his face when the pair arrived told Eli that as well as downloading the material, he had also read some of the files. Eli explained to him the drawbacks of opening his mouth and repeating anything that he had seen. But just to make sure he understood, Ringer explained it once more. After a number of hours studying the contents of De' William's memoirs, Eli split the information into two groups. The first, which he reckoned to be a bit soft on the effect it would have should it be made public, he downloaded on to one disc. This would be used as a taster should they need, it so as not to release all their bargaining power. The second containing the remainder was anything but soft. This was damning stuff, the type of information that ruins careers, brings down governments and, worse, gets men killed. Eli had to do quite a bit of editing to ensure that his name and the identities of many of his colleagues were removed. It was obvious from the way the information had been formatted that De' William had planned to reveal several extracts in the newspapers before the book's release to hot up more interest. As he delved deeper he had to admire the quality of the Colonel's writing and wondered why he had gone out of his way to deliberately upset the establishment. With a bit of tweaking and names hidden behind a few pseudonyms it could have been turned into a very good, albeit close to the bone, novel. At any rate, in the format the Colonel had intended it to be released, it told Eli one thing -, that he was justified in killing him, and that he had done it just in time.

For the rest of the week Eli and Ringer placed copies of the discs in secure places. Some were left in safety deposit boxes and with solicitors, others with friends, all with strict instructions what to do and when to do it. By Friday they were done and Eli was happy that their backs were finally covered. Now more relaxed, he decided to stay the weekend and spend time with his daughter before returning to Belfast on Tuesday in time for their next meeting at the farm.

A short distance from Eli's house, almost next door in fact, was a park with a few swings, a seesaw and a climbing frame. He had a lot of good memories there from the past, involving his wife and both their children. Before the accident they would often use it when he was at home on leave. His wife would always pack a picnic to make it special, even though it was just a few hundred yards from their front door and the four would spend many a summer's afternoon there, kicking the football around.

On Sunday morning he had talked Kitty into visiting the park with him but she wasn't exactly willing company.

"Aren't I a little bit old to be pushed on the swings, Dad?"

Kitty was a typical twelve-year-old who thought she was a teenager on her next step to being an adult. She had inherited all her father's mannerisms but luckily not his looks; those all belonged to his late wife, Kitty's mother Carol.

"You're twelve-years-old, my girl. Which means you're not too old for your old dad to push on the swings, so just humour me."

"Can't we just go for a jog instead; we're wearing our track suits."

A jog! Are you 'avin a giraffe?" exclaimed Eli, while

quickly returning the cigar he was about to light back into his pocket. "I want us to get a bit of 'gentle' exercise and some fresh air, not take part in the London marathon. This tracksuit is like that black leather jacket I have hung up in the hallway. I might wear it sometimes, but it doesn't mean I ride a Harley Davison!"

Kitty, even at her young age, was a bit of a health freak. She loved having her bran and muesli for breakfast and went for after-school runs with her friend, who lived a bit further down the lane. Eli was just glad that she was still eating meat and hadn't turned into one of those anaemic looking girls that won't touch anything with a face.

"If you stopped smoking those smelly cigars like the one you have in your pocket we 'could' do the London Marathon this year."

He gave his daughter a sideways glance.

"How did you know I had a cigar in my pocket?"

"Because you always do, Dad, it was just an educated guess."

The words 'chip off the old block' came to Eli's head.

"Well, seeing as how you know I have it..." He lit the cigar whilst trying to blow the smoke away from his ozone-friendly daughter. "What do you want to do the Marathon for, anyway? Why not do the Boat Race, that's more up my street, sat down using your upper body strength." Eli, trapping his cigar between his teeth, stretched out his arms as though exercising, then tensed his biceps in a Charles Atlas impersonation. Kitty giggled, thinking how silly her dad looked.

"You can't just enter the Boat Race, Dad. You have to go to either Oxford or Cambridge University."

"Well, you could go there, you're smart enough."

"Even if they did let me into one of them, they definitely don't allow girls on the rowing team. Don't you know anything, Dad?"

The proud father smiled at his daughter's cocky answer. He wasn't aiming his sights too high for her; she was smart, and could very well end up at a top-level university.

"Well, you'll have to go there and change that, won't you? There's nothing my daughter can't do if she puts her mind to it." Following his boastful statement he puffed proudly on his cigar whilst Kitty wafted the smoke away and they both headed for the swings. "Do you remember the times we used to have here, with your mother and your brother? The sandwiches she would bring and those chocolate cornflake buns you used to make together the night before."

"I do, Dad, but it makes me sad. Every day when I pass the park, to and from school, I think of them."

"Is that why you didn't want to come here this morning?"

"Partly, but I also didn't want any of my friends seeing me playing on the swings."

Eli laughed. At twelve years of age, image was everything?

"And I suppose you'll be embarrassed being seen with me as well then."

"No, my mates think you're cool, with you being in the army and all that. It's just the swings that are a bit childish, but I know you like coming here to remember how things were, so I don't mind. I cry a lot when I think about them, so I know it must be hard for you, Dad."

Eli's heart almost pumped through his chest with pride at his daughter's words. He had brought her here to talk about how she was feeling but had ended up being consoled himself by her. He pushed with his left hand, sending Kitty higher on the swing whilst holding his cigar in his right, before placing it in his mouth so he could wipe away the tear that was forming in the corner of his eye.

"What about the house, does it hold too many memories for you?"

"It does, but Auntie Pat says that it's the past that makes us what we are, and that Mum is always watching over me there. I know that's her way of making me feel better but I feel sorry for Auntie Pat as well, she must miss her sister and nephew."

"Of course she does, love, that's why she takes good care of you, because you're the only family she has. What I mean is, though, do you want me to sell the house and move us to somewhere different? Maybe we could move further in to the country where we can make a fresh start and new memories."

"Not just yet, Dad, let me finish school and take my exams first. We'll talk about it again in another four years."

Eli asked and got an answer. He had trained men in the army that didn't make grown-up decisions as quick or as well as his daughter did.

"Well you let me know when you've decided what we're doing," Eli answered with a proud chuckle and a little bit of sarcasm, giving Kitty a stronger push on the swing so he could miss a shove and take a puff on his cigar.

"When we do move, Dad, we won't leave Auntie Pat, will we? We'll take her with us, won't we?"

"Of course she can come with us, but when you leave school and go on to university she might want to go her own way and live her own life. She's still young enough to meet someone and maybe have children of her own."

"Why don't you and Auntie Pat have children, Dad?. Then we can all stay together and I'll get another brother or sister."

His daughter's words came as a bit of a shock and staggered her father a little. In Kitty's mind, though, she could see nothing wrong.

"Kitty, I don't think you should be thinking things like that. I hope you haven't said anything similar to your Auntie."

"No, I thought I would run it by you first."

"Well don't run it by anyone else. I think I preferred you when you were playing with dolls and things were a lot less confusing."

"But Auntie Pat's pretty, dad, and you're not that much older than her. If you lost a bit of weight from your belly and stopped smoking those smelly cigars, I bet she would let you take her out for dinner."

"Buy her dinner? Is that what happens these days? When I met your mum all she got was half a lager and a bag of jockey's whips on the way home. At the week-end for a treat and if I could afford it, we would go for a Ruby Murray down the old star of Bengal."

"Auntie Pat doesn't like spicy food, Dad, she says it plays havoc with her Farmer Giles!"

A smiling father thought again, 'definitely a chip of the old block.'

"Listen to me, my busy-bodied little girl. Your Auntie Pat and I aren't going to be having dinner or anything else for that matter, so get it out of your head. I brought you here because I was worried about how you are. I see now that I should be worried more about what they are teaching you at school, and how much television you've been watching."

"Don't worry, Dad, Auntie Pat explains everything to me, not school. She says that I am better off knowing about life, the good and the bad. Then I know the things and the people I should avoid."

Eli shook his head. The rate Kitty was growing up scared him, but he could see the sense in Pat's reasoning that a child should be prepared.

"Come on, Dad, push me higher."

"You've soon changed your mind. You thought swings were for kids a minute ago."

"None of my mates are about, so I might as well enjoy it."

He looked around the park after Kitty's words, enjoying the view as he had done so many times before, but something caught his eye. Two men, about fifty yards away were entering the gate and the sight of them immediately had the hackles rising on the back of his neck. The suits they were wearing were totally out of character for a Sunday morning stroll in the park and they were paying himself and Kitty far too much attention. Checking his perimeter he noticed another man in the tree line to his right. Reacting slowly and calmly, he grabbed the chains that supported the swing and brought it to a halt.

"What's up, Dad, are we going home already?"

"Kitty love, do as I say. Get off the swing, come behind me and lay on the floor."

She did as her father asked without question. At the same time as drawing his weapon, Eli knelt down in front of her, making himself a shield but also a smaller target. He took aim at the two men approaching, who immediately raised their hands and stopped.

"Mr Moon, we're MI5, we need to talk to you."

"Put your hands behind your heads and clasp your fingers together then turn around," Eli ordered.

"Mr Moon!"

"Do it now, or I will drop you both on the spot." The order was repeated, sternly. The two men complied and turned around. Eli put his left arm behind his back and patted his daughter reassuringly on her head. "Stay there, love, and don't move until I tell you." He moved towards the men and placed his weapon against one of there heads. "Now, both of you turn with me and face those trees at the other end of the park." Eli rotated the pair, putting them between himself and the third man he had spotted in the tree line. "Kitty when I say now, get up and run behind me. Ok?"

"Yes, Dad." Eli scoped the area before giving the order.

"Now." Kitty moved as fast as she could to cross the short distance and take cover behind her father. "Who's your mate over there in the woods?" he asked of the uninvited pair.

"There's no one with us, Mr Moon."

"Liar, shouted Eli, "I'll put a double tap straight in your nut if you don't tell me the truth, I made him at the same time as I saw you two."

"I promise you, Mr Moon, we are alone. I don't doubt that you saw someone, but whoever it is, isn't with us."

Eli looked at the last position in the trees where he saw the figure. Who ever it was had disappeared. Maybe it was just somebody taking a walk in the park, or a dog walker. Or maybe it was the sight of him drawing his weapon that made them vacate. Either way he wasn't taking no chances.

"Mr Moon."

"Stop calling me that," I'm trying to think.

"We were told to call you it by Fletcher."

"Fletcher. What does he want this time?"

"He wants you to come to a meeting in the city." The reference to Fletcher, and the Mr Moon name gave weight to him believing who they were, but he needed more convincing before he relaxed.

"Both of you, slowly lower your arms, fasten the middle button on your jackets, then put your hands by your sides."

When the two men had performed the task, Eli pulled their jackets from their shoulders and down to their waists, trapping their arms by their sides. Spinning them around once more so they were back facing him, he relieved them of their standard issue weapons from their standard issue shoulder holsters, confirming in his mind that they were who they said they were.

"My identification card is in my wallet if you want to see it," one of the men offered in an attempt to clear up the misunderstanding.

"That won't be necessary, only Box 500 would carry a piece of shit weapon like that. They're prone to more stoppages than a London bus. You've obviously never been in a fire fight. Besides, I recognise you both now from the Hereford meeting."

"I presume then we can relax now and get dressed." The MI5 men weren't happy at being trussed up and their experience questioned. Eli nodded his head, allowing them to straighten themselves up. "We need you to come with us."

"Am I under arrest?" enquired Eli as he put his

weapon back into the waist band of his tracksuit bottoms and covered it with his top.

"No, but Fletcher, said that we have to bring you."

"Sorry lads, that's not going to happen. You can tell Mr Fletcher that Mr Moon can't play out today because he is spending time with his daughter, who I now have to explain to the reason why I carry a weapon tucked inside the waist band of my Adidas."

"We're sorry about that."

"You should be," Eli, replied angrily. "Approaching me on open ground without making yourselves known was amateurish and unprofessional." Eli was foaming that people who were supposedly on his side could be so slack. "I don't know who trained you pair of mugs, probably the same man that trained Fletcher, but the cemetery is just around the corner if you carry on like that. Now go back to your boss and tell him that I haven't changed my mind, and if he wants to speak to me in connection with De' William's death it will have to be whilst I'm under arrest. Now pick up your weapons and start walking back the way you came."

Feeling slightly scolded, the two men retrieved their arms from the ground where Eli had placed them and began to walk towards the gate. Eli followed behind with Kitty, while still keeping his eye on the woods where he had seen the other person. He believed the MI5 men were alone but he thought the appearance of the figure too much of a coincidence not to be related. Outside the park the two men climbed in to their Government Issue, black vehicle and drove away under the watchful eye of both father and daughter. Eli, knowing that questions were going to be asked, looked down at his daughter, who was staring up at him with a mischievous look on her face and one of those questions on her lips.

"Dad?" she began, before her father cut her short.

"Don't ask."

He knew what was coming. Taking hold of her hand, they set off walking back towards their house.

"But dad, can I tell my friends that you carry a gun? Then they will think you're even cooler."

"Tell nobody nothing, Kitty. 'Loose lips sink ships' as your old Granddad used to say. Your lucky he's not here to hear your blabbering mouth, or unlucky actually, because he would have loved to meet you."

"Did Granddad carry a gun dad?"

Eli's attempt at removing the weapon from his daughter's mind didn't seem to be working.

"Yes when he was in the Army, but he never told anyone about it or the things he did." The loving father gave his daughter a pat on the head. "You're just like your Granddad. He would keep himself fit running and doing press-ups and sit-ups. He also loved to swim but there were no fancy big pools in his day. He had to make do with the River Thames. He would have been proud of you doing your running and wanting to do the Marathon, but not if you went blabbing about things you shouldn't, like me carrying a weapon."

Kitty thought for a moment, trying to picture her granddad, and how he may have looked when swimming the Thames. She wasn't sure whether she believed her father; even at twelve she knew a tall story when she heard one, and she had heard plenty before from her dad, especially when he was using the story to get a point across.

"Ok Dad, I won't mention it, not even to Auntie Pat."

"Good girl. Why don't you ring your friend from down the road, what's her name?"

"Debbie."

"Yeah, Debbie, give her a ring and ask her if she wants to come around and listen to the charts this afternoon. You do listen to the charts, don't you?"

"Of course we do."

"When I was a kid we used to tape the charts. We would stop and start the tape machine so that we only got the songs and not the presenter's voice."

"Well, we just download them these days dad."

"Yeah, I've heard about that downloading thing."

"Anyway, I'll call Debbie when we get home, but I won't tell her about your gun, Dad. Or about the two men in the park with guns either."

Eli stared at his daughter, who was looking back at him with another mischievous look and grin.

"Wind your neck in," was his fatherly advice.

Back at the house Kitty took the remote handset from the phone in the hallway and disappeared upstairs. From the kitchen, Pat heard them coming in and shouted through.

"Do you want a tea, Eli?"

Pat, short for Patricia, was a lovely woman. She was four years younger than her sister Carol, which made her five years younger than Eli. She was of average looks with a good figure but her gentle nature had made her a doormat in several failed relationships. For the past two and a half years she had lived in Eli's house, looking after Kitty, stepping up to the plate as a good sister, auntie and godmother would do. It was a situation that worked for everyone after the tragic accident. Pat had recently left her last home and had been renting a flat. Kitty needed a woman's touch and Eli needed space and time to grieve and continue doing his job. There had never been anything between the pair, he had never even looked at another woman, let alone his late wife's sister. The situation in the house was purely one of convenience, but Eli's conscience bothered him at times. He couldn't help feeling that he was no better than the men she had known because he was using her like a live-in baby sitter.

"Yes please," he replied to her offer. "No sugar though."

"Since when, you've always taken sugar?"

"Since people keep mentioning my jelly belly lately."

"That wouldn't be Kitty, with her knew fitness regime, would it?"

Pat obviously heard it every day, even she had been told to shed a few pounds to make herself more presentable.

"She seems to think that if I lose a bit off my gut and stop smoking that women might find me more attractive."

Pat passed Eli his tea; the mention of him and women seemed to quieten her a little.

"Well she has got a point, a stone off the middle wouldn't do you any harm, and those cigars must be killing you. I bet they are the equivalent to smoking five cigarettes at a time. It's a wonder your teeth are still in such good nick."

"That's the Army for you, a good dental and health plan."

"Well if Kitty, has given you her approval to go out with other women I suppose that's half the battle. Has she got anyone in mind for you?"

Eli looked at Pat, thinking the question was a bit loaded.

"She's had the same conversation with you, hasn't she, about me and you getting together, I mean?" Pat nodded whilst drinking her tea. "I'm sorry Pat, she doesn't mean any harm."

"I know she doesn't. That girl has lost more than most adults have to cope with and now she's happy with our situation she's just trying to make sure she doesn't lose it as well."

"Still, I'm sorry; I'll have a word with her. She shouldn't be talking that way."

"Why, is the idea of me and you off-putting?" Eli was

a little caught out; there was nothing wrong with Pat, far from it. He just didn't expect to be having this conversation on a Sunday morning. "Don't get me wrong, I'm not trying to move in on my dead sister's husband. It's been nearly three years and we've never even had so much as a cuddle, even to comfort each other in grief. I've lived with you longer than I have with any other man before. I know everything about you, from your quiet moods right down to the skid marks in your underpants, and there's nothing that puts me off. I know you don't love me in a relationship way, but if you think that there might be room in your heart for that to change, and you could believe as I do that we would be doing nothing to be ashamed of, then I wouldn't mind; in fact I would be very happy if you invited me out to dinner sometime. But if you don't want to take our relationship in that direction, I completely understand. We will carry on as we are, at least until you leave the Army or Kitty has finished her schooling."

Eli didn't reply straight away. He had never heard Pat speak her mind this way, but he respected her for talking straight.

"So Kitty even mentioned the dinner bit as well, did she?"

"I think she has it all planned out," replied Pat, who despite laying her cards strongly on the table, could hardly control the butterflies in her stomach. Although the offer was one with no hard feelings, she wasn't looking forward to a refusal.

"We'll go for dinner then, the next time I'm back, if that's ok with you. Where would you like, it's been years since I last dined out so I'm a bit out of practice?"

"Anywhere, really!" Pat's face broke in to a smile of relief and happiness. "But not an Indian though."

"Yeah, Kitty said you don't do well with spicy food, she mentioned you get too much grief from the old Farmers." Pat's smile fell away as her face turned bright red with blushes. "Don't worry," added Eli with a wink. "I know a good fish restaurant."

His joke saved her embarrassment but she still took a big drink from her cup to hide her face. Eli, now having a better feeling about the morning, thought it the right time, seeing as how they were in an honest mood to get a few other things off his chest. He walked to the back door in the kitchen, opened it and sat on the steps that led to the back garden. Taking the half-smoked cigar from his pocket he lit it and asked Pat to sit down beside him.

"You don't mind, do you?" he asked, indicating the cigar in his hand.

"I told you I don't. You need to cut down though."

"I will, when I'm out of the business I'm in and I don't need them to help me think." He smoked his cigar and did exactly that, began to think. Then he told her what was on his mind. "In the next few weeks I'm going to be getting up to a bit of skullduggery," he began to explain. "After that I'm retiring from the Army and everything else. I want us to travel the world, buy a house abroad and do all the things a family should do – you, me and Kitty." Eli's inclusion of Pat in the mention of a family brought the smile right back to her face.

"Sounds great," she beamed. "But why do I think there's a catch?"

"What I'm doing next, if it was to go wrong, could get

a little messy. There's nothing for you to worry about. You don't know anything so there's nothing you can say wrong if anybody asks but there are a few things you need to know." Eli paused as Pat took a drink from her tea, wondering what he was going to say. "Over the years I've always been paranoid after the accident that Kitty wouldn't have enough money to survive, should anything happen to me." Pat listened carefully, knowing Eli's tone was serious. She had never been privy to anything he did in the three years in the house but she knew from her sister that where Eli's business was concerned that Three Monkeys was the best policy. "This house, for instance," he continued while taking a puff; "it's owned, lock stock and barrel. There's only the bills to pay each month and they're on direct debit from my bank, so no matter what happens to me or how long I'm away, you and Kitty will always have a roof over your heads. The deeds are in Kitty's name, I transferred them after her mother died and put you down as her guardian until she is twenty-five."

"You're here, Eli; she doesn't need me as a guardian.

You're not going anywhere. When you speak like that it makes me feel like I've just had a break in life only for it to be taken away."

"Just listen, Pat, the worst scenario has always got to be covered, it's simply a part of life." He squeezed Pat's knee, reassuring her that what he was telling her was important and needed to be said. "Do you see the metal pole that the washing line is attached to?" Eli pointed down the garden but there was no need, Pat used it every week and knew exactly where it was.

"Yes, what about it?" she asked, wondering where the conversation was going.

"Well on a sunny day at 2 o'clock it casts a shadow and at the end of that shadow about twelve inches below the ground an ammunition box is buried."

"Did you put it there?" Eli nodded whilst taking another smoke.

"Two and a half years ago after the accident I took the payout I got from the insurance and every other penny I had at the time and bought gold; not bullion or anything, just normal rings, necklaces and bracelets, stuff that could be easily sold on by you and Kitty, should you need money if I weren't around. There's not a single item in that box worth less than five thousand."

"And how much is in there?"

"About four hundred and fifty grand's worth."

"Why Eli? Why not just use a bank?"

Pat couldn't see the reasoning behind his extraordinary actions.

"Because the insurance pay-out was only a hundred and fifty. I needed the amount to be much more so you and Kitty would have enough to survive. The rest of the money I used was hooky and unaccountable so it couldn't be shown. Don't get me wrong, there's money in the bank and there's more policies on me but the government has a habit of freezing things if you get killed whilst undertaking certain illegal activities. I've just made sure that all Kitty's' eggs aren't in one basket, that's all."

"It's a lot for me to take in. I'm not sure I can handle all this information."

"Well I've told you now and I feel a lot better knowing my daughter will be looked after."

"With all that money, do you need to be taking any more risks?"

"In the words of Rocky Marciano, 'one more round.' I can't hang my gloves up until I've done this thing I have to do."

Pat looked at Eli, for the first time in a different light, finally getting a vision of just how deep he really was. She couldn't say she understood him but she could tell by the way he spoke that he was going to do this thing, and that nothing she could say would stop him.

Chapter Ten

Deaf and Dumb

"What do you fancy for your tea tonight?" asked Roisin. It was Tuesday morning and the pair were at the breakfast table, coming round over a morning cuppa. The conversation was a little sparse; it seemed that Michael wasn't the only one with things on his mind.

"Why do women ask their husbands that question? I mean, what man knows what he wants for his tea, fifteen minutes after he's just got out of bed. I don't even know if I fancy any breakfast yet, he let go a sigh to follow his words. Roisin lowered her cup and looked across the table at her husband, wondering what his little outburst was all about.

"You need to go back to bed and climb out of the other side, ye narky bleeder."

"I'm just saying that it's a stupid question. Anyway, don't worry about me. I'll get something with the lads because I'm going to be a bit late tonight." Roisin looked again, this time as though he had forgotten their anniversary. "What?" he asked, thinking he had something to answer for "I won't be that late. If you like, make me a bit of whatever it is you have and I'll throw it in the microwave later." With her look unchanged Roisin got up from the table and carried their cups to the sink. "Oy woman, I wasn't finished with that," he complained as the remainder of his morning cuppa was thrown down the drain.

"This Tuesday night thing is becoming a bit of a habit isn't it," she shouted over the noisy clanging of the cups that were now being vigorously washed. "It can't be work, you came in stinking of whisky last week."

Michael wondered what had brought on the sudden change in her mood. It had been happening a lot lately and he was growing tired of treading on egg shells.

"It is work; we meet to plan the job we're doing. Last week I stayed to discuss a few things with Eli, and we popped the cork on a bottle."

"Are you sure?" she asked with a disbelieving tone in her voice.

"Am I what woman, what sort of a question is that? I think it was you that got out of the wrong side of the bed this morning, not me. In fact, you've been in a twat of a mood all week? I had a drink last week with Eli, that's all. I can't believe I'm even having this conversation. If this is what I get for taking you into my confidence – jealousy and suspicion – then I wish I'd have left you in the dark."

Roisin backtracked a little.

"It was just a question."

"No it wasn't, it was an accusation. Jesus woman, what am I supposed to have done wrong now, and when did I find the time to do it? Did I do it between working at the building site or the bar? Or was it between planning Ireland's biggest robbery, Peewee's apprenticeship, Ma's bingo, or your fucking hairdressers?"

"Alright you've made your point, I was only asking. Can't a woman get a little jealous when she's feeling a bit insecure?"

"Insecure. Insecure about what? What have I done to give you reason to doubt me?"

"You're always somewhere else lately, I don't know what you're getting up to."

"You know exactly what I'm getting up to, because I told you last week. Roisin, what the fuck is up with ye, you're talking stupid? I hope that doctor hasn't been prescribing you any of that Prozac shit, because I'll ruin his fucking life if he has, see how he likes it."

Roisin tried to calm herself and offered an excuse.

"Take no notice of me, it's just my hormones."

"I was going to say, you're not usually this bad when you're on your bike." She looked, blankly.

"What bike?" she asked.

"Ye know, the old menstrual cycle. You're not usually this bad when the decorators are in."

Roisin's face quickly reverted to its previous angry glare.

"There is no bike as you put it, or any decorators. And the reason that I have been in a twat of a mood, as you also put it, is because there hasn't been for over three months."

Michael had to pause for a moment to think about that one. He was never top of the class in maths but he could work that one out on his fingers.

"Yes Michael Flynn, I'm pregnant. Ye bleeding thoughtless idiot!" Michael, was speechless, not knowing how to react to the news. "I was going to cook you something nice this evening," she continued, "and break the news to you then. But you won't be here because your off doing God knows what with your new Cockney friend."

Michael still sat gobsmacked, not only at Roisin's language, but because she had finally got the one thing she wanted the most, and it had made her insecure.

"You never seize to amaze me, woman. As far as I'm concerned it's great news, the best news. How long have ye known?"

He got up and went to hug her. She could see he

was clearly delighted with the news but couldn't contain herself and burst into tears. Michael guided her back to the kitchen table and sat her down.

"Come on babes, this is happy news. I don't understand what's wrong with you, isn't this what we've been hoping for. God knows we've tried enough, I've never known a woman ovulate so much."

This time Michael's joke brought a smile to Roisin's face as she wiped the tears from her cheeks.

"I am happy," she reassured, "but are you sure it's what you want. You joke about me ovulating now, but is that how it was, have I pushed you into it?"

"Don't be stupid, I was up for it just as much as you, if not more, if you know what I mean."

Michael put his arms around his wife and cuddled her with all the love he had. He wasn't the greatest at understanding women's problems, the crying certainly had him confused, but Roisin wasn't just his wife, she was his best friend, more so than Danny, Dermot, or Sean, so when something was upsetting her, it upset him too. Trying to get in touch with his more sensitive and feminine side, he attempted to come up with a diagnosis that would explain the way she was feeling.

"I know it's a little early but perhaps it's some sort of post-natal depression that's affecting you."

Roisin looked at her husband in disbelief that he even knew the meaning of the words post-natal.

"I think you've been tuning in to Woman's Hour a bit too much on that radio of yours at work. And its pre-natal, by the way."

Oh ye, Michael thought.

"I'm only trying to help, babes. It's hard to understand why you're so upset given the news."

"I'm going to get fat,"

Her worries were voiced in a squeaky voice, as the waterworks were turned on again. Michael raised his arms as Roisin's head fell on to his shoulder.

"Well of course you are. Women usually do when they're going to have a baby. What's wrong with that?"

Michael was almost laughing whilst giving his reassuring answer.

"You're already not paying me a lot of attention lately. How will it be when I've put on four stone."

"Four stone! Fuck me, woman, is it mine, or Sean's? I don't have to ring Dermot, do I, and ask him where you get them blood tests done?" Roisin gave him a loving slap on his shoulder. "I've never looked at another man since the day I met you. You know that." Michael kissed her on the forehead. He knew that everybody looked, but like her, he had never leapt. "And I must have been paying you some attention or else how did you end up in the state you're in. This baby isn't the second coming, you haven't had an immaculate conception?"

"You know what I mean."

Michael did know what she meant but he was still struggling to understand it. He tried to carry on with the jokes to get her smiling again.

"The weight won't bother me either. I'm not afraid of a big woman, especially if some of the weight you put on goes on your chest."

Roisin looked down at her cleavage, taking Michael's reassurances the wrong way.

"What's wrong with my chest, you've always been happy with it before? You always said that I had gorgeous tits."

"I've never been anything else but happy, but a little more wouldn't hurt," he said with a cheeky grin, but knowing he was on thin ice.

"I know what you mean," she replied. "I've often thought the same about you."

Michael, didn't click straight away about what Roisin had said, but when he did, her 'touché' answer brought a smile to both their faces, and an end to the discussion.

"Listen, I have to go out tonight, but Friday we'll have a bit of a drink at the bar and celebrate with all our friends and family. And don't worry about me looking at any slimmer women. If we get caught pulling this job I'll get a ten stretch inside. Then the only thing you'll have to worry about is me watching my 'Deaf and Dumb."

"Deaf and dumb, what's that?" she asked.

"My bum, my arse. It's rhyming slang. I think I'm listening to Eli too much."

"Isn't that where this argument started?"

Michael sighed at her added jibe.

"Babes, if we don't plan this robbery properly, we'll probably end up getting caught. Then little Finbar will be in long trousers before I get out of jail."

"So you've known that you're going to be a daddy for all of five minutes, and you've already named the child and decided it's going to be a boy?"

"I have indeed, so don't go making me out to be a liar."

"And what if it's a little girl, what will we call the baby then?"

"Catherine of course. That will put us in the good books with Ma, giving us a quiet life, and a babysitter for the next sixteen years." Michael pushed Roisin back to her feet and towards the kettle. "Now you don't have to start taking it easy just yet girl, so make me another cup of tea. Somebody threw my last one down the sink, and I'll have a slice of toast as well, I've just time before the lads pick me up."

Roisin did as he asked without any comment. She

decided not to spoil the soon-to-be-dad's moment and took pleasure in watching him sit at the table with a smile on his face to match her own.

"So you're not going to tell anyone until Friday night, not even Danny?"

"Not even Danny," confirmed Michael, "or my mother for that matter, which will probably get me a thick ear later. Everybody's usually in the bar Friday nights anyway, listening to Fatty, so it shouldn't take too much manipulation to make sure that they are this week."

"Well how about forgetting your tea and toast and taking me back to bed for a quickie, I'll let you leave your boots on."

Roisin opened her nightie to make the offer more appealing. Michael looked at his beautiful wife and then at the kettle, exaggerating the movement as though it was a big decision.

"Leave off woman and make the tea," he joked. "What are you after? Twins?"

Chapter Eleven

Educating Roisin

Eli stood outside the farmhouse door smoking and greeting the lads as they arrived. Michael hung back so as to be the last one in line, hoping to have a quiet word with him before he finished his cigar.

"Your look a little tired, fella," he observed. "Have you been overdoing it a bit?"

"It was a busy week but me and Ringer had our business under control by Friday afternoon so I decided to mix it with a bit of pleasure and spend the weekend at home with the bottle."

Michael looked confused.

"What, you were on the hard stuff?"

"No," Eli smiled. "The bottle of water – daughter."

Now Michael smiled.

"To say you're English, you don't speak much of it." Now they both smiled together. "Anyway, that's nice to hear; was everything good?"

"Brilliant as it happens, I haven't slept so well for ages. I think I may have got too much of a good thing though, that's why I'm yawning now. That and the long drive back. Ringer drank a skinful yesterday so I did the honours. My daughter is growing up so fast, though. It's scary, she understands things that at her age I hadn't even began to think about."

"Tell me about it," agreed Michael. "My brother Peewee, who you met the other week is only just sixteen and a cheekier little fucker you'll never came across."

Eli nodded in total agreement while pulling a face as if to say 'you can say that again'. "He won't read a book or a newspaper," Michael continued. "And he didn't even bother turning up to do his exams before leaving school. Mind you, he was always being expelled from that place for fighting but you should hear him argue the toss with Dermot and Sean when he's winding them up at work. There are words that come out of his gob that the only other place you'd hear the like would be if you tuned in to Prime Minister's Question Time."

"Does he watch a lot of telly?" asked Eli, taking an interest.

"All the time, but he never watches any old crap. He prefers that National Geographic channel, and anything to do with engineering or history."

"I bet he's dyslexic," said Eli, thinking he recognised the symptoms.

"Dyslexic? Do you think so? I suppose it would explain a lot."

"It explains everything, including the fighting. The other kids don't understand it, you see, which isn't really their fault. How are the kids supposed to know any better if the teachers don't? Young Peter, being dyslexic, would already be frustrated because he was lagging behind, then one of the other kids takes the piss so he punches them on the nose. I bet he's got a good memory as well."

"Like an elephant," confirmed Michael. "He never writes anything down, it doesn't matter if he's going for the sandwiches or building materials."

"That's because dyslexic people train their memories. They don't know that they are doing it at first, its just the body's natural instinct to overcome a problem. They tend to remember things by linking the words they want to remember to pictures. It's called word association. By bringing up a picture in their mind it leads them to the answer or whatever it was they were trying to remember, whether it be an important date in history or just a telephone number."

"How do you know so much about it?"

"I grew up with the same problems that I think your little brother has, except in my day they didn't have such a nice word for it, I was tagged as a remedial. Even on the door at school it said remedial class, there was no getting away from it. I was fighting every day in the schoolyard. The biggest break I got though was when my dad took me down to join me up because the Army entrance exam was multiple choice. Like your brother I wasn't thick, all I had to do was put a tick next to the correct answer. I scored nearly a hundred percent!" Eli smiled as he reminisced.

"I didn't realise," said Michael, in a guilty tone. "I've given my little brother a whole heap of gip over the years for not doing his homework."

"It's not your fault. Like I said, if the teachers at school don't spot it, how the hell are you supposed to know? If you want to do something about it, get in touch with an agent that books turns for the pubs and clubs, Fatty should know one. Book a memory artist to play at O'Reilly's Bar and whilst he is there get him to have a word with young Peter. What he teaches him about word association and training his mind will put him in good stead for the rest of his life."

"I'll do that," Michael acknowledged before pausing. "I think maybe I should see one of them fellas myself. I've forgotten now what it was I was going to ask ye."

"You were probably going to ask me if the meeting with Joe Ninety went well, and do I have our bargaining tool? The answer is yes, so hopefully our backs are covered."

Michael smiled as their conversation was broken. The others were anxious to get the meeting started.

"Are we holding the meeting out here or inside?" asked Ringer, sticking his still-hung-over head out of the door. "Hurry up, will you, I don't think I can take much more of Sean and Dermot's bickering. If we don't get started soon I'm going to strangle the pair of them."

Eli raised his eyebrows while looking at Michael as if to say he's not joking, before finishing his cigar and throwing it onto the frost-covered grass that blanketed the farm and the surrounding fields.

"Come on. We'd better get in there, he's obviously vexed. He just spoke more words than he did for the whole trip driving there and back from London."

Inside, Sean and Dermot were still at it as they entered. Sean ceased his verbal assault mid-sentence and turned his attentions on them.

"Fuck me, what have you been doing out there, we're freezing our fucking nuts off sat here waiting."

"Sean, wind your fucking neck in. And Dermot, until you stop rising to his insults he's not going to stop throwing them in your direction." Eli put them both in their place, thinking a bit of a wake-up wouldn't do them any harm this close to the robbery. "I know how fucking cold it is, Sean, but it hasn't stopped Errol and Oneway being out every night for the past week, keeping an eye on the manager's house and his movements. And they aren't doing it from some nice warm car with the heater on either, they've been under a bush laid in the snow and the fucking frost. Now in the absence of Errol and Oneway, who are at this moment doing that very thing, which means I haven't had chance to talk to them since my return, how did you get on this week? I.e., did you get the van, and Dermot, how far have you got in your preparations?"

It had been a while since the pair had been given a bollocking of such magnitude. The last time was in London four years ago when they jointly stole Michael's Chinese spare ribs from the fridge.

"The Sprinter is in the barn. It's almost brand new so it should do the job we want it for, no problems."

"Good," replied Eli, before looking at Dermot.

"Everything's complete," he started, "I had to make some changes to the plan where the detonations were concerned. The secondary explosions that will scatter the flour once the bombs are in the air will now take place automatically – five seconds after the initial blast that launches them. We did some figures to estimate the speed and velocity they will be travelling at and we've calculated that they will be at a height of around two hundred feet when that occurs."

"What was the reason you decided to make the changes?"

"Simply because Errol would need another set of hands to do his job properly. Detonating each explosion manually would have meant using two different remotes, working on two separate wavelengths at the same time as holding a pair of binoculars to his head and relaying to us what is happening on the street. I don't doubt that Errol is good at his job but it would only take one slip and a wrong button pressed, and the whole robbery would be fucked."

Eli was happy and impressed by Dermot's command decision.

"Well, you'll get no argument from me, Dermot, my old China. That's your department, so if you're happy, so am I. What do you think, Michael?"

"Dermot knows his stuff, he'll see us right." Sean, even after his bollocking, couldn't help pissing on Dermot's bonfire with another witter.

"Fucking teacher's pet, he'll be bringing you a fucking apple next week, and who the fuck's been teaching you words like velocity?"

Eli shook his head; 'You can't change Sean' he thought to himself. To him, bollockings were like water off a ducks back.

"Ok, moving on to next week and the day before the robbery," continued Eli. "We'll meet here again at two o'clock, so have your dinner first, because we're not cooking anything. Sean, if you don't think you'll be able to get all the way through to Monday morning after the robbery without eating, bring some sandwiches with you."

Sean, not realising that Eli was taking the piss, put his thumb up as though he was confirming the most important part of the plan. Eli continued.

"The clothes you wear for the robbery, along with the paint sprayers' suits, will be burned when we get back here. That includes your footwear and underpants, so don't go wearing your favourite daisy roots (boots) or your Y-fronts if you want to keep them. We'll all have a shower and then change into the spare clothing I want you to bring with you. Nobody is leaving this farm after the robbery until every speck of flour and strand of DNA has been removed or burnt, is that understood?"

"You'd better leave your security blanket at home, Dermot," interrupted Sean. "You won't be able to sleep if we burn that!"

Eli again shaking his head, looked across at Danny, then Michael, as if to say 'what do you do?' Danny and Michael were smiling, they thought the joke was funny. Eli, again continued. "When, and only when, I am satisfied that nothing can tie any of us to that bank, we will all leave, and you lads will go back to work as if nothing has happened and you simply had a lie-in that morning."

"What about the money?"

"Thank you, Dermot, I can always rely on you to remind me about that. The money will stay on the farm, along with the Mercedes Sprinter, until we return after a safe period of time to divvy up."

"How long do you call a safe period?"

"Well how long would you say Dermot?"

"A month may be two."

"A year," Eli enlightened.

"A year?" repeated Danny, "Isn't that a bit dangerous? Anyone could stumble by. Kids, the police, nosey fucking neighbours. By Tuesday morning that van is going to be the best known vehicle in Belfast."

"Nobody will find the money or spot the van because the money will be inside the van and the van will be inside a big hole in the floor of the barn that Sean will dig on Friday when he brings your JCB. After the robbery, he'll backfill the hole, covering the vehicle, and there it will stay for a year until we return. The farm is on a three-year lease and every now and then you lads can have a drive down just to make sure the place is secure."

"A year?" repeated Sean, "It'll be like torture."

"Better the torture of knowing the money is there, but not being able to spend it" added Michael. "Than the torture we would receive from the IRA, if you were caught spending any of it."

He summed up the reasoning for the long waiting period perfectly.

"As you know, lads," resumed Eli, pretty much continuing along the same lines. "It's not doing the robbery that's the hard part, most places are wide open to thieving bastards like us. It's staying out of jail to enjoy the spoils, or as the case may be in this instance, staying alive to spend it." He gave the Irish lads a look, along with time to think, but they didn't really need it. None of them were arguing because they knew he was right. "In the meantime," he advised, "if you need any money, go to a bank. Only this time, borrow it. If the banks won't lend you it, give me a ring. We still get our regular donation from our friendly neighbourhood Notting Hill Yardie, Allan."

"Fuck me, is he still paying ye?"

"Of course he is, Sean, that's one fish that won't get off the hook. He'll pay until the day he dies and as I said before, if we have anything to do with it, he'll get a telegram from the Queen. But the point that I am trying to get across is to not give any fucker any reason to look at you." He received a round of agreeing nods for his wise words. "Right, we'll meet back here next Sunday at two o'clock, except for you Sean. We'll see you here sometime Friday with the JCB. Leave the beer alone next Saturday as well, lads. I want you all clear-headed when you arrive here next Sunday."

"The lads and me are having a few drinks at the bar Friday night," added Michael, "that'll be our last until after the robbery."

This was obviously one of the subtle hints Michael had told Roisin about. His way of making sure the lads were in the bar to hear them break their baby news.

"Well don't celebrate too hard, there's more than

one way of drawing attention to yourselves. Michael, before you go." Eli turned and took two mobile phones from a drawer. "I got two pay-as-you-go phones when I was in London. Take this one just in case there are any last-minute problems and you need to get in touch. There's only one number registered in it, which belongs to the phone I have, and vice versa. Don't use it to call any other number, then if it falls in to the wrong hands, nobody can tie it to you. Bring it with you next Sunday and after the robbery we'll mag to grid them both with the rest of the stuff."

"Mag to grid, you've lost me."

"Sorry, I keep forgetting that you weren't in the army, not the British Army anyway. Mag to grid, it means to get rid of something. It's a term from map reading when you plot a bearing onto a map that has been taken on a compass, a magnetic bearing to a grid bearing, mag to grid. What you're getting rid of is the magnetic variation. If you go the other way, from grid to mag, you add it."

Eli did his best to explain the saying but then didn't

know why he'd bothered. It wasn't as though the Irish lads were ever going to need it.

"I'll remember that one, the next time I get lost in Belfast," quipped Sean.

"So long as you don't get lost next Monday morning, I couldn't give a monkey's what you remember, but I do know one thing you won't forget."

"What's that?"

"Your sandwiches."

Sean smiled and winked with a raised thumb.

Nothing did go wrong that week. If anything, their only problem was that there wasn't enough time in it. They were busier than ever finalising work so they could close up the site for the holidays, and then after work trying to find the time to do their Christmas shopping. It was on all of their minds that they could well be spending the festive season behind bars, so they were taking extra care with the presents they chose for their families and loved ones. Michael though, was at a slight advantage with Roisin. She knew all about what they were getting up to, so he didn't have to buy her any exuberant gifts to cushion the blow, but he did consider buying his mother a life time membership to the local Mecca Bingo.

Friday night in a busy O'Reilly's bar, an unexpected guest was about to enter. Eli walked through the door and was immediately spotted by Danny, from his usual position at the end of the bar. He nudged Dermot, who was stood next to him, and caught the eye of Michael, who followed his look towards the door and their arriving surprise guest. They all wondered what he was doing there, and immediately had the same thought – that something was wrong.

Eli moved from the door, making his way through the punters towards Michael and Roisin. He acknowledged Danny and Dermot at the bar and let on to Sean, who was busy belting out an Elvis Presley song on the Karaoke. As he approached, Michael had to make the decision whether or not to distance himself from Roisin, so they could talk privately, or introduce the pair.

"Good evening, Michael, and I presume this lovely lady is your beautiful bride, Roisin."

Roisin, turned to see a very smartly dressed man, holding his cigar in one hand and a small gift wrapped box in the other.

"You must be Eli, the mysterious man that my husband spends all his time with and comes home drunk, talking in rhyming slang. Michael didn't mention you were coming tonight but I'm glad you did. I was hoping one day to get a chance to thank you for saving his life."

"I think you'll find we saved each other's, but you're welcome anyway." Michael, whose predicament had been solved by the pair doing their own introductions, was still confused by the visit.

"What are you doing here Eli? Not that it's not nice to see you of course but there's nothing wrong, is there?"

"Nothing's wrong. If there was I would've rang you. I just thought I would drop in for a quick brandy and give you both this present." He passed Roisin the neatly wrapped parcel and took a smoke of his cigar while supporting a big cheesy grin. "Open it," he continued. "I'll get the drinks in." He went to the bar where he was served by Babs. "A large Courvoisier please, darlin', four pints of Guinness for the lads, and whatever it is that you, Roisin and Michael's mum are drinking."

"Cheers, that's very kind of you. You're a long way from home aren't you?" said Babs, recognising the southern tones of a fellow Londoner. "In fact, don't I know you?" she asked.

"You do," Eli confirmed. "I used to come in your old boozer, the Rose and Crown, up Notting Hill. I worked on the building site next door for a while, that's how I know the lads. Eli's the name."

"Barbara, but just call me Babs, I'm Danny's partner."

The pair shook hands across the bar.

"He's a very lucky man, Babs. Did you get a drink?"

"I'll have a gin and tonic, but don't tell Danny, he doesn't like me drinking them!"

"Knock yourself out, girl, I won't tell him. I'm good at keeping secrets." Babs fetched Eli's double brandy from the optic and placed it in front of him with a smile.

"Lavvly. Now there's a score for the round. Keep

the change and get yourself another one of those 'G n T's, alright, my love?"

Eli turned back to Michael and Roisin, who had opened the package and stood with a small white beautifully bound Bible in her hand.

"Eli, it's gorgeous, is it for Christmas?" she asked.

Eli leaned forward, obviously about to say something he didn't want anyone else but Michael, and Roisin, to hear.

"No, it's for the baby's christening, and his or hers first Holy Communion. Its antique, I bought it from a book store last week when I was in London."

Roisin backhanded Michael in the chest.

"You said you weren't going to tell anyone until tonight."

"I didn't, I swear."

"Well then how."

"Don't ask," Michael answered, cutting Roisin short, before himself leaning forward for some privacy. "Hang on a minute, Eli," he said, quietly looking for answers. "Not only do I not know 'how' you know that Roisin is pregnant, but now you're telling us that you knew over a week ago. I've only known for four days myself."

Both he and Roisin stared at him, waiting for an explanation.

"Well," Eli, began slowly. "When I first came to see you in the cellar that Friday morning, we had already been in Belfast for over a month, sorting out the farm and things. So now and then, just to make sure that everything was alright with you all, ie, we followed you sometimes if you know what I mean." Roisin, looked at Michael as Eli talked, realising that there was a bit more to this Cockney fella than met the eye, and a lot more than Michael had told her. "Anyway," he continued while taking a drink. "One day, when I walked past Roisin, after she had come out of the chemist, I spotted the pregnancy test sticking out of her handbag. Then three days later, when we saw her visit the clinic, we put two and two together and came up with a bun in the oven." Roisin was gobsmacked. Michael was silent and Eli took another drink and a smoke.

"Who the fuck are ye?" Roisin asked shocked. "And why do you follow people about?"

"Don't worry about it, babes, he does it all the time," Michael reassured her. "I'll explain it to you later. Here, get that down ye."

Michael passed her the orange juice from the bar that Eli had bought her, attempting to change the subject. At the other end of the bar Babs was delivering the two Guinness to Danny and Dermot.

"Your London friend from the building site bought you them. He seems like a nice man, why haven't you mentioned him before?"

Danny paused before answering with a searching question of his own.

"Did he say anything to ye?"

"Only that you were a very lucky man," she answered whilst giving him a wink. The G 'n' T was kicking in already. Turning to serve another customer, she left the big man none the wiser as to Eli's visit.

"What the fuck is he up to?" said Dermot, as the pair took a drink from their fresh pints before looking back over at Michael and Eli, where Roisin was still studying the lovely gift.

"So do you like the present?" Eli asked. "We all chipped in for it – me, Ringer, Oneway and Errol."

Roisin, who had knocked back her drink in one, wishing it was something stronger, again looked at Michael as if to say 'who the fuck are Ringer, Oneway and Errol'.

"Don't ask," Michael repeated. "It's best if I explain it to you later." Michael gave Eli a dirty look. "You're enjoying this aren't ye."

Eli just smiled cheekily.

"Had you been following all the lads or was it just Michael and me?" Roisin was wondering if they were the only ones that had been singled out for the big brother treatment.

"No, we followed the others as well. But don't take it the wrong way. It's something we had to do before I approached Michael, to make sure he was in the right frame of mind to do the work. I don't get my kicks out of watching you do your shoe shopping."

Roisin accepted his words with a smile, but was interested in what else he knew.

"And did the others get up to anything worth talking about?"

Eli, knowing that his wife was prying looked at Michael for guidance as to whether or not he should enlighten her anymore. He was in one of his Cockney lairy and mischievous moods when he enjoyed shocking people with things they didn't know. He'd had a bit of fun with them with the baby news, which he had said quietly so nobody else heard, but the present of the Bible was from the heart.

"Go on, you might as well tell her' said Michael. She won't leave you alone now until you do, and you've spilled your guts about everything else."

Eli took another drink, finishing his brandy before passing Michael, his and Roisin's empty glasses.

"I'll go to the bar then, should I?" he said, taking the hint. Roisin smiled at Eli, awaiting some juicy gossip.

"Come on then, whilst he's at the bar," she egged. "Dish the dirt."

Her bubbly personality and smile made Eli laugh. She was a beautiful girl that lit up the room with her smile and she and Michael made a beautiful couple. They were going to make great parents, which made Eli reminisce about how good he once had it. It also made him more determined that nothing would go wrong with the robbery, so they could raise their child together.

"Right, Danny and his better half have got a thing about doing it outside in phone boxes and the park," he revealed first.

"I know about all that," answered Roisin, "Babs is always dragging him into the open air for a shag." Roisin smiled cheekily while revealing a bit of information of her own. "That's not the only place she likes him to make love to her either. And I'm not talking about their special spot behind the trees! I hope ye have something better on Sean."

Eli, whilst figuring out what she meant, moved on to her next victim.

"Sean. Which could explain the other reason for his weight loss. Visits a lady of ill repute, twice a week on the Creggan estate."

"I know about that too. It was me that put him on

to her. She's an old schoolmate of mine, bringing up two kids on her own so she does it to make a bit of extra cash. And she's not a lady of disrepute. Fatty is her only customer, if you can call him a customer and not just a paying fuck buddy. She does it because she's a friend of mine. It helps them both out and kills two birds with one stone. You're not very good at this whistle-blowing stuff, are you, Eli?"

'Obviously not,' he thought to himself, looking at Roisin, and also thinking how looks can be deceiving.

"What have you got on Dermot," she whispered. "He's the one that plays his cards close to his chest."

"Dermot is seeing the old chesty bird from the café again, or he might have never stopped for all I know."

"That wee bastard. He's back shagging that old slapper Greasy Deasy. I knew he was up to something."

"So you didn't know about that then."

"Not a clue," she replied.

Eli gave a big smile of relief and had another puff on his cigar, having restored his reputation. Obviously his years of SAS training hadn't gone to waste.

"What's the crack?" asked Michael, returning with the drinks. "What did he tell you?"

"Nothing that you need to know about," she answered, whilst looking up the bar at Dermot. Seeing Roisin's glare, Dermot suddenly came over all paranoid.

"Haven't you got something you should be announcing?" said Eli to Michael. "You'd better get on with it before someone else guesses your news, seeing Roisin drinking orange juice. When my wife was pregnant she used to drink Mackeson on a night out, but I don't think they sell it anymore."

"I'll have a few Guinness later. If I drink this all night I'm going to end up looking jaundiced."

"I'll do it now," replied Michael, looking at the time. "Where's Ma, we'd better make sure that she's the first to congratulate us or there'll be hell to pay."

"Don't say it like that, Michael. Ma's been waiting for this day just as long as we have."

"Longer you mean. She was after me getting you pregnant a month after I met ye. She bought me a pair of silk boxer shorts to put me in the mood."

"That's because your mother isn't as stupid as you. She knew a good thing as soon as she saw it. And I never saw you in any silk boxer shorts."

Michael was in trouble again. Eli left them to it. He could see the couple were about to do their thing so he moved down the bar to have a last word with Danny and Dermot.

"How's it going Eli, what brought you here?"

"Just a quick visit, Danny, concerning something you'll find out about in a minute when Michael's made his announcement. Oh and Dermot, Roisin wants a word with you."

"Me, why? I mean what? I mean, did she say what it was about?"

He gulped as he swallowed worryingly.

"Search me." Eli's shrugging of his shoulders and upturned hands didn't cast much enlightenment. "How should I know?" With a cheeky twinkle in his eye he knocked back what remained of his drink whilst Dermot's paranoia grew. "I'll see you Sunday, chaps. Don't forget, I want you bright-eyed and bushy tailed. We have to make sure that everything's shipshape and Bristol fashion. Be lucky."

Leaving Dermot with another stare to wind him up some more, Eli walked out of the door, puffing on his cigar and enjoying a giggle to himself.

"Why do Londoners always talk in rhymes and riddles instead of just telling you straight out what's on their fucking minds?"

"I don't know, but if he wants me bright-eyed and bushy tailed, he shouldn't have bought Babs those G 'n' T's. Just look at her, she's getting frisky already. She'll have me up all night. And it's freezing outside. And that telephone box stinks of piss."

Dermot wasn't listening to Danny's complaints about Babs and their demanding G 'n' T fuelled sex life. Eli had given him his own food for thought.

"I wonder what Roisin wants to talk to me about?"

"Ah lighten up," said Danny, giving him a slap on the back. "I'll put your name down for the Karaoke. You can sing that song, Santa Claus is Coming to Town, because he will be Monday morning!"

Chapter Twelve

The Robbery

Sunday afternoon at about two-twenty-five, the Irish lads, full of expectancy arrived at the farm. Sean had been there on Friday to dig the hole in the barn and the JCB was now parked up at the side of the same, waiting to refill it after the robbery when the money and the van were inside.

"You're late," said Eli, as they entered the farmhouse.

"We had to stop off at the KFC to get Fatty some supplies. It was your idea remember. He didn't fancy sandwiches."

Sean clambered through the door and put three

party buckets on the table before sitting down to devour a drum stick that he had already liberated from one of the tubs. Eli, stepping forward and leaning over lifted the lid on the bucket that he had already opened, just enough to see what was on offer.

"Hot wings," he said with a lick of his lips; "my favourite." He ripped the lid off completely and grabbed a couple of pieces, then passed the bucket back to Oneway and Ringer, who made short work of what remained. The other Irish lads grabbed one of the other buckets before Sean jumped back up to retrieve the third.

"Greedy fuckers, I asked you before I went in if you wanted anything."

Sean, clutching the third bucket to his chest, wasn't happy when suddenly finding himself on short rations. Errol, who had been securing the front gates, was the last man to enter the room. Seeing the food, he walked straight over to him, peeled open the lid on the last box and took a handful.

"Cheers Fatty, I love KFC."

Sean, was mortified and looked inside, trying to work out how many pieces were left for himself.

"I thought you couldn't eat it unless it had been killed in a certain way," said Michael to Errol.

"Ye." Added Sean, hoping for its return.

"I don't eat pork but I love chicken. It doesn't matter to me how it met its end. But I will say a prayer and thank the chicken for its sacrifice, if it makes you feel better."

"So you drink Guinness, and you're not bothered if your food hasn't had its throat cut. And, you fight for what you think is right," Michael added, summarising Errol's beliefs. "Fuck me, if you start eating fish on a Friday you could be a Catholic."

Errol smiled. He knew Michael, didn't mean any disrespect with his joke.

"Don't be converting me Michael. I've just bought a new prayer mat and it comes with a twenty-year guarantee," Errol said with a sarky grin.

"Right, gentlemen," Eli interrupted. "I know it's Sunday, but can we leave the Songs of Praise chat for another time. I want to go over the plan once more, this time filling in all the blanks." The lads all shuffled their backsides on their seats, getting comfortable to listen to what he was about to say. "For the past two weeks Errol and Oneway have watched the manager's house every night, and on a Sunday he likes to go for a drink with his wife down to their local pub. This, hopefully, will give us our means and time of entry. They usually go out at about seven-thirty and arrive back home some time around eleven. Dermot, you get the good job of keeping an eye on the manager and his wife tonight at his local. Here are some pictures of the pair taken this week by Errol and Oneway. There's also one of the car they drive." Eli walked around the table and passed Dermot the snaps. Dermot snatched the photos whilst giving Eli a dirty look. "What the fuck's up with you?" he asked, catching everyone's attention. Dermot looked around the room, it was obviously something he didn't want to discuss in front of the others.

"I'll talk to you later."

"Talk to me now if there's a problem. You're not still

moaning about having to wear the Santa Claus suit are you?"

"No, it's got nothing to do with that. It's about you telling Roisin on Friday night that I'm still seeing Liz Deasy on the side."

"Well I had to tell her something to shock her, she knew more than me. What are you worried about? I made it up, it's not true." Dermot didn't say anything, instead he just started to study the pictures.

"You dirty little fucker," said Sean, jumping in; "you're riding old Greasy Deasy again, aren't ye. You kept that one fucking quiet. I thought you were joking the other week."

"Ye, and it still would have been quiet but for London's answer to fucking Nostradamus here gazing in to his crystal fucking ball and blabbing it to Roisin." Everybody in the room gave a little laugh at Dermot's description of Eli. "It's not funny, I got a right doing Saturday in the bar. They were three-handed giving it to me - Roisin, Babs and his mother." Dermot pointed at Michael like his finger was a loaded gun.

"What were you doing in the bar? I thought we agreed there was to be no drinking after Friday night."

"I wasn't drinking, this was in the morning. I went there to get my coat that I left the night before and I walked in on them, sat around drinking tea. And guess what they were talking about? All that was missing was a caldron in the middle and a few pointed hats."

"Well, Dermot, at least you're not paying for it like Fatty is, up the Creggan Estate." Sean with opened mouth, stopped mid-drum stick, wondering how the fuck he knew about his secret rendezvous! Eli, left him in suspense. "Right let's get back to the plan. Dermot, you take the phone that I gave to Michael and we will call you when the manager and his wife leave the house. You can then call back when they leave the pub, which will give us plenty of time to take up position in his garden and await their arrival back home. If, however, they change their routine and go to a different pub we will simply move in at ten o'clock and wait for them. Just in case they change their routine entirely though, and decide not to go out at all, I've taken the precaution of digging out one of my old disguises, an RUC police uniform. If needs be I will knock on the front door. When we have them under control we enter the house and take care of the parents. We will have to move very quickly if we do this, because the house is bound to be fitted with panic buttons connected to the local plod shop because of his job at the bank. With any luck they will be asleep in bed, the parents I mean. We then separate the occupants, tying up the wife and parents upstairs, and the manager in the kitchen down stairs. Don't forget to blindfold him and stick a pillow case over his head, and don't forget also that Michael is the only one that speaks in his company. When Dermot arrives at the house we'll leave Michael to take care of the manager while the rest of us leave to make ready the vehicles." Eli now walked over to the wall once more and pointed out the area around the Falls Road. "We'll put the decoy cars carrying the explosives into position just before first light. The third vehicle, loaded with bricks and a smoke bomb, will be placed here," he pointed to a position on the map. "This will happen before we return to the farm to pick up the Transits and the Sprinter. As I said before, when we do the job, I will drive the red Transit, Ringer will drive the blue one and Michael the green. Errol and Dermot have sprayed the three vehicles in these colours because it'll be your vehicle's colour that Errol will use to talk to you when communicating from his position on the roof. We don't want any names floating around the airwaves, being picked up by some CB buff on his scanner. When we set off for the bank in the morning, me and Ringer will take different routes and head for the centre. Sean, you'll have already left in the Sprinter with Danny in the back, and Oneway will follow you, driving Michael's van, the green Transit. You three will go back to the manager's house and pick Michael up. He'll will take charge of his vehicle. Oneway, you'll get into the back of the Sprinter with Danny. Dermot, by this time, you will already be on your way to the bank with the manager in his car. Now, and this is important. Make sure you arrive there at seven o'clock sharp as normal, and that at all times during the journey that your face is covered by your white beard and moustache."

Dermot nodded.

"And that goes for the rest of you. I want you to drive with your hoods up, face masks on and the sun visors down. There'll be plenty of cameras on the way there, not just on the street outside the bank. Now we all know the timings and what we have to do, so has anybody got any questions?"

There were none. Eli, had it covered and Michael's silence told him that he hadn't missed a thing, but in true Seven P's style, Eli went over the plan once more, and once more again after that.

They left the farm at five o'clock to make there way to Downpatrick. Dermot was on his own and headed straight for the manager's local, whilst Michael, Ringer, Oneway and Eli, headed for the house. Sean, and Danny stayed at the farm with Errol, giving him a hand to test the headsets they would be using one last time. Their hour-long journey started in the light, but as they approached their destination the winter evening slid into darkness, accompanied by a light fall of snow. Eli went forward in the woods opposite the manager's house, leaving the others in the vehicle hidden down a track. When he got to the place that Errol and Oneway had been using for the last two weeks, he immediately noticed that the manager's car was not in the driveway. A single set of tracks could be seen in the snow fall coming out of the gates, which turned on the road in the direction of the pub. He rang Dermot to tell him that their man may already be there.

"He's here," said Dermot, answering the phone and speaking before Eli had chance. I'm in the car park; I spotted his car as soon as I turned in."

"He's started early," Eli replied; "he must have something on his mind. Maybe the thought of being involved in a robbery and having his family kidnapped has given him the taste for a few extra pints. Go inside Dermot and grab yourself a drink. When you've clocked his boat race give me a missed call to confirm it and then we'll wait for your call later when he leaves."

Dermot wondered what a clock and a boat race had to do with it but he knew what he meant. Eli made his way back to the car to re-join the others.

"That was handy," he said, climbing in to the car. "He's already at the pub. That saves me sitting out there. Freezing my fucking Jacobs off."

"Tell me about it," said Oneway, who had just done two weeks of it. Eli took the phone out of his pocket and checked it had a signal before placing it on the dashboard. Moments later it rang twice, then cut off.

"That was Dermot, confirming that our man is in the pub," He conveyed to the others. "All we have to do now is wait until he leaves and Dermot rings again."

For the next few hours of waiting they must have smoked a hundred fags whilst going over the plan again and again, until the mood was lightened by Danny re-telling Fatty's jokes about the Kitty Kat killer and Nelson Mandela. Just after eleven o'clock, the phone started to vibrate and ring on the dashboard.

"He's leaving now," said Dermot, speaking quietly as he watched the pair from the other side of the pub. "I think his wife will be driving, he's well-oiled, and she has the keys in her hand.

"Well it's a good job that we'll be there to make sure he gets up for work in the morning," replied Eli. "Don't follow them back, Dermot, she might panic if she sees your headlights in the mirror. Give it ten minutes before you leave, and when you arrive here, hide your car down the track next to ours."

"Ok."

"Right chaps, they're on their way. Their route from the bar will bring them back from the right, so we'll enter the garden from the left and rear, that way they won't see any of our foot prints in the snow. Oneway, you know the area better than anyone, so you lead the way, Balaclavas on, lads, let's go."

They made their way as Eli had said, via the left-hand side of the house, and entered the grounds by scaling a small wall. In the garden there were several bushes, two of which bordered either side of the front door and were perfect for their needs. They took cover behind them and waited, using the time to throw snow back over any tell-tale signs of their presence around the threshold. Within ten minutes the manager's car was at the gates and his wife was opening them to gain entry to the drive. After driving all the way in, she climbed back out, telling her husband to be careful of the slippery surface in his drunken state. Her warning was unheeded, as he was no sooner out of the car than his feet, in one movement, went from underneath him to above him as he crashed to the ground, landing on his back. His wife rushed to help, skating her way around the front of the car, hanging on to the bonnet for support. Her anxiety was eased when she heard the sound of her husband's drunken giggles and watched as he attempted to make an angel in the snow with his arms and legs.

"Get up, you fool, I thought you'd broken your neck."

The manager, apparently uninjured, started to sing, and as his wife helped him back to his feet he threw his arms around her, revealing his undying love.

"Shush, you'll wake mum and dad," she said, whispering as she struggled to support and guide him in the direction of the house. Then, within the ten wobbly steps it took for them to get from their car to their front door they were pounced on by the reception committee and subdued. Now, with the keys to the house in Eli's possession, entry was simple. In a matter of moments, Ringer and Oneway had found the parents, who were bound, gagged and locked in one of the bedrooms out of the way along with their daughter, the manager's wife. The manager, who could hardly stand up, was taken into the kitchen and cable-tied to a chair before being blindfolded and a pillow case placed over his head. As Michael closed the door to the kitchen, leaving him on his own, Dermot arrived at the house carrying his Santa Claus suit.

"There's no need for us to be here any longer," said Eli, now they were all alone. "Get changed into your suit," he added, pointing at Dermot, "and we'll take your clothes with us back to the farm. The others will be back here with the vehicles at six, so have the manager ready to move by then."

Michael gave Eli the thumbs up as Dermot got changed. When Eli, Ringer and Oneway had left, Michael opened the kitchen door but didn't expect to see their captive asleep, snoring with his head bobbing up and down inside the pillow case.

"What now?" said Dermot, looking over Michael's shoulder? "Should we wake him up?"

"Nah, let him sleep. We'll watch some telly and wake him at five in the morning to give him the third degree. At least everything we say then will stay fresh in his mind. We could even set our alarms and get some sleep ourselves."

Through the night, back at the farm, the preparations continued. Sean ticked over the engines on the vehicles to make sure they were ready for their morning run and Eli once again took the remainder of the team through the plan. By first light they had delivered the three cars to their positions just outside the city centre. Errol, changing the plan, had decided to detonate the two cars containing the explosives remotely in his line of sight, just to make sure that no innocent passers-by were hurt in the blast, after noticing a worn stretch of grass that looked like it could be a short cut to the local school. The third, containing the bricks and the smoke bomb, he left on a timer, which left him just over thirty-five minutes to cover the distance between the Falls Road and his position in the building opposite the bank. At five o'clock, back at the house, Michael woke the manager, who after realising it wasn't a dream, complained of an aching back.

"What are you doing here?" he asked mumbled through the pillow case over his head. "You're not supposed to be here until tonight."

Their suspicions were confirmed, he was obviously involved, or, he and his family had been threatened so he had no choice but to co-operate.

"We didn't trust you. We thought your bottle might go." Michael laid out the bluff, giving the manager plenty of rope.

"I won't lose my bottle, everything's prepared. The money's all stacked and waiting, twenty-six million in used notes."

Michael turned to look at Dermot, who was stood in the doorway behind him. They were both smiling at the amount mentioned and Dermot mouthed the words 'fuck me'. Michael continued with the pretence.

"If you weren't going to lose your bottle why did you feel the need to go get pissed last night? You don't usually do that. You were told not to change anything about your routine."

"Ok I got a bit drunk, but that doesn't mean I wasn't going to go through with it."

"Well we're here now, and we do the job today."

"You can't, the money's not down at the loading bay, its still in the bank vault. It will take too long to move it."

"There's been a change of plan, we're going to pull the job this morning, taking the money straight out of the vault, and straight out of the front doors."

"That's impossible. The police!"

"Don't you worry about the police, or how the job is going to be done." Michael cut the manager short and jabbed his fingers in his ribs to make him pay attention. "All you need to know is that the deal remains the same and your family will be held until after the robbery. When, if you keep your part of the bargain, they will be released unharmed." Michael repeated the warning and each word was accompanied with another jab in the ribs. "*Do... You... Understand*?

The pillow case moved up and down as the manager nodded in agreement.

"Where are my family, are they ok?"

Michael let go with the back of his hand, striking the manager across the head. The man yelped with the unexpected blow.

"I'll ask the fucking questions. Not you," growled Michael, enforcing his position before falling a little soft. "They're fine, but when we leave to go to the bank they will be moved to another address. Follow my instructions and do the job this morning correctly and they will be released later, as agreed, unharmed."

"I will. I've told you, I wasn't going to back out."

"Just so long as you know that if you double-cross us, you won't know where your family are and neither will the police. You'll never see them again."

"I swear I will go through with it."

"Ok, now listen carefully. There's another man here in the kitchen standing behind you."

The manager automatically attempted to turn his head as though he would be able to see through the blind fold and the pillar case.

"He's in disguise, dressed in a Santa Claus suit. He'll ride to work with you and you'll get him into the bank at the same time as you and your assistant, before any of the other staff arrive. What's the name of the man you meet on the steps in the morning?"

"Doyle, his name is Jimmy Doyle."

"Has he got family and where does he live?"

"He lives in Newtownards with a wife and two kids."

"Good, then tell Mr Doyle that my friend here is a promotional Santa Claus sent at the last minute by Head Office. Make it convincing, because if you don't get him inside, as I've already said, you'll never see your family or anyone else again. Do you understand?"

Again Michael jabbed him in the ribs.

"Yes I understand. There's no need for all of this. I will do what you want me to do. I swear."

"You make sure you do because I don't want my friend having any problems with you on the way to the bank, or inside with this Doyle fella."

"He won't, I swear."

"Good. Now once you're inside, and you and Mr Doyle have keyed in your pass codes to open the vault, he will be tied up and you will be a good little Santa's helper and assist my friend to bag and stack the money near the front entrance." Again the manager nodded his head. "Now in a moment I'm going to remove the pillow case from your head and take you upstairs. I'll let you talk to your family so you can reassure them that everything is going to be alright before you get washed, shaved and changed into your work suit. Once you've done that we'll go over the plan again before you and Santa get in your car and drive to the bank." Michael turned back to Dermot, telling him to put on his white moustache and beard, before pulling his own balaclava over his face and removing the pillow case and blindfold from the manager's head. "This is Santa, who'll be accompanying you this morning."

Dermot stepped forward. The manager, still blinking at the introduction of the light, looked at him in disbelief, unable to believe that there was actually a person dressed in a Santa Claus suit in front of him. Dermot, though, left him in no doubt that the situation was no joke.

"Now you listen to me. I don't want any trouble out of you this morning, and remember, we've been watching your movements for over three months now, so any deviation from your usual routine will result in you losing a lung and your wife losing a husband." With his hand in his pocket holding the replica gun, Dermot pushed it into the man's chest. "Now, you make sure that your man Doyle does as he's told, and that you wave at the fucking camera as you always do when entering the bank. Is that clear?"

The manager was clear about two things. It was clear that he was fucked. And it was clear that they knew everything.

Sean, and Danny were the first to leave the farm, heading for the manager's house with Oneway following behind in the Transit that Michael would later be driving. Ringer and Eli didn't leave until shortly after seven to travel the short distance directly to the city and the Northern Bank. Dermot by this time had already arrived at the bank along with the manager and immediately began to spread some Christmas cheer, true to character. The assistant waiting at the bank doors was completely taken in by Dermot and the manager's reason for him being there, and the three entered under the watching eye of the cameras without a fuss. After a wave from the manager, of course.

At seven-twenty the two car bombs were detonated under Errol's watchful eye, causing a massive police presence to converge on the Fall's Road area of the city. At seven-thirty the smoke bomb in the back of the decoy car was activated, creating more of a headache for the police and straining them to their limit when having to cordon off the area surrounding it. At seven-forty Errol had now arrived at the building opposite the Northern Bank, and with his control pad in hand was ready to fire the mortars. At seven-forty-five Ringer arrived bang on time in the blue Transit, carrying the first of the mortars, and before Ringer had finished moving into position and switched his hazards on, Eli arrived at the top of Bedford Street to the left of the bank, blocked off his side of the road and switched his on. At seven-forty-eight, Dermot, in the Sprinter, and Michael, in the green Transit, pulled up at the lights, first and second in the queue in front of Errol's position. The drivers in the few cars behind Eli's red Transit were growing impatient, sounding their horns and shouting complaints because he had blocked the street. Errol, seeing the commotion, knew it would take Sean at least another thirty seconds to get into position and decided not to wait for the signals to change.

"Big boy in the white van," he radioed. "No one's going to give you a ticket. Don't wait for the lights, move in to position now."

Sean, realising he was the subject of Errol's order, drove through on red and Michael behind him angled his vehicle towards the target and switched on his hazards.

Sean swung the big Mercedes out to the right, mounting the kerb for a moment to give himself enough room to execute a U- turn. A bus shelter stood outside the bank a few metres above its doors, so he mounted the kerb on the other side and drove the Sprinter between the shelter and the building. Any closer and he could have leant out of the window and made a withdrawal from the cash machine. Then before turning his hazards on, he looked into his wing mirror to see Ringer's vehicle at the top of the hill behind him. A hundred yards to his front, Eli's vehicle was parked, and now had several of the drivers from the cars behind him gathered around, shouting for him to roll it backwards onto the kerb, out of the way. Eli just sat quietly in his paint sprayer's suit and mask, ignoring their yells. Sean then glanced to his left at ten o'clock, where Michael's vehicle was receiving the same treatment. In line with his character, he started to giggle to himself, thinking how quickly the irate drivers were going to scatter when the fireworks started. He switched on his hazards, pissing himself at the thought. It was time for Errol to take command.

"Brace yourselves, gentlemen," came his warning over their headsets.

BOOM, BOOM, BOOM.

The deafening noise echoed around the enclosed streets as six flour bombs, two from each vehicle, were sent hurtling in to the sky above the area of the bank. Adding to the explosion was also the noise of the exploding van tyres as they disintegrated under the enormous pressure of the blasts. Every pedestrian dove for cover as cars that could move were driven away at speed from the blast area. It must have been a frightening time for the locals, who wouldn't have heard anything like it since the end of the Troubles.

BOOM, BOOM, BOOM.

The six parcels exploded at their given height with more of a duller sound than the first, but it was still loud enough to rattle the fillings in your teeth. A covering of white flour now blanketed the area and slowly began to fall onto the streets below. As the first specks began to settle on the window screens of the vans, Ringer, Michael and Eli climbed out and started to make their way towards the bank. Every step they took their vision became more and more impaired by the thickening substance, until the point that anything more than three metres in front of them became invisible. Ringer, arriving at Sean's Sprinter first, opened the side door of the vehicle, releasing Danny and Oneway, whilst Eli and Michael headed straight for the bank doors. Sean took up his position to the front of the vehicle with Oneway to the rear. The vehicle and the bank were now like one sealed unit. Dermot opened the doors with the manager at his side and pointed at the bags of money already stacked in the entrance, waiting to be loaded in to the van. Danny and Ringer set to it immediately as Michael and Eli followed Dermot and the manager back to the vault.

"Has he given you any fucking trouble?" said Michael, pointing at the manager, aiming his question at Dermot.

"No. He's done well," he answered. Much to the

manager's relief, who recognised Michael's voice from being his captor earlier that morning.

"Good." The manager got another jab in the ribs. "You can carry on impressing us by packing the rest of that money fast."

He did just that, helped by Dermot, as Errol's voice entered their ears.

"Get ready lads, I'm sending up the second batch."

BOOM, BOOM, BOOM.

As the explosions rattled through the building, Errol relayed more instruction.

"That's two boys, you need to move quickly, this stuff's falling fast. I estimate you have two minutes before I send up the third and pull you out."

BOOM, BOOM, BOOM.

Sounded the new packages as they exploded high in the sky, delivering their cargo, which immediately began to fall and merge, with the first replenishing the cover. Everybody was doing their job and doing it fast. The money was leaving the bank quicker than a line of coke up a supermodel's nose. Eli and Michael ran the distance between the vault and the doors with each bag as it was handed to them. When Dermot threw the last bag to them, he shouted 'that's it' and raised his thumbs. Michael grabbed Doyle the assistant, who Dermot had bound earlier and helped him to his feet before bouncing the ankle-tied man to join the manager in the vault. Eli began his final preparations to leave by scoping the floor area, making sure that they weren't leaving any incriminating evidence.

"The third lot are going up." Again, Errol was in their ears.

BOOM, BOOM, BOOM.

"That's the lot lads, get into the van now."

Errol gave the order strongly, knowing they were going to need as much cover as possible to make their getaway.

"You heard the man," shouted Eli, repeating Errol's order through his headset. "Move. Now!"

BOOM, BOOM, BOOM.

The final airborne blasts rocked the building, shattering several windows and causing Michael and Dermot to take cover for a moment.

"Fuck me," cried Michael, his words muffled from behind his mask, "I think you overdid it a bit with the size of those last charges."

"I did it on purpose," shouted Dermot, "just in case any of the public out there started to get brave."

"Come on, let's get the fuck out of here." Michael, returning to his feet, grabbed hold of the vault door. "Throw in the replica."

"There's no need, I never had to show it, they didn't give me any trouble. As far as those two are concerned we were unarmed."

Dermot tapped his belly, indicating that the replica weapon was still safely tucked away inside the jacket of his Santa Claus suit. Michael nodded and slammed the door shut. As they raced across the bank towards the doors, Eli was at the entrance, beckoning the pair with his arm. Dermot jumped into the back of the van as Eli and Michael tried to close the large doors but they were unable to do so because of the mounds of flour that had formed as it drifted inside.

"Leave it," he shouted, "it doesn't matter."

Michael followed Dermot into the back as big Danny threw several cans of CS gas around the street. Eli tried to join Sean in the front but was quickly pushed back.

"Get back out and wipe the windows," he shouted. "The fucking wipers won't move under the weight of the flour."

Eli jumped back out of the van and furiously attacked the screen, removing the heavy Chapatti flour which covered it. Errol's voice came over the radio again.

"Come on lads, you need to get moving, this stuff is starting to thin out up here."

He'd moved from the office after the final blast and was now on the roof, ready to guide them safely out of the city. Eli, after clearing the obstruction, jumped back in the passenger seat next to Sean.

"For fuck's sake, Fatty, don't turn on the washers," he shouted, "or we'll end up with a giant fucking naan bread all over the screen!"

Sean, smiling under his mask, put the van in gear and set off slowly, returning the way he had come, now driving the wrong way down Donegal Square West.

We're moving now," radioed Eli. "How do we look?"

"I can just see you," answered Errol from the roof-top, looking down through the rapidly clearing flour onto the street below. "The green Transit is coming up on your left, there's just enough room between it and the traffic island for you to squeeze through."

"Did you get that," asked Eli looking at Sean.

"I heard. How are we for room at your side?" he asked, concentrating on the gap at his.

"You're good here. Keep going as you are."

"That's it, lads, keep coming, you're nearly through," encouraged Errol. "Carry on then down Bedford Street, past the red Transit."

Sean did as Errol, instructed and as they passed what remained of the van Eli had driven, their vision improved to around fifteen yards.

"Carry on slowly at that speed whilst I see if there's anything for us to worry about."

Errol from his high vantage point over the buildings and streets around him, searched with his binoculars for any sign of trouble. Standing at the corner of the roof he looked to his right first.

"Right, listen in. May Street is blocked all the way up to Donegal Square and the bank so there's nothing going to bother us from there. In the other direction we've got two police cars approaching from the Fall's Road end, coming the wrong way down Howard Street. They're going to run into the same problem so they won't bother us either." He turned lastly to look in the direction that the group were travelling. "Bingo," he said, spotting some oncoming problems on the horizon. "About a mile in front of you, approaching along the Dublin Road, we have three more police vehicles converging fast." Errol quickly consulted his street map to choose a suitable diversion to get the van out of sight. "Take your second right on to Franklin Street and then your first left down McClintock Street." Errol watched as Sean made the turns, disappearing from his sight and hopefully the oncoming police. "Follow the road around to the right on to Clarence Way and park up fifty yards short of the junction." No sooner had they come to that point than the three police cars with sirens screaming sped past in front of them heading towards the bank. Errol checked that the road was now clear before giving the lads the go-ahead to proceed on their original course. They continued to the junction and turned right, bringing them back onto Bedford Street and on to the Dublin Road. "Keep your speed under the limit, big man." Errol kept talking calmly to Sean, hopefully keeping him the same way. "When you pass the university I'm going to lose line of sight so you'll be on your own, so don't do anything stupid like getting a pull. Join the West Link Road at the first junction and make your way home."

It was obvious that the police would trace the vans' movements after the robbery from the CCTV pictures that were taken before the first mortars were fired. The plan was to leave the centre by any clear route in the opposite direction of the farm. Then once they were out in the country and away from any cameras to skirt the city back to their hideout. After five minutes travelling east along the West Link Road, virtually all the flour had blown from the vehicle, leaving a thin fog behind them. Once on the back roads, Sean just followed his nose whilst Eli listened to the van radio, which was tuned into the local station hoping for any early information. Errol was also still keeping them informed of the scenes outside the bank via their headsets.

"We're about to leave the West Link Road and will probably be out of range soon," radioed Eli. "What's the situation back there?"

"It's not what you would expect," informed Errol. "The police have stopped at the perimeter of the fallen white flour and are evacuating the people. They're not going anywhere near the bank. They seem more concerned in cordoning off the area and the people within it."

"Ok, see you ba." The radio went dead, they were out of range. Eli would have to wait for the rest of his update until later.

Back at the farm the Mercedes and the money inside it were quickly buried in the pre-dug hole inside the barn. The bails of hay stored there were then moved across and re-stacked on top of the freshly turned earth, before they all stripped off in the yard, and their boots and clothing were collected to be destroyed. Everybody gave themselves a quick hose-down in the cold December sun to get rid of any signs of flour and afterwards Sean gave the JCB the same treatment, the difference being that the machine's parts didn't shrink in the cold winter air and water! Within an hour the Irish lads were leaving the farm in their vehicle and digger to go to work as though it was any other day. Eli, Ringer and Oneway carried on cleaning the farmyard and the road outside of any signs of fallen flour, but the thin cover of frost and snow helped with that job. A few hours later Errol turned up. He'd slipped out of the building and away from the area of the bank just in time. He brought back a report that the use of the flour had continued to serve their purpose long after the robbery had been committed. Their little ruse with the Anthrax had indeed worked its magic because that is exactly what the authorities mistook it for, an Anthrax attack. The whole area was evacuated until police forensics wearing protective clothing tested samples and declared it safe. In fact it was several hours before they realised that the bank had been robbed and that the suspicious substance and car bombs were just an elaborate cover for the crime. Several hours in which a second snow fall had occurred, making any traces of the flour impossible to follow.

Not counting the forty-five minutes Dermot was inside the bank, the rest of them were there for less than five. The robbery had gone like a well-planned military operation, which of course was exactly what it was. For

Eli, it was an accumulation of over four years of waiting, information gathering and planning. Bringing in the Irish lads as partners was a brilliant move and one he had planned a long time ago back in the Heathrow warehouse. Apart from a few cases of breathing problems and sore eyes, the early evening news reports on the television and radio didn't mention any serious injuries to any of the public. The manager and his assistant were eventually found and released, as were his wife and her parents, who contrary to what Michael had told her husband, were never moved from their home. As Eli would say, the plan had more front than Woolworths and more bluffs than Frank Muir. All it needed was eight men with balls and a couple of tons of Chapatti flour. The man who was going to wake up with the most on his mind was the manager. Not only would he be grilled all night by the police but when they had finished with him, the IRA would quite possibly want a little word.

Chapter Thirteen

Worst Nightmare

The bus drew along side the stop where Kitty and her friend Debbie got off on their way home from school. It was nearly four o'clock and the two girls' spirits were high, having just broken up for the Christmas holidays. As they idled their way along the lane towards their houses, they talked of the things they were going to watch on the television and the presents they hoped to receive.

"Are you coming to my house later to do your home-work, or should I come to yours?" asked Kitty.

"There's no rush," answered Debbie," why don't we do it after Christmas and the New Year is over?

They didn't give us much to do. They never do over Christmas"

"I can't. Auntie Pat makes me do it straight away. She'll want to check it before I go to bed tonight."

"Ok, then, you come to mine," decided Debbie, "have your tea first and I'll see you about five o'clock."

As the girls sorted out their timings they arrived at the gate to Debbie's house, which was first on the way. They gave each other a wave before Kitty broke into her usual jog to cover the three hundred yards past the park and on to her house, which was the second and only other house on the lane.

"Kitty!" her Auntie Pat yelled from the kitchen. It was four-thirty and the food was ready. Midweek, when there was just the two of them, Kitty and Pat would eat at the breakfast bar in the kitchen, but at weekends, especially if her dad was home, they ate at the dinning room table. Pat got no answer from her call but there was nothing unusual in that. Kitty would always put her music on in her bedroom when she came in from school and changed out of her uniform. Pat took two sets of cutlery out of the drawer and placed them next to the plates before going to the foot of the stairs to call her again.

"Kitty, your tea's on the table, hurry up."

Again there was no answer, and what's more, she couldn't hear music or any other of the usual after-school noises that came from upstairs. She hadn't seen Kitty come in from school but there was nothing unusual about that either. She often went straight upstairs to get changed without telling her Auntie that she had arrived home. The house was quite big and the first time Pat would see her most nights was when she came down for her tea, usually in her tracksuit. Pat made her way up the stairs and along the landing towards Kitty's room, calling her again along the way. Still there was no answer, and when she opened the door to Kitty's bedroom she found it empty with no signs of Kitty being there, since it was tidied it earlier that day. She thought it strange but put her being late home down to the fact that it had been her last day of school. Returning back downstairs to the kitchen she thought about covering Kitty's food with foil but decided to ring Debbie's mum Susan first. Pat and Sue, as well as Kitty and Debbie, were good friends and would often visit each other's houses for coffee and a good gossip after the girls had left in the morning. Again it wasn't unusual for either girl to get lost in the other's house.

"Sue, it's Pat, is Kitty there?"

"No, Pat."

"They must be doing something after school," Pat replied, thinking that neither of the girls was home. "I wish they'd let us know when they are going to be late."

"Debbie's here, Pat, eating her tea. She got home the same time as usual. Why, is Kitty not back yet?"

"No, I just presumed they had been held up, with them breaking up for the holidays."

"Just a minute Pat, whilst I ask Debbie." Susan shouted through to her daughter, who was sat in the living room with her meal on her lap, watching telly. "Debbie, Pat's on the phone, was Kitty kept behind at school or something?"

"No mum, we came home together. She's coming around here after her tea to do her homework with me."

"Pat, she-"

"I heard," she interrupted. "Let me check the whole house again, I'll ring you back."

Pat, still not too worried, returned to Kitty's bedroom and then moved on to all the rooms upstairs, but there was no sign of her. Coming back down the stairs she checked the coat rack for her school bag and coat but they weren't there either, she had obviously not returned to the house.

'She must be outside,' Pat thought to herself, 'She must have her headphones on listening to her music, it was the only answer. Where else could she get to between Debbie's house and theirs?' Going through to the kitchen she opened the back door to the garden, which revealed nothing at first sight. She searched the garden shed and then began to rummage amongst the bushes and trees as though searching for a mising pet. Realising how silly her rummaging was, she walked down the side of the house, calling Kitty's name. Her calls were starting to show signs of strain and worry, the whole situation was totally out of character for her niece and now things were, unusual. She was now at the front of the house, walking down the garden path towards the lane, where she turned to look back at the house. Both doors and most of the windows were open, it was obvious that Kitty wasn't inside, nor anywhere close. From her position she could hear Susan coming along the lane from her house, also calling for Kitty. They met halfway, level with the park, and without saying anything to each other, ran into it, still calling. The park was deserted and it was starting to get dark. Pat's stomach suddenly felt empty as the most enormous feeling of woe came over her.

"This isn't good, Pat," said Sue, weighing things up and getting the same feeling. "They both got off the bus together and Debbie watched Kitty set off, running for your house."

Sue felt terrible for suggesting the worst but it had to be said. The fact was that in the few hundred yards between their two dwellings, Kitty had gone missing.

"Something's happened to her Sue, I know it has. What if somebody's taken her?"

Patricia's fingernails were at her teeth as her eyes welled at the horrific thought.

"Don't think that way Pat, she's probably already back at the house. You go back there and check again, I'll go and have another word with Debbie to make sure she's not covering for her because she's out with a boy or something."

Both women ran back out of the park and then in opposite directions down the lane to their houses. Susan wasn't going to have another word with her daughter; she had already checked that she wasn't covering for Kitty. Debbie had confirmed that they got off the bus together and walked as far as her gate, which told Sue that something wasn't right. She was going to ring the Police, she knew Kitty's movements as well as she knew her own daughter's and this was all wrong. She could also see Pat was about to crack and wanted to make sure that an ambulance arrived along with the Police.

"What service please?" asked the operator.

"Emergency, I need the Police and an Ambulance," she replied with a quiver in her voice. "My friend's Niece is missing, and I think she's starting to go in to shock."

"What's her name?"

"My friend's name is Patricia Cummings. Her niece is called Kitty Moon."

"And how old is Kitty?"

"She's twelve; she didn't come home from school."

"And have you checked with her school and her friend's houses?"

"Yes, yes, we've done all that," Sue shouted, cutting short the operator in her frustration, "She got off the bus with my daughter and has gone missing in the few hundred yards between her house and ours. There's no mistake, please hurry, I've got to go back to her aunt. Get them here now."

Sue shouted Pat's address to the operator before slamming the phone down.

"Debbie," she called, looking for her daughter. Debbie, who didn't yet understand what was going on, had been stood behind her mum, listening to her frantic call and was now herself close to tears. Sue grabbed her and bent down to squeeze her tight. "Do not go out of the house, do you understand."

"Yes, mum."

"And if the police or ambulance comes here first, send them to Pat's house, do you understand?"

Young Debbie nodded her head as she began to cry at the scary situation. Her mother gave her a kiss and stroked her cheek while thanking God that her daughter was home safe. She kissed her before running out of the door to make her way back down the lane.

Back at Eli's house Patricia, had returned with the tears now pouring from her eyes and frantically began to search the whole house once again. The more she searched and found nothing, the more her fears grew. Finally, returning to the back garden and coming up empty, she collapsed to the ground, sobbing with her face in the grass and calling Kitty's name. Susan found her there when she arrived and helped her back indoors and onto the settee in the living room.

"No, Sue," said Pat trying to get back to her feet,

"I've got to keep searching. My God," she exclaimed, "I need to ring the police."

Sue put her hands on Pat's shoulders, pushing her back down to the couch.

"I've done that, they're on their way. They'll be here soon and they'll find Kitty straight away, you'll see."

Sue, being a good friend and neighbour, was trying her best to keep herself composed so as to be strong for Pat, but in the pit of her own stomach she feared the worse. It wasn't easy for her either, she had known Kitty all her life, in fact she was present at the birth because Eli was away somewhere with the Army at the time. She had been best friends with Kitty's mother Carol, before she died, so she was as close as anything to being an Auntie herself.

Pat's body was now shaking inside and out. A feeling of guilt was falling upon her as though it was all her fault. She started to sob again as she thought of Kitty's father.

"What about Eli?" she cried through the tears. "If anything bad has happened it will kill him. She's all he's got. He won't be able to take any more loss, and it's all my fault."

"Don't think that way, Pat," Sue comforted. But the whole situation had become too much for Kitty's aunt, who started to convulse, her eyes rolling in her head.

"Mrs. Cummings, it's the Police and the Ambulance Service, can we come in?" The police had arrived and were making themselves known, calling from the front door.

"We're in here, come quick, please, she's not doing well."

The police and the ambulance men rushed in, hearing Sue's calls. The medics entering the room immediately recognised that Pat was going into shock and jumped to her aid.

"Come in to the kitchen, love, out of the way," a police officer said to Sue. "She's in safe hands now. The paramedics will take care of her." Sue followed the two police officers, a woman and a man, into the kitchen. "Do you know the young girl that's missing well enough to give us a description," asked the policewoman.

"Yes, she's my daughter's best friend, and I've known her all her life."

"Well, let's get that done first, then we can get her description out over the radio to our officers on the ground."

Sue gave an accurate description of Kitty, and of the school uniform that she was wearing. She also found them some recent photographs from around the house. She gave them some background on the family and explained how Pat had fitted into things since the death of Kitty's mother and brother. By nine o'clock that evening it was pitch black and Kitty hadn't returned home. The police, having learned more about the family, realised that it was totally out of character for the young girl to disappear, officially escalated the disappearance from a missing persons status to a possible abduction. The people in charge were upgraded also and a detective inspector was soon on the scene and was brought up to speed by the WPC who first arrived.

The Inspector was called Clegg. He was an old-time copper in his fifties, supporting a well-groomed silver moustache that matched the hair on his head and his shimmering blue eyes, both of which, in a tired way, reflected his long service and good conduct. He took pride in his appearance and always wore a shirt and tie, and at this time of the year was seldom seen without his light brown rain coat. In recent years he had seen more than his fair share of children going missing but it wasn't just on his patch, sadly, It was the same all over the country. It wasn't going to change either, not while misguided do-gooders were standing up for the human rights of the paedophiles and rapists, and not that of the women and children whose lives they destroy, and end. He actually yearned for some old time villain to nick, a good old blagger like a safe cracker or a bank robber. Anything other than the car thieves, burglars, drug dealers and sicko's he had to put up with today. He didn't condone any type of crime but given the choice he would turn the clock back in a breath to a time when child abductions were a seldom heard-of crime. A time when neither his hair nor the deep blue of his eyes had faded.

"She obviously never got home for her tea, poor little sod," the Inspector observed, looking at the two untouched plates of spaghetti bolognaise on the breakfast bar. Clegg moved around the kitchen, opening a few of the cupboards and drawers before looking in the fridge. He took one of the several bottles of spring water from the second shelf and opened it to take a drink. "It's a nice home. Clean and tidy, and she's well fed, there's enough grub in the fridge to feed me for a month. I can't see any reasons down here for her to want to run away. Do we know which one is her bedroom?"

"Upstairs, Sir," answered the WPC; "at the back of the house. I'll take you to it."

He followed his officer out of the kitchen and along the corridor to the stairs. Passing the living room where he noticed the aunt was starting to move on the settee, after being heavily sedated earlier by the paramedics.

"The lady on the couch, what's her name?" Clegg asked, following the WPC up the stairs.

"Patricia Cummings, Guv, she lives here and takes care of her niece whilst the father is away. According to the neighbour he was on compassionate leave from the Army after his wife and son were both killed in a car accident, but he returned to his unit earlier this year."

"Poor bastard," commented Clegg, "and now this."

A window shed light on the landing at the top of the stairs. Clegg looked out of it onto the garden at the side and beyond to the park and the other house on the lane.

"Is that where the neighbour lives that gave you the information?"

"Yes, Sir, a Mrs Susan Wright. It was between her house and this that the girl went missing."

"I presumed the park was one of the first places checked."

The inspector pressed his face against the window to get a better view of how far the park extended. His vision was impaired by darkness, the only light being given by the street lamps.

"The two Constables downstairs, Smith and Jones, gave it the once-over Sir. "Are you taking the mick?"

"About what, Sir? I know they definitely checked the park."

"The names of the two constables. When I was young, Smith and Jones were two outlaw cowboys. BBC 1, Monday night, 9 O'clock. I never missed it."

"I don't remember that, Sir."

"And why should you, you were probably in nappies in the Seventies." The WPC smiled. "Anyway, it was a good programme. What else did they get up to, Constables Smith and Jones.

"They also checked the woods that surround the park. They got through most of the undergrowth and were satisfied that the area was clear but they were hampered by the fading light." The Inspector took his nose from the window and carried on along the landing, following the WPC towards Kitty's room and passing two others. He stopped and looked behind him at a third door, which obviously belonged to the front bedroom.

"Whose are these rooms?"

The WPC turned around.

"The one at the other end is the father's. The second is empty, it's a small box room that they use for storage and the third next to the daughter's is the aunt's."

Clegg nodded his head and walked back along the landing towards Eli's room. He opened the door, keeping hold of the handle, and leant inside. The décor was slightly dated but like the rest of the house it was spotless. Clegg looked across at the bedside table, where two photographs, one of a very pretty lady with dark hair and the other of a young boy in his rugby kit, sat angled towards the bed.

"Who turned on this bedroom light?"

"I did, Sir," answered the Constable, "I thought if the girl was hiding somewhere because of troubles with her aunt, she might come back if she thought her father was home."

The Inspector was impressed with her line of thinking, and realised when praising her that he didn't know her name.

"Good thinking Constable….."

He hung on to the word, prompting her to tell him her name.

"It's Potts Sir, Polly Potts."

"Well then, Constable Potts, seeing as how you seem to be on the ball. What does this room tell you?"

WPC Potts had already looked around the room earlier when switching on the lights, but still leaned forward to look over the inspector's shoulder.

"It struck me earlier, Sir, when I saw the photos at the side of the bed that there was nothing going on between the girl's father and her aunt."

Again Potts was on the money, correctly noticing what Clegg had already spotted and coming to the same conclusion.

"It may not mean anything," added Clegg, "but at this stage in the investigation any possible reasons for the girl's disappearance have to be looked into."

Clegg closed the door and followed the WPC back along the landing to Kitty's room. He entered slowly, trying to get a first impression of the place in the house where Kitty probably spent most of her time. WPC Potts stayed at the door, waiting for more questions from the inspector, who sat on the end of Kitty's bed, still studying his surroundings.

"Have you had a look around, Constable, for a diary or anything that might shed light on her disappearance?"

"I've had a look in all the places I would have hidden mine when I was her age, but to be honest with you, Sir, I don't think she's a diary-type person. From what the neighbour told me she's more of the sporty tomboy, not the girlie diary Barbie type. And in my opinion, Guv I don't think she has run off. It was a long shot when I turned her father's bedroom light on because my gut tells me she's been abducted."

Clegg thought about what the WPC had said, again respecting her opinion. He took one last look around the room and headed back for the stairs.

"Unfortunately Potts, I think you're right. What about the father in the Army, do we know anything else about him?"

"He's called Eli Moon, Guv, but apart from that we don't know much else. In the first place we haven't been able to question the aunt yet because of the sedation, and secondly, they seem to be having a bit of trouble accessing his details back at the station."

"Well we need to find him," said Clegg, stopping at the top of the stairs and looking at his watch. "Its nearly ten o'clock now and I'm changing the word possible to a definite abduction." Clegg sighed, as though Kitty's disappearance was a fault on his part. "Come on, let's see if the aunt is well enough to talk yet. Perhaps she can tell us how to get in touch with Mr Moon."

Clegg and the officer Potts went downstairs, with the inspector giving everything from pictures to ornaments the once-over as if they might tell him a little bit more about Kitty, and where she had gone. Entering the living room where Pat was now sat up, still sobbing and groggy, he did the same there. After one or two turns about the room he tapped the paramedic on the shoulder and beckoned him to the doorway for a talk.

"Is she capable of answering a few questions yet?"

"Do it now, Inspector, but make it quick. I'm going to give her another sedative, strong enough to knock her out for the night. She's dangerously close to having a heart attack."

"Good idea," agreed Clegg. "As soon as I've finished, get her up to bed. One of my officers will stay with her tonight. Thank you for your assistance."

Clegg gave the medic a tap on the back and moved towards Kitty's aunt. Bending down on one knee, he took hold of her hand and began to talk to her in a soft voice.

"Pat, love, my name is Detective Inspector Clegg. I'm in charge of the search for your niece Kitty, and I promise you that everything that can be done, is being done. Now we've got everything we need to help us find her from your neighbour but we need to get in touch with Kitty's father, Mr Moon. We seem to be having a bit of trouble getting a fix on him, so we could really do with your help."

Pat raised her head and slowly wiped the tears from her eyes, before pointing at the small table to her right that the phone sat on.

"What, over here in the drawer?" asked Clegg. Pat bowed her head while attempting to lean across, only to be stopped by Clegg. "Stay still, I can get whatever it is."

"There's a card with a number on it," she said quietly and slightly slurred.

The Inspector reached across and opened the drawer, finding only a pen, a pad and a solitary card with one word and one number on it. Being an old soldier himself and good at his job he soon put two and two together.

"Right Pat, one of my officers and the medic are going to take you upstairs where you will be comfortable. We need you to calm down and get some sleep. Can you do that for me?"

Pat didn't say anything or make any movements. Her face crumpled up, showing her pain, as more tears fell from her eyes. Clegg tapped her hand and climbed back to his feet as the WPC and the medic took over and helped her upstairs to her room. The inspector followed them down the hallway but continued out of the front door, whilst pulling his mobile from his pocket. The number on the card was for a landline and the word typed above it simply said, Hereford. Clegg dialled the number, which was answered immediately.

"Headquarters, can I help you, Sir."

The greeting on the phone was typical of any Army

camp and brought back memories to the inspector of his time in the ranks.

"Hello, my name is Detective Inspector Dick Clegg. It's very important, and of the utmost urgency that I get in touch with a Mr Eli Moon. I believe he's one of yours."

"Are you available on this number, Inspector, all the time?"

"Yes, this is my mobile number."

"Good, I will pass on the details of your enquiry and someone will be in touch as soon as possible."

"Thank you."

The short and precise conversation was ended and Clegg replaced the phone in his pocket as a car pulled up outside the house and his Sergeant got out.

"Where have you been, Patterson? I've been here nearly an hour, you must have got the call at the same time as me."

"Yes, Guv, I was already at the nick when the shout came in concerning the missing girl, so I decided to go straight to records and see if we had any persons of interest living in the area."

"Paedophiles, you mean?" guessed the Inspector, with a sickened look on his face.

"Yes, Sir. The computer coughed up three names, I'm having them picked up right now so they will be down the nick later for you to question."

"Ok, well done."

"I didn't have much luck with the father though, Guv," continued Patterson. "The computer didn't want to know when I keyed in his details."

The Inspector put his hand into his pocket, pulled out the card he had retrieved from the drawer under the telephone and passed it to the Sergeant. Patterson first looked at the blank side and then turned it over and read what was written.

"It's not much of a business card. Hereford. What does it mean, Sir?"

"It's not a business card, Sergeant. And it means, if my suspicions are correct, that the young girl we are searching for has a father in the SAS. That's why we can't get any information on him. Anyway, I've rang the number and somebody is going to get in touch with me, so you aren't the only one whose been quick off the mark tonight."

Clegg gave Patterson a look letting him know that he was too old a cat to be done by a kitten. Patterson, who'd been the inspector's sergeant for over two years and knew him well, just shook his head and passed the card back.

"What now, Sir, the description of the girl is out to every car and officer on the beat."

"Firstly, I want you to get at least ten officers with powerful torches down here to search the park next door properly. It was done earlier by a couple of the lads but I want it doing again. Then we'll go back to the station and question those three sick bastards when they are brought in. Before that, though, I want you to go inside and tell the PCs that are on guard and that pretty WPC Potts upstairs not to answer any questions about the father if any press turn up. In fact, get one of those constables out here. I know its cold but I don't want anyone getting down this garden path. We'll speak to the Superintendent back at the nick and tell him that we want to go public with this one as soon as we have spoken to the father. There's no point in mucking about, this girl has definitely been abducted. The quicker we get the public helping us with our enquiries the better, and that can only be done with a statement to the press."

"So we're ruling out any involvement from family or friends, Guv?"

"Well I haven't had time to speak to the neighbour and her daughter yet, who from what WPC Potts tells me, seem to be the only friends they have, but the auntie is definitely out of the equation. I've heard some false statements and seen some crocodile tears in my time but that lady is definitely not putting it on." Sergeant Patterson nodded to the inspector's conclusion, before entering the house just as the medic was leaving. "And put the kettle on," yelled Clegg, as the medic approached him.

"I've given her something to help her sleep, Inspector. She's out cold now and she'll stay that way until the morning. I'll put a memo in for one of our team to call back first thing and monitor how she is."

"Thank you again, I don't think she would have made it through tonight without your help. She might not be the girl's mother but she's certainly going through a mother's pain."

The medic appreciated the inspector's words and left. Patterson came back out of the house, closing the door behind him.

"The WPC's going to stay with her tonight, Sir. I'll organise a relief for her in the morning."

"Good. Did you put the kettle on?"

"No. Do you want me to?"

"I shouted you."

"Sorry, Sir, I didn't hear."

"Never mind. We'd better get back to the nick anyway. We can have one there while we await the arrival of the three undesirables."

Clegg and Patterson left the garden as one of the constables took up position at the gate. It was that time at the beginning of any missing persons/abduction that the inspector felt his most worthless. What needed to be done was being done, both on the ground and back at the station. He wanted to quieten the house down now, so that on the off-chance that Kitty had simply been doing something she shouldn't and thought she was in trouble that she might find it a lot easier to come home with just one Bobby on the gate.

Arriving back at the station, Clegg was in the process of climbing out of the vehicle when his phone began to ring.

"Hello, D.I. Clegg speaking."

"Inspector, this is Lieutenant Colonel Mike Roberts. I understand that you've made an enquiry after one of my men, Sergeant Major Moon?"

"Yes, Sir, it's not good news I'm afraid. His daughter has gone missing, and it's looking more and more likely that she has been abducted."

"My God, I don't think Moon will be able to handle this. Are you up to speed with the history of his family?"

"Concerning his wife and son, yes, Sir. But right now at this early stage, time is of the essence. We need to make a press release but I can't do that until the next of kin has been informed."

"I understand the situation, Inspector. Sgt Major Moon's location at this time is not known to me but all of our men carry pagers for just such an emergency. I will activate his immediately and inform you as soon as I have given him the news."

"Thank you, Sir, I don't envy you that job."

Clegg had forgotten how many times he'd had the daunting task of delivering such heart-wrenching news to the parents of missing children.

"A word of advice, Inspector," offered the Colonel. "When you meet Moon, you may be better listening rather than talking. He's the type of unassuming person that you don't meet every day."

"I gathered from your Hereford location Colonel, that he's more than just your average squaddie."

"Have you ever been a member of Her Majesty's Forces, Inspector?"

"I did my bit, Sir, a long time ago."

"Then you know exactly what he is. Sgt Major Moon is a highly decorated soldier and the most respected member of our Regiment. He's a streetwise man that has fought his way from Aden to the Falklands and every other conflict that has threatened our country. I'm just saying, tread carefully under the circumstances."

"I understand what you're saying, Colonel, but I've got a job to do, and like Mr Moon, I'm also good at that job, so I hope he'll understand when I get on with it. One question does spring to mind though, Colonel."

"What's that Inspector?"

"Is he armed?"

"Always, and there will be several weapons hidden in strategic places around his house. They won't be visible to the eye, but believe me they are there, and they will be loaded so warn your officers."

"Thank you, Colonel. I'll wait for your call."

Clegg replaced the phone in his pocket and followed Patterson into the station. He thought about what the Colonel, had said but he didn't have time to worry about how Eli might react. Finding Kitty was the only thing on his mind, and after the Colonel had spoken to Eli, it would be the only thing on his too.

Chapter Fourteen

A Friend in Need

At the farmhouse, back in Belfast, it was approaching eleven o'clock. Eli and the lads had been sat down for the last hour or so, having a well-earned drink after repeatedly cleaning the farm and the land outside, removing any trace of anything pertaining to the robbery. The television was tuned in to the local news channel and another report was coming in.

"Listen lads," shouted Oneway as he grabbed the remote and increased the volume to hear the presenter.

(Television News reader) "More now on what was first believed to be a terrorist attack in the centre of Belfast today. It has now emerged that the substance first thought to be Anthrax was in fact a type of flour, and the police now realise that it was used as an elaborate cover for a bank robbery after the discovery this afternoon at the Northern Bank of the manager and his assistant locked in the vault. The police have no statement at the moment but are anxious to trace a white Mercedes Sprinter van, seen here caught on camera blocking the doorway to the bank moments before the substance was fired in to the air and the camera's vision was disabled."

The footage of Sean's manoeuvre was shown on the television, accompanied by a cheer from Oneway.

"Look at that, Eli, we've found somebody that drives worse than you," he joked as Sean's vehicle mounting the kerb was broadcast across the country.

"At that point," said Eli, pointing at the screen, "I was surrounded by irate drivers telling me to move my fucking van. All I could think about was Sean, getting stuck under that fucking bus shelter. He's obviously a good judge at squeezing through tight spaces, because when he came down that path I couldn't see any daylight between the bank, the van, and the bus stop."

"He did his job well," said Ringer, "you asked him to get as close to the bank doors as he could and the boy delivered."

"Turn the telly down, Oneway," interrupted Errol. "I can hear somebody's bleeper going off."

All four of them went in search of their pagers, knowing how important the incoming message could be. Eli went to his overcoat, hung on the back of the door.

"It's me, lads," he said, as the noise grew louder when he pulled back the lapel to get to the inside pocket. Bringing up the message, he read it out loud as the others listened. "Ring Charlie Oscar at HQ" (Commanding Officer at Headquarters).

"Fuck me, you don't suppose we've been rumbled already, do you?"

"Nobody knows what we did today, Oneway," answered Eli. "Even if they suspect something they can't prove fuck all, but the easiest way to find out is to ring Sterling Lines." Eli went back to his coat and removed his mobile from his other pocket.

"I hope they don't want us to go to war," commented Errol. "That would be just our luck, shipped out to God knows where with just over a month of service left and twenty six million quid buried out the back."

"If it was anything like that all our bleepers would have gone off," Eli said, before raising his hand, letting the lads know he had been connected.

"Sergeant Major Moon, here responding to my alert."

"Yes Sgt Major, I will put you through."

"Eli. Mike Roberts here, how far are you from my position?"

Eli knew immediately that something was wrong; officers only dropped the formalities of rank and put you on first-name terms when they were going to give you some bad news.

"About four and a half to five hours Sir. I'm just doing a spot of fishing with the lads up north. Why Sir, do you need us back at the lines."

"There's no easy way of saying this but you need to stop what you are doing and get home immediately."

"Home Sir, or HQ."

"Home, Eli, it's your daughter, Kitty. I'm sorry to tell you that she's gone missing."

"Missing? What do you mean, missing?"

Eli could barely put a question together at the initial shock of what he'd been told.

"I don't know the full details but they are taking it seriously. Just get yourself home ASAP. A police inspector called Clegg is in charge and he'll be waiting there for you."

Colonel Roberts didn't want to mention the word abduction, but it was the first thing that sprung into Eli's mind. He dropped his hand and the phone to his side, ending the call. Shell-shocked, he tried to compose himself, for a moment almost forgetting how to speak.

"What is it, who's gone missing?"

Errol's words brought him from his daze, but the signs of his disturbing news were visible in his shaking hands.

"ELI? WHAT IS IT?" shouted Ringer, making everyone jump, but having the effect of getting an answer.

"It's Kitty. Kitty has gone missing. I've got to get back."

There was a silence while Eli turned in several directions but moved nowhere, unsure of what to do next. He put his hand on his stomach, as though feeling the emptiness inside, and at the same time steadied himself by using the table to lean on. His friends had never, ever seen him not in control of his faculties, or any situation.

"Right," interceded Ringer, taking command of the situation, "Oneway, get the Rover and bring it to the door. Errol, pack Eli's bag whilst I pack my own. I'll drive him back to London. If we hurry we'll make the midnight ferry. You and Oneway stay here and watch points; I'll call you tomorrow and bring you up to speed with what's going on."

The plan was agreed, and the three of them jumped into action as a dazed Eli stood motionless. Within minutes he and Ringer were racing to the docks to catch the midnight ferry from Belfast to Liverpool. Ringer knew that words were no good right now but felt he had to say something to reassure his friend that everything would be ok. Eli said nothing in response, so Ringer adopted his usual mode of saying nothing. Eli, oblivious to his surroundings, was in a world of torment. With his head resting sideways on the window, he stared into an empty void with seemingly no help nor hope. At this moment in time there was no light at the end of any tunnel. Just the word paedophile, which he struggled to erase from his mind.

'Kitty was too wise and strong', he thought to himself, 'to fall for the snide approaches of a pervert.' He knew Debbie was the only real friend she had, but he clung to the hope that there may be someone else he didn't know about, maybe even a boyfriend that she had kept secret from him. He would settle for any reason for her disappearance other than the one he struggled to banish from his thoughts, even pregnancy at her young age, so long as she was safe. A feeling of deja vu came over him, remembering the death of his wife and son. After receiving that news whilst serving in Afghanistan it took him two days to get home in the back of a Hercules transport plane. Then he had to stay strong for his daughter, knowing she was the only one to survive the crash. This time he was struggling to grasp anything to keep himself afloat, a reason to live apart from the obvious – 'revenge.' If his worst fears were realised though, and Kitty's life was taken, then they may as well save a bit of time and bury him at her side, because his life would be over. His mind jumped between worry and memories, guilt and remorse, unable to concentrate on one thing, because each was more painful than the other. His head was cold from resting against the window, but lines of sweat occasionally rolled down his face, joining tears on his cheek. It had been a long time since Eli had even spoken to God, let alone asked for any favours, but in the course of the journey he prayed and bargained with everything he had for the safe return of his daughter.

Morning had broken by the time the pair arrived at Eli's home. Inspector Clegg had been there for almost two hours awaiting his arrival after the Colonel had told him that he had been informed and his expected time of arrival.

"Mr Moon, my name is Inspector Clegg." Meeting Eli at the doorway, he held out his hand with the greeting. "I'm in charge of the investigation."

Eli swapped the holdall he was carrying to his left hand and accepted the shake.

"Come into the living room, Inspector, we need to talk in private."

Eli discarded his bag in the hallway and continued on to the lounge, with the Inspector following. He paused for a moment to look at a large framed photograph that hung on the wall showing himself, his wife, and their two children. It had been taken in happier times five years earlier, which now seemed a century ago. When Clegg entered the living room behind him and tried to close the door, he realised that their private conversation concerned three people when Ringer entered behind him.

"What news have you got of my daughter, Inspector?"

"Nothing yet," answered Clegg, with a hopeless tone marring his voice; "I'm hoping to get a bit of a response from the public when Kitty's disappearance is aired on the morning news in about an hour's time, but so far our enquiries haven't yielded anything. It's such a secluded lane that you live on that witnesses are in short supply."

"What about the local child molesters, Inspector, how many of them have you had words with."

The Inspector wouldn't normally go into those details with the parents of a missing child. In fact he would try to steer them away from those thoughts entirely, but he knew when he met Kitty's father that trying to fob him off with the usual 'we'll handle it' line wasn't going to work.

"Come on Inspector, I know what the worse scenarios are. And I've just spent the whole of last night thinking thoughts that no parent should ever have to think, so there's no need to pussy foot around."

Clegg turned from Eli and looked at Ringer behind him, who tilted his head, awaiting an answer.

"We pulled in three locals of interest last night. I questioned them and their houses were searched. With nothing found and nothing to charge them with, there was nothing more we could do and they were released."

"You may have done everything you can do, Inspector, but our hands aren't quite as tied as yours."

"Mr Moon, I know what you and your friends-" Clegg again looked over his shoulder at Ringer- "are capable of. But taking matters in to your own hands, no matter how untied they are, isn't something I can allow."

"We can do it with your co-operation, Inspector Clegg, or without it. All the information contained in your computers can be accessed by us at Hereford, but I would rather not waste time driving down there right now. Now, I think we have much more of a chance of finding my daughter if we are both in the same camp and singing off the same hymn sheet."

The inspector knew that he was probably right. Besides, why should he be bothered about three convicted paedophiles getting a good hiding if he let their names and addresses slip? He also knew Eli wasn't joking about having access to their computers, so he was going to find out anyway. Pulling his notebook from his pocket, he tore out a page containing the relevant information and offered it to Eli. Eli shook his head and looked over the Inspector's shoulder towards Ringer, who stood with his hand outstretched. As Clegg turned and passed him the note he couldn't help noticing the hard, warlike look of Ringer's hands and face, but scarier than that was the look of excitement in his eyes as he studied the names. Ringer left the room without a word being said, leaving Clegg with just one question.

"What will he do to them?"

"He'll torture them, and then ask them some questions about Kitty's disappearance. If they don't tell him anything he'll torture them again and repeat the questions. If they still don't tell him what he wants to know he'll torture them again, and then strangle them before getting rid of the bodies."

Clegg didn't know what to say. He now realised that his statement earlier of knowing what Eli and his men were capable of wasn't entirely true. His worries weren't for the paedophiles though, who were soon to get their comeuppance, they were for his job and his pension. Eli also sensed his fears.

"Don't worry, no one will ever know you gave us those details." Eli put the Inspector's mind at rest. "My sister in-law Pat, how is she?"

"Upstairs, asleep in bed. The paramedics had to sedate her after she went into shock. She blames herself, but obviously there was nothing she could have done to prevent what happened. There's a WPC with her who'll let us know when she wakes up. In the meantime I suspect you could do with a cup of tea, Mr Moon, I know I could."

Eli nodded his head in agreement and led the way through to the kitchen.

"How do you take it?" he asked, searching for some cups.

"NATO," replied Clegg, using the old Army term meaning milk with two sugars, and tipping Eli off to his previous military life.

"So you did a bit yourself, Inspector."

"Nothing on your lines," he admitted; "just three years in the signals."

"Don't sell yourself short Inspector, an Army that can't communicate can't organise itself, and an unorganised Army is easily defeated."

Eli finished making the tea and pushed one towards Clegg, who wondered who the third cup was for. He watched as Eli picked it up and carried it down the hallway and out of the door, giving it to the constable standing guard on the gate. Actions speak louder than words and Clegg learnt a lot about Kitty's father in that action. Even with his mind obviously battered with thoughts of what might be happening to his daughter, he still considered the troops – the policeman stood in the cold. Eli returned and picked up his own cup before going back to the lounge, with the Inspector following.

"When the news of Kitty's disappearance airs this morning my Superintendent will give a statement. If Kitty isn't found we want you to make a plea the day after."

"No," was Eli's immediate answer. "There'll be no appeals, Inspector."

Clegg expected every parent to do anything that may get their child back but Eli's situation was a little different.

"I suppose we could wait until your sister in-law feels up to it, if it's revealing your identity that's the problem."

Eli turned while taking a cigar from his pocket which he didn't light; Kitty and Pat didn't allow him to smoke in the house. He placed it on the mantelpiece next to a picture of his daughter, which stood next to the ones of his wife and son. He took a deep breath, knowing that every decision he made right now could mean life or death for his daughter, but he had to follow his gut.

"Inspector, if I thought that standing in front of a firing squad on national television would get my daughter back I would do it. But it won't. I've seen other parents on television pleading for the safe return of their children and never heard of any of them being set free. All that crap is just some psychologist's pathetic theories that if a kidnapper knows details of the families involved that it will in some way make him feel some empathy and sway them from molesting and murdering their captive. It may be a good tactic when dealing with and negotiating a hostage situation, but all it probably does when dealing with sick bastards that take children is turn the abductor on even more. Paedophiles want to see people beg and cry in front of them, it feeds their need to feel dominant and not inadequate, and that's why they pick on children."

Eli stopped talking for a moment to take a drink of his tea, giving Clegg a chance to question his reasoning.

"Aren't you taking the place of those psychologists when you put your own opinions into practice, Mr Moon?"

The inspector was trying to defend the police's tactics but at the same time he had to agree, he had never seen a child set free after an appeal.

"The difference is Inspector, as I have just stated is that your way doesn't work. My way is of an opinion derived and learnt from living life, not from reading some university textbook. You could describe my job these last few years as being a people watcher. Learning their every movements, mannerisms and daily routines while building a profile of a target. When you've studied your target long enough, and well enough, the slightest change in any of their traits will trigger an alarm bell. That's why it's old fashioned police work that will find my daughter Inspector Clegg, in other words, you and your Bobbie's on the ground. Spread your circle and target known offenders, making sure that your officers investigate any reported strange movements. I'm here now drinking tea because I know there's nothing I can do. As leads and information come in, I can help you, and sometimes go that bit further, as my man Ringer is doing right now. I won't interfere with what you do but when you do find my daughter, hopefully alive, the person that took her is dead. If she is not alive, the person that took her is dead. Either way, the person that took my daughter, is dead. I advise you at that point not to interfere with me or get in 'my' way."

Clegg didn't even offer an argument; it was no more than he would want to do himself if it were his daughter. His children were all grown up, though; it was his grandchildren that he worried about these days.

"Maybe that's the way all paedophiles and rapists should be treated. Perhaps then there wouldn't be so many. A visit from your friend what's-his-name."

"Ringer," answered Eli.

"A visit from your friend Ringer would soon send them all scurrying back under their rocks. The problem is that when we do catch them the judges can only give them light sentences, and even then they claim forty-three's."

"Forty-three's what's that?" asked Eli, ignorant of the term.

"Forty-three's? It's the number of a prison rule. The rule states that any prisoner considering themselves to be under threat of bodily harm from the other inmates because of the nature of their crime can ask to be segregated onto a protection wing."

"So what you're saying is that on this wing they are

under no threat, so prison holds no deterrent for them apart from the loss of their liberty for a few years?"

Eli summed up the situation pretty much as it was.

"Exactly," confirmed the inspector. "They get TVs, videos and three square meals a day, plus a wing full of other sickos to swap stories with and polish their techniques for when they reoffend. Most paedophile rings are raised from within the walls of prisons. Then, when they get released we have to give them a new address and we're not allowed to tell their neighbours that they have a monster in their community."

"It's not right," said Eli, as he looked to the ceiling, where sounds of movement could be heard from upstairs.

"In the old days," continued Clegg, "prison was a daunting place for paedophiles and rapists. They would get hot chocolate thrown in their face each evening and a good hiding given to them as soon as they got out of the hospital wing from the last one. You see, back then, the deterrent was the other prisoners, not the sentence. Now they have nothing to fear inside because when they claim rule forty-three's, they are protected. Prison for them these days is more like Butlins, without the redcoats and the swimming pool."

Eli drank his tea, pondering the inspector's words and the injustice of it all, as more noises came from upstairs.

"I think my sister in-law is awake. I'll go up and re-assure her that everything is going to be ok. She needs to know that none of this is her fault."

"That's a good idea, Mr Moon, it's about time I was getting back to the station anyway. The news is going to go out soon and I want to be near the phones for any information."

"Call me Eli, Inspector; we can't keep calling each other Mr. What's your name?"

"Dick," answered the Inspector.

Eli turned from his position in the room and walked to the door. A slight smirk formed on his face as he turned back to Clegg.

"On second thoughts, maybe we should just stick to Inspector where you're concerned."

He left the room and began to climb the stairs. Clegg, called, stopping him mid-flight. There was something bothering him that had to be voiced.

"Let's hear it."

"I know from your Colonel that you're always armed, and he tells me that you've probably got an endless supply of weapons hidden around the house."

Eli, sighed.

"Colonel Roberts is a nice man, but like all officers he talks too much," he answered.

"All I'm trying to say is when news does come in that someone has been apprehended, don't fly off the handle and put any of my officers in danger."

Eli, hearing some more noises coming from Pat's bedroom, walked back down a few of the stairs to distance himself and get a bit closer to Clegg, keeping their conversation private.

"Inspector, when you do catch the person responsible, there isn't a prison or a safe house in the land where he, she or they will be safe from me. So I won't be flying off any handle. You should also know that when I draw my weapon there won't be anybody getting killed that doesn't deserve to be dead."

Eli turned back around and continued his assent of the stairs. Clegg paused for a moment, watching him disappear, before leaving the house. It was his duty to safeguard the welfare of his officers and although Eli, hadn't relinquished any of his weapons, the subject had at least been broached. Besides, he believed him when he said that he hit what he aimed at.

Eli knocked on Pat's door and entered. The WPC stood up from the chair in the corner and began to fasten the couple of buttons she had loosened on her tunic. It had been a long shift for the young female constable after being first on the scene the previous afternoon, so she'd tried to make herself comfortable in the awkward chair to grab some sleep whilst Pat was sedated.

"Sorry," said Potts, "it's been a long night. You must be Mr Moon."

"Relax," replied Eli, "Why don't you go downstairs and make yourself a drink whilst I have a word with her? If you want a wash to freshen up there are some towels in the cupboard before the bathroom."

"Thank you, Mr Moon, and I'm sorry about your daughter."

"Don't be sorry, Constable. It's not your fault, and neither is it her auntie's. If anyone, if what your D.I says is correct it's the system that is to blame, making it too easy for these sick F..." Eli stopped himself from swearing in front of the young lady. "Well, you know what I mean. But don't worry, I'll get her back."

PC Potts nodded, hoping with all her heart that he would, then left the room as Eli sat down on the bed next to his sister-in-law. He held her hand, waking her from the intermittent sleep she'd had since the sedatives had begun to wear off. Immediately, she began to sob at the sight of him, and his touch on her hand.

"Eli, I'm so sorry."

Eli stroked her head pulling back the hair from her face and squeezing her fingers.

"Shush Patricia, None of what has happened is your fault. You've got nothing to be sorry for. I'm here now and the police are putting out an appeal on the news this morning. Kitty will be back with us in no time, you'll see."

"She didn't come home from school, Eli." Pat was still drowsy, and a lot of what she was trying to say was gibberish and slurred. "Her tea was on the table, and I looked everywhere."

"I know, there's nothing that you could have done so you've got to stop blaming yourself. Now you get some rest and I'll wake you later with something to eat."

Eli placed Pat's hand back under the covers and kissed her on the forehead. He could feel her pain even beyond his own, adding to his sadness, anger and frustration. Still he found the strength to control his feelings, knowing he must stay calm for his daughter. Although it had been the last thing on his mind, it had been nearly two days since he himself had slept, and he was starting to feel the weariness in his body. He walked into his own room and drew the curtains, before lying down on the bed whilst clutching the portrait of his wife and son to his chest. Tears began to roll down his face from his closed eyes. His sorrow was silent as memories rushed through his head, and once again he spoke to God, and asked his wife and son to keep Kitty safe.

Chapter Fifteen

Ringer's Catch

PC Potts, after receiving no answer from her knocks, entered Eli's room. Carefully she walked over to his bed, where she found him fully clothed and sleeping on top of the covers. Removing the picture from his chest she replaced it on the bedside table, remembering its place from the day before. Eli awoke, and for a moment, everything was normal, before the reality of the situation came flooding back.

"Mr Moon?" Eli rolled onto his back and focused on the PC's face. "Detective Inspector Clegg asked me to wake you. He's sending a car to pick you up in about an hour."

Eli sat up and put his feet on the floor before dropping his face in to his hands.

"Open the curtains, would you, please?"

Potts did as he asked, allowing the midday sun to light up the room. Eli shaded and rubbed his eyes before running his fingers through his hair and looking down at his watch through squinted eyes.

"Twelve-fifteen. Is there any news of Kitty?"

"I don't know Sir, the Inspector said to wake you so you could get a shower and have something to eat. There's a car coming in an hour to take you to the station."

"I'll have a cup of tea, forget the food."

"The Ambulancemen have been here this morning to check up on Mrs Cummings. They made her drink a protein shake because she hadn't eaten since yesterday. They left a couple of packs in the fridge, I can make one of those for you if you like."

Eli looked at the Constable, turning his nose up.

"Just tea, please."

"Mr Moon, last night you told me not to be sorry

because you were going to get your daughter back; what good will you be if you're malnourished?"

He looked up at the spunky WPC, appreciating her attempts to rouse him.

"How come you're still here?" he asked, realising that Potts had put in a long shift.

"It's better if Mrs Cummings, in her state, wakes up to a face she knows. I got a bit of sleep last night, so I offered to stay. I hope you don't mind but I took you up on your offer this morning and used your bathroom to freshen up. Now, Mr Moon, what about that breakfast?"

Eli rubbed his chin, feeling the bristles whilst checking his dishevelled clothes.

"I suppose I could do with a wash and change," he admitted; "but don't go over the top with the toast. I'll have two slices, with butter, not marge."

"You get yourself cleaned up, Mr Moon. I'll make you egg on toast and a cup of tea."

He watched as Potts left the room, knowing she meant well.

Forty-five minutes later, a car arrived to take him to the station. He had managed to eat most of the food and felt a lot better on the outside after his shower and shave. He still didn't know the exact reason why the inspector wanted him at the station, but he hoped after their conversation in the early hours that he wasn't going to try and talk him into making an appeal. During the journey his phone rang. Ringer was the caller, wanting to bring him up to speed with his findings.

"I drew a blank on any information relating to Kitty, but I got several other names, one of which was given by all three men as a major organiser in the sick world these fuckers live in."

Eli didn't know whether to be disappointed or not. He hadn't found out anything pertaining to Kitty, but on the other hand it could mean that there was another explanation to her disappearance. One less haunting than his worst nightmare of paedophiles being involved.

"I'm on my way to the police station. Why don't you meet me there and run the names by the inspector."

"No, I'm already on my way to our headquarters. I'll

run the names through the computers myself, it will be quicker. If I get any information about Kitty, then I'll inform the inspector. Until then, or you need me, I'm on a mission."

Ringer ended the call leaving Eli knowing that a lot of overdue justice was going to be dished out around the capital that day. At the station Eli was met at the door near the front desk by Clegg.

"What's going on Inspector? People keep treating me like a mushroom. Nobody is telling me anything, and I don't like being kept in the dark."

"Please, before we talk, I need you to check your weapon."

"Why."

"Please Sergeant Major, check your weapon at the desk. I promise you there is no bad news."

The Inspector called Eli by his Army rank, hoping it would add weight to his request. The desk sergeant listening to the conversation looked at Eli, wondering who he was, and wondering why he was carrying a weapon. Eli put his hand into his pocket and pulled out his Browning 9mm. He pressed a button on the weapon with his thumb, releasing the magazine into his left hand. He pulled back the top sleeve and showed the surprised desk sergeant the empty chamber before placing the weapon and the magazine down on the desk in front of him. Thinking that was it, the desk sergeant picked up the weapon and magazine, only to be handed another four full clips.

"Now what's going on?" asked Eli, growing impatient and anxious for news of his daughter.

"Come with me, there's somebody waiting for us in my office."

Clegg led the way down the corridor to his office where a familiar face sat at his desk.

"Fletcher, what the fuck does Box 500 want? I haven't got time for any of your shit right now."

Eli, immediately presumed that Fletcher was there concerning Colonel De' William's death, or trying to re-cruit him again. Either way, this wasn't the right time.

"I've brought you some information. I'm here to help Sergeant Major, nothing else."

Clegg nodded at Eli, confirming Fletcher's reasons, and as he made his way to his chair, he began to fill him in with the details of what had occurred.

"In the early hours of this morning we interviewed the driver of the bus that dropped your daughter and her friend off after school yesterday. He gave us a description and a partial index number of a car he had seen on the lane at that time. He remembered some of the numbers because he said the man sat inside was acting rather strange."

"Who and where is he?" asked Eli, with the veins already beginning to bulge in his neck.

"Please, stay calm Mr Moon." The inspector's eye's locked with Eli's, his stare almost pleading for some patience that he knew he would be unable to give himself, if the tables were turned. "Please stay calm Eli; and give me time to explain what has happened."

Eli, not unsurprisingly vexed, gave way to Clegg's words. Clegg, seeing the allowance in his demeanour, continued.

"We ran the plate and brought in the owner for

questioning this morning. He has no previous for anything like this, in fact, he doesn't even have a record, not even a parking ticket. After searching his property and finding nothing we were just about to let him go when Mr Fletcher here from MI5 turned up.

Eli turned towards Fletcher, wondering what his angle was.

"Well what do you know about this mug that they don't?"

"He's on our hit list, Sergeant Major, as a person of interest. As are you, for certain discrepancies that we are unable to prove."

Fletcher's sarcasm wasn't appreciated and Eli's look told him so. Fletcher, quickly continued, backtracking by explaining his reasoning.

"What I mean is. He didn't show up on the police records, but when the inspector's men keyed in his details it triggered an alarm at our end. You know how it works when you put a tag on somebody. Computers don't differentiate between the good and the bad. It just spat both your names out because you were both on our list.

I was just as surprised to hear of your connection as you are to see me here now."

Eli, accepted his explanation, but Fletcher wasn't off the hook yet.

"Who is he, and what does he do?"

Eli knew that the Mi5 man had all the answers; he wouldn't be there otherwise. Fletcher stood up and placed his briefcase on the desk. Opening it, he pulled out a picture and placed it on the table.

"This is a surveillance picture taken of the man that the inspector has in custody."

Eli turned as though the cells were right behind him and he was close enough to get his hands around the prisoner's neck.

"His name is Ahmed Khan. He's a drug importer and distributor here in London for a Libyan man, called Barra Hussein."

Fletcher passed a second picture of Hussein climbing into a limousine surrounded by bodyguards outside the Libyan Embassy in London.

"What's the connection, and why abduct Kitty?" Eli

was confused. "And what's your interest? It can't be just drugs, MI5 aren't interested in narcotics."

"There is no connection to you, not that we are aware of. It's all coincidental as far as we can tell, and not personal. By that, I mean that your daughter wasn't targeted. And our interest in Hussein is because besides drugs, he is one of the biggest arms dealers in the world. Anything from land mines to tanks, but he specialises in supplying extremist groups and terrorist organisations. Anything that can't be detected by air-port security, such as C4 plastic explosives and Glock Seven hand guns, which are made from porcelain."

"I know what fucking Glock Sevens are made from, you prick," interrupted Eli, growing impatient with the skirting conversation. "I had eggs for breakfast this morning Fletcher. I don't need any more to suck on."

Fletcher, swallowed the spit in his mouth.

"Of course not, I'm sorry," he apologised, feeling like he was treading on the shells of those eggs.

"Give me the connection Fletcher, or I'll walk back down that corridor and get my fucking Browning."

"Hussein has another side line." Fletcher began to cringe as the next word left his lips.

"Yeah. What?" Eli, wide eyed, waited for an answer. Fletcher, again swallowed the spit in his mouth not wanting to give it.

"Slavery."

"SLAVERY!" Are you taking the fucking piss? You're telling me that my daughter has been abducted by a fucking slave trader?"

Fletcher, still cringing, gave a confirming nod. Eli, turned to Clegg. The blood pressure in his face was almost glowing around his bulging eyes as the veins in his neck began to throb.

"Get that fucking cunt out of that cell, and in front of me now."

His shout echoed around the halls of the station, causing officers to stop what they were doing and look towards the inspector's office.

"Eli!"

"Don't fucking Eli me Fletcher. I want fucking answers. And that cunt Khan is going to tell me what I want to know. I'll skin that bastard alive. Get me a scalpel, a pair of pliers, and a set of fucking bolt crops."

Fletcher, visualising what each tool and implement would be used for, pleaded with Eli for his attention.

"Please listen, Sergeant Major. We've known about and followed Hussein for over five years, but we've never been able to get to him. You yourself must have been down the same road many times in your career, so you know what we have been up against. Now look back at his picture and you'll see why."

Eli, panting with anger, grabbed the picture and once more cast his eyes upon it. Immediately, he noticed what Fletcher was hinting at – the diplomatic seal and flag on the limousine that Hussein was stood next to. Releasing the picture, he pushed it back towards the MI5 man.

"He's a diplomat, so fucking what?"

"You're hurt and angry, Sergeant Major, and we can all understand that. But you know what it means as well as we do, he's untouchable whilst covered by his immunity."

Eli growled with frustration.

"I'll show you how fucking untouchable he is when I put a round through his fucking nut."

"And what about our diplomats abroad if you did kill him? It would be open season on them."

Annoyingly, it wasn't hard for Eli to see the flaws in his own angry plan. He looked up in acceptance of more information which allowed Fletcher to continue.

"Now, both the inspector and I know that you're not going to consider anyone else's safety but your daughter's, and I for one don't blame you for that but, if you go off half-cocked, and her rescue isn't done correctly, then there's a good chance that you will never see her again, and a lot of our diplomats will be in danger also."

Fletcher continued to press his point, hoping that Eli would see the sense in his reasoning.

"Our problem is that even if we had the advantage of knowing where he was holding her, there still isn't a judge in the land that will grant a search warrant on a diplomatic residence. But before we even get that far, we don't even know if he 'has' actually got her or not.

After all, Khan, in the cell next door could have been on your lane for any number of reasons that are totally innocent."

"So which way do you think we should play it?"

Fletcher gave a slight sigh of relief. At least Eli sounded like he was willing to listen.

"Well, firstly we need to know that that the suspect Khan, actually did take part in the abduction of your daughter. If he admits that, then I think that we can safely assume that she is now in the hands of his boss, Hussein."

"He's right," concurred Clegg. We need his admission so we know that we are not barking up the wrong tree. Speed is everything at the moment Eli, and I know how stupid I sound saying that to you but we haven't got the time to be chasing a red Herrin."

Eli, obviously knew it, and again looked at Fletcher to continue.

"Then, we have to find a way of bringing him out into the open so we can catch him red-handed and discredit him. Once our suspicions are made public, this will embarrass his country, who will drop him like a hot potato and his diplomatic immunity won't be worth a toss."

Eli didn't like it, but he knew Fletcher was right. He began to calm down slightly, for the first time seeing maybe, just maybe, some light at the end of the tunnel. The situation was now changing into a dilemma. The good thing being that it was now falling in to his area of expertise.

"So if Khan admits his involvement, you believe that my daughter is alive and being held in one of Hussein's properties protected by his diplomatic status." Fletcher again nodded. "And how many properties does he have?"

"He has six altogether, four inside the city and two more just on the outskirts in the country."

"And in the five years that you have been watching this Hussein, have you learnt enough about him to predict his next move?"

"He will move the girls in his limousine from the house where they are being held, straight to the airport and on to his private jet. The car and the jet, like his properties, are covered by his diplomatic status and beyond our jurisdiction. In the short distance he and his entourage are out in the open whilst walking from his car to the plane we are still powerless because he disguises them in burka's or Hijab's and passes them off as his wives. We believe at this point that the abductees are drugged but with no visual clarification of their identity we dare not intercede. In this day and age you know what an outrage it would cause if we were to lift one of the burka's and insult one of his wives by getting it wrong."

"Well that just breaks my fucking heart, thinking that some woman in the interest of national security may have to show her 'boat race' to prove her identity."

"It's a shit law, Sergeant Major, but until someone in government has the backbone to change it, the burka is always going to be used as a means of escape."

Fletcher's words added to Eli's frustration but he knew from experience that any difficult situation could be manipulated with the relevant information and a good plan. He turned to the Inspector and Fletcher with a different look on his face.

"I want to know which airport his plane is at. The tail number and the exact location it is parked on the hard standing."

"The airport is Heathrow," answered Fletcher. "I'll find out the rest and let you know."

"So this mug Khan you have in the cells. What's his position in Hussein's set up?"

"He takes delivery of all the drugs and arms that Hussein ships into this country. If there's anything to be shipped outwards, he also takes care of that, but this is the first time that we have ever known him to abduct a young girl for him. Hussein has another team for that."

"Well it will be his last fucking time, I promise you that."

"Remember, Sergeant Major, we still don't know if he has anything to do with your daughter's disappearance. And we need to know what he knows about Hussein, so don't go losing your rag because he's no good to any-one dead."

After Fletchers words, Eli took a little walk around the room, deep in thought.

"What has he told you so far?" he asked, looking at the inspector.

"Nothing," answered Clegg. "He waived his right to a solicitor and since then has just replied no comment."

Again Eli paused for a second to gather his thoughts. He knew what needed to be done to make Khan talk, but the question was how far would Fletcher and the inspector go with his form of interrogation. Kitty's life was on the line and there was nothing he wouldn't do to get the answers he needed, but he needed those answers quickly. He didn't have the time to play Khan's no comment games.

"What do you and Box 500 want from this, Fletcher? You're being a bit free with the information about Hussein not to have something up your sleeve."

"We only want to work with you on this, Sergeant Major. We both have our own agendas here. You want your daughter back and we want Hussein. This has dropped into our laps purely by mistake and as I said, was only brought to our attention when the inspector's men accessed Khan's details."

Eli looked at Clegg, who once again confirmed what Fletcher was saying.

"I know how you feel about working with MI5," Fletcher continued, "but we need to join forces and pool our resources to come up with a plan. As I said, we need to discredit him in the eyes of his government, which will force them to disown him. Once he has lost his diplomatic immunity he won't have a friend in the world. You will get Kitty back and we will throw the book at him and put him away for a very long time which will mean that his arms dealing days will be over."

Eli again took time to think about what Fletcher had said before making a decision. He had made his feelings about working with MI5 quite plain on their previous meetings but this was different. He couldn't afford to alienate them this time. He needed all the help he could get.

"What about you, Inspector?" Eli, looked back at Clegg. "Are you going to run with us on this, or are you going to stand behind me quoting the prisoner's rights every time I get a little rough."

"I'm getting a bit too old to run, Eli, but I think I can manage a steady jog," he answered. "Besides, I can't get into any trouble if you mistreat the prisoner. I ceased to be in charge the minute MI5 got involved, so my arse is covered."

Eli managed a little smile. He was beginning to like Clegg, but he still had his reservations about Fletcher.

"Ok," he agreed, "but we do it my way, with no arguments."

Fletcher and the inspector both nodded in agreement.

"Right," said Fletcher, getting the ball rolling, "let's get Khan into an interview room and see what he has to say."

"No," replied Eli. "The Inspector has already tried that and got nothing. I told you, we do this my way. Get him into a vehicle, we're going for a ride."

"Where to?" asked Clegg.

"Hereford. Now you get him prepared for the journey. I want him released on bail with no charges. Then

I want him in the back of a car ready for the trip. Now I'm going to make a phone call, can you handle Khan?"

Clegg nodded.

"Good."

Eli left the office and walked down the corridor to retrieve his weapon before going outside to make the call.

"Ringer, what's your location?"

"I'm on my way back from HQ. I've got some addresses to go with those names the first three gave me."

"Forget them for now and turn around. Meet me at the airstrip and bring a big chute. We've got a man here that doesn't want to talk. I think a game of catch will make him a bit more cooperative."

"What's gone on, is there any news of Kitty?"

"There's been a breakthrough but I'll explain later. By the way, what did you do with the three mugs whose names the Inspector gave you?"

"They're in the back, they won't be bothering any more kids."

Eli knew that Ringer didn't mean that he had warned them off.

"Well get rid of them on the way and call ahead to arrange the plane."

As Eli talked, a vehicle pulled up to his left. Clegg and Fletcher were in the back, either side of Khan, and a constable was driving. "I've got to go, Ringer, I won't be able to talk for the next few hours because I will have company in the vehicle. The Inspector, and a member of Box 500. You ring Errol, fill him in with what's gone on, and find out if there have been any problems at that end. You can bring me up to speed when I see you in a few hours."

Returning his phone to his pocket, Eli walked to the car and opened the driver's side door.

"Get in the other seat, Constable. I'll drive. I'm going to need something to occupy my mind rather than the thoughts of ripping that fucker's head off."

The officer did as he was told and as Eli climbed behind the wheel he looked back and came face to face with the man who had abducted his daughter.

"I'm the father of the young girl you snatched yesterday. We're going on a long drive now and at the end of it I want you to tell me everything you know. If you don't, you will die. If you do, you'll live and go to jail. Until then I don't want to hear you breathe."

"I've changed my mind," said Khan, breaking his silence, now realising that this wasn't normal police procedure. "I want to see a solicitor."

"No. No. No," Eli, tutted with a shake of his head. "You child-abducting perverted cunt. It's too late for that now. As far as anyone in that police station is concerned you were released on bail ten minutes ago. Where we are going now there are no solicitors, no rules, and for you, no help. You're in my world now, you fucking depraved fucker. Whether or not you come out of it depends on the information that you give me to secure the return of my daughter."

Eli, whilst fitting his seat belt, maintained his glare at Khan through the rear view mirror, waiting to see if he did have anything to say.

"No comment," said Khan defiantly, returning to his original stance, probably thinking that Eli's words were just a police ploy to scare him into talking.

Arriving at the Hereford airstrip, Clegg and Fletcher, wondered what they were doing there. When Eli had said Hereford, they immediately took it that he meant that they were going to the 22nd Regiment Headquarters at Sterling Lines. The sight of a Hercules warming up with its propellers spinning wasn't what they expected at all. And they certainly didn't expect to see Ringer walking off the lowered back, wearing his jump suit.

"Everybody out," ordered Eli. When they were outside the vehicle, Ringer walked straight towards Khan, recognising that he was the prisoner because he was handcuffed to the inspector.

"You'd better undo them, unless you're coming with us."

Clegg, immediately reached into his coat pocket for the key and handed over Khan. Khan, knowing that whatever was about to happen wasn't going to be good, began to struggle and launched his knee towards Ringer's crotch. Ringer was ready for the attack and pushed Khan backwards against the car whilst gripping and twisting the clothing around his neck with his left hand. Pulling him quickly back towards him sent Khan's head into a whiplash movement before it was met by Ringer's hard skull, sending Khan's nose in four different directions. Khan, semi-conscious, was thrown over Ringer's shoulder before the words brutality could leave the inspector's lips. Walking back onto the Hercules, the cargo doors closed behind them and as the plane began to taxi down the runway, Fletcher and Clegg looked at Eli, waiting for the punch line. Eli, who could sense their gaze upon him, didn't offer one.

"Isn't that plane a bit big for this little airfield?" noticed the inspector.

"It is," confirmed Eli. We normally just get picked up here by helicopter and taken to Brize Norton, but there are too many prying eyes there for what we are doing today, so Ringer borrowed a Herc. Don't worry, there's plenty of flat grass at the end of the strip."

"You just borrowed a Hercules." Clegg smiled, thinking it wasn't exactly a cup of sugar.

"Yeh. How else are you going to get one? Do you

know how much those things cost? I dread to think what favour the RAF lads will ask in return."

The Hercules, with a tremendous roar, and taking advantage of the extra land at the end of the airstrip, took to the skies and as its engines faded into the heights, Clegg's phone rang with his Sergeant, Patterson, on the other end.

"Go ahead Patterson. What have you?"

"Sir, you're not going to believe this, but those three suspects we brought in for questioning in the Moon case-"

"The paedophiles."

"Yes Sir, the paedophiles. Well, we've just had a notification from Herefordshire Police that they have been found dead in a roadside ditch. It seems they had a tip-off where to find the bodies."

Clegg didn't have a problem believing it, in fact he had been expecting this phone call since Eli explained what Ringer would do.

"Do we know what the cause of death was on the three men?"

"The report states that the first indications are that they appear to have been badly beaten, tortured and strangled. And it's definitely a revenge attack by somebody who knows about the crimes they had committed."

"Does it state why they suspect that?"

The inspector's questions were to satisfy his curiosity as to the lengths Ringers exacting of revenge would go.

"Because before they were strangled their penises were cut off and stuffed down their throats."

Clegg paused for a moment, picturing in his head the deaths the three paedophiles had met. Even though they deserved what they got, as a police officer it was still hard for him to accept.

"Are you sure they were separated from their parts before they were killed?"

"Herefordshire have sent some pictures through with the report, and judging by the amount of blood I can see around the three victims' groin areas, I would say it took place before death, whilst their hearts were still pumping. It's pretty gruesome stuff, Sir. Whoever did for them did his job well."

"Ok sergeant, you know the routine. Take charge at that end but don't worry too much about following up. Just let Herefordshire deal with it."

"What do you mean, Sir?"

"Just take it from me Patterson, and don't ask questions. I'm not having the lads out chasing their tails searching for something that isn't there. Go through the motions and don't drop any bollocks but wrap it up quick."

Clegg ended the call and returned his gaze to Eli, who had heard most of the conversation.

"He enjoys his work, your man Ringer. I hope that Khan isn't going to end up the same as the other three."

Eli looked back at the inspector.

"Don't worry yourself, Inspector, over the fate of three perverts. We have been dragged into this mess so we might as well do a little bit of cleaning up whilst we are here. As for Ringer, he knows we need Khan for information, he won't kill him yet, but you can't blame him for taking things a bit personal, after all, he is Kitty's godfather."

Clegg, clearly shocked, had to ask the question.

"What on earth made you pick him as a godparent?"

Eli almost managed a smile to go with his answer.

"If anything ever happened to you, and you needed your wife and children protecting, wouldn't you choose him?"

Clegg didn't answer. He just joined Eli with his you've-got-a-point look, as they both turned skywards to look at the plane, which was still climbing in a circular route to reach its required altitude.

"What's the point of all this, Sergeant Major?" asked Fletcher, also looking up. "Khan's not going to talk just because he's threatened with being thrown out of a plane."

"Keep watching gentlemen. Your questions will be answered in a moment. And by the way – nobody is threatening anything."

Inside the plane, the cargo hatch was being lowered as they passed over the airfield now at the acquired height. Ringer, with his eye on the jump lights, walked over to Khan and unstrapped him from his seat. Khan looked at the single parachute hung up on the side of the fuselage. Ringer, with a gritted smile, shook his head, giving the prisoner his first inclination as to what was happening next.

"Have you anything you want to tell me that will help get my goddaughter back?" he asked.

Khan said nothing. He just shook his head adamantly from side to side, still not believing, or maybe simply hoping that this was all part of some elaborate ploy to make him talk. Or maybe he simply didn't know anything that would shed any light.

"Fair enough," accepted Ringer, who, as far as he was concerned, was left with no choice but to continue with his interrogation.

With the rear door now fully open the noise from the air rushing past became deafening. Ringer, taking hold of Khan dragged him to the rear of the plane giving him a wonderful view of the Herefordshire countryside. Khan, obviously forgetting his plea of silence, began to scream and struggle as much as any man would who was about to be ejected at eight thousand feet without a parachute. The green light flashed, giving Ringer the go-ahead to release his package. Preparing for the move, he clasped his left hand around the back of Khan's collar and with his right he took a good tight grip of the back of the belt around his waist.

"Are you sure?" Ringer asked, in a move out of character, giving Khan another chance to rethink his stance. Khan, stupidly, stuck by his guns, sealing his fate. After a short run-up he was thrown out of the back of the plane like a sack of spuds, and as his screams faded into the distance, Ringer casually put on his parachute, lowered his goggles, and ran off the back in pursuit. With his arms tucked by his side he darted towards Khan, who was tumbling in the distance, still screaming as he approached terminal velocity.

"Who's come out of the plane?" asked Fletcher as the two shapes fell towards them.

"The first one will be Khan," informed Eli. "And the second one, well that will be my pal Ringer."

"Do we know if Khan knows how to use a parachute?" asked the inspector, innocently not realizing what was going on.

"It doesn't matter if he does, or he doesn't," answered Eli. "He's not wearing one!"

Fletcher and Clegg both looked back in to the air as Eli started to walk towards the hanger.

"What's he going to do?" asked Fletcher. Eli stopped to answer before joining them in their skyward gaze.

"Hopefully, Ringer, who is wearing an oversize chute to compensate for the weight, will catch him and bring him down safely. You see you were correct, Fletcher. A man isn't going to talk just because we 'threaten' to throw him out of a plane, but I think he will if we actually do it."

Eli continued onto the hanger to set up a table and some chairs ready for the interrogation, while Fletcher and Clegg looked back into the sky, hoping Ringer's hands were a lot better than the English cricket teams had been all that summer. The two men looked at each other, both realising that they couldn't watch and turned to join Eli inside the hanger. A short time later, through the large doors entered Ringer, with his parachute gathered up over his left arm, and the back of Khan's collar in his right hand. Eli pointed at the chair he had placed facing the table and Ringer dumped Khan on it. Eli walked over to Khan, taking a deep breath of the air that surrounded him.

"Is that Eartha Kitt I can smell?"

The experience had caused Khan to soil his trousers, which was exactly the effect it was supposed to have. Eli bent down, bearing the stench, to bring himself and Khan to eye level.

"As I told you earlier, the young girl that you abducted is my daughter. Your little excursion from the aircraft should be enough to make you realise that the only chance you have of living is to help me get her back. If you do not give me immediate, and truthful answers to all my questions, or if you wish to stick to your earlier position of no comment, I will take pleasure in torturing you, driven by the thought of the terrible things that may be happening to my little girl.

Then you will be taken back up in the plane and this time no one will be jumping out after you. There was only one chute in that plane, and that has just been used."

Khan was obviously in no doubt that Eli meant what he said and these weren't just some police scare tactics but he still looked up at Inspector Clegg as if to say, 'is this legal'.

"Don't look at the inspector," said Eli, answering his unasked question. "With all due respect to him and his officers there is fuck all they can do to help you. I told you, you're in my world now, mine and his."

Eli looked at Ringer as Khan followed his gaze. Ringer glared back like a pit bull that had tasted blood, the adrenalin from the jump still pumping around his tightly coiled body.

"You see," Eli resumed, "you're the minor now, and we are the fucking predators."

Eli left his eyes locked with Khan's in a momentary silence before landing a huge disorientating slap on his face. The shock startled Khan, but the ensuing onslaught terrified him as Ringer took a hold of his head and sank his teeth in to the jugular part of his neck while pressing his fingers into his eyes.

"You fucking mug!" screamed Eli. "Where's my daughter? Where did you take her?"

Khan, screamed with fear.

"Alright, alright, I'll tell you everything."

He quickly folded under the well-rehearsed attack that they had used my times before in their interrogations. Ringer released his hold, he hadn't drawn blood. The feel of his teeth was enough to make his point.

"Where did you take her?" repeated Eli.

"I called a man, she was transferred into his car."

"Carry on, what's this other man's name."

"Hussein, but you don't understand he's a-"

"We know all about Hussein, and what he fucking is. Where did he take her, and where is she now?"

"If you know who he is, then you know why I've never been to any of his properties, especially the Embassy."

Eli paused with his questioning, realising again why Hussein had been such a problem for MI5.

"What does he want with my daughter?" Again Eli stopped; the rest of the question was something he could hardly contemplate, let alone let pass his lips. "Is he a paedophile?"

"No," replied Khan, with a shake of his head. "That's not his motive, he uses the children to pay for the weapons he buys in Arab countries. They have to be virgins to fetch a good price. Whilst she is still in this country she will be untouched. But if he gets her on a plane, then..."

Khan didn't finish. And although his answer disgusted and churned Eli's gut, he did find some relief that Kitty, by the sounds of it, was probably unharmed and still alive.

"When he tries to leave, what will be his destination?"

"Usually he will fly to one of three countries: Morocco, Northern Cyprus or back to Libya."

"How long before he goes?"

Khan blinked his eye's trying to regain his sight after the relief from the pressure of Ringers fingers.

"My Eyes," he complained.

"Never mind your fucking eyes you cunt. Answer the question. How long before he leaves the country."

"You never know with Hussein what he will do, where he will go or when. He doesn't trust anyone, and he's well aware that he is under surveillance. He uses his diplomatic status like a big security blanket and he knows he is untouchable behind it."

Khan was confirming about Hussein what Fletcher, had already said. Eli contemplated his options, growing more and more frustrated because he was coming up short of a plan when it really mattered. He walked away from the meeting for a moment, using the large space of the aircraft hanger to have a little walkabout. The tipped heels of his brogue shoes echoed in the vast space as they clicked on the ground with every step. For the second time since he received the news back at the farm in Belfast of his daughter's disappearance, he reached into his pocket and pulled out a cigar, but this time he lit it. As he enjoyed the first few puffs, putting his mind in to thinking mode, Ringer came by his side to supply him with a thought.

"Listen to me," he said with his hand on his friends shoulder. "If we knew where this Hussein fucker was keeping Kitty, it wouldn't matter how many diplomatic seals were hanging on the door. Or how many men we had to kill to get her back, you know that." Eli nodded in agreement. "But if we did go for it, and somehow got the wrong premises, we would be tipping this Hussein cunt off that we were on to him and we would probably end up locked up on political charges, leaving that bastard to leave the country alive, and with our most precious possession." Eli again nodded, listening to what his friend had to say.

"So what's your plan? Because I'm struggling here to come up with something that will save her."

"I haven't got a plan, that's your department. I've got an idea."

Eli looked at Ringer, hoping it was a good one.

"Let's 'ave it then, because as I said, I've got nothing, and I never felt so fucking useless in my life."

"I know, mate," Ringer said, replacing his hand on Eli's shoulder. "Now obviously we haven't got the time to go down the usual routes to find a way to get to Hussein. So my idea is this. With the help of our little flying friend over there, and everything else at our disposal, we have to make one for ourselves."

Eli, intrigued with what he was hearing, turned and looked at Khan, and then back to Ringer.

"What's on your mind?"

"We give him a big enough reason to stick around, and then wing it with a plan as we go. We know he's a smuggler, and what he sells. Let's put in an order large enough to grab his attention and use the time created to locate Kitty."

Eli carried on walking but after a few steps stopped, and stood motionless. A few puffs of smoke rose from his position before he turned back towards Ringer. A smile, probably of relief, formed on his face. The foundations had been laid by his friend, but now a full-blown plan was beginning to come together in his mind. He nodded his head as he walked back towards Khan, now patting Ringer on his shoulder, as he passed.

"Oy, Khan," he shouted while kicking the leg of the

chair that the prisoner was sat on. "You've arranged the shipping of drugs and arms for Hussein sometimes. Yes?"

"Yes," replied Khan; "all the time, that's my job."

"Do you ship the stuff yourself or do you have an agent."

"I use an agent."

"Has Hussein ever met that agent?"

"No, he doesn't meet anybody, he never gets his hands dirty."

"What sort of money would make Hussein stick around? What amounts are involved in his usual deals?"

"If its drugs, maybe one or two million, for weapons five or six for small deliveries, all the way up to a hundred million for armoured vehicles and tanks. He likes to gamble at the casinos, so any good amount will grab his interest."

"Is he a ladies man, does he like prostitutes?"

"No, he's into boys. Not kids, young men in their twenties."

"You mean he's a fucking 'iron." Khan, looked at his captor, confused.

"An iron huff, puff," explained Ringer while passing the captive and giving him a slap on the head.

"Yes," confirmed Khan quickly, fearing that another onslaught was coming. Once again Eli, took a moment for contemplation.

"What's on your mind?" asked Fletcher, wondering where this was leading. Eli, before answering, looked at Ringer, who gave him a nod, confirming his backing for whatever plan he had arrived at. Eli took a puff of his cigar as the cogs turned in his head. He began to explain.

"Khan here is going to ring Hussein and tell him that an IRA splinter group have approached him to supply them with ten million quids worth of arms and ammunitions. Tell him if he asks," Eli continued looking at Khan, "that they can't go to their old suppliers because of the peace agreement that now exists in Northern Ireland. If he asks how you know these Irishmen, you will tell him that they have been buying 'his' cocaine through you for years, and that 'you' can vouch for them. You're going to introduce me as your shipping agent and tell him that I want five kilos of pure for moving the stuff."

"I've told you," answered Khan. "Hussein won't meet anybody."

"He'll meet me, because I won't be the one asking. It will be the Irish lads with the ten million that will ask for the meeting."

"All that will take too long," interrupted Fletcher. "You can't pose as a shipping agent, you'll need wagons and warehousing, not to mention that your plan depends on finding ten million quid. It would take me a month to get the necessary release forms signed for that much money. Hussein won't stick around forever; he will be well on his way and in God knows what country by the time you've put your plan into action."

For the first time in two days, Eli almost smiled.

"Fletcher, calm it with the negative waves. I'm not talking because I like the sound of my own fucking voice. The wagons, the warehousing and the ten million quid are all covered." Eli again looked at Ringer, who was well on board with where his friend was going with his plan. "All we want from you and the inspector is your cooperation. We've got the wagons and the warehousing, but when Hussein wants the weapons moved from whichever country they come from, you will have to make sure they clear customs at both ends without any hiccups because a shipping company is the one thing we don't have."

"That's no problem," confirmed Fletcher, "but there is one other thing you haven't got."

"What's that?" asked Eli.

"An IRA splinter group."

"No, I haven't, but like a Hercules plane, Ringer and I know where we can borrow one." Eli gave Ringer a wink and now did smile at Clegg.

"But you don't understand," shouted Khan from his chair. "Hussein will not meet anyone."

"Yes he will," ensured Eli as he again smoked his cigar with his confidence growing in his quickly thrown together plan. "He will have to, when the Irish won't go through with the deal unless they meet all parties involved so that they can confirm their identities. If they are happy with everything they will promise to place more orders later for both drugs and arms. But just to make sure that

Hussein goes along with their request, they won't ask for the meeting until after the shipment is on its way. That way, if he refuses, the Irish will pull out, and Hussein will be left with a container full of weapons worth £10 million that he will have to pay for himself." Eli again looked at Clegg, Fletcher, Ringer, and even Khan for a reaction to his plan. It was pulled from nowhere and was off the cuff but he had a good feeling about it himself, and he was the one with the most to lose.

"I'll give you all the help I can to make it work," said the inspector, giving it his full backing; "anything to get your daughter back."

"Thank you, Inspector, that's much appreciated."

Eli now turned back to Khan to deliver the final ultimatum.

"Now then, are you going to go along with our little ruse in return for your life and a lighter sentence? Or are you going back up in that plane with my friend here to collect some more frequent flyer miles!"

Khan looked at Ringer and without hesitation gave his tired reply.

"I'll do whatever you ask."

Jetlag was affecting him.

"RIGHT," said Eli. "We need to get the ball rolling but I'm not setting the wheels in motion at our end until we know Khan here can deliver at his. Inspector, get him his mobile phone."

Clegg, did as he was asked, retrieving the prisoner's personal belongings from the constable, who was sat waiting in the car outside. "When you want to get in touch with Hussein, do you ring him direct?"

"Yes," answered Khan.

"Is his number in your phone?"

"Yes."

"And what name is that number under?"

"Libyan. It's under the name Libyan, for obvious reasons."

"Libyan, good. And what does he call you?"

"Nothing. He thinks I am beneath him, so he doesn't have to call me by my name. In fact, he thinks all men are beneath him."

After Khan's words Eli began to gather a picture of his new foe, Hussein. The Inspector came back with the phone and gave it to Eli.

"Key code," he demanded. Seeking to confirm Khan's story.

"1966."

Eli entered the code and typed the name Libyan in to the contacts. The name was there. It seemed that Khan was telling the truth and maybe he could deliver what he had said. Leastways, it was enough for Eli to move things further. It was time to mobilise the lads and bring them up to speed. He rang Belfast.

"Eli, what's happening, is there any news of Kitty?"

Back at the farm, Errol and Oneway had been waiting for his call.

"Plenty, my friend, but right now I need you to send Oneway to get the Irish lads there at the farm with you. I need to speak to you all as one. I'll ring back in four hours."

Errol looked at his watch. He wanted to know more

but knew by the haste in his friend's voice not to ask questions and to do as he was told.

"Ok, its two o'clock now, I'll have them here for six."

The call ended and he was beckoned by Fletcher, who informed him that he and Clegg were leaving the base and setting off back to London. Khan, however, wasn't making the return trip. He wasn't going to be let out of their sight until all this was over and, hopefully for him, Kitty was safely back in her father's arms. The alternative, which Eli dare not contemplate, would mean him being left to Ringer's devices, in a situation that Khan, wouldn't want to contemplate either.

At six o'clock, back at the farm the Irish lads had arrived. They had no idea what had gone on since the robbery. Each of them had spent the last three days with their eyes and ears fixed to the news, listening to what was Ireland's biggest headline since the signing of the Good Friday Agreement. Whilst they waited for Eli's call, hardly a word had been spoken after they were enlightened by Errol of the disturbing news. Michael also decided to tell his mates a little bit more about Eli's life concerning the loss of his wife and son so they could fully understand the even greater impact this would be having on him. They each tried to put themselves in his position, which of course was an impossibility to imagine how he must be feeling. Bang on six the call came through.

"Eli, its Michael speaking. Errol, and Oneway have filled us in with what's gone on. What do you need from us, anything fella, just name it?"

"Put the phone on loud speaker, Michael, so all the lads can hear me." Michael did just that and put the phone on the table.

"Go ahead, Eli, we're listening."

"They've taken my daughter. She's caught up in some fucked up political situation that stops me from barging in, not that I have any idea where they are holding her. I've come up with a plan, but for it to work I'm going to need all of your help and against everything we said about leaving the money from the robbery alone for a year, I need ten million of it."

Eli didn't like asking favours or anything else for himself. He paused, expecting a bit of silence while the Irish lads made up their minds.

"I'll go back to the site for the JCB," shouted Sean with an immediate response.

"Give us a couple of hours and we'll be ready to move by about nine," added Danny.

"Eli, it's Dermot. Don't worry about anything this end, we'll be with you soon, with the money you need."

"Thank you, Dermot."

The lads had questioned nothing. Eli realised it, and would never forget it.

"There ye have it, Eli. We're all behind you. Whatever you need."

"Thanks Michael, thanks all of you."

"Forget it, Fella," interrupted Sean. "We set out six years ago to steal a hundred grand, so if there's any change from this we'll still be up on the deal. Just tell us what you want us to do."

"Ok," Eli agreed in a soft voice of acceptance. "First of all, I need the four of you, and Oneway, to come over on tonight's ferry. Don't worry about customs, the way has been cleared and Oneway will flash his ID card if there are any problems."

"We'll be on that ferry. Don't worry."

"Thanks, but that's not the whole of it," he continued with another request. "When you get to this end I'll be asking you to put your lives on the line again."

"Eli, you're the man with the plan, just count us in, no questions." Michael confirmed the Irish participation but wondered if there wasn't more to Kitty's disappearance. "You don't think that this is in any way a reprisal because of our recent withdrawal from a certain bank."

"No, it's a Libyan diplomat who deals in weapons and drugs, and also, which is the part that concerns Kitty, the slave trade of young girls. There is no connection that I am aware of between me and her disappearance. Kitty was simply in the wrong place at the wrong time, but it's personal now."

"What about me Eli, what's my job."

"Your job, Errol, is to take the van loaded with the money and meet SBS Harry at Dingle beach. He's going to pick you up at the same place he dropped us off and bring you back."

"What time."

"0300 hrs, tomorrow morning."

"I'll be there."

"Good. I will see you all back here lads. I'm sorry about the short notice but time is of the essence."

With that call over it was time for Khan to start proving to Eli, why he shouldn't be separated from any of his vital organs. Given back his phone and under a watchful eye, he called the diplomat Hussein and explained who the Irish were and what they wanted supplying. Khan, with the pretence that he had more than one supplier, offered Hussein the first choice on the deal but said he would have to go elsewhere if he couldn't guarantee delivery by the following Monday. To wet Hussein's whistle and to tempt him even more into the deal, he told him of the ten million in cash the Irish were bringing with them when they arrived in the country on Friday.

Eli wanted Hussein backed into a corner, where if he waited for a deposit, he wouldn't be able to supply the weapons on time and meet the dead-line. To make the deal he would have to order the weapons now, and use his own money or guarantee. It was a trap baited by greed and Hussein willingly walked into the arrangement; the ten million pounds was just too tempting for him to refuse.

The diplomat didn't know at such short notice if he could get his hands on that amount of weaponry, but he knew he could source most of it, so he had offered to top up the delivery with narcotics to compensate after Khan vouched for the Irish lads as old customers of his in the drugs trade. Eli was happy with the way the first call had gone. It was always a good sign when the mark you were trying to trap was coming up with ideas to make the deal work. In Eli's mind the greed-baited trap had snared its quarry. The diplomat would have to accept the meeting with the Irish lads now, otherwise he would be left with an expensive container full of weapons and drugs with no buyer and a bill to be paid.

The next morning Inspector Clegg arrived at Eli's house around nine. One or two reporters were gathered outside, seeking an interview, which of course they weren't going to receive. Kitty's disappearance had been reported regularly on the news and inevitably it had made that morning's papers which is of course what the Police wanted. Clegg pushed past the constable on the gate rather irately on his way to speak to Eli, who was in the kitchen making his sister-in-law some tea and toast. She was feeling a bit better now that she had been brought up to date with what was happening and in Eli's words, there was light at the end of the tunnel. He had told her as much as he thought he could to give her confidence that Kitty would be back with them soon. He only wished he was as confident in his own heart, but at least something was happening, which had raised his spirits slightly.

"Do you know where I have just come from?" asked Clegg, standing over Eli as he spread the butter on the toast.

"Good morning, Inspector. Would you like a cup of tea?" he offered, making no guesses at Clegg's previous location and reminding him of his bad manners.

"Yes, sorry. Good morning, but I've been down the morgue since seven o'clock this morning, looking at the three men your mate Ringer left in a roadside ditch, so you must be able to understand how I'm feeling."

"Men, Inspector? I'd say that was the wrong term for anyone that raped and killed children. Monsters, I'd say, suits them better. Now do you want a cup of Rosy Lee or don't you?"

Clegg, sighed. He was obviously compassionate to Eli's situation but what he had just seen disturbed him, as it would any straight thinking man.

"Eli, I am being serious, your friend has got problems. The way he throws people out of the back of planes, tortures them and feeds them their own genitals before strangling them doesn't show signs of a psychopath, it confirms it."

"Seriously Inspector? Eli gave what can only be described as a 'Give Me Strength' laugh. "You think I'm not taking things seriously?"

Clegg immediately regretted his choice of words as Eli shook his head whilst taking a plate from the cupboard to put the two slices of toast on. He didn't normally allow any ill-speaking about any of his three friends but the inspector wasn't casting abuse, he was just doing his job. Playing by the book wasn't going to work in this instance though. They didn't have the luxury of being able to waste time while police constables went knocking door to door for information, but Eli didn't see that as Ringer's fault, and he wasn't going to have him blamed for doing his job.

"Ringer prefers the garrotte as a method of killing," he defended. "That's where he gets his name from. He's a soldier inspector, not a psychopath. He often has to kill people silently without the use of a weapon, and he is only practicing what he has been taught, and remember, he was following my orders, although the action of shoving their cocks down their throats was all his own doing. But don't take that as a sick act on his part. What he's doing is sending out a message so that the next paedophiles he questions will be in a more talkative mood. As for those three men, they are off the streets and no longer a danger to any child.

They're not free to reoffend only to be caught again and put through the process of being given another light sentence and serving their time protected by that Rule 43 you told me about. What's more, before they died they gave Ringer several more names, one of which they all mentioned. A name that does not appear on your police computers as a person of interest. In fact, you have nothing on him at all. Now, Inspector, do you want a cup of tea?"

"Yes," replied Clegg, wondering how many more bodies were going to turn up. Eli made him a fresh brew before taking the tea and toast he'd already made upstairs to Pat. When he returned, he had some more advice for Clegg, although he thought it a suggestion.

"Why don't you work with Ringer on this, Inspector? I don't mean face to face or anything. I mean work with him by releasing a statement to the press giving details of the three men and the brutal manner in which they were purged, although you might want to use the word slain? Say that you think you have a vigilante on the loose that is targeting sex offenders and paedophiles, after somehow getting hold of their details and home addresses. If nothing else, those particular types of crimes in this area will drop dramatically, because every sick bastard will either go running for the hills or be locking themselves in doors. It could save the lives of a lot of children."

"What about your man Ringer, won't it put him in danger if these people are expecting that they could be next?"

"Don't worry about Ringer, Inspector, I'm quite sure he'll be on his guard but he's in no rush to deal with the others, now we know they had nothing to do with Kitty's disappearance. But he'll be very touched when I tell him you were concerned about his welfare."

Eli gave Clegg a smile.

"Why is he bothering at all, we got the information we needed out of Khan yesterday. Why not just pass on the names to us and let Vice deal with it."

"It's the old Magnus Magnusson syndrome, Inspector."

"Magnus Magnusson, what's he got to do with it?"

"Ringer's started, so he'll finish. He never leaves anything half-done, it's just his way. And I think this bee is well and truly in his bonnet. Don't worry, when the time comes for you to be involved, he'll pass on his information."

Clegg wasn't used to having so little control over a case, but there again he had never worked alongside members of the SAS Regiment and MI5. It was becoming bigger than anything he had ever been involved in before. The talk of diplomats and gun-running weren't normal everyday police work for him and being party to a prisoner being thrown out of a plane defiantly couldn't be found anywhere in the policeman's interrogation handbook.

"Have you moved any further with the plan?" he asked.

Eli, before answering took a drink of his tea. His heart was ripped, his nerves were at their end but still, he was in control of his actions.

"Khan made the call to Hussein late last night, and he seems to have gone for it as though it was any other deal. There again, why shouldn't he? As Ringer said, he's a smuggler and Khan is his go-between, so it should be business as usual. At any rate the ball is now rolling and he's got plenty to think about other than trying to leave the country with my daughter. The rest of my team are on their way as we speak. And with them they have ten million quid, and four Irish friends of mine that are going to pose as the IRA splinter group."

"You've obviously got everything you need at your disposal."

"Not really." Eli gave his answer some thought. "I've been lucky Inspector. Lucky to have friends that have at their disposal everything I need. I don't know what I did to deserve them but it is a very humbling situation when men drop everything and are willing to risk their lives for you and your family."

"Well it seems to be coming together. Let's hope your luck holds out for your daughter's sake. You haven't known me long but you've only to ask if you need anything more from me."

"You humble me as well, Inspector, and I will need you to do your part as the plan unfolds. In the meantime just keep your ear to the ground and let me know anything that Fletcher gets up to behind my back. You won't realise it, but Box 500 aren't to be trusted."

"Why do you refer to MI5 as Box 500? You're always calling them that."

"It's just the number on the pigeon hole back at HQ where any memos meant for them are left. Box 600, is MI6.

"Whilst we're on the subject of Fletcher, he asked me to give you this."

Clegg passed over a note containing the tail number of Hussein's private jet and its position at Heathrow airport.

"Good," said Eli, reading the note. "At least now we can cover his means of escape."

"What about the other thing Fletcher mentioned, the wagons and the warehousing?"

"That's something I'm going to sort out this morning. I'm off to see an old Yardie friend of mine who has exactly what we need. He'll lend it to me no problems; he'll do anything for me, my mate Allan.

Eli made the comment with his tongue firmly in his cheek. Clegg wondered how on earth Eli could have a Yardie as a friend.

"Where's Khan now?"

Clegg was wondering if he was already in a ditch.

"Don't worry, he has a lot more parts to play in the plan so he's alive, for now. Ringer has him somewhere safe but he's not leaving our sight until I have Kitty back home in the same condition."

"And then what will be his fate?"

"If she's unmolested he will be handed over to you with a signed confession. If not, I will be his fate."

The Inspector looked over his cup whilst taking a drink of his tea. He didn't blame Eli for the revenge he was seeking, but there was a fine line between being the avenger and becoming as bad as the people you were reaping it upon.

"Is there anything else you need from me now?"

"Now you've given me Fletcher's note, I have two other favours to ask. When I leave here this morning I won't be coming back until this is all over. I don't know if this Hussein mug watches television but the last thing I need is for the cameras outside getting a glimpse of me and blowing my cover. Get that WPC who was here to move in and stay with Pat. She was good at her job and they get on well."

"Potts," said Clegg remembering her name, "I'll have her back here straight away."

"I also need you to put your armed response team on full alert, they must be ready to move at a moment's notice under the leadership of one of my men, probably Errol, who you will meet later."

"That can be arranged. Anything else?"

"Yes, I also need eyes on his jet, twenty-four hours a day. It has to be done covertly, so put your best surveillance team on it. If any ground crew go near it looking like they are preparing it for flight, I want to know. And if Hussein even approaches Heathrow Airport then the plan is out of the window and he's a dead man. Fuck his diplomatic immunity. They can do what they want with me, so long as my daughter is safe."

"Consider it done. I'll return to the station now and put all that in to motion."

Clegg finished his tea and headed for the door.

"One more thing, Inspector." Clegg stopped and turned. "Thank you again; I know you're taking risks by overstepping your boundaries."

"You're welcome. But don't forget, your friend Fletcher is the fall guy in all this. That's who I'll be blaming anyway. I'm not losing my pension for no one."

"I agree Inspector. I can't think of a more deserving patsy, but you need to learn that Box 500 never let themselves be the fall guys in anything.

"I gather that you have had plenty of dealings with them in the past," surmised Clegg.

"Not as much as they would have liked. They are a different breed, Inspector, and not to be trusted. They don't go through the ranks like we had to do, or learn from the knocks that life dishes out. They go straight from a silver spoon life into the corridors of power and end up making decisions on the running of the country they know nothing about."

"Well once this is over and we have your daughter back safe, I doubt if I'll ever have reason to work with them again."

"That goes for the both of us, Inspector. I wouldn't be working with them now if it hadn't been for Kitty's abduction."

Clegg raised his hand and left.

A short time later that morning, Eli had to take care of another heart-breaking situation – saying his goodbyes to Patricia, his sister in-law. It was going to be hard, but it was necessary. He entered her room and found her laying on top of the bed, eyes wide open and staring into space. He knew that she wasn't coping and was barely hanging on. He knew she needed him to stay by her side but he couldn't, because what they both needed was missing, and he had to go and get her back. Again, in loss he was unable to grieve. As before when he had to be there for Kitty, Pat needed him now. The weight on his mind was unbearable, but his need to save his daughter overcame everything.

Sitting on the bed he held her hand while again, he reassured her that none of what had happened was her fault and that it would all be over soon.

'I will get Kitty back, I swear it,' he whispered in her ear. But it was action not words that was going to solve this problem. And that meant digging deep and getting on with what needed to be done. With heavy heart he kissed her on the forehead and placed her hand by her side. Still she lay motionless as a single tear fell from her eye and the word sorry fell from her lips. When he left, Pat was filled with the overwhelming feeling that they were saying goodbye for the last time. She knew that if he didn't return with Kitty in his arms that he wouldn't return at all.

Chapter Sixteen

My Old China Allan

Evading the few reporters that were outside the front of the house, Eli left via the back door. He climbed over the fence at the end of his garden and made his way across the field that ran alongside the park. When he reached the road he flagged down a taxi and instructed the driver to take him to Notting Hill.

Arriving back outside the Palm Cove Club was a bit of a trip down memory lane for Eli. He was going into his bargaining mode so he took a cigar from his pocket and lit it whilst surveying the street. Behind him, where what had been the building site where the Irish lads had worked now stood a completed multi-storey car park, servicing a large shopping mall. At the far end, as always, was the Rose and Crown and opposite was the Chinese takeaway, where unbeknown to Michael and the lads was the location from where he and his team had set up their OP (observation post) in the upstairs room to keep an eye on them whilst they worked. A drug dealer still stood in the doorway but it wasn't the Rastafarian from years ago. He had obviously moved on, or further up the ladder in the Yardie's empire. As he puffed on his cigar he climbed the steps towards the club doors. It was cold, so leaving his hands in his pockets he kicked the base of the doors with the toe of his Brogue shoe. Then repeated the action moments later when growing impatient. Eventually the small hatch opened and the big bald shiny head of Robbie the giant doorman popped out. Still occupying his original position, he had obviously advanced nowhere in the last four years.

"Do you know who I am?" asked Eli, through his cigar-gripping teeth. Robbie shook his head, having not had the pleasure of his company four years previous. "Well I'm your fairy godmother who keeps the wicked policemen away from your door. Now be a good chap and go tell your guvnor, 'Allan' that his old soldier friend wishes to speak to him."

Robbie, picked up an internal phone that hung on the wall whilst outside Eli looked up at the camera with a big grin.

"Let him in," instructed a voice down the line. Allowed entry, Robbie led him towards the office. Eli surveyed the room as he crossed it, taking note and familiarising himself with the surroundings that hadn't changed much since the last time he was there. Not that he had taken much notice on his previous visit. He was too busy that time watching Michael, and waiting for the ideal moment to make contact. But basically, nothing had changed. The Yardie certainly didn't believe in any re-investment in his premises. The same crappy button-back seating was still in need of some good upholstery cleaner but the dated John Travolta era disco ball had been swapped. Unfortunately, it was for some more up-to-date rope lighting and some even more annoying flashing rave type fixtures.

"Is it the cleaner's year off?" he joked sarcastically. Robbie, sucking his teeth in response, opened the door and then the internal security cage into the stair well. One thing was different there: at the top of the first flight leading to the roof, another security gate had been bolted into place to prevent the arrival of any more unwanted visitors. It was definitely a case of the gate being shut long after the horse had bolted. Robbie pushed open the door to the office and Eli stepped inside where the Yardie had been watching his arrival on the numerous security cameras.

"Soldier boy," he said, giving a derogatory greeting. "If you're here for your money you're early man. Where be Uncle Tom you usually send." The Yardie's description of Errol was meant as an insult to any black man that did the bidding of a white person. Eli knew it was an insult to his comrade and friend but let it pass in light of the more pressing matter he had come to discuss, but it would probably cost the Yardie the next time they met.

"I'm not here for money. In fact, I'm here to save you some, in return for a little favour."

The Yardie lit up a spliff, joining Eli with his cigar.

"You mean you want something and I'm not able to refuse you."

"Well that's about the gist of it, Allan, but I'm willing to forego six months payments for the favour. That's a saving of six hundred grand to you."

"And what's the favour you want from me?"

"I want the use of your warehouse and wagons for the next week."

"And if I refuse."

"You're not stupid, Allan. You've had a good run for the last four years under my protection. There hasn't been a copper or a sniffer dog through those doors. You've had a free hand on this manor and all that's down to me."

Eli puffed on his cigar before adding a little jibe.

"You could use the six hundred grand you save and give the club a bit of a refurbishment."

"I just did it last week."

The Yardie returned a joke of his own, not to be outdone by the cheeky cockney's banter. But he knew

Eli was right, and his services were cheap at a hundred grand a month, especially as his life was thrown in as part of the deal. The dealer at the end of the road in the doorway of the Chinese was making that much on his own, and the Yardie had twenty more peddlers just like him around the town.

"One year," he re-negotiated, "without no payment and the warehouse and wagons are yours."

The Yardie, true to form, tried to haggle a better deal. Eli was having none of it. It was important to him that his Caribbean friend didn't know just how much he really did need his facilities. He could do without his interest on top of everything else that was going on at the moment.

"I might as well buy the place at that price Allan. Three months," he amended, cutting the deal in half.

"Three, you said six. Ye talking stupid man."

"Well you fucking started it, now do we have a deal at six or don't we, and I won't tell my mate Errol that you called him an Uncle Tom. Now we've been down this road before Allan, so just say 'Yeah man' and I'll get out of your face."

The Yardie pulled hard on the oversized roll up whilst taking his time to answer, but he knew he had no choice so he called big Robbie in to the room.

"Yeah, Boss," said the giant answering the summons.

"Take a few men and empty the warehouse of any shit. When it be clean leave the keys in the trucks and in the front doors. Go do it now."

The bouncer moved towards the door.

"Robbie,"

The big man stopped and turned.

"Ye Boss."

"I want that place cleaner than my teeth."

As though pushing home his point he gave the giant one of his gleaming white smiles before looking back at Eli, to seal the deal.

"By four o'clock soldier Boy, the place be yours for one week, but don't come back asking for any more favours. I pay you your money each month because I have too, not because I want to do business with you. Just send back your boy in six months when the next payment is due."

Again the Yardie had a go at Errol, as he also tried to put Eli in his place. Eli had got what he came for, so he allowed the Yardie his soapbox for the moment.

Another part of the plan was now in place and he was getting ever closer to getting his daughter back. As he left the club and Robbie closed the doors behind him, he checked his watch. It was two o'clock. He decided to continue with his trip down memory lane and call at the Rose and Crown. He wasn't particularly in the mood for a drink, or rather he was but he knew it wasn't the right time. The pub, though, was as good a place as any to wait for Ringer to pick him up.

Nothing had changed inside the Rose either, apart from the prices, which he realised when he received less than two quid change from a tenner when ordering a double brandy. By three thirty Ringer was outside the pub, honking his horn with Khan safely secured in the back seat. He climbed in the front while looking between the headrests and giving him a long hard stare. It was just as well he hadn't had a few more drinks because the sight of Khan made him want to separate his eyes from their sockets. They headed off on their way to the Yardie's Heathrow warehouse and it wasn't long before Khan's phone rang, which Ringer had in his pocket. He pulled over to the side of the road and passed it to Eli, viewed the screen and then passed it to Khan, accompanied by the muzzle of his Browning 9mm leaving him in no doubt as to the next move if the call didn't go well. Khan answered the phone, playing his part perfectly. Hussein, initiating the collection, gave him the location and the number of the container of arms. He was going ahead with the deal as though it was like any other, and once again, if you could call it that, luck was on Eli's side. The container was in Belgium, less than a two-day turnaround, which meant if a vehicle set off today the load could be back in England by the night after, which was Friday. If it went in to the weekend the docks wouldn't load, which would mean Kitty, remaining captive until Monday, and that thought obviously didn't sit well in Eli's head. All that was needed now was for Errol, Oneway and the Irish lads to arrive with the ten million.

The next move was to ring Fletcher to pass on the details of the container received from Hussein via Khan. It was up to him to clear the way through customs so it could be picked up and brought back without any problems. That was Ringers job, and when they reached the Heathrow warehouse he immediately began to prepare one of the wagons for the trip.

By six o'clock he was on his way to Hull to catch the evening Rotterdam ferry. He just had time before leaving the warehouse to shake hands with the other lads that had arrived from Ireland. Everything that could be done at the moment had been. Everybody and the money were accounted for and the next move could only be made after Ringer had collected the container and it was safely on its way back to this side of the water. Only then would the trap be set to snare the diplomat.

After four years the Irish men had their separate thoughts at being back in the place that nearly saw their demise. A thousand witty comments and jokes bounced around the inside of Sean's head but he refrained from making them public under the circumstances. Eli gathered everyone around and began to explain what had happened, and what had gone on so far. Khan, bound and vulnerable, sat in the back of the Range Rover as they all simultaneously looked at him whilst Eli explained to them his involvement in Kitty's disappearance.

"Your head must be fucking battered, fella," said Michael seeing the weariness on his face.

"It is, but I'm thinking positive that things are coming together slowly but surely, and now you lads have arrived I won't see it any other way than I'm going to get my daughter back."

All the lads nodded their heads, trying to look just as positive.

"I've booked us all in a hotel down the road. If we stay close together things will be easier to organise. There's nothing we can do now until Ringer has control of the shipment, so you might as well relax and get a good night's sleep."

"What's our next move once Ringer has the container?" asked Dermot.

"We get Khan to ring Hussein, and move the goalposts to put him under pressure. He'll tell him that you've arrived with the ten mill but you're not willing to hand over any of it, or go ahead with the deal, unless you meet everyone involved. That includes him and the shipping agent, namely me. You see, the problem is that Hussein never meets anybody or gets his hands dirty. He always stays behind the security of his diplomatic immunity, leaving all those arrangements to his lackeys, one of which is Khan here."

The group again looked at Khan inside the vehicle, adding to his discomfort.

"So what will change this time, why will he meet us?" asked Danny.

"Two reasons, big man. One, Khan will tell him that because of who you are and what's at stake you need to be sure that the people that you are dealing with are who they say they are and that this could be the first order of many. Two, if he doesn't agree you'll simply pull out. That would mean him being left with a very expensive container of weapons paid for out of his own pocket and he won't want that. So long as we make the call after Ringer has cleared British Customs he's fucked. I'm counting on his greed and love of casinos to sway him into letting his guard down. It's all a matter of timing."

"What's so important about the meeting, Eli?" asked Michael. "What good will it do? He'll be clean as a whistle, prepared and surrounded by his Hench-men. If we try to jump him there and bollocks it up it won't get us any closer to your daughter. In fact, it could make her situation worse."

Eli lit another cigar as the others watched. The next part of his plan wasn't exactly what they expected.

"The meeting is purely to bring us all face to face," he explained. "I will argue about my payment for shipping the container to strengthen the illusion of who I am. We will then get into an argument in front of

Hussein, letting him know that we don't like each other and when I leave you will tell him that you intend to have me checked out. Tell him that you have somebody bent over in the force that will run a check on anyone for a few quid."

"To what end?"

"To the end, that you are going to grass me up, shortly before the exchange back here at the warehouse."

"Grass you up, for what?"

"Don't worry, Sean, I won't take it personal. You won't be telling him what I am, just who I am, i.e., Kitty's father. Hopefully he will put two and two together and realise that he has my daughter but I have his shipment. With so little time before the deal goes down he will hopefully be forced into making a few mistakes, one of which may be to lead us to Kitty. Also, by giving him this info it'll make him trust you more."

"What if he wants to know the name of our tout?" asked Danny. "We can't just make one up. He could have his own informants in the force to check if the person exists."

"Good point," accepted Eli. "You can tell him that your informant is a Chief Inspector called Clegg. He's a good man, and he's in our corner."

"Fuck me, Eli, there's a lot of fucking hopefuls in there, to say they are coming from a man that lives by his seven P's."

"It's the best I've got. If you can think of anything to enhance the plan I'd appreciate the input."

For all his wishing, Michael didn't have anything miraculous up his sleeve, but he was going to do everything he could to help Eli, get his daughter back.

"What's our cover in all this?" he asked. "Who does this diplomat Hussein think we are."

"Well, this is the good part about the plan. They say that when you are telling lies that you should stay as close to the truth as possible, so this should go down a treat." The lads looked wondering what he was getting at. "Hussein," Eli continued, "thinks that you are an IRA splinter group who want the weapons to rekindle the Troubles in the province. He also thinks that you are long-time customers of Khan's on the drugs side, which is how he was able to vouch for your validity. And he's been told that I am one of the regular shipping agents that Khan uses here in London."

"At least our cover story will be easy to remember."

"I hope so Dermot, because we can't afford any slip-ups. If we do get him to attend the meeting he'll be scrutinising everything and looking for anything that doesn't ring true."

"So what's your angle?" asked Danny.

"My argument at the meeting will be that I'm not being paid enough to ship arms that will end up in the hands of the IRA. It's important that we play it out in front of him so that he believes who we are without question."

Danny and Michael knew what had to be done and the scenario they had to portray.

"We just wind the clock back a few years and act like it's the Eighties, when we were deadly enemies."

"That should do it Danny, but you must do to me whatever it takes to make Hussein believe you hate me. Enough for him to feel comfortable enough to hand my daughter over to you."

Danny himself wasn't comfortable with any of it, but he agreed.

"I'll do it, for ye daughter."

"Good man," replied Eli, with a forgiving nod and a wink.

Dermot, broke a silence brought about by sick and perverse thoughts. Unwanted thoughts, of the world Hussein and his associates lived in.

"What's on the cards for the rest of tonight?

"Nothing for you lads, go get yourselves a couple of beers and relax. Visit your old mate Mactazner at the Harp of Erin or grab a Ruby Murray. We'll meet in the morning for breakfast. Oneway, I want you to stay here with Khan, whilst Errol and me go get the weapons we will need."

"I'll do that," said Errol, changing the plan. "You and Oneway go get the weapons. I'll stay with Khan, and interrogate him some more in a few different languages. If he's lying about anything, I'll get him to slip up."

"Fair enough," agreed Eli. "Danny, have you ever fired a machine gun."

"Does Dolly Parton sleep on her back?"

"She probably does," he agreed. "But this is no ordinary machine gun, it's a GPMG (general purpose machine gun)."

"I've fired the American M60."

"Well a Gympie is heavier under fire, much more powerful and repetitious. It takes a lot of strength to keep it under control whilst firing it from the hip, which is why it's going to be your weapon."

"I can handle it."

"I know you fucking can. That's why I'm giving it to you."

Eli, was giving Danny his uplifting talk that he would give to any soldier under his command before going into battle. Danny, smiled, knowing his responsibility.

"Now, Hussein goes everywhere in his Limousine, and you can bet your arse that its armour plated with bulletproof glass, but a few rounds out of a Gympie at close range and it will soon falter. Oneway, will run you through its workings and the stoppage drills, but basically it's a case of cock it, point it and let the fuckers 'ave it."

"I've told you Eli, i can handle that," repeated Danny, looking forward to getting his hands on the weapon.

Eli, gave a look of acceptance, confident with the big man's capabilities.

"What do we get?" asked Sean excitedly.

"You get a nine millimetre, the same as the rest of us. Apart from Ringer, he's the sharp shooter. It will be his shot that sets the ball rolling. None of us will move until he has taken out the man that poses the biggest threat. After that it's up to us and our quick reactions to beat them to the draw."

Eli looked at the lads, who seemed fired up for the challenge. He was touched by the fact that the Irish were there, and once again impressed by their willingness to get stuck in, even when there was nothing in it for them.

"One more thing before we go," Eli continued. "Here's a photograph of my daughter, Kitty, we obviously don't start firing until she is out of the way. We have to find some way of getting Hussein to release her to you. In fact, Sean, I want you to stay in the car and guard her once she's inside."

"Leave it to me. If it looks like you're losing the fight I'll drive her out of there and fuck the lot of ye."

Sean put it crudely, but that would be Eli's wish.

"Don't even wait to see how the fight's going Sean. Just get my daughter to safety as soon as Ringer fires that first shot."

"Like I said, leave it to me."

The conversation was deep. The Irish lads were being careful of what they insinuated but certain questions had to be asked.

"What will make him hand her over to us?"

Eli took another smoke from his cigar. Parts of what had to be done sickened him to the stomach and he already knew that the lads weren't liking it either. He looked back at Danny, knowing it was going to be him that would play the part of a sick bastard.

"You're going to have to make him think that you are interested in her. Use the dislike that Hussein by that time will believe we have for each other as a way of getting him to throw her in as part of the deal."

Danny didn't answer, but he knew what he meant.

For a straight-thinking man it was a difficult line of thought.

"And another thing," added Eli, looking at Michael and pulling a package from his pocket. Here's a couple of CDs marked A and B. If this does go tits up you could well find yourselves charged with the exact crimes that we are trying to portray, and I don't think I will be around to help you. Disc A contains enough information to get you released from any prison so long as you have Disc B as back-up. Keep the second disc in a place where no body will ever find it. Don't tell anyone about it or make copies. If the information on it becomes public then you've lost your bargaining position and they will add blackmail and treason to your charges." The Irish lads looked at each other. It was never easy working with Eli, but he did cover his back and the backs of his men.

"So these discs are our get out of jail free cards for the bank robbery," presumed Michael.

"They still are," answered Eli. "We're not out of the woods with that one yet, but I'll leave it to your discretion when and where you decide to use them as your trump card."

Eli, took another smoke on his cigar with something else on his mind.

"Oh, and there's one more thing that I want to say."

They all looked at him, waiting for his next words.

"Thanks for coming here, for bringing the money and for backing me up without asking any questions."

The lads nodded, they were probably the most unlikely team anyone could have ever put together but a team they were, and together they stood. If you were to cut one of them now they would all bleed, and the wrenching that was tearing Eli's stomach apart was being felt by them all.

Chapter Seventeen

The Meet

Again, just for a few moments, everything was fine, as if he had just woken up on any normal day under the covers of a warm douvet. Then, as every other morning since his nightmare began, the stomach churning realisation that his daughter was missing would blanket upon him.

'Kitty, how was she?' he thought to himself. 'How had she slept? What sort of a father am I for sleeping whilst my daughter is in the hands of kidnappers? Was she scared? Of course she's fucking scared, she's twelve years old, you dickhead, Eli, where's your fucking brains? What if anyone has been harming her? If they have I'll skin them alive and kill every fucking member of their families. This is all my fault. I'm her father and I wasn't doing my job. I wasn't there to protect her after all she has been through. Fucking Army, what was I thinking doing extended service? I should have left when her mother and brother died, not left it to her auntie to pick up the pieces. What sort of a fucking father am I?'

Eli's thoughts were tearing him apart. The urge to get up and go searching Hussein's properties was overwhelming, but he had to be strong and resist the temptation. It won't be long now, he reassured himself. Ringer will be back soon and we can set the ball rolling. Where was Ringer, he thought? Where was he and how was he progressing with the load. He knew he had made the ferry the previous evening and that he would have loaded the first thing that morning. By now hopefully he would either be clearing Dutch customs or already on his way back. Leaning off his pillow towards the bedside cabinet, he flicked the switch on the back of the kettle before throwing back the covers and grabbing his dressing gown. He walked to the bathroom and swilled his face whilst drinking some water from the running tap. Cupping some more of the liquid in his hands, he washed it over his forehead, sweeping his hair until his hands were on the back of his neck and he was staring in to the mirror at his unforgiving reflection.

'Get a grip of yourself Eli,' he whispered to himself, still looking in the mirror. The moisture from his breath misted his reflection, which he partially cleared with a wipe of his hand. 'Kitty's, depending on you, and you need to be at the top of your game.'

Almost giving himself a kick up the backside, he discarded his dressing gown and jumped into the shower. Once refreshed and back at the sink brushing his teeth he thought about what Kitty had said, and he heard her words as though she were stood next to him.

'If you smarten yourself up a bit, Dad, Auntie Pat might fancy you a bit more.' A smile formed around the brush and paste in his mouth. A tear joined the smile but he quickly snapped himself away from returning to those thoughts. He rinsed his mouth and returned to the bedroom to finish making his tea. The shower had brought him round and the brew tasted good. Both of them put him in a more positive mood about the day's outcomes.

'Think positive' he told himself whilst dressing. 'Hussein doesn't intend to kill Kitty, she's worth nothing to him dead or molested. He can't go anywhere anyway without me knowing, we have his plane covered. If he tries to leave I'll kill him at the airport and get Kitty back. Both ways he's a dead man and I'll get my daughter back.'

His phone rang, breaking his positive thoughts. It began to vibrate and move around the bedside table. After tucking the last of his shirt into his trousers he picked it up and answered the call.

"Mr Moon, its DI Clegg."

"It's Eli, Inspector, what news have you?"

"My men watched Hussein's plane last night around the clock and nobody went near it. I also have a twenty-man armed response team at the ready and located at my station."

"Thank you, Inspector. I've no news for you as yet I'm afraid, but I'll keep you informed as the day goes on. Hopefully my man Ringer will arrive back sometime this evening. If he does I'll try to make it go down tonight, if not it'll be a long wait until Monday."

"Ok, I'll wait for your call. Let's hope he makes good time."

At the station the Inspector, himself wasn't doing any slacking. He wasn't in that early in the morning because he was keen to make a good impression. He was there because he hadn't been home. The couch in his office often came in handy for him to grab a few hours rest when he was on a big case, and this case was just about as big as it got. Not just because of Kitty's abduction; unfortunately those type of crimes crossed Clegg's desk far too often. But couple it with the mutilated bodies of three paedophiles, a gun-running Libyan slave trading diplomat, MI5, and the SAS co-ordinating a joint rescue mission and this was a monster case. And now the icing on the cake was that he had an IRA splinter group running around on his patch, and it amounted to a pretty big problem. He also knew that the outcome wasn't going to be a quiet one, not with Eli dishing out the justice. He was cringing with every report that came in to the station.

Eli finished getting dressed and went downstairs to join the others for breakfast. The thought of eating still did nothing for him, but it was where he had arranged to meet the rest of the lads. Everybody was up and ready apart from Errol, who had spent the night at the warehouse, guarding Khan. They sat down and quietly discussed the plans for the day, and as the hour approached ten the call came that they had all been waiting for.

"Ringer, tell me something good, such as you've loaded."

The others around the breakfast table listened to the call and watched Eli's face for his telling expressions.

"Loaded, and on the ferry," came his reply, putting the smile back on Eli's face and telling the lads that they were in business. "I slipped the Dutch load master a few quid to get me to get me through first. I've been on the water for over two hours. By my reckoning I should be back at the warehouse by four."

"Why didn't you ring me earlier?"

"I didn't want to wake you on the off-chance you were getting some sleep."

"Thanks, I did manage to get a little bit last night, but knowing you are on your way back has perked me up. Listen, I need to know the instant you clear customs at this end, so we can make the call to Hussein. Also, I'm going to try and set the meeting for tonight, so let me know immediately if you run in to any hold-ups with the traffic. Other than that, I'll see you about four at the warehouse."

"We're due to dock shortly after mid-day. I'll call you as soon as I've driven out of the ferry port."

"Ok, drive carefully we can't afford no fuck ups."

Eli ended the call and looked at the others around the breakfast table. They were all ready and keen to get on with what needed to be done.

"What now," asked Michael?

"Now we go to the warehouse. As soon as we receive Ringer's call we get Khan to call Hussein and move the goal posts. In between time we clean our weapons and prepare what we can for this evening. After the call we can address what Hussein has said and together discuss our next move."

Silence followed his words because none of them had anything to say. The situation was now a waiting game of the worse kind, where cool heads and strong nerves – and for Eli, internal strength – were the order of the day. At any rate the format had been agreed, and as six barely-touched breakfasts were pushed to one side, the commitment of the group could not have been stronger. Even Sean had only managed a small nibble on a slice of toast, obviously feeling apprehension at the situation. But like the others he was afraid for Kitty's life, not his own. The team moved off to Heathrow with one thought in their heads, to do whatever it would take to get Kitty back and fuck the consequences.

When they reached their destination Eli found a quiet corner of the warehouse to afford himself some privacy so that he might ring home and find out how Pat was doing.

"Hello, the Moon residence. WPC Potts speaking."

"Hello, Constable Potts, this is Mr Moon speaking. How is my sister in-law coping?"

"She was a lot better when she woke this morning, Sir. She actually made me a cup of tea."

"Good. Has she eaten anything?"

"Only some toast Sir, but I'm going to make her a cold lunch soon. She can have it when she wakes."

"Thanks, Miss Potts. Your care and attention's much appreciated."

"It's my pleasure, Sir. Anything that helps you and your family get through this situation. And Sir?"

"Yes?"

"Mrs Cummings told me about what you had said to her, about promising to get Kitty back. It was those words that gave her the strength to get out of bed this morning."

"I hope I don't let her down."

"She doesn't think you will, Sir. She said that you're the type of man that does what he says."

"I hope so, Constable. God knows I hope so."

"It's just that we know who you are, Sir, and what you do. We also know that this investigation is taking a different route to what our inspector would normally take, so he must be behind you. I just wanted to say that we are all behind you as well, Sir, if that's ok?"

"It's fine, Constable, and again, much appreciated."

"Give them hell, Sir. There's plenty of room in that ditch for more of those bastards." Potts' strong words were obviously heartfelt and brought a welcome smile to Eli's face.

"You'll go far, Constable Potts. It's a shame that the people running this country don't think the same way as we do. Anyway, take care of yourself and Pat, and make sure she eats."

"I will, Sir." From an unexpected place Eli had found a great uplifting. His short conversation with the young WPC had replaced his faith and given him the encouragement that so far all the consoling pats on the back from his friends had failed to produce. Perhaps it was because their concerns, all though genuine and heartfelt, were also predictable. Whereas the words from the constable had come out of nowhere.

At one o'clock Ringer called back. He had cleared customs and was pulling out of Hull on the M62. It was time for Khan to make the call. Everything depended on this conversation; if Hussein didn't go for the meeting they were back to square one. The whole team made a circle around Khan, who stood in the middle with the phone to his ear like a bull's eye on a dart board.

"There's a problem," he said, starting the conversation with Hussein.

"Have the Irish arrived with the money?"

"Yes."

"Is there something wrong with the load?"

"No, the container has just cleared customs without a hitch. It will be at my agent's Heathrow warehouse around seven o'clock this evening."

"Then what's the problem."

"The Irish. They won't part with any of the money until they have met all parties involved."

"That's impossible," dismissed Hussein. "You know that."

"I told them that, but you know the Irish," returned Khan. "It's been a few years since they were customers in the weapons trade but you know how paranoid they are, especially of each other."

"It can't be done. We've completed our part of the bargain, they either take delivery or I will find another buyer."

Things weren't going too well. Knowing his life was on the line, Khan needed to put the pressure back on Hussein.

"That's not all we have to worry about. The agent won't meet anybody either. He's more paranoid than the Irish and he knows we are shipping arms, not drugs. He wants the container out of his premises by tonight and he wants double what we normally pay, ten kilo not five."

"The deal's off," shouted Hussein, infuriated. "I'll ring you with an alternative location for the container to be moved to. Tell the agent he'll be paid the agreed five kilo and find someone else for future shipments."

Hussein killed the call dead, leaving Khan in the warehouse in a predicament that would surely mean his end. There was complete silence and Eli's heart could almost be heard hitting the floor.

"That leaves us with no alternative," said Michael, coming to his conclusion after hearing Hussein's refusal. "Split into four two-man teams. Choose the four most likely locations he may be holding your daughter and hit them simultaneously. It will give us close to an eighty percent chance of finding your daughter."

"That's not a good plan," replied Eli. "It's probably the only one left open to us but it will either mean death or life in prison for you lot."

"I wasn't offering, I was telling," Michael sternly reiterated.

"And me," said Danny. "After all, this could be my distant cousin we're going to rescue."

His participation was volunteered with a smile, gratefully received by Eli. Dermot, and Sean followed the lead followed by Errol and Oneway, who volunteered Ringer in his absence, pointing out that he would probably take the two remaining addresses on his own. Eli was knocked out by their unselfish offer and wondered what he had done to deserve such comradeship, especially from the Irish lads who owed him nothing but simply didn't give a fuck.

"Right, Khan," said Eli, turning to the captive. "If you want to live, you better give us your best educated guess as to the four addresses where Hussein may be holding Kitty." Eli had hardly finished talking and Khan had hardly time to swallow his last piece of spit down his dry throat when his phone rang. It was Hussein, obviously ringing with the new location for his container to be taken.

"Answer it and keep up the pretence," said Eli to the nervous and sweating captive, "I don't want him spooked." Khan did so, picking up the conversation where it had been left.

"Ok, give me the new address."

"Forget that, I'll go to the meeting."

In a shock turnaround, Hussein put the light back at the end of Eli's dimly lit tunnel.

"But it will be held on my terms at my room in the diplomatic hotel, next to the embassy in Knightsbridge."

Everyone could hear what he was saying and silently raised their thumbs, rejoicing at Hussein's change of heart.

"There' a metal detector on the front doors of the hotel, and my personal guards will be there to search them as they enter, so tell them to come unarmed, and I want the Irish to bring me half of the money as a deposit. The shipping agent is your man, and your contact. If you can't get him to agree to attend, that is not my problem. The Irish can take it up with you, but I'll have completed my end of the bargain. Those are my terms, and the meeting will be at six this evening. I know it's short notice but I don't want any tricks." The call ended, leaving Khan, along with the others, breathing a sigh of relief.

"We've got him," shouted Eli with a clenched fist, letting his locked-up emotions run free as a small amount of the weight on his shoulders was lifted. For a moment he thought his plans were smashed, but suddenly he had been thrown a lifeline.

"Right, gather round," he instructed with a new found zest; "you as well, Khan, you lucky fucker. You've got a reprieve for now but if you don't continue to play your part convincingly, you'll be the first man nutted."

When Eli used the term nutted, he wasn't referring to a clash of heads. He was talking about two nine millimetre rounds from his Browning entering Khan's head in quick succession.

"I know what I have to do," he answered. "It is damage limitation for me. I understand that."

"Have you got any family, Khan?"

Danny, stepped forward and menacingly towered over the man they all wanted to kill. Khan, stared up at the powerful Irishman but revealed nothing.

"It doesn't matter, you don't have to answer," continued Danny. "But know this. They will grass themselves up when they turn up at your funeral. And then, when you are deep in the ground, they will be systematically tortured and murdered in revenge for what you have done. By their relationship and paying their respects to you they will be signing their own death warrants. But if we get through this and get Kitty back, you will live. It may be in jail, and it may be in a wheelchair, but at least you'll be alive."

Eli looked at big Danny, who was growing in his estimations by the second.

"I won't let you down. I understand the implications," answered Khan.

"I'm not sure you do."

Dermot, now foreseeing a way of guaranteeing Khan's compliance had a little plan of his own to offer.

"Eli, can you get me a piece of C4?"

"What's on your mind, and how much are you talking about?"

"Just a small piece, the size of your little finger but big enough to hold a detonator that I can link to a receiver. I'll hide the transmitter in the heel of your shoe. Don't worry, it won't go off by accident; it will take a good hard stamp to complete the circuit, which will send a signal to the receiver, causing the charge to explode. The detonator is non-ferrous and the rest of the components are plastic and invisible to metal detection, so they should pass through the security of the diplomatic hotel."

"And where are we going to put this charge?" asked Eli, intrigued.

"Around Khan's knackers'," answered Dermot, smiling at the shocked captive. "I figure because he works for them he won't be searched like you. If he decides to try and tip Hussein off, a simple stamp from you will seal his fate and the small blast should disorientate Hussein's guards, giving you a fighting chance."

Michael smiled at Eli, who smiled at Danny, who smiled at Sean, who called Dermot a sneaky little geek whilst giving him a pat on the back.

"Get on with it," said Eli, liking the idea and looking at Khan, who didn't seem to share his enthusiasm. "Oneway, get Dermot the stuff he needs."

Eli, circled his position in a moment's silent thought. So far, he had done everything he could to secure the return of his daughter, but he needed to make sure that to Hussein, everything seemed kosher. For the first time that day he lit a cigar as the planning cogs in his mind began to turn.

"Right, this is how things will go this evening. Danny and Michael will arrive at the meeting at five to six. Sean and Dermot, you will be our back-up. I want you positioned outside at a safe distance from where you can watch the hotel entrance."

The lads nodded"

"You will be armed, and you'll also have our weapons that we don't take inside with us. Once me and Khan arrive, just after six, be prepared to enter should you hear his Crawford's Cream Crackers being blown to smithereens. That will mean that things have gone tits up and I've had to put my foot down."

Eli's description brought a smile.

"Fight your way in, and we will do the same coming out. Hopefully we'll meet somewhere in the middle."

Eli looked at Khan, who looked away. There was no light at the end of any tunnel for him, and no one in the room gave a fuck. "Michael and Danny, you lads use the time you have alone with Hussein before we arrive to sweeten him up with a bit of the old Blarney talk. Once we're inside we'll will go into our disagreement and play it by ear. It's important that Hussein never gets the time to analyse anything and realise that we're in it together."

"Eli, you're the one doing too much analysing."

Michael had to say something about the way the situation was being dissected.

"Calm yourself down," he continued. "You're only worrying because you know all the answers. Hussein has his mind on the money, that's why he's accepted the deal and agreed to the meeting. The reason he's having it in the diplomatic hotel is because he's covered by his immunity and it ensures his safety, not because he suspects anything."

"Michael's right," agreed Danny. "We know what you have to lose and why you're nitpicking, but if you're not composed enough to see this through we'll have to replace you in the meeting with Oneway, who can control his emotions."

The lad's words calmed Eli, bringing him down a

gear to a more controlled pace. Nodding his head in agreement, he took a smoke of his cigar and in his mind re-analysed the situation. For a start, Hussein had unknowingly done him a favour by calling the meeting for six; it left the evening with plenty of time to complete the deal, which would put Kitty within his grasp all the sooner. At his point, Hussein couldn't suspect anything, the deal thus far apart from the meeting was no different than any other that Khan would have set up in the past, and he had covered his arse by holding this meeting within the boundaries of his diplomatic immunity. Steadied and thinking more clearly, he continued with the evening's plan.

"Right lads, I'm sorry about that. You were right to pull me but I promise you I will see my end through. I won't let you, or my daughter down."

"We know that," reassured Michael. "What's next?"

"Well, me you and Danny know the job we have to do inside the hotel."

That end had been covered.

"Right now though, Errol and I are going to the police

station, where he will take charge of the police firearms unit and bring Inspector Clegg up to speed. We will also get Fletcher from MI5 to meet us there."

"Eli, if it's all the same to you, I'd rather us Irish lads didn't meet this Fletcher fella. I don't like the sound of those initials, MI5."

"You're not a bad judge, Michael," agreed Eli. "I'd rather not have anything to do with them myself but without them this time I would never have found out who was holding my daughter. The sad truth though is that we need them, because after the meeting when you make the call to Hussein, grassing me up, it's then that I'm hoping he'll lead us to Kitty. That being the case, we're going to need Fletcher and his MI5 clout to enter diplomatic premises. Don't worry; I'm going to leave him with Errol and the firearms team. The closest we should get to Fletcher tonight is on the end of a radio."

Michael and the lads, with no other choice, had to go along with the plan. Their reluctance was only born out of a lifetime of mistrust for any government agency, but the same could be said for their mistrust and fear of the SAS, and look where they were now.

"Michael," Eli continued. "Whilst I'm gone I want you to separate five million from the money to give to Hussein. I'll be bringing back two holdalls to carry it in, both fitted with transmitters. Hopefully Hussein will take it with him when he leaves the hotel. It'll be a lot safer to track him from a distance than having to do it visually."

"Don't worry," assured Michael. "Me and Danny'll come up with something during the meeting to try and make sure he does, but I think we'll be making a mistake if we give him half the money. For a start it shows weakness on our part if we give him what he asks for, and five million wouldn't even fit in six holdalls. Plus the more bags we arrive with, the less likely he is to take them with him, whereas if we take two million in two bags, they're easier to carry and he probably won't let them out of his sight."

Eli smiled.

"I said in that warehouse four years ago that you were a tricky bastard, young Flynn. And I was right."

Michael accepted Eli's praise with a tilt of his head.

"You're bang right. Two million it is then. Oneway, Khan is now your problem. I want him cleaned up and dressed smart for the meeting. Take him back to the hotel and make him have a shower and a shave, take big Danny with you so he doesn't try anything, and pick up the stuff Dermot needs whilst you're out. Dermot, you get your little device made up and we'll all meet back here at four and wait for Ringer."

"What should I do?" asked Sean.

"Sean, I want you to rearrange the warehouse. Basically, we need a kill zone. Move all the trucks down to the bottom end so we have a large open space where we are stood now. When Ringer arrives, I want him to park the trailer lengthways, effectively cutting the warehouse in half. Make sure there's a large enough gap between the rear of the truck and the wall so the doors can be opened. This gap will also give Ringer a clear line of sight to Hussein and his men. Pile pallets on this side along with the forklift, so we can use them as cover, and when you arrive for the meeting tonight, make sure that you park your vehicle by the side of them. When Hussein arrives in his limousine, that will only leave him the area by the wall and the rear of the truck for him to occupy, and only his limousine to take cover behind. As I said, his vehicle will be armoured but if he takes cover behind it we can ricochet our shot of the wall to get to the bastard. If he manages to get inside his limousine, he won't be able to shoot at us, but he'll think he's safe. That is, until Big Danny steps out with the GPMG."

Sean acknowledged what he had to do and set about his task.

"I'll also bring some radios back with me for tonight. We'll use our own names instead of call signs. Once Hussein is on the move there'll be a lot of chat, it'll avoid confusion."

Eli and Errol moved towards their vehicle but were stopped by Dermot.

"Eli," he called.

Eli turned to see Dermot pointing at his feet. Not understanding, he spread his hands out, palms turned upwards.

"Give me a dolly blue Dermot. What you after, my son?"

"I need one of your shoes, unless you have another pair back at the hotel that Oneway can pick up."

"I have, but they don't match these trousers," he replied in a sarcastic tone, whilst sliding the right one from his foot. "It's a good job there's no holes in my socks," he added, throwing the footwear to Dermot and lightening the mood for a moment.

At the station, Eli was first to hop through the front doors, where he, and Errol were greeted by Clegg.

"Don't ask."

Eli stopped, what he thought would be the inspector's obvious question. Clegg, not noticing anything unusual, put aside his puzzled look and introduced Errol to the firearms team he would be taking charge of. Leaving them to get acquainted, Eli followed Clegg to his office, where Fletcher was waiting for their arrival.

"Is Khan still alive?

Was Fletcher's first question. Eli, sighed and looked

at Clegg, who now realised what he meant when he said, don't ask.

"Is that what you thought I was going to say?"

Eli answered his query.

"That, or would I leave my weapon at the door. And, I did think for a moment that being the observant inspector that you are that you might ask me why my right shoe was missing."

Both Clegg and Fletcher, looked down at Eli's foot, then raised their heads with a question on his lips.

"Don't ask," Eli repeated, and assured them both of Khan's health and that so far he had been cooperative as their link to Hussein.

"So what's our next move?" asked Fletcher. "You haven't exactly kept me up to date with what's been going on."

He was feeling a little left out, which of course he had been.

"That's because until one o'clock today there was nothing to report. What you do know, because you arranged it, is that the weapons are now on our soil. What you don't know is that since they landed that Khan has arranged a meeting for six o' clock this evening at the Libyan Embassy hotel."

"How did you get Hussein to come out of his hole and agree to the meeting?"

"That's not important. The point is, he may have accepted it but he's obviously still cautious because of where he's having it. It's up to me and my team to convince him at that meeting that we are who we say we are, so he relaxes and goes through with the deal."

"How on earth have you arranged it all so quickly?"

Fletcher had tried for years to get Hussein in a compromising position but he hadn't even got close enough to smell his aftershave.

"When your daughter is kidnapped by gun-running slave traders, you don't exactly need a rocket lighting under your arse to make you get a move on. The plan is basically what we came up with at the airfield. We put a deal under Hussein's nose large enough to keep him interested. Then as Ringer put it, we winged the rest as it came along."

Eli filled in the parts he wanted Fletcher to know, leaving out most of his plans concerning the warehouse and the Irish, concentrating instead on the six o'clock meeting and his plan for Hussein, to hopefully lead them to the property where he was holding Kitty. He explained that he wanted both the inspector and he to stay with Errol and the firearms team, shadowing the evening's goings on, and ready to come in as back-up at a moment's notice.

"I can't tell you anything more at the moment and I won't know anything until after the meeting. I'll bring everyone up to date with our next move over the radio.

"I don't have a radio," said Fletcher, as though he thought he should have.

"I'm afraid we only have four. They're the ones we normally use that have been linked on their own wave-band. Obviously Errol will be in charge of yours. For your orders and location whilst tonight's meeting is taking place talk to him, you're both part of his team. The other three will be split between myself, Oneway and the other team."

"Who are this other team?" asked Fletcher.

"Again, that's not important."

"On the contrary Sergeant Major, I think I should be aware of what's going on and who is involved."

"On the contrary, Mr Fletcher, if I thought that informing you of the identities of all parties involved would add weight to me getting my daughter back, I would do so. But it doesn't, so I won't."

Fletcher was, as usual, beginning to piss Eli off, and he couldn't see the point in him being there any longer. He made his exit, leaving Fletcher full of questions and not happy with his downplayed role. On the way out he gave Clegg a wink to give him confidence in the forthcoming events of that evening and mouthed the words 'watch him' whilst flicking his eyes back towards the MI5 man.

It was four o'clock and the group were once again gathered at the warehouse with only one person missing – Ringer. At four-fifteen he rang Eli's phone to explain that he was being held up by the one thing that he couldn't pay, threaten or coerce in to helping his journey go any faster, the M25. It was their first setback but not a major one. He would rather the container was secure at the warehouse before attending the meeting but there was nothing that could be done now. He would just have to keep his fingers crossed that it would be there for Hussein later. Like most other parts of the plan for the past two days, they were once again going to have to wing it and play it by ear. Time now though to check the things they did have control over.

"Dermot, have you done with my shoe? I've felt a right Billy Hunt, limping about all day."

"I have it here. Don't worry, you won't set it off by accident. It will take a very hard stamp to make the connection. I've zip-tied the charge around his ball sack, just in case he tried to remove it."

"Oooh, i bet you enjoyed that," joked Sean whilst pulling his Larry Grayson face.

"Fuck you, Fatty, it had to be done." retaliated Dermo, at his snide remark before continuing. "The only way it's coming off is with a pair of snips, or you stamp your heel."

"Good work Dermot, and wind it in Sean, it's time to get serious. Anyway, I see you've been busy. You've got the place exactly as I asked."

"As soon as Ringer arrives I'll get him to park up over there and your kill zone will be complete."

"Good lad. Danny, Michael, how's the money coming along?"

"All packed in the two bags you provided, we just managed to get a million in each one."

"Sorted. And the trackers, how's the signal?" Eli looked at Oneway.

"Both are working perfectly and sending out a strong trace."

"Cushty." He was happy, and showed it by rubbing his hands together. "Have I forgotten anything?"

"Just the weapons," reminded Oneway. "But Sean and Dermot have sorted them. I let them do it, seeing as how they will be in charge of them tonight."

"Nice one, lads. Are you happy?"

Sean, and Dermot both nodded.

"All the weapons are loaded and in the vehicle," Sean added.

"Good. So we're ready to go."

"We are," replied the lads.

Eli looked around with something on his mind.

"Before we do," he started.

"Eli, we're ready," interrupted Big Danny, knowing he was about to voice his appreciation. They could all see how emotional he was becoming. "We know you're grateful for our help, just as grateful as we were four years ago when you let us walk out of this warehouse. But we need to ask you again if you're able to pull this off tonight because if you're not we've been through it all with Oneway, and he can take your place.

Eli, paused for only a split second.

"No, I'm ok, lads. I just wanted to say thanks, that's all."

"We know. Now grab Khan, and let's get to the embassy. By the end of this evening we will have your daughter back, my friend."

As Eli and Khan stood in the elevator rising to Hussein's penthouse suite, Eli seized his last chance to deliver one final piece of advice.

"Don't fuck this up," he warned, looking into Khan's eyes, then moving his gaze down to his shoes. "Or I'll be on my heels quicker than the chorus of River Dance."

Khan glanced down at the polished brogues on his captor's feet, not needing to be reminded about Dermot's little safeguard strapped to his balls. The lift bell rang, indicating that they had arrived, and as they stepped out onto the floor the time was shortly after six and there was no going back. Everything was ready and everyone was in position. Michael and Danny were already inside with Hussein and the two million. Sean and Dermot were outside, watching from their vehicle, and nearby at full readiness were Errol, Clegg and Fletcher with the firearms unit. As they approached the hotel room door the two men guarding it stood up from their chairs either side of the entrance and searched Eli thoroughly. Khan was allowed to enter the room first, followed by Eli, who took a deep breath of composure before coming face to face with Hussein. As the door closed behind him, as always, he made himself aware of his surroundings. The suite was of a stately standard and took up most of the hotel floor. The reception room they were stood in was lavishly decorated in uncomfortable looking chaise longue style furniture and a large desk commanded the main position in front of some French windows, leading to a balcony. In the middle of the room stood Hussein, and behind him off towards the corners were two more of his bodyguards. Eli's stomach rumbled with hunger for the diplomat's throat but he controlled his impulses and acknowledged him with a simple nod of the head. To Hussein's right were Danny and Michael. Eli immediately began his well-rehearsed verbal onslaught on the pair.

"Who the fuck are these two mugs?" he shouted, pointing angrily. Hussein looked at Khan for an explanation to Eli's outburst.

"These are the buyers," Khan explained, answering Eli's question before looking at Hussein to answer his.

"The only way I could get him to attend the meeting was to give my assurance that it would be between you two alone. He wouldn't agree to meet the buyers. I had no choice but to lie."

"Yes, and the reason I told you I didn't want to meet the other party involved is because these fuckers could be anybody."

Eli again pointed at Michael and Danny. He then grabbed hold of Khan by the neck, vexing his anger and making the show look good in front of Hussein. An act wasn't too hard for him to portray. It was something he had wanted to do since first seeing him at the police station.

"You've been dealing with each other for years," choked Khan, forcing the words through Eli's tight grip. "You just didn't know it because it's my job to be the middle man."

"Well why didn't you keep it that way?"

"Come on, let him go," interrupted Michael. "It was us that insisted on this meeting. We insist on knowing and meeting people we are dealing with. It wasn't important before with the drugs, we just let Khan do his job, but now we are dealing in weapons the stakes are much higher."

Eli released Khan from his hold and turned back towards Michael, and Danny.

"Exactly," he said. "That's why I want paying a lot more, and I want extra because you're fucking Irish."

"Have ye got a problem with that, Englishman?" Danny asked.

"No problem. I just don't like the Irish, at least not the ones that wage war against the British."

Danny moved towards Eli, stopped by Michael's arm being stretched across his chest. Together they were painting a believable picture for Hussein.

"These are the gentlemen that the shipment belongs to," said the diplomat, uttering his first words in an attempt to calm the situation and introduce the two parties.

"The shipment belongs to me until it's paid for," corrected Eli. "It will arrive in my warehouse about eight-thirty tonight and it's not leaving until we agree on an amended price and I'm paid in full."

"The payment is five kilo, as usual," reminded Hussein, looking at Khan for confirmation. "Why should I pay any more?"

"I want three times that," haggled Eli. "Double for moving weapons, and triple because I now know those weapons are for the Irish."

"You're telling us that you'll ship drugs but you develop a conscience when it comes to shipping weapons?" shouted Danny.

"I'm not telling you fuck all," answered Eli with equal aggression. "You're not paying my wages, but to answer your question there's a difference between shipping something that may kill someone and something that will kill someone, especially when those weapons could end up being pointed at British soldiers. I might be a scumbag drug importer but I don't like the thought of being labelled a traitor no more than you would."

"Your conscience is irrelevant," added Hussein, stepping between them. "The shipment is here now and these gentlemen have brought the deposit I requested."

"Not quite," admitted Danny. "We only had two bags and we could only fit a million in each, so your deposit is two million, not five. Even if we'd have had more bags we wouldn't have been able to carry them. We struggled with one each as it was. The other eight is safely tucked away though, and will be brought with us when we complete the deal."

The diplomat didn't look too put out. In fact, he used the situation to make a point of his own. He looked at the said bags in the centre of the room.

"As you can see, Mr Moon, none of us seem to be getting what we expected, but I for one will not let it ruin our business. Today I found myself agreeing to a meeting that I wouldn't normally attend and all because my man Khan vouched for you as his agent, and these men as long-standing trustworthy buyers. Now I've lowered my guard and rules, and forfeited more than half my deposit, so I'm sure you can lower your price so we can proceed."

Eli, seemingly uninterested in Hussein's words, turned to face Khan.

"First of all you lie to me by telling me that this was a private meeting between your gaffer and me. Now I find out that every fucker knows the ins and outs of the cat's arse about me. I told you Khan, no fucking names."

"I had to tell them," he answered, defending himself once again. "The Irish wouldn't complete without this meeting and knowing more about you."

"If you had told me it was arms inside the container in the first place we wouldn't be having this meeting because I wouldn't have accepted the job, then people I haven't met before wouldn't be throwing my name about like a used fucking rag."

"If they'd said they wanted the meeting in the beginning I wouldn't have accepted the job either," Khan explained for the benefit of Hussein. "I know the rules, yours as well as Mr Hussein's."

"Mr Moon, as I said, it's irrelevant now. I'll pay extra but not treble."

"Double then," countered Eli.

"Ten kilos is too much also, but I will make you one

offer. Three hundred thousand in cash, now. You can leave this meeting with that amount in your hand. You would be making the profit that the five kilo would bring without even having to sell anything. But I warn you, if you do not except my offer I will call the deal off, and I will have Khan remove the container tomorrow."

Eli paused as though thinking, making it look good before accepting with a condition.

"Ok, but I want the container moving tonight. I don't want those weapons around me any longer than need be."

"Once you have been paid and the rest of the money is in my hands the container is no longer my problem, it will belong to our Irish friends here."

"Well we want to see it first," said Michael, jumping in. "The rest of the money will not change hands until after we inspect the load, and then it still needs delivering to Belfast."

"Nobody mentioned Belfast to me," said Eli, looking back at Khan. "If you want that container delivering there it will cost you another three kilo, not cash, and that's non-negotiable. And I want it tonight when you inspect the load."

"We haven't got three kilo, not in London anyway," informed Michael. "And we only have enough money to complete the deal we've already done with Mr Hussein."

"Why not just take some more money, Mr Moon. It will make things easier," said Hussein. "Let's say another two hundred thousand," he offered.

"I have regular customers to supply," explained Eli, keeping up the pretence. "If I miss a delivery they'll go elsewhere. I need at least three kilo."

Michael and Eli had baited the trap. They now stayed quiet whilst looking towards Hussein to offer a solution, hopefully one that would hang him.

"Have you got any you could lend us?" asked Michael of the diplomat. "After all, we're shelling out ten million this evening."

Hussein, after a little contemplation, agreed.

"Ok, I will supply you with the coke you need. At least that way we can put this deal to bed." He turned towards Khan, unhappy with the proceedings. "If you ever put together another transaction as disorganised and flimsily as this I will have you shot." Hussein voiced his dissatisfaction with his man but in his own frustration he was going in the direction he was being led. "I will bring the three kilo with me to the warehouse where we will all meet again at nine o'clock for you to inspect the weapons. Once you are happy with the delivery you will pay the rest of what you owe me, so make sure you have the money with you. Is that agreeable?"

"Don't forget that works both ways, Mr Hussein," returned Michael. "We'll bring the rest of the money with us and we'll be more than happy to pay the agreed price so long as we are happy with the shipment. But if we're not then we expect that deposit back, with the three hundred thousand replaced that you pay him."

"Don't worry about the shipment, you will be more than happy with the weapons," he assured.

"Just the same, bring the money with you.

Michael looked and pointed at the two bags as he repeated his terms.

"We don't want to have to come back here to get it later, but if we have to, we will."

Hussein, whilst agreeing to Michael's condition, looked at Eli for his approval but Eli knew that he still had to weave one last piece of the web.

"Why don't we meet where you are picking up the drugs," he suggested. "I'd prefer that to the warehouse."

"No," replied Hussein. "The warehouse is where the container is so that's where we will meet and complete the deal."

Eli again waited, making his pause noticeable. He wanted Hussein to be able to think back on this moment later, giving him cause for suspicion as to his motives.

"Ok," he finally agreed. "Pay me the three hundred thousand and you've got a deal."

Hussein turned to one of his guards and nodded his head before looking at the bags the Irish had brought. The man walked forward and counted out the money before putting it into a separate bag and giving it to Eli, who before leaving with it and Khan, reminded Michael and Danny of what they owed him.

"The container belongs to you now. I want that three kilo of pure uncut by tonight or I'll dump it by the side of the road."

Michael, looked at Hussein with his arms outstretched by his side as if to say, 'What is this man's problem?' Hussein raised his hand slightly and then lowered it, indicating to Michael to calm down and that the drugs weren't a problem. Danny continued the ruse once Eli and Khan had left the room by taking his phone from his pocket and making a call.

"Khan is going to be coming out of the hotel in two minutes with another man," he said whilst Michael and, more importantly, Hussein, listened to his words. "Take a picture of this man and send it to our contact with the name Eli Moon, as an attachment."

Sean was on the other end. He was expecting the call and knew to him it meant that Eli and Khan were leaving and the meeting was going well. To Hussein, the call was the next part of the trap.

"Why have you done this?" he asked, intrigued.

"As we said," Michael answered, "we don't work

with anyone that we haven't had checked out. We've known and dealt with Khan for years and we obviously know who you are but we know nothing of the agent and for some reason his name rings a bell. Moon is a common name in London, so it could be nothing, but we have a man high up in the police force that will run his details through Interpol. The search is a lot quicker and more precise with a picture so Danny has instructed one of our men outside to acquire it."

"What if he has no criminal record?"

"It doesn't matter. If he has a driving licence or any other official document, even a gym membership with his picture on it, his arse is tagged."

Hussein nodded his head and pulled an approving face, thinking that this resource could be very useful.

"How quickly will you get your reply?" he asked, curious.

"Within the hour," answered Danny. "Long before our next meeting at the warehouse. We pre-warned our contact that we would be sending the details, so it shouldn't take long. If you want we will ring you if there are any problems."

"Do so," replied Hussein. "And maybe you could let me use your contact some time. There are a few people I would like to have checked out myself."

"Not a problem," said Michael with a smile. "Just do us a better deal with the price of our consignments in the future. We can't buy more weapons from you if we're not making enough profit on the drugs."

"It's a deal," agreed Hussein, returning the smile and growing more comfortable in the presence of the Irish. "Maybe I will even let you have the three kilo you need as a show of good faith."

"That would be a good start to what we hope will continue to be a long and lasting relationship." Hussein, still smiling, probed a little more.

"This contact of yours, you say he's quite high up in the ranks."

"He's a detective inspector in the Met, but that's all we're going to tell you right now. Like I said, do us a good deal in the future and our resources will become yours."

With Hussein eating out of his hand, Michael asked for his number so he could call him later. Hussein gave him his card along with a handshake before they parted company.

Chapter Eighteen

All or Nothing

Danny and Michael returned to their vehicle, which was parked a few hundred yards up the street from the diplomat's hotel. From their position they could see the front entrance and, in its light, Hussein's limousine. Inside their vehicle, though, they found that not much observing was going on as Sean and Dermot were in the middle of yet another one of their petty arguments.

"What the fuck are you two bickering about now?" asked Michael, climbing in the front seat.

"It's that fat chain-smoking fucker," ranted Dermot. "It's been one fag after the other for nearly an hour."

Michael and Danny, who both had a tab in their

hand, got rid of their cigarettes to avoid adding smoke to the fire. Michael picked up his radio to report that they too had left the meeting but not before resolving the disagreement.

"Fatty, open your window and stop winding Dermot up, and if the pair of ye don't find something else to argue about I'll get Danny to remind you of where your solar plexus is again."

"I'm not thick like Fatty Keenan here. I didn't need to be shown last time and I still don't."

"Good, then where the punch lands won't come as a shock to you will it, ye complaining gobby fucker."

Michael gave them both a bollocking stare before putting the radio to his mouth.

"Eli, this is Michael, over."

"Go ahead, Michael."

"The meeting finished well and he gave us his number. We're back with the others now, watching his limo."

"Good. I'm on my way back to the warehouse. This is where it starts, fellas. We'll see now if Hussein believed our acting enough to take the bait."

"You're analysing again," replied Michael, who knew that the meeting had gone well. "Whether or not he plays the game after we make the call later remains to be seen, but we know he doesn't have the drugs with him that he needs to complete the deal, otherwise he would have given them to us when we were inside. That means he must have them at one of his other safe houses, and when he goes to collect them he will be giving us another address to hit later. But right now I can tell you he's well up for it, don't worry about that."

"I hope you're right, Michael. Errol, did you copy all that. Give me a sit rep, over (situation report)."

"You're coming in loud and clear, you as well Michael. We're out of sight around the corner from Hussein's Hotel. I've split the firearms team into two. The inspector's with me, and I've put Box 500 with the second team and vehicle."

"Smart move," complimented Eli, knowing Fletcher didn't have one of their radios and couldn't hear the conversation. "How's the signal from the two money bags."

"It's strong," answered Errol, looking down at the laptop on his knee, showing a satellite view where at the diplomatic hotel's location a red light flashed, "but there's been no movement yet."

"Ok let's stay off the radios now until Hussein makes his move. I'll check in with you all again when I reach the warehouse and speak to Ringer. Eli out."

Eli looked across at Oneway, who was driving and then into the rear at Khan, who was handcuffed to the hand grip above the door.

"Put your foot down, Oneway, our time window is closing," he said as they passed the signs for the airport, which brought to mind something else that was causing him to worry. "When we get to the warehouse I want you to return to Heathrow airport and take charge of Clegg's men there. If Hussein heads for that jet."

"Nobody," interrupted Oneway, "will be getting on that jet. Not Hussein, and certainly not Kitty."

Oneway's assurance was accompanied by the acceleration of the vehicle to well over a hundred miles an hour, speeding them towards the warehouse. It was only a few miles beyond and fifteen minutes had it covered. Their timely and swift arrival coincided with the welcoming sight of Ringer, and the trailer entering the warehouse doors. Eli showed him where to park in the pre-prepared spot whilst Oneway unlocked the cuffs and offloaded Khan.

"Where do you want him?" he asked, leading him by the shackles.

"Give him here."

Eli took charge of Khan and the key for the cuffs before dragging him towards the wall and a pipe to secure him to. Oneway went to speak to Ringer, who was climbing out of the unit and stretching his legs.

"I'm off back to the airport to make sure Hussein doesn't try to leave by his private jet. Keep an eye on Eli, he's questioning every move, I've never seen him so unsure of himself."

"Can you blame him?" replied Ringer. "I'm surprised he's even been able to put a plan together never mind see it through. If it was my daughter missing I wouldn't be able to control myself like he has. I'd have pulled

Khan and Hussein's fucking heads off by now and probably fucked everything up. I think our mate has more strength than we even realised. Don't worry," he added, patting Oneway on the back; "if we do our jobs as we always do then things will turn out ok."

"Right lads," said Eli, returning. "Oneway, airport. If Hussein heads in your direction we'll be with you ASAP to back you up."

"Like I said," reiterated Oneway with some conviction. Nobody's leaving on that jet."

The three friends shook hands before Oneway returned to his vehicle and reversed out of the warehouse.

"Look in the back of the other motor," said Eli, pointing Ringer towards the second vehicle. "We brought your sniper's rifle. When the time comes, position yourself at the bottom end of the warehouse in the shadows and take out the main threat."

Eli stood where he hoped Hussein's limousine would end up and pointed to the back of the building. Ringer retrieved his weapon from the back seat and began to remove the telescopic sights. The weapon was nothing fancy, just a simple bolt action 303, but once zeroed to its firer it was deadly accurate and delivered a round equivalent to a modern 7.62. The sighting system was new though, an L42 scope, but Ringer wouldn't need it at such close range within the warehouse.

"I trust that so far things have gone well," gathered Ringer with a fingers' crossed look.

"They've gone as good as I could have hoped, thanks to your idea."

"Well, things are moving, that's the main thing. Where's the rest of the lads?"

"The Belfast lads have got visuals on Hussein's hotel and limousine. He hasn't moved yet. Errol has taken charge of the police firearms unit, which he's split into two groups. The second of which he has attached Fletcher to, so he can't hear any of the chatter over our radios."

"That was a good move from Errol."

"That's what I said. We also used two of our tracker bags for the money, and so far the transmitters are working perfectly."

"Who's got the receiver?"

"Errol in his vehicle, I'm just about to give a radio check then we wait."

"So everybody is ready and in position."

"Yes." Eli's nodded answer was still without conviction.

"Good," Ringer replied sternly, whilst working the bolt action of his rifle, making sure the chamber was empty. "Then trust in yourself. Trust in your men, and get a grip of the situation. Pull yourself together, Eli, I intend to get my goddaughter back tonight and kill every fucker that contributed to her disappearance. Now get on that radio and let the others know that you're in control."

Ringer's bollockings were very rare but when they came they were short and to the point, as this one was with a 'get on with it' look. Eli, doing just that, pulled the radio from his jacket pocket but Michael's voice got there first.

"Come in Eli, this is Michael, over."

"Receiving you Michael, go ahead."

"Hussein's driver is in the limo, it looks like he's ticking the engine over, warming it up for his boss."

"Ok, sit tight. Errol, Oneway, did you copy Michael's last?"

"Errol here, received and ready to move."

"Oneway here, received and understood. I'll be in position at the airport in five minutes."

"Ok, everybody, this is it. When Hussein moves I want Michael's team to follow him first. Let's see where he takes us before we make the phone call. If he heads straight for my position he must already have the drugs, but if he has to go get them from somewhere else he may tip us off to the house where he is holding Kitty. Michael, tell Sean not to get too close. Hussein shouldn't become paranoid until after the call, but that doesn't mean his driver isn't switched on and won't have his eye on his rear mirrors. Remember, we have him on tracker so if you lose him, Errol can guide you in. Eli out."

Sean, at the wheel, took the smoking tab from the corner of his mouth.

"Does he think I haven't done this before?" he said, referring to Eli's comment.

"He's just nervous, that's all. Wouldn't you be if it were your daughter?"

Sean nodded his head, agreeing.

"It's an unimaginable situation that he's in," added Michael.

"His guts must be in knots, the poor bastard," said Danny from the back.

"Not for much longer," interrupted Dermot, pointing at the hotel. "Someone's on the move, I presume that's Hussein the slimy fucker."

"That's him," confirmed Danny, as the four of them looked across to see Hussein climbing into his limousine and two of his men placing the bags in the boot with some other luggage.

"Eli, Michael here, over."

"Go ahead, Michael."

"Hussein's on the move and he has the two bags of money with him."

"Cushty," Eli replied, ignoring radio protocol and voicing his relief over the air.

"Hang on, there's more," Michael continued. "He's

also loading a couple of suitcases. It looks like he's going on a trip."

Eli, not answering, dropped the radio from his ear to his chest and took a deep breath. Again he questioned his coverage of Hussein's jet and the airport. Turning towards Ringer, he was once again given that motivating look, telling him to get on with it.

"It doesn't matter where he thinks he's going, lads," Eli replied with power in his voice; "we know different. Oneway and the inspector's men have his exit at the airport covered, so concentrate on the jobs you've been given. The plan's a good one, and I trust you all to carry it out. Errol. is the movement showing up on your monitor?"

"We've got him. I'm switching the GPS tracker from satellite to street map now, over."

"He's pulling out now."

"Ok Michael, you're in the seat. You give us the commentary and the rest of us will listen in."

As Hussein's limousine left the hotel frontage, the lads sat motionless in the darkness of their vehicle.

After a safe distance Sean pulled out, giving the vehicle plenty of lead.

"He's joined the main thoroughfare at Knightsbridge Green and is now heading for Piccadilly Arcade," relayed Michael.

"Well he's going the wrong way for the airport," pointed out Eli. "Stay with him, lads."

"He's heading to the right around the Arcade and down Grosvenor."

"Get a bit closer, Fatty," shouted Dermot, driving from the back seat; "you're going to lose him."

"Stop fucking worrying. Did I interfere when you were making ye shoe bomb earlier? Ye little fucking chemistry geek."

"Shut the fuck up, the pair of ye," growled Danny, giving Dermot a punch on the leg and Sean an ear warmer. "Keep your eyes on that limo."

Michael got back on the radio as Hussein's vehicle turned once more.

"We're now heading south on Lower Grosvenor, passing the Victoria Palace Theatre. Hang on, he's switched to the inside lane and he's doing a left; fuck, I didn't see the sign."

"Don't worry, Michael," interrupted Errol., "I have him on the GPS street map. You're heading down the Vauxhall Road towards the bridge. Just concentrate on keeping him in sight, I'll keep a track on where you are."

"I should have put someone that knew London in the trace vehicle," said Eli to Ringer. "If the tracker hadn't have worked we could have been fucked."

Eli saw his miscalculation as a mistake and wondered how many more he had made.

"The Irish lads won't lose him," Ringer replied while looking up at the A-frame of the roof supports for a suitable sniper position. "Sean's a good driver, he knows what he's doing."

Eli gave an agreeing nod as another message came in.

"The limo's crossing the water now. We'll be over the bridge about ten seconds after."

On his monitor, Errol could see the movement as Michael described it.

"We're going through a tunnel now, he's turning right at the Vauxhall Tavern on to the South Lambeth road.

"Don't get too close, Michael, I have him."

"Ok Errol. He's now turning right again under another bridge on to Parry Street."

Eli knew London like the back of his hand and he didn't need the tracking monitor to visualise from Michael's description exactly where they were.

"He's carrying straight on at the next lights and joining Nine Elm's."

"Someone light me another fag," asked Sean. "I've nearly finished this one."

Danny, from the rear, lit one and placed it in his brother's mouth as he extinguished the last one in the ashtray.

"He's slowing," said Sean, with the fresh fag bouncing in the corner of his mouth.

"He's slowing," repeated Michael over the radio. Now he's indicating right towards the power station. What the fuck does he want there?"

Errol could see on his laptop that the area was enclosed and warned the others.

"Michael, drive straight past, don't follow," he advised. "There are only a few industrial units down there and only one entrance. They will notice you for sure if you turn the corner after them. Find a place to park and sit tight. He has got to come back out on to Nine Elm's"

"Drive twenty yards beyond, Fatty," said Michael, slapping Sean's arm with the back of his hand and pointing at a suitable place to pull over and park. "Danny, take the radio, I'm going for a look. Tell Errol to pull over and wait."

Michael jumped out of the vehicle before it had even stopped whilst Danny relayed his instructions to Errol.

He crossed the carriageway between the fast-moving traffic, back to the entrance that Hussein's limousine had been driven down. Peering around the corner into the darkness, there was nothing on the road in front of him. Breaking into a slight jog, he continued down until reaching another street running to the right. Down it, not twenty yards away, the limo was parked outside a large lock-up. Nobody was in sight and he couldn't see inside the limo because of its blackened windows, but there was light coming through the upper windows of the lock-up, so it was obvious someone was inside.

"Danny, what's going on, where's Michael?" Eli asked, hearing the change of operator.

"He's gone on foot after Hussein. We're parked up on Nine Elm's."

"Eli, this is Errol, over."

"Go ahead, Errol."

"There are no other exits from that area. Hussein has to come back out where he went in, which means he's gone there for a reason. I've zeroed in on the signal and I've got the exact address. I think we should leave half the firearms team here with Fletcher, and storm it when he leaves."

Eli didn't make a decision straight away. Walking a circle in the middle of the warehouse, he puffed on his cigar, mulling on the options.

"Wait out, Errol," he said over the radio, then looked at Ringer for any input.

"We're not sure of the number of occupants inside

the premises," said Ringer, unsure of Errol's plan. "If one of them were to get a call off to Hussein he would definitely have it on his toes."

Eli, nodding in agreement, continued to circle and smoke.

"Eli, this is Michael, over." Eli, relieved to hear Michael's voice and eager to know what was going on, quickly answered the call.

"Go ahead Michael, what's the Bobby Moore?"

"One of Hussein's men entered a lock-up. When he came out he was carrying a small sports grip; if you ask me they've just picked up the drugs."

"Well done. Did you see if anyone was in the lock-up?"

"I only saw one other person, who let Hussein's man out."

Michael was slapped on the shoulder by Dermot, who pointed back to the entrance.

"Hang on, Hussein's limo is back at the junction."

"He's indicating to come in our direction," warned Dermot, watching the direction he was turning in. "Get down."

Michael, Danny and Dermot lowered themselves in the vehicle, whilst Sean sat still, casually smoking his cigarette with one eye on his mirror watching the limousine as it approached and passed them by.

"Ok, lads, he's gone," he said, letting a few more cars come between them before continuing the pursuit.

"We're on the move again, heading the same way along Nine Elm's."

"Ok, Michael, you're doing brilliant, keep it up lads. Errol, I want you to continue but leave Fletcher and his team there. I want them to storm the lock-up Hussein just visited, but not yet. I repeat, I want them to hold position and await my orders."

"Roger that. Hold position and await your order."

Confirming his receipt of the message, Errol put down one radio then picked up another, which was his link to Fletcher and the second vehicle to relay the order.

"We're joining the Battersea Park road." Michael was becoming anxious; they were en route to Heathrow and time was running out. "If I'm right and he has picked up the drugs then he's probably going to join the M4 and head to your location. I think this is a good time to make that phone call."

"Stand by, Michael. Errol, sit rep."

"On our way. We have Hussein's signal, let Michael make the call."

"The limo's turning right over the river towards the Chelsea Embankment. Eli, it's now or never."

"Ok, Michael, if they head for the M4 make the call."

The next thirty seconds of radio silence were excruciating for everyone involved. The timing of the call was critical, and a part of the plan that had to be initiated, but it held the most trepidation for Eli.

"Ok, lads, we have crossed the river and are heading for the M4 on the Warwick Road. It's time to make the call."

"I agree. Right Michael, drop back a bit further so you're well out of sight and do your stuff. Errol?"

"Go ahead."

"I want you to catch up on the Irish lad's position."

"Roger that," he confirmed.

Michael took his mobile from his pocket and keyed in

the number, copying it from the card Hussein had given them earlier. Sean reduced his speed, allowing several vehicles to pass as a few miles behind them, Errol, the inspector and the remaining half of the firearms team sped forward to catch up, as Michael mentally ran through the call he was about to make.

In the limousine, Hussein, who believed up to this point that everything was running smoothly, answered his phone to the number with no name.

"Mr Hussein, this is Michael Flynn. I have news of our friend the shipping agent."

"Yes, Mr Flynn. I trust there were no surprises."

"None at all," answered Michael, sounding full of confidence. "He is who he says he is and his business is beyond repute."

"I thought so," replied Hussein. "My man Khan has used him for many years and we have never had a problem. How long will it be until you reach the meeting point?"

"About thirty minutes, we should be there on time."

"Excellent, we will do good business tonight and in the future."

"We shall indeed," replied Michael. "Oh, by the way, I was right about recognising his name, I knew it rang a bell, but it is of no significance."

"What do you mean?" asked Hussein. "Where have you heard it before?"

"It was just something on the news that I watched in the hotel room about a young girl called Moon that had gone missing this week in the London area. It turns out that she's the shipping agent's daughter. I'm getting to like him better by the minute. He must be a proper callous bastard to be doing business with us whilst his daughter is missing, or have a good reason. Maybe he's expecting a ransom note and needs the money. Normally I would feel sorry for the man, but given his attitude to us Irish he can go fuck himself."

Hussein's curiosity was pricked, arousing his suspicion. He didn't like coincidences especially when they occurred whilst a big deal was going down.

"Mr Hussein, are you there?"

"Yes, I'm sorry, I was just thinking about a few things."

"Is there anything wrong?"

"No," replied the diplomat after a pause. "Everything is fine. Proceed to the meeting and I will see you there. Don't worry if I'm a little late, I have a stop to make along the way. And don't say anything to the agent about what you have told me concerning his daughter."

"Ok, Mr Hussein, we'll see you at the warehouse."

The call was made and there was nothing anyone could change now. Michael had done a good job of planting the seed but he had no control as to how Hussein would react to it. He picked up his radio to bring the others up to speed.

"The call's made Eli. I think it went well."

"Ok, Michael. Errol, what's Hussein's position?"

"He's still on the Great Western Road, about to join the M4 motorway."

"Ok let's see what he does. Oneway, are you ready at the airport?"

"Ready and waiting, everything is covered here."

In the back of the limousine Hussein was going over in his mind the recent happenings, concentrating mostly on the earlier meeting at his hotel. He trusted Khan implicitly and saw no difference to this deal and the numerous others they had put together over the years. What did jump to his mind was remembering earlier that Eli had tried to shift the meeting to the property where he was picking up the drugs. 'Why' he asked himself. He didn't know the names of any of the young girls who had been abducted on his behalf. Why should he, to him they were just a commodity the same as the drugs and the weapons he dealt in. But if one of the girls was the shipping agent's daughter it would explain a lot and change everything. Picking up the limousine intercom phone, he spoke to his driver.

"Have you noticed anything suspicious behind us?"

The driver, as always had been vigilant during the journey and had seen nothing out of the ordinary but looked in his mirrors once more to make sure.

"No sir, everything is normal."

"Ok, leave the motorway on the next off ramp and

head for the lodge at Chiswick. Take note of all the vehicles that follow you."

"Yes sir, understood."

Hussein's driver hit the brakes and swerved across three lanes just in time to make the turn-off, causing several vehicles to move out of his way. A few hundred yards behind, the Irish lads relayed what they saw.

"Eli, he's off and making no attempt to hide it. He's just crossed three lanes like something from the Dukes of Hazzard."

"OK Michael, do not follow, I repeat do not follow. Carry on and join me at my position."

"Ok, understood and heading your way."

"Errol, move up and take over, let's see where he's going. Fingers crossed he's going to lead us to Kitty."

"We're about three miles behind but we have a strong signal on the GPS. He's now going around the roundabout and is almost coming back on himself along Chiswick High Road."

Back in the limo, Hussein was making another call, this time to the lock-up where he had just picked up the drugs. In the lock-up a man named Nassim answered the call.

"Nassim, is everything ok there?"

"Yes, Sir, did you forget something?"

"No. Go outside and check the surrounding area. Have a good look, not just a glance."

Hussein's man did as he was asked and went to the door of the lock-up. He turned on the outside lights and began to walk up and down the surrounding streets, relaying his movements to Hussein and describing what he was seeing. Eventually he walked all the way down the entrance road to the Nine Elm's but like the rest of the area there was nothing out of the ordinary to report.

"Everything is as it should be Sir, there is nobody about. What exactly am I looking for?"

"If you would have seen it, you would know. Go back to your work, secure the doors and call me immediately if anything untoward happens."

Hussein put down his mobile and once again picked up the limo intercom.

"How is our rear, are we being followed?" he again asked the driver.

"No, Sir," he replied, again checking his mirrors. "Only two cars followed off the motorway but neither of them stayed with us. I also got them close enough at the roundabout junction to look at the drivers. They were an old couple and a young woman, nobody of interest."

"Good, carry on but keep your speed steady, make several stops just to see if anything stands out. Pull into the next petrol station and park somewhere where there is plenty of light."

"Yes Sir," answered the driver.

Hussein had only one more call to make. Going back to his mobile he rang Khan. Eli was ready for the call and had Khan unchained, well rehearsed and shadowed by himself and Ringer. As the phone rang he passed it to him.

"Don't fuck up," warned Eli. At the same time Ringer's hand fell on his shoulder. But with a small charge of C4 still strapped to his testicles, and Ringer stood next to him, Khan had no intentions of getting anything wrong.

"Where are you, and can you talk in private?" Hussein asked.

"At the Heathrow warehouse waiting for you, Sir, and yes I am alone. Why, is there a problem?"

"The shipping agent Moon, what is he doing?"

"He's in his office filling out the paperwork to send the container over to Belfast."

"Is he, or has he been acting suspicious?"

"No Sir. why do you ask?"

"I'll tell you why, you fool. The girl you brought me, where did you snatch her from?"

"Hemel Hempstead, I watched her get off the bus and stopped her on the lane."

"And what were you doing there?"

"I had been to a meeting earlier that afternoon with Moon the shipping agent to discuss the shipment. Why, what difference does it make?"

"You idiot, the girl you snatched is his daughter! She was on her way home from school."

"What?" exclaimed Khan in a believable tone. "She was just a girl on the street. I had no idea."

"The question is, does he know we have her and if so what is he planning and are the police involved?"

"He can't do," answered Khan. "You've seen Moon when he is angry. He would have killed me if he knew anything. He's been a bit short-tempered this week but that was because I lied to him about shipping weapons. Which is exactly the reason why he wouldn't dare involve the police in anything that brought them sniffing around his business. He'd get thirty years."

"Just the same, I don't like the fact that he tried to change the meeting to one of my premises. It makes me think that he was trying to get me to show my hand. Make sure you're armed and get ready to cover Moon when we arrive. I'm not coming to that meeting without some leverage. Can we trust the Irish to back us up if Moon tries anything?"

"No problems," confirmed Khan. "They don't want to fall out with you, they need those weapons and more in the future. Moon isn't exactly their favourite person either. I don't think we should worry about whose side they will be on if he tries anything."

"Who's on the phone?" shouted Eli with his hand at the side of his mouth, mimicking a distant call from across the warehouse.

"It's Mr Hussein, apologising," shouted Khan. "He's going to be a bit late but he's on his way."

Hussein could hear what was being said; falling for the ruse, he created one of his own.

"Tell him that I am having trouble getting hold of the drugs the Irish need to pay him."

"He's having trouble getting the stuff for the Irish," repeated Khan, "but he won't be long"

"Well, tell Mr Hussein that without the stuff the only place that container is going is for a float down the river, and the Irish can go fuck themselves."

"Tell him that I heard what he said, and I am on my way." Khan once again repeated the message. "Now have a good look around that warehouse inside and out. The only surprise when I arrive wants to be of my creating. I will ring you again when I am five minutes away."

Eli took the phone from Khan's hand. He had done

well but got no thanks, just his handcuffs replaced. Eli, going back to his radio, called Errol.

"Errol we've had the call from Hussein, he's obviously suspicious but he seems to be going ahead with the meeting, so don't lose him."

"We've got him. He's now leaving Chiswick Road and joining Acton Lane. He keeps pulling over, obviously to see if he is being followed. Hang on, he's pulling over again this time, it looks like he's pulled in to a petrol station." Hussein's driver had done as he was told and pulled in to a well-lit area of the station forecourt. His bodyguards climbed out and one of them opened the rear door.

"I'm not getting out," explained Hussein. "I want you all to search the outside of the vehicle. Check the underneath and the wheel arches and don't forget behind the bumpers. You're looking for anything that doesn't belong, like a transmitter."

Hussein was leaving nothing to chance. He knew all the tricks of tracking and surveillance, as he would do, having supplied most of the specialist equipment used for it.

"The car is clean, sir," reported one of the guards after ten minutes of searching.

"Very well, we will proceed to the lodge."

As they pulled out of the petrol station Errol got back on the radio.

"He's on the move again."

"What were they doing all that time?"

"I don't know. We are a mile back down the road out of sight, but I know they stopped at a petrol station because it shows up on the street map. Their reason for stopping may have been something as simple as they were getting some fuel."

"Don't tell me they left the motorway just to get some petrol."

"No, they are continuing along Acton Lane, so they're going somewhere important."

"Well wherever he's going it must be close. It's eight forty-five now."

"Hold on a second, Eli," interrupted Errol. It's possibly closer than you think, because he's entering the grounds of a lodge opposite the Acton Green common. We're going to get closer to get a visual."

"Ok, but be careful, this could be the place where he's holding Kitty."

"Roger that. Errol out."

"Michael give me sit rep."

"A what rep?" repeated Michael, confused.

"Sorry," apologised Eli, forgetting they weren't in the army. "Give me a situation report. Where are you and what's happening?"

"We're passing the airport now. We'll be with you in ten."

"Errol have you got any closer?"

"We've got a visual on the lodge but it's surrounded by a high wall and trees with solid wood gates, we can't see anything inside."

"Ok, hold fast in that position. I'm going to play a hunch that after Michael's call that the lodge is his one and only stop, and that when he leaves there he'll be coming straight to the warehouse. I think he's holding my daughter there and he's called to either confirm her identity or to pick her up and bring her with him to use as leverage. When Hussein is five minutes away from the warehouse he's going to ring Khan back to make sure everything is safe. As soon as he makes that call I'll tell you of his impending arrival. At that point, I want you and your team to hit the lodge and Fletcher's team to hit the lock-up. You have to be in and in control of both properties before anyone has a chance to make a call and warn Hussein. Do you understand?"

"Don't worry Eli, we'll be all over them like a rash. The sergeant in charge of the other team is very capable and I've supplied them with some stun grenades and explosive charges for the doors."

"Ok Errol, you know what has to be done but just for the legal side get the inspector to ring his station and report seeing armed men at both addresses and that he intends to follow up on the sighting."

"Anything else?" asked Errol.

"Just good luck, my old friend."

"Understood, Eli. But luck has nothing to do with it.

Let's give these bastards what they deserve and give them it hard. Errol out."

Eli now set about his final preparations within the warehouse. Going to the vehicle, he collected a bag and brought it back to where Khan and Ringer stood. Taking out two nine millimetre hand guns, he checked the magazines were full and the weapons were cocked and ready to fire before placing them between the pallets he was planning to later take cover behind. The next weapon he took from the bag was given the opposite treatment. This one was cleared, making sure it was empty before Eli leaned forward and tucked it inside Khan's waist band with some more advice.

"When you do as Hussein has told you and cover me with this weapon, remember it's not loaded. He'll also expect you to frisk me and take mine." Whilst talking, Eli took a fourth weapon from the bag and gave it the same treatment, making sure it was free of ammunition before placing it in his own waist band. "And this one's not loaded either," he added, giving Khan a look that said there was nothing he hadn't thought of.

"And I'll have you in my sights if you make any move towards those other weapons in the pallets," added Ringer, pushing home his point by jabbing the end of his rifle in Khan's ribs.

"Eli, this is Errol, over." With a rush of anticipation he answered the call.

"Send, over."

"Hussein is on the move again, circling the common and going back towards the M4 along Acton Lane."

"Did you manage to see anything when he left?"

"Negative, the gates just opened and closed behind him."

"Ok, wait out."

Eli halted the conversation with Errol when the darkness of the large double warehouse doors was broken by the headlights of an incoming vehicle. It was the Irish lads arriving, and as prearranged, Sean parked up a few yards from the row of pallets.

"Ok, Errol, the Irish lads have just arrived so we're ready here. Keep tracking Hussein until he's out of range and move both firearms teams into position."

"Roger that, Errol out."

"Oneway, you're up, he could be coming to you next."

"Everything is covered here. The inspector's men have the place locked down tight and I've taken the added precaution of sabotaging Hussein's jet. I've now taken up position back at the slip road. If he comes off to head for the airport I'll follow him in and we'll take them out as they debus. If he carries on towards you, I'll join the M4 and follow him to your position."

Oneway was parked at the top of the slip road, with a good view of the passing vehicles on the M4. For cover he had his hazard lights flashing and his bonnet raised to make it look like he was a broken-down motorist.

"Eli, this is Inspector Clegg, over."

"Go ahead, Inspector."

"Both teams are in position. Errol has left me in the vehicle in charge of the radio and the tracker. I just thought you might like to know that Hussein has re-joined the M4 and is now approaching the airport turn-off."

"Roger, Inspector. Oneway, did you copy that, over?"

"I copied. He hasn't passed me yet. Wait out, over."

Oneway watched the passing traffic, looking for the large limousine that would hopefully stand out from the other vehicles.

"He should be with you about now, Oneway," said the inspector, still following Hussein's progress.

"I have the subject in sight, gentlemen. He's doing a ton straight past me, it looks like he's keeping your date, Eli."

"Ok, Oneway, follow him in at a distance but do the last quarter of a mile on foot. We don't want him spooked by the lights from approaching vehicles once he's inside the warehouse."

"Good thinking. I'm on my way."

"Inspector, come in, over."

"Yes Eli, I hear you."

"Keep your men at the airport on full alert. If things go wrong here he could still make a dash for it."

"Ok, I'll pass that order on."

Almost immediately Khan's phone began to ring. It was Hussein, giving the call he said he would give when he was nearby. Eli got back on the radio before giving Khan the phone.

"Inspector, tell the teams to go now. Hussein is calling Khan, so his phone is engaged, it will stop anyone from calling him."

"Roger, Eli, it's a go." Now he pressed answer on the phone and put it to Khan's ear.

"Khan, can you talk?" Hussein asked.

"Yes Sir."

"Describe to me the situation where you are."

"The Irish are already here, four of them in total. The two you met earlier, a smaller skinnier man and a fat one who hasn't got out of the car, I think he's the driver. The other three are checking the load, and Moon is watching them. They sound happy with the merchandise you have supplied. I've checked everything inside and out. Everything is as it always is. I haven't seen anything suspicious or out of the ordinary."

"Ok, but I still want you to cover Moon when we arrive, I will be there in five minutes."

Eli made a rolling motion with his hand, wanting Khan to keep Hussein talking to give Errol and his teams more time.

"Are you sure it's his daughter, Sir?" Khan asked, attempting to extend the conversation. "The only thing that seems to be bothering Moon is that he's having to deal with the Irish."

"We'll find out soon enough," answered Hussein. "Until then, keep your eye on him."

"Do you want me to have my weapon drawn? Moon is armed as well, it could cause trouble."

"No, don't do anything that might raise the tension before I get there."

Eli removed the phone, ending the call, and got back on the radio.

"Inspector, Hussein will be here in five minutes. I need answers fast."

"You'll have them as soon as I do, Eli. All hell has just been let loose here."

Eli paced and puffed for the next two minutes that felt like an hour. He stared at the radio, willing it to bring him news while looking through the warehouse doors for signs of Hussein's vehicle. Taking the key from his pocket he removed the handcuffs from Khan's wrists and threw them to the back of the warehouse.

"Eli, this is Errol, over."

"Talk to me Errol, what the fuck's happening?"

"Both properties were entered and contained, nobody made any calls. The other place is full of drugs, it's a proper fucking cutting factory, but Hussein's man there won't be doing any more of it."

"What about the lodge, Errol?"

"The lodge is definitely where he keeps the young girls, we had to kill four of his men here, plus we have two wounded prisoners."

"Is kitty there, is she safe?" Eli asked in desperation.

"No, but I think she was. We've rescued four teenagers and one of the girls told me that there was a fifth until Hussein's visit. By the description she gave me, I think it was Kitty."

"The bastard has her," said Eli with gritted teeth, "and he's bringing her here. Errol, leave the firearms team to clean up there and get here with the Inspector. And sorry for not asking but are all our lads ok?"

"All good Eli, there a good set of lads this firearms team."

"Nice one."

From the doors Dermot broke the call with his shout.

"We've got company, I can see some headlights coming down the road, it can't be anyone else but Hussein!"

"Errol, got to go. The Libyan's arrived. Right everybody, switch your radios off and get rid of them, this is it."

Eli placed his behind the pallets, where his weapons were, and Michael chucked his into the car at Sean, who put it into the glove compartment. Eli stayed near the pallets with Khan, slightly behind him, and the Irish grouped about fifteen yards to his right alongside their vehicle.

"Dermot," shouted Eli. "Jump in the back of the trailer as though you're still checking the load and leave the doors wide open so they don't block Ringer's view." Dermot ran across the floor and did as Eli had said.

"Ringer, do you have your line of sight?"

"I have it.

"Good, let's do this."

As Hussein's limousine entered the warehouse it was parked exactly where it had been channelled. There was a few seconds delay before two doors of the vehicle that faced the wall opened and two of his men got out. The first, armed with an Ouse sub-machine gun, rested it on the roof and took aim across the warehouse at Eli and the Irish. The second, carrying only a handgun, also used the car as cover but turned his attentions on Dermot in the back of the trailer.

"You, get your hands up," he was ordered in an Arabic accent, "and the rest of you do the same."

Dermot did as he was told as the rest of them followed his lead. Khan, as ordered, had already drawn his weapon and was holding it to the back of Eli's head, who now, like everybody else, had his hands raised. With everybody covered Hussein, now feeling safe, got out of the vehicle on the side facing the group.

"What the fuck's going on?" shouted Michael. "This

better not be a double cross. Our people know we are here, you'll be hunted down and butchered if it is."

"Calm down, Mr Flynn, it's just a security precaution. Attending meetings is all new to me but I assure you my precautions are not against yourself, it's our friendly agent that has me worried."

Hussein turned his attention to Eli, who quickly responded.

"Your shipment has been delivered, Hussein. The Irish have inspected it and are happy. All that is left to do is for you to give me the three kilo and I'll send it to Belfast. The paperwork is on my desk, all filled out and ready to go. What's your problem?"

"You, Mr Moon. You are my problem." Hussein stopped before explaining his actions any further. "Have you searched him?" he asked, looking at Khan. Khan tucked his own weapon back in his belt and using both hands patted Eli down, making it look good before eventually finding the planted Browning inside his waist band. Khan chucked the weapon out of the way under the wagon, then returned his own back to Eli's head.

"Was that meant for me?" Hussein said rather smugly, while pulling a weapon of his own from his pocket. "The problem is not of your making, though, Mr Moon," he continued. "Unfortunately that was a miscalculation of Khan's."

"What's all this about, Hussein?" interrupted Danny. "We came here to do a deal, not to play guessing games."

"It's about the young girl you mentioned earlier. The one you heard about on the news that is missing, his daughter."

"What about her?" asked Michael joining in?

Hussein, instead of answering, turned to his limousine, opened the back door and produced Kitty, followed by another of his guard. She was blindfolded and sobbing with fear at Hussein's rough handling and she could feel the cold weapon he now held to her head.

"Kitty," shouted Eli. With his arms outstretched he lunged forward reaching for his daughter but was stopped by Hussein raising his weapon.

"Daddy," she cried, hearing her father's voice, "Daddy."

"Calm down Kitty, nobody is going to hurt you. Let her go Hussein, or I'll or."

"You are in no position to make threats Moon."

Hussein's body guard gripped Kitty tighter while making a point of holding the gun to her head.

You knew I had her, Moon," the diplomat continued. "That's why you tried to change the location of the meeting. You were hoping that I would lead you to her and at that meeting you were going to kill me with that weapon or take me hostage to exchange."

"Look Hussein, you have what you wanted," haggled Eli. "Take the weapons and the money you gave me. Keep the drugs as well, I'll ship the container to Belfast for nothing, just give me my daughter back."

"I'm afraid that won't be possible. You've got a bit of a temper. I wouldn't want you coming after us once your daughter was safe."

"Daddy," cried Kitty again, hearing Hussein's words.

"Don't worry Kitty, everything's going to be alright." Eli tried to calm his daughter. It broke his heart to see her that way but they were so close to an end he had to hold it together.

"How did you end up with his daughter?" asked Michael, still building a portrayal of an impartial group.

"It was Khan who decided to kill two birds with one stone. After a meeting with Moon, on his way home he abducted the girl not realising who she was. Fortunately I found out just in time, thanks to you and your source at the Met. If you hadn't have found out I think Mr Moon had different plans for us all. Why else would he be carrying a weapon?" Hussein looked back at Eli to ask another question. "I'm curious, Mr Moon; how did you find out that Khan had taken your daughter?"

He didn't answer straight away, not wanting to come across as too eager to reveal information. Hussein, seeing his reluctance, looked at his guard who again gripped Kitty tightly and pushed the gun harder into her head. Kitty's screams shook Eli, who once again stretched out his hands.

"Alright, alright," he succumbed. "It was the partial description of the car the police had been given to them by the driver of the bus that Kitty got off. I saw the car Khan was driving that day, the colour was unusual and the description too close to be a coincidence. But it was only two days ago when I asked the police if they had any new leads that they told me about the bus driver's sighting. By that time the weapons were on there way, and I'm disgusted to say that I didn't want to involve the Police because if they arrested Khan they might find out about what we were up to and the other things we had done in the past. A simple cross-reference of our telephone numbers would have told them that we knew each other and aroused their suspicions. Besides, I couldn't be sure, so I intended to find out tonight, but I wasn't going to kill anyone, I swear. I was just going to use the weapon if you did have my daughter, to make you release her."

Eli was doing a good job of making himself sound like a weak and desperate man.

"But how did you know it was me that was holding your daughter?" Hussein continued to probe, wanting all the answers.

"Khan," replied Eli. "We got drunk together a couple of years ago and he let slip some of the other things you and he got up to. As soon as I heard the description I remembered the conversation but didn't want to believe it."

The diplomat looked at Khan with anger in his eyes for his loose lips. Khan, who obviously had never said anything, could only offer a feeble excuse.

"I don't remember saying it, I must have been drunk."

"I'll deal with you later," growled Hussein.

"So what now?" asked Michael changing the subject? Eli was doing well answering Hussein's questions but it was about time he was thrown a lifeline. "We need to get a move on," he added.

"Kill Moon," ordered Hussein, looking at Khan and pushing Kitty back towards the limousine.

"Whoa whoa whoa," said Danny, stepping foreword. "What about our load. Don't get me wrong, you know I don't like this fucker, but if you kill him, who's going to deliver that container to Belfast?"

"He's right, Mr Hussein," said Michael, backing Danny up. "We need him alive, he's no good to us dead and he won't do as he's told if he thinks he's never going to see his daughter again."

Hussein thought about the situation. Normally he would have no loose ends because he didn't meet anyone else, so now he had, he didn't want to leave any.

"What do you have in mind?" he asked, looking at the Irish.

"Give us the girl to make sure he delivers the container," continued Michael. "When he does we'll hand her back and obviously we never do business with him again. In the meantime we've checked the shipment and we're very happy, so we'll pay you the rest of the money. It's all in the vehicle there, eight million quid, being guarded by another one of our men, Sean."

Sean raised his hand as Hussein looked at him. He then turned slightly to look over his shoulder as though he was looking at the money behind him.

"The last member of our team, who you haven't met, is Dermot." Michael was doing the introductions, trying to make Hussein as comfortable as he could in their presence. "That's him in the back of the truck, checking the shipment."

"Everything is good here," added Dermot to the charade. "We've got more than our money's worth."

"As an added bonus," Michael continued, "you can also take back your five hundred thousand *and* keep the three kilo. Moon can't say anything because of your relationship in the past and if he's any sense he'll be thankful that he has his daughter back and forget the whole thing. But if you kill him that means we're out because without him we can't move that load and that means we want our money back." Hussein, still pondering the situation, wasn't convinced and Danny could see it.

"Give her to me," he said with a smile, "I'll take good care of her, I like them young and fresh myself."

"Leave her alone, you Irish bastard," shouted Eli, "she's only a child."

"If there's grass on the pitch she's old enough to play ball games," replied Danny, his comments intending to give the impression that he shared the same sick perversions as Hussein's customers in the slave trade. "Now shut your fucking mouth, Englishman." He walked over to Eli and hit him on the jaw, sending him flying behind the cover of the pallets. Taking the weapon from Khan's hand, he followed through out of sight of Hussein and his men and pretended to knock Eli out with a pistol whipping. Standing back up he continued the show by sticking the boot in which sounded a lot worse than it was. "He won't be bothering anyone for a while," he said, implying that Eli was out for the count. Again Kitty cried for her father, knowing something was going on but unable to see anything. Danny, on a roll, threw the weapon back to Khan and walked towards Hussein. "Give her to me," he whispered so kitty couldn't hear. "When Moon has delivered our goods to Belfast, I'll have some fun with the girl and then kill them both." After his words Danny looked at Hussein with a devilish smile before taking hold of Kitty and dragging her from the guards grip. "I'll throw her in the back of our vehicle," he added whist dragging a screaming Kitty across the room. Hussein was still unsure that her release was what he wanted but was overwhelmed by Danny's presence and found himself going along with the move. Behind the pallets, Eli had crawled into position and retrieved the weapons he had earlier planted; despite a sore jaw he was ready for action. As he looked across to the doors he could see Oneway had arrived and was crouched in the corner with his weapon drawn taking aim at Hussein's guard. He smiled with relief as he got a narrow sighting of Danny, dragging Kitty towards their car. She was kicking and screaming like the fit fighter she was, unaware that she was being led to her safety. As Danny lifted her in to the back of the car he took care to guide her into the foot well behind the passenger seat. Still screaming, she was steadied by Sean's hand being rested on her head as he whispered her name.

"Kitty, don't be scared, you're safe now," he assured. "We're friends of your father's, we're here to help."

Danny now took hold of the GPMG that was laid along the back seat. It was going to be awkward to get the large weapon out of the vehicle before he was noticed and once he had, the warehouse was going to turn into a war zone.

"Be careful, brother," advised Sean, who was looking towards Hussein and his men out of the corner of his eye, "the fella with the machine gun is watching your every move."

Danny, giving it no further thought, used a reversing movement to free the weapon from the confines of the vehicle. Once clear he began to spin, fetching the muzzle towards his target. Hussein's guard, seeing the movement and the weapon, started to react, bringing their sights onto his position. The first shot rang out, but it wasn't from Danny. The shot emanated from above, it was Ringer, delivering a round to the biggest threat, Hussein's machine-gun carrying body guard. The man's head disintegrated like a melon being struck by a cannonball, sending chunks of skull against the wall behind him. The second shot was from Oneway at the door, which took out the other guard behind the vehicle before simultaneously everyone else began to react. Khan and Michael, dove for cover behind the pallets from where Eli was now rising with a weapon in each hand, sending numerous shots towards Hussein, who was diving back into his armour plated limousine to join his remaining guard who, with the same thought had already beaten him to it. Sean, as ordered was reversing his vehicle at speed out of the warehouse, getting Kitty to safety, whilst Danny covering their exit began to spray the limousine and everything near it. The deafening sound of the G.P.M.G filled the warehouse as the heavy rounds pounded on the armour plating and the bulletproof windows which lived up to their reputation for only a moment before succumbing to the massive onslaught of the powerful repetitions of the weapon. The remaining guard, unable to get to the driver's seat because of the internal security window, had no choice but to get out of the vehicle next to the wall and take his chances that way. It was a mistake. Two rounds entered his body, one from Ringer, taking out half of his chest, and the second from Oneway, coming the other way and entering his back. Hussein, now caught alone inside the vehicle, was left to Danny to finish off. A box that had contained a belt of five hundred rounds was attached to the weapon he was firing and Danny held his finger down tight on the trigger until every one had been spent cutting the limousine and Hussein to smithereens. At the end of it, whilst the echoes still rattled around the room, the group gazed upon the vehicle, which now resembled a piece of Swiss cheese rather than a prestige motor vehicle? As Ringer, with his rifle slung across his back, dropped from the overhead beams, Eli checked that everyone was accounted for.

"Where's Sean, and Kitty?" he shouted to Oneway at the door.

"The last time I saw him he was doing a handbreak turn and heading in the direction of the gates," he replied.

"Don't worry, he's got a phone, I'll ring him," said Michael, pulling out his mobile. Eli joined Ringer at the limo tiptoeing amongst the body parts, double-checking that all four men were dead and that there was no one else hiding inside the car.

"Eli," Michael shouted, holding up his phone, "it's Kitty, she's ok." Eli ran to speak to his daughter.

"Ringer," he shouted as he did and pointing to Khan. "Make sure that fucker doesn't go anywhere."

Ringer walked over and pulled Khan from behind the pallets, bringing him into the centre of the room. Khan looked at his massacred former boss, who lay in the back seat of the limousine like a two hundred piece jigsaw.

"Lay down spreadeagled and kiss the ground," Ringer instructed, forcing him downwards before going back amongst the bodies and removing the weapons out of temptation's way.

"Kitty are you ok? Are you unharmed." Speaking to his daughter for the first time, Eli could hardly contain his relief.

"I'm ok Dad, what about you? I heard all those shots as we were leaving. I was scared you'd been hurt."

"I'm fine, sweetheart, just a bit of jaw ache that's all."

Eli looked at Danny, who still stood with the GPMG in his arms looking, like a Gulliver-sized Rambo.

"Sorry, fella," he replied. "I had to make it look good."

Eli smiled and gave the big fella the thumbs up.

"Listen, Kitty, the man with you is a friend of mine called Sean."

"I know Dad, he's explained everything. We're going to the drive-through KFC."

"That's good, babes, are you hungry?"

"Not really, Dad, but I think Sean is." Eli lowered the phone from his mouth and looked at Michael.

"My ears are still ringing with the sound of gun fire and Fatty is already ordering a party bucket," he said in a disbelieving tone.

"It doesn't surprise me," joked Michael. "Doing handbrake turns always gave him an appetite."

The two smiled as Eli returned to his call.

"Kitty, put Sean on darling, and I'll see you shortly."

"Eli, don't worry, we're both ok."

"That's good Sean, you did well but I don't want you to bring Kitty back here, there's too much slaughter here for a young girl's eyes. Take her home to her Auntie Pat, that's the best place for her now.

She knows the way. Put her back on, I'll tell her what to do."

"Yes Dad?"

"Kitty, give Sean the directions to our house, he's going to take you home."

"What about you, Dad?"

"I won't be long, sweetheart, but your Auntie Pat has been ill since you were taken. She needs to see you and give you a big cuddle. There's nothing else in the world that she'd want more right now."

"Ok, Dad, but hurry home, please. There's nothing I want more than a cuddle from both of you."

The proud father smiled. Kitty had a way of making his heart pump in his chest.

"I will. But there's something else I have to ask you."

Eli composed himself in preparation to ask the unthinkable. The lads looked in his direction, knowing the next question on his lips. He needed to know, because if it was a wrong answer, she needed to go to the hospital first.

"Has anyone touched you? You know, sexually."

"No, Dad."

Eli's face glowed as the colour returned to his cheeks. The weight from his shoulders flowed away and as he looked at his friends there was only one thing he could say.

"Thank you, from the bottom of my heart. From me, my daughter and her Auntie Pat. We all thank you."

It was the only payment any of them wanted, and it meant more than any reward, but as always, Ringer had his mind on business.

"Eli, we need to get a move on. We're surrounded by a shitful of mess here that needs cleaning up."

Eli took a look around the room, weighing up his next move. As he did, Errol arrived with Clegg, who couldn't believe what he saw when entering the warehouse, but still had his priorities in order.

"Eli, your daughter. Is she safe?"

"She is, Inspector, thanks in a large part to you, and I won't forget that." Clegg, accepting the thanks, walked towards the limo which was now becoming an unapproachable area as the blood pool grew.

"How are we going to explain this," he asked trying to figure out which bits belonged to Hussein.

"First things first, Inspector. We need to clean up a bit around here before we start explaining the what's, whys and whens."

"You're going to need more than a mop and bucket for that lot," replied Clegg, once again looking at the limo and its surroundings.

"I don't mean that sort of cleaning up. Oneway, go to the office and collect that five hundred thousand. Dermot, paddle over there and get the money out of the boot of the limo, that's if there's anything left of the bags after Danny's sharp shooting." Dermot, climbed down from the back of the truck where he had stayed and taken cover, pulled his jeans up around his ankles and began to wade through the clotting blood as Eli, turned to the next business on his agenda and looked down at Khan.

"Ringer, take that piece of shit away and end its fucking life."

"You said you would let me live if you got your

daughter back," pleaded Khan, climbing to his knees. "You said I would go to jail."

"Porridge for you," replied Eli, angrily. "What, for some of those cushy Rule 43's? Not fucking likely."

"Eli," called Errol, interrupting. "Let me deal with Khan. Ringer is busy with you here, and he doesn't need any more corpses adding to his body count. I need to go back to the lodge and the lock-up to debrief the firearms teams. We need to make sure that the case against Hussein is faultless at all points or it could come back to bite the inspector on his arse. Remember he made the call and gave the go-ahead for us to enter. I can get rid of Khan later, once we know that he has nothing that's any more use to us."

Eli, looked at Khan, seriously considering simply nutting right there and throwing his body in the boot of what was left of the limmo. Errol, knowing what was going through his head once again interrupted.

"Eli, we may need him.

"Ok, but I don't want him found. The only burial he deserves is a shallow grave."

Errol grabbed Khan and dragged him towards the doors, where he was thrown into the back of a van. Inspector Clegg thought about interceding but after what he had seen already and the scene that lay in front of him he decided to turn a blind eye. It was no more than Khan deserved anyway. Turning his back on his removal as though if he couldn't see it, it wasn't happening, brought him face to face with the Irish and Dermot, who was returning from his money collecting duties.

"All the money's accounted for and in the back of your vehicle, the whole ten million. And there's an extra bag containing three kilo."

Dermot held up the bag Hussein had collected earlier from the lock-up.

"Nice one, Dermot, now go in the limo and see if you can still find some of Hussein's fingers intact. Put his prints on all the bags then give it to the Inspector. They will go as evidence to build a case against Hussein, along with the container of weapons. Also, do the same with the three hundred thousand we supplied and make sure you use his right thumb. That way it will look like Hussein counted the money at one time. That's for us to keep though, a little bit of evidence we might be able to make work for us as a diversion."

Dermot smiled, knowing exactly what Eli was thinking. It could end up looking like Hussein, besides dealing in drugs, weapons and being a slave trader, also had his hand in robbing banks in Belfast.

"So who are these chaps then, Eli?"

"These are three friends of mine, Inspector, the fourth is driving Kitty home to her Auntie, and that's about as much as I think I should tell you."

"I understand, say no more but I would like to know how I am supposed to write this one up. It's not going to be easy."

"Nonsense, Inspector." Eli took a cigar from his pocket and lit it; he was obviously getting back to his old self and about to go into thinking mode. "It'll be a piece of cake," Puffing strongly to get it well lit, he looked around the room as though wondering where to start, before taking the two weapons he had used from his waist band and cleaning them of all fingerprints. He gave a look to the Irish lads and Oneway, who followed him in what he was doing. Eventually all the firearms were placed on the floor in a row at Clegg's feet, apart from Ringer's rifle, which he would never relinquish. The Inspector, after looking at the array of weapons, looked at Eli for an explanation. "Get the serial numbers on those weapons assigned to some of the members of your firearms team. Then when ballistics do their scientific bit it will prove that they did the killing during the course of their duties. Put the breaking of the drug and paedophile rings down to a long and ongoing investigation by the Metropolitan Police. Your gaffers will be glad of the publicity and the clear-up rate, and it will secure their silence. I wouldn't be surprised if you didn't get a promotion out of this, Chief Superintendent Clegg?" Clegg smiled at his sudden raise in rank. "Also, let Fletcher and Box 500 take credit for the information supplied on Hussein and the smashing of the gun-running syndicate. That should keep them happy and earn you a few friends in high places." Clegg was enjoying listening to Eli's portrayal of the events. The way he was talking, before the night was over he could end up a Commander. "Now here's the good part," said Eli, continuing to cover everything and taking another smoke. "Release a statement saying that Hussein got away and is wanted for questioning in connection with all these offences. Also, get the young girls you rescued from the lodge earlier to identify him by his picture as the man that abducted them. That, along with the drugs factory at the lock-up, plus the three kilo in this bag which 'you' found in the limousine covered in his fingerprints, will cause the Libyan government to drop him like the hottest potato we ever cooked up. Everyone will be a winner, Inspector, and if no fucker makes a statement to the contrary I'll defy anyone to prove it didn't happen that way."

Clegg looked gobsmacked at Eli, who was holding his cigar in his teeth, surrounded by a smile. He turned to the nameless Irish, who also smiled and gave him a reassuring wink. They had heard Eli's rolled-off-the-top-of-the-head scenarios before and accepted it as a natural thing. Oneway and Ringer didn't give a fuck; whilst Eli had been talking they had had been busy shovelling Hussein's body parts into bin bags, so he couldn't be accounted for when the coroner arrived.

"Well, Inspector," said Eli, releasing some smoke. "Are you going to go along with it, or are you going to fuck up a perfect bit of bullshit by telling the truth?"

Clegg looked around the room at all the mess and mayhem. The banging of Ringer's shovel on the ground made him turn to see him using it as a cutter to chop one of Hussein's legs in half because it was to big to fit in to the plastic bag. It dawned on him, as if he didn't already know, what a terrible world we lived in. But the sickness and depravity wasn't of his making, nor was it Eli's or any of his men. It was people like Hussein and Khan that made it that way, and to beat them at their own game you had to get down and get dirty.

"Fuck it," he said, coming to a decision. "I'm sick of playing by the rules. I'm sick of paedophiles and rapists getting light sentences in cushy cells with TVs on protection wings. Thanks to you and Ringer over there, this is the best clear-up rate I've ever had. In fact, in a week you've done more than I ever have and at no cost to the taxpayer."

Clegg paused for a while; although he found the situation upsetting, it was quite satisfying as well.

"My statement will read exactly as you just explained it, you have my word on that. In the meantime, you lot had better get yourselves away from here. Fletcher will be here soon and I've got to arrange some good men that can keep their mouths shut to take your place."

"Good," replied Eli, "but there's one thing left to do to set the scene." He walked over to the weapons Ringer had collected belonging to Hussein and his men. Selecting the Ouse machine gun first, he sprayed the pallets and a portion of the wall behind. He repeated the process with the smaller arms that the other two guards were carrying before walking towards Clegg with the Glock Seven that Hussein had produced.

"What was all that about?" Clegg asked after the noisy display.

"The fire fight was too one-sided," explained Eli.

"We don't want some high-priced lawyer arguing that it was a massacre because they didn't return any shots."

"So what about the weapon in your hand, aren't you going to fire that as well?"

Eli looked at the Glock in his hand and answered the inspector's question.

BANG came the noisy shot as Clegg doubled up in pain and fell to his knees as the round entered the fleshy part of his waist line.

"What the fuck?" shouted Clegg with gritted teeth, holding back any further cursing.

"Get up, Inspector, it's only a flesh wound, just a little piercing through your love handle to add a bit of weight to your report."

Clegg got back to his feet, holding his side and looking for an explanation from Eli, who after another puff was only to happy to oblige.

"Forensics will prove that Hussein's fingerprints are on this weapon. Ballistics will prove that his weapon fired the first shot that wounded you. That will prove that Hussein was here before he did a runner. The case against him is now air tight. There will be a massive manhunt for a man who is actually in six bin liners in the back of our Rover, soon to be treated to a diving lesson from our mate SBS Harry. You get a few months on the sick with full pay and at the end of it I shouldn't wonder if you didn't get a trip to Buck Palace to pick up a gallantry medal from Queen Lizzie herself. And I've been there to pick up my Queens Gallantry Medal. It's a great day out. Your wife will love it."

The Inspector, gobsmacked, speechless and wounded, smiled whilst looking at the blood on his hand and spoke his last words.

"See you, lads."

A lot of respect was left with Clegg by the two teams as they climbed in to their vehicles, but it was Ringer's words that summed up their days work as he shook the inspector's hand.

"When you're done here Inspector, go visit the families of those four young girls you rescued tonight. That will put Hussein and any other thoughts that you might not have done the right thing out of your mind."

Chapter Nineteen

Loose Ends

Everywhere that Kitty had ever wanted to go. Everything that she had ever wanted to do with her father but couldn't because he was too busy with his job was all done over the next couple of months. Eli, Kitty and Pat became a family and put everything to do with Hussein behind them. Hussein, though, stayed front-page news for quite a while. The tabloids absolutely slaughtered him, printing information concerning the gun-running and drugs conveniently leaked by high ranking members of the Met and MI5. The charges made against him for his links to the slave trade were the most heinous in the public eye, and the one million pounds offered by an anonymous donor through one of the large newspapers for information leading to his capture had everybody in the country looking for him, thus keeping the interest at a high. It could be that the unknown person offering the reward knew that he would never be found. Fortunately, only one man was in a position to claim that reward but SBS Harry was too busy playing darts at the Legion to go diving for bin liners off Canford Cliffs and Poole Harbour.

Eli, though, still had some unanswered questions about what went on. Tiny things in the back of his mind that he couldn't put his finger on that just didn't add up. But now was Kitty's time, everything else could wait. But given time he would figure it out.

The Irish returned to Belfast and back to work. Each day's graft brought them closer to the following Christmas and the retrieval of their half of the bank robbery money, which had been returned to its burial place in the barn on the farm. The robbery made big news for the whole of that year and it was going to stay that way for many years to come. The only man ever arrested on suspicion of being involved in the robbery was the manager, but even he was eventually released without charge. The best news of that year was that on the 11th August Michael and Roisin became the proud parents of a bouncing baby boy, who they baptised 'Finbar, Eli, Flynn'.

Clegg did indeed make Superintendent, which stopped him from retiring. He also received a medal from the Queen for his bravery above and beyond the call of duty whilst being wounded during the apprehension of Hussein's men. In his acceptance speech he vowed never to rest until he had apprehended and brought to justice the disgraced diplomat, Hussein.

His achievements didn't stop there. Later that year he received an anonymous call to a house fire. It was an unusual request for an inspector to attend such a thing, but the caller was quite insistent he should be there. The funny thing was that when they broke down the door of the smoke-filled property the cause of the problem was just a magazine that had been jammed in a toaster. When the smoke cleared and the house was checked, Clegg, with his men and the Fire Brigade, found a ghastly and familiar sight in the living room. On the floor lay three men, each having been badly beaten and tortured before having their genitals hacked off, stuffed down their throats and strangled. A fourth man sat unconscious in the chair covered in the other three men's blood and holding the knife that was obviously used for the mutilations in his hand. The room was full of magazines, CDs and videos showing disgusting images of child pornography, some of which showed the four men taking part. Clegg was sickened and needed some air. He walked to the front door and took a deep breath. Looking across the street he noticed a familiar Range Rover and in the driver's seat a familiar face. He crossed the road to the vehicle and rested his arm on the roof above the driver's open window.

"Hello, Ringer," he said. "It looks like you've been busy again."

"Just some unfinished business Mr Clegg. Once I start something I like to see it through."

"Eli said that about you. So why did you set the fourth man up and leave him alive?"

"He's the man you don't have on your computers. From what the others told me he's a big cog in the wheel of an international paedophile ring. When he wakes up he's willing to talk and tell you everything he knows. If he changes his mind and suddenly develops amnesia just threaten to release him on bail, he knows what will happen the next time I get a grip of his Gregory Peck."

"So you're going to let us deal with it now?"

"Its all yours, I've done my bit. Besides, Eli's back next week and we have something else that needs our attention."

"Not on my patch, I hope," joked Clegg, putting his arm through the window and shaking Ringer's hand. Ringer at the same time gave the inspector a card with a number on it.

"If you ever need to get in touch. We can't be contacted through Hereford no more. We are all officially civilians now."

"Thank's. But I hope I never need it."

"Well its there if you do and by the way. In a cupboard in the kitchen there's a plastic bag containing three hundred thousand pounds from a certain bank robbery in Belfast last year."

Clegg's jaw dropped.

"You're joking, aren't you? You mean that was you lot."

"Don't ask questions, Superintendent, you know the score. Of course it wasn't us, its Hussein the diplomat's prints that are all over the money, not ours."

Clegg smiled, showing his agreement to the favour he was being asked.

"Leave it with me. I will make sure that the link is made and it gets plenty of tabloid coverage."

"Good man," answered Ringer, returning the smile.

From the door of the house one of Clegg's officers called for him.

"Sir, he's waking up."

Clegg turned to acknowledge the officer and by the time he turned back around Ringer was already on his way. It was the first time that the two had parted and the inspector was left smiling.

The bringing down of Hussein's network didn't do Fletcher's career any harm either. He was rewarded with a promotion and he was making quite a name for himself within the walls of MI5. Life was looking pretty good for him; at least it was until he returned home one evening in November.

He pulled into his driveway in the row of suburban detached houses and entered the front door, discarding his briefcase and coat. Heading for the kettle first he switched on the light in the kitchen and took a cup from the cupboard. As he dropped in a tea bag and reached for the sugar he became aware of a strange smell. Sniffing the air, he left the kitchen and headed for the living room, identifying the foreign odour when nearing the door as cigar smoke. Pushing the door slowly open, the light from the hallway brought sparse illumination to the room. Fletcher squinted, trying to focus his eyes on what was an unbelievable and ridiculous sight. In the middle of the room, a man was tied to one of his dining room chairs with a pillow case over his head. His first thought was to turn and run back through the front door, but the overwhelming urge to pull off the pillow case and see who it was underneath kept him pinned to the spot. Edging slowly forward into the room he switched on the light, confirming his eyes weren't deceiving him. As he reached forward, ever closer to the hood, the door was closed behind him. Fletcher froze in his stance as the unmistakable sound of a Zippo lighter being flicked and lit came from behind him, and the smell of cigar smoke filled the room. Fletcher dare not make a move in case it turned out to be his last, but he was pretty sure, whilst not knowing the identity of the man in the chair, that he knew the identity of the man behind him. It was Eli.

"Alright Fletcher, you conniving, scheming git. How's your luck?"

Fletcher's world could almost be heard collapsing around him. He was obviously in trouble but still couldn't help wondering who was in the chair. Slowly straightening up and turning around he came face to face with Eli.

"Sergeant Major Moon, what's all this about?"

"Cut the bullshit Fletcher, and take a seat."

From the adjoining dining room Ringer entered with another chair and placed it facing the captive. Fletcher, after being urged, sat down, and Ringer took up position next to him, adding to his discomfort, whilst Eli stood behind the hooded man, looking over his head towards the increasingly worried MI5 man.

"Have you ever debriefed your troops, Fletcher?"

"Troops, I don't know what you mean."

"No, I don't suppose you would. You probably came straight from Oxford or Cambridge into your job in the intelligence service. Not the military service."

Eli puffed on his cigar, but not in his usual lairy manner, this was a more serious almost angry movement as he stared in to Fletchers eyes.

"I never thought I would have to debrief my own daughter, but I did. Not all at the same time of course. Obviously I didn't want to be too full-on and bring back any disturbing memories about her ordeal, so it was just once or twice a week at first whilst we were away.

Gradually I pushed a little more as her abduction became easier to speak about and she began to open up. She's a tough little nut, my Kitty. My heart pumps with pride when I think of how well she handled herself."

"Eli, what's all this got to do with me?" Fletcher asked, pleading ignorance. "And who is this?" he added, pointing at the man in front of him.

"Save it Fletcher, you fucking mug. I know everything. Kitty told me that when she was abducted she had a hood stuck over her head, a bit like our friend here." Eli slapped the captive, causing him to move and moan. From his muffled groans it was obvious that he was gagged under the pillow case. "But she could still hear everything that was being said in the car. First she heard a phone number being dialled on a mobile, you know how you can hear the different buttons being pressed because they each have their own sound. In that call there were only three words spoken. 'I have her' was all that was said in an English accent. She said the man sounded a bit like her uncle Oneway, a deep Yorkshire-type accent. Then when a second call was made soon after, the voice sounded Asian. Well, she didn't actually say Asian. She said he sounded like Mr Patel. The nice man who owns the corner shop, but I knew what she meant. And this time, he said, 'I have a girl for you'. The thing is, she swears there was only one man in the car with her. At first, I thought that my daughter must be mistaken. Which would be understandable, considering she had just been snatched off the street and thrown into the back of a car with a bag over her head. But then I thought 'what if she was right?' You see, my daughter is very bright. I didn't raise no idiot. So what if our recently departed gun-running, drug dealing slave trader Khan wasn't who he said he was, and 'was' in fact, the man behind the two voices in the car. But why, I asked myself? What would be the reason? Why would Khan pretend to be someone else?" Eli, again took a long drag from his cigar whilst watching Fletcher's changing face. "Then it came to me," he continued whilst exhaling. "What if Khan was like Ringer, and me, or Oneway here?" Oneway now entered the room from his position outside where he had watched Fletcher's arrival. Fletcher was now surrounded, and from his lowered position began to feel a little claustrophobic.

"Like you in what way," he asked, still portraying his ignorance.

"Undercover, you snide public school bastard. Quit it with the, 'I don't know what you're talking about' attitude Fletcher. I know you were behind my daughter's abduction. And I know you did it to get me to do your dirty work and get rid of Hussein. What I don't know is why, but I'm going to find out."

Eli's anger hit boiling point as he ripped the pillow case from the head of the man in the chair. Fletcher's jaw dropped on to his chest. 'SHIT' was the word that filled his thoughts. The revealed man in front of him was Khan. Still alive, and blinking with the sudden light. He groaned through the large plaster over his mouth as he shook his head violently from side to side. Fletcher was the first thing that he had seen since being hit over the head and thrown in the boot of a car earlier that day. The surprise of seeing Fletcher soon turned in to fear as he looked up and saw Ringer next to him, bringing back unpleasant thoughts. More fear was to come as Eli walked in front of him and ripped the plaster from his mouth, causing Khan to wince as the hairs on his face were removed with it. Eli blew a long stream of smoke into his face, causing him to cough and tug at his bindings. Returning to his original position behind Khan, Eli resumed his stare at Fletcher and continued talking.

"I needed answers, but dead men tell no tales as they say, and that's what I thought Khan was. So I put it to the back of my mind and finished our holiday. That's when you were almost off the hook, Fletcher. You nearly got away with it, you slippery bastard, but whilst I was away my discharge papers came through, as did Ringer's, and Oneway's, and more importantly Errol's."

Fletcher now realised how Eli had come about his information.

"So despite signing the Official Secrets Act, Sgt Bogal got his discharge papers and decided to tell you everything."

"He's my friend, Fletcher. How long did you think he would keep a secret like that? And I don't think what you did can be covered by the Secrets Act. Besides, that's not why he didn't tell me straight away, he was thinking about my daughter. He knew what I would do, and that wouldn't have helped Kitty at the time. Then after it was all over she needed me and the time to recover. She needed that holiday. That's the only reason he held back." Eli took a smoke from his cigar as the wheels turned in his mind. "I should have sussed you right from the start but I wasn't thinking straight for obvious reasons. It wasn't just the things my daughter said, there were other things that nagged at me. I even answered my own question when I said to the Inspector that I wouldn't be working with MI5 if it weren't for my daughter being missing. Then there was something else long before Kitty went missing. Something you said at our first meeting at Headquarters, that didn't fit with your usual vocabulary. It was as though you were repeating something you had heard someone else say."

"What was that?" asked Fletcher, intrigued as to his faults.

"You called me a barrow boy. It was the same term used a few weeks earlier by a certain demised Colonel, right before I put a round in his nut and blew his fucking brains half way across his study carpet."

"So you admit it was you who killed De' William."

"You bet your fucking life it was me. I ended that grassing fucker's life. The point is, Fletcher: what were you talking to him about? And why was I part of that discussion?"

Fletcher wasn't one for parting with information, but he knew if he didn't give Moon some answers that he could well end up deceased, like the Colonel. He rubbed his face with his hands and looked at Khan before starting to explain in the hope of creating some damage limitation.

"The dark cloud the Colonel was under when he was forced to take early retirement was that he was suspected of doing under-the-table deals with Hussein back in the Nineties. When a situation arose of concern we were forced to approach De' William for information. He agreed to help us but in return we had to agree not to stop him from publishing his tell-all book."

"The information in that book would have put a lot of men in danger," Eli interrupted. "What did De' William know that would compensate for that?"

"A few months ago," Fletcher resumed, "CIA intelligence obtained satellite photographs of an Al Qaida training camp located deep in the desert. From those pictures, two men were identified as belonging to an Irish Republican group. The men were there teaching Al Qaida tactics they had successfully used against British forces in Northern Ireland, such as car and roadside bombs, IEDs (improvised explosive devices), anything that could be successfully transferred to the desert surroundings and used as an effective weapon against our troops. But that wasn't all. Further intelligence revealed that Al Qaida was going to back the group to restart the troubles in Northern Ireland in the hope that it would overstretch the British forces. When you came up with your plan in the aircraft hanger that day, you had no idea how close to the truth you were."

"This Irish Republican group you mentioned, you must be talking about the INLA (Irish National Liberation Army). They're the only ones with an axe to grind after having their noses put out by the Good Friday Agreement."

"The two men were former members of the INLA, although it's not known where their allegiances lie now, but we do think that their motives are drug-related and not political. We have had confirmation from one of our Irish touts that Al Qaida shipped them over a ton of drugs to fund the buying of weapons they will need. That's why it was so important to take down Hussein now after all these years of trying."

"Hussein was not the only arms dealer," interrupted Eli. "There's plenty of others in the shadows that will fill his boots. The Irish will just go elsewhere."

"He was the only one they had dealt with before. It would have been a natural act for them to go back to their original supplier. But now they are having to find someone else. It has given the Irish the time they need to deal with it."

"The Irish government are going to deal with a para-military group themselves?" said Eli, in a disbelieving tone. "That will be a first."

"I'm not talking about the government. When I say Irish, I mean Sinn Fein. They like how things are in Ireland at the moment, and in Spain, on the Costa Blanca. They own properties there, businesses, even whole commercial centres that they rent out, so it's in their interest to make sure that things stay the way they are. They don't want to be leaving sunnier climates and having to return to rainy Belfast to start fighting again. They will out the group to make it look like it was dealt with internally and without any British or American involvement. That way they strengthen their seat on the Irish Council, and we keep our intelligence in Al Qaida. The Americans gave the order that Hussein should be removed but it had to be done in a way so as not to tip off the Irish, or Al Qaida, that we were on to them. The Yanks gave the order as though it was a simple task, without realising that we had been trying to take Hussein down for over ten years. We infiltrated his organisation five years ago with Khan, but still we couldn't get him to make any mistakes."

"So you kidnap my daughter, blame it on Hussein and sit back and watch the fireworks. Who came up with that little cracker?"

Fletcher, without hesitation, threw the blame at the dead Colonel.

"It was De' William's suggestion. You know he wasn't a fan of yours and he knew the situation with your family. He knew about Hussein using kids for currency and he knew what you would do if he took your daughter. To him it was the perfect solution. Not only would we get rid of Hussein but we would get rid of you too. The idea was rejected at first, but when you again refused our offer of working with us when we questioned you at Hereford HQ over the Colonel's death, a second order came from above, that time was running out and we were to proceed with De' William's plan. A plan which would now work out even better because now he was dead we didn't have to give him anything back."

"You fucking wankers," cursed Eli, finding it hard to control his temper with the realisation that he had been used. "And you wonder why I wouldn't work with you. You talk about abducting a young girl as though it was nothing."

"Compared with killing a Princess, abducting a young girl 'is' nothing to MI5 and Six, and they will always use the S.A.S Regiment to do their dirty work?"

Fletcher's condescending and snobbish return wasn't received well by Eli, who had taken about as much as he could.

"Wrong answer Fletcher, because to me my daughter isn't nothing, she's everything. Ringer, knock that mug out."

Fletcher, hearing Eli's order, automatically looked up at Ringer, which was a wrong move, because he raised his chin to the perfect angle for his incoming knuckles. A crushing blow sent Fletcher from the chair to his living room carpet and out for the count. Eli now turned his attention to Khan, who braced himself for some of the same treatment.

"I presume Khan isn't your real name?"

"No," he answered, dropping the phoney accent for his own Yorkshire twang. "It's Carey, Mark Carey."

"You're not known to us from the Regiment, Carey, so how did you come to be working undercover for Box 500."

"I was recruited straight out of training twelve years ago. They wanted me because of my Asian looks and the languages I spoke. I was only nineteen and didn't know any better. They made it sound as though I was going to be the next James Bond. Right now though, I'm wishing that I had refused, and gone to my own Regiment. I could have been doing something I was proud of, and having a beer with my mates like a normal soldier. Whatever you do to me, and I know you're angry but I want you to know that I am sorry for abducting your daughter but I was ordered to do it. Being undercover as part of Hussein's group has sickened me for the last five years. I'm just glad it's all over."

Eli couldn't stay angry with the man. He could obviously relate to what he was saying and knew that when he had abducted Kitty that he was only doing what he'd been told to do. He'd been picked as a young man like an apple from a tree, a favourite tactic of Mi5 recruiting, which Eli had seen many times before.

"How do you know our man Errol?"

"We met briefly when I was learning to speak the language in Morocco. That was when I had first been earmarked to infiltrate Hussein's group. MI5 knew he spent a lot of time there and that he spoke the language, so they decided that the best way for me to become fluent would be to live there for a year and converse with the locals. I didn't recognise your mate in the warehouse, but I'm fucking glad that he's got a better memory than me."

Carey looked at Ringer, knowing that if Errol hadn't interceded that day in the warehouse that he would definitely have done him in, and not in a nice way.

"Untie him," said Eli. "He's just a soldier like us, following orders."

Ringer pulled a knife from his pocket and cut the bindings attaching Carey to the chair.

"Thank you," he said, quickly rising to his feet. "And whilst Fletcher is still unconscious," he continued, "I want you to know that he's a lying bastard. He was happy to go along with the plan to abduct your daughter and he was pissed off when your plan was a success. He and De' William came up with the plan together, hoping you and Hussein would kill each other, then he was going to have it reported as a drugs deal gone wrong. He wanted to disgrace you both. That way, he believed he would satisfy everyone involved, especially Al Qaida and the INLA, that Hussein's death was not suspicious."

Eli looked down at the unconscious MI5 man on the floor. He hadn't finished with him yet, but now after what Carey had just told him he was going to be treated to something extra special. Looking at Oneway and Ringer, he moved to the next part of his plan.

"Put Fletcher in the chair and remove his shoes and socks. Make sure he can't move his legs."

Oneway and Ringer picked up the limp body and

fastened it tight to the chair, minus his footwear. Eli left the room and from the sounds emanating from the kitchen, he was searching the cupboards and drawers for something that he couldn't find. In the living room Fletcher was coming around, with the help of some water from a vase that used to contain some flowers being poured over his head. Once awake, he realised that he had changed places with Carey. Struggling to free himself from his bindings, he was stopped by the sight of Eli, coming back in to the room carrying what he had been looking for.

"What's that?" he asked in a terrified tone, meaning what was it for, and why was Eli carrying it in his hand.

"You should know," Eli, grinned. "It's your hammer. It's for hammering things like nails."

Eli waved the weighty tool under Fletcher's nose, close enough so he felt a slight breeze from its passing.

"But in this case," Eli added, "it's for toe nails." Fletcher looked down at his feet, only now realising that his shoes and socks had been removed.

"No," he began to beg. "No please. I didn't want to take your daughter. I was against it from the beginning."

Eli moved in front of Fletcher, and tossed the hammer in his hand.

"Do you think my daughter begged?" he asked of Fletcher, who was starting to blubber at the thought of what was about to happen. "When she was young if she got scared I used to sing nursery rhymes to her. Her favourite was the one about the little pigs going to market." Eli bent his right knee, lowering himself towards Fletcher's feet. "Hello little pigs," he said, looking up with a sadistic grin on his face.

"No, Moon. Please God, no," continued the begging. Oneway grabbed the pillow case that had been used to cover Carey's head earlier and stuffed it in Fletcher's mouth. Fletcher began to snort through his nose as he hyperventilated, searching for air.

"I'll sing it to you," said Eli, raising the hammer then starting from left to right he began the pounding his toes in a timed sing along with the rhyme. "This, little, piggy, went, to market." Each word was emphasized to coincide with a blow. Fletcher, screaming his muffled yells, turned his head whilst Ringer kept count to make sure that Eli hadn't missed any pinkies. "And, this, little, piggy, stayed at home." The second five digits on the other foot were subjected to the same treatment as the rhyme was continued. Fletcher, still screaming, threw his head from side to side, sending water from his tears and sweat about the room. Eli moved the hammer back to the first foot to continue the second verse of the rhyme. "This, little, piggy, had, roast, beef." Now he revisited the other. "And, this, little, piggy, had none. Fletcher was now once again unconscious after passing out with the pain. He slumped motionless in the chair, in a room without sympathy. Eli stood up, a little out of breath after his exercise, and removed the gripped, almost bitten in two, cigar from the corner of his mouth. "I'm going to have to cut down on these fucking things," he said with a slight pant and turning to Carey. Carey, still a bit shocked after witnessing Eli's form of justice, stood with an obvious look of relief on his face that he was no longer the occupier of the chair. "If you've still got a taste for undercover work after tonight, take your selection for the Regiment, I'll put in a good word for you. Not that you'll need it, I'm impressed that you didn't come clean and blow your cover when Ringer threw you out off that plane, even if you did shit your pants. Now fuck off and get out of my sight."

Carey didn't need telling twice. He left the house, not sure that he was cut out for that type of work anymore. Eli dropped the hammer, which landed at Fletcher's feet.

"Come on, we're done here," said Oneway, pulling the gag from Fletchers mouth. Ringer nodded in agreement before cutting the bindings that tethered Fletcher to the chair. On their way out Eli showed one piece of sympathy by lifting the phone in the hallway, dialling 999 and saying ambulance before leaving the receiver off the hook on the table. After that he only had one thing left to say.

"Be Lucky, Fletcher."

Outside the house, Errol, who had purposely stayed out of the proceedings had brought the Range Rover to the front door. As his friends climbed in he waited for answers.

"Well?" he asked. "Did you find out what you needed to know?"

"Yeah, everything's cushty. Come on, let's go to the pub."

"No Eli, did you find out that I knew nothing about what was going on with Kitty until Oneway and me walked in to the warehouse that day with the Irish lads and I recognised Khan?"

"Errol, I know you didn't. That's not what this was all about. I wasn't trying to get proof that my mate didn't cross me."

"I need to know you have no doubts in your mind. I came across Khan, working undercover in Morocco, about six years ago. When I saw him in that warehouse I couldn't believe it, but I couldn't say anything until I knew what was going on. When Khan told me what Fletcher had done, I knew if I told you that you would go off your nut and kill him. I had to let you see the plan you had come up with through to make sure we got Kitty back safe and sound."

"Errol, I know, we all know. You made a command

decision and ran with it, and it was the right one as was proved be me getting Kitty back and Hussein getting shot to pieces."

"And you know why I had to save Khan from Ringer. He was just a young undercover soldier doing his job."

"Errol, for fuck's sake, I know, we've just let him go ourselves and he's called Carey by the way. Now can we go to the pub? I'm starving. For some reason I could just eat a bit of tenderised steak. And I'm buying the beer, all night."

"No you're not. I am."

Oneway's interruption and statement was something that the other three had never heard pass his lips before. They all turned and looked at him in disbelief.

Don't look so surprised. After what I've just seen in there," he explained, "you're not taking me out, and getting me hammered!"

Chapter Twenty

The Healthy Option

A couple of weeks before the following Christmas, Eli had made arrangements to meet the Irish lads back at the farm outside Belfast for the final divvy up. By the time he arrived the money had already been retrieved and stacked in one million pound piles on and around the kitchen table that they used to plan the robbery a year earlier. Kitty and Pat were with him and as he drove the vehicle around the back of the barn to where the lads were congregated watching Sean backfill the hole for the third time, Kitty climbed out with a present she had brought him to say thank you for looking after her when they last met. She held out her hands which contained Sean's favourite pass time, apart from smoking and drinking, a KFC party bucket. Leaning out of the cab to retrieve the gift he smiled with happiness at the sight of the young lady, but true to form decided to have a little fun.

"I don't suppose you've got one of your dad's cigars for after, have ye? I'm in a mood to celebrate."

"I've given them up," said Eli, overhearing his request.

"What, completely?" replied Sean, shocked and disgusted.

"Completely," confirmed Eli. "It's part of the new healthier life style that Kitty and Pat have got me on – cycling, jogging and swimming. I feel like a new recruit again."

"You'll kill yeself," were Sean's thoughts on his new regime.

"Don't listen to him, Eli," advised Michael, "Ye look grand. Peewee," he shouted looking for his brother. Peter stuck his head out of the barn. "Come here and show Kitty around the farm whilst I talk to her dad."

Peter didn't look happy.

"There's nothing to see except cow shit," he replied, turning his gaze back to watching the JCB.

"Then show her that, it shout be right up your street your always talking it."

Peter, giving Eli a long cheeky stare, remembering him from the year before, did as he was told so the conversation could get down to business. Kitty looked at her dad with a few blushes showing at being thrown in to the young boy's company.

"It's ok, love," he reassured. "Go with him, but don't stand for any of his lip." The pair set off down the yard after young Peter had passed back another one of his dirty looks.

"Is Peter not a bit young to be around all this?" asked Eli.

"The wee fella's seventeen now, he's got to learn the crack sooner or later, and more importantly he has to learn to keep his mouth shut. He starts Engineering College next month in London. I don't want all those Cockney wide boys thinking they can pull the wool over his eyes."

"I doubt that, if our last conversation is anything to go by. I suppose you're right, though. Kitty's sixteen next, and she already has me and Pat jumping through hoops."

"Anyway," said Michael, getting down to business. "Danny and Dermot are just after finishing the count and there's just over sixteen million left after the ten you already have."

"How is it after its year in the ground?" asked Eli.

"It's a bit damp and smelly but it's nothing that an hour under Roisin's hair dryer won't sort out."

"Why don't you just buy a big tumble dryer and throw it in for ten minutes, a hundred grand at a time," suggested Eli. "Throw in a few squirts of air freshener and no one will be any the wiser as to its location for the last twelve months."

The Irish lads looked at each other, wondering why none of them had thought of that.

"Fuck that," said Sean, "We'll buy a fucking launderette and do the fucking lot in one go."

With the Irish now smiling, Michael asked Eli what to do with his share of the remainder.

"Keep it," he replied with a shock revelation. "We don't need it. We have the ten, plus the other from before, and Yardie Allan has started paying his monthly dues again."

"Well what did ye come here for if it wasn't for the money?" asked Dermot.

Eli, gave him one of his lingering stares, one that would normally be accompanied by a smoking of his cigar.

"I came to see my mates of course, and to wish you all a happy Christmas. And I'm taking Kitty over the border to show her Mountmellick, where all her Irish ancestors came from, the Moss's and the Dunns and of course the Keenans or the Kinahan's as we used to be known in the old days."

"Three million fucking quid," said Danny. "It's a lot to give away."

"Well I figure if I ever need a U-boat big man, I can always come back and see you lads."

"U-boat," guessed Sean. You mean a sub. I'm getting better at that Cockney talk."

He got his fags out and placed one in his mouth before offering them around, stretching his arm out towards Eli.

"I've told you, I've stopped. You might as well do the same because they're going to ban it in the pubs within the next three years."

Sean's cigarette dropped in his mouth.

"Ban smoking in the bars?" he repeated, looking at the pack in his hand like he could be losing a best friend. "I don't believe that."

"If you don't believe that, Sean," answered Eli, "then don't believe anything I've ever told you. Right lads, I'm off. We have to make Mountmellick by night fall."

Eli, called to his daughter to join Patricia back in the car and after shaking each of the Irish lads hands, he joined them before lowering his window and voicing some last advice.

"Remember this my treasonous comrades. Now that you have the money, you've got to live to spend it, and as soon as you start spending it, people are going to notice. If you want my advice, I would sell up and get out of Ireland to somewhere that you are not so well known. But whatever you do keep switched on and remember those 7P's because I don't want to lose any of my mates because they got sloppy."

The lads knew his words were voiced because of worry and concern, but there only reply was to raise their hands in a good-bye motion.

"Be lucky, chaps."

"Eli," shouted Michael. "You owe me a name."

Eli smiled as though accepting his debt but now wasn't the time for Michael's revengeful education.

"There's plenty of time for naming grasses, but not right now. Chill out for a while, smell the roses and spend some time with your family. We will see each other again and I will fill in the blanks."

"Don't leave it too long."

Eli could see that Michael didn't want to let it go. He was like a dog with a bone and eager to put things right.

"Do you remember when we shared a bottle in that kitchen before the robbery?"

"I do,"

"That night I told you a lot about myself and the Falklands but I didn't tell you that one slipped through our fingers. A bastard that committed atrocities against innocent people, young and old just the same as the man whose name you want to know but this fucker killed thousands of students and even stole babies. His name was Menendez. He was the commander in charge of the Argentine forces and we had him but we didn't know at the time what he had done, otherwise we would have nutted him before the top brass got involved. It was only when we talked to the prisoners, his own men who hated him that we learned who he was and what he had done back in Argentina as the head of the secret police. The government though, they knew and they let him go. Why, who knows but what I do know is that sometimes, something's are bigger than we are and although it doesn't seem fair we have to let things go."

Michael for a second pondered Eli's words.

"So you think I should let this Tout, the British Government had. This collaborator who murdered innocent Irish people go because the situation is bigger than I am?"

Eli, for once short of a word simply shrugged his shoulders before Michael continued.

"So tell me. If you ever saw him again, this Menendez. Would let it go?"

Eli smiled.

"Of course not. I'd kill the bastard."

Eli pulled away, leaving the four Irish each with their own thoughts in a silence that lasted until his vehicle had disappeared down the drive and out of the front gates. As usual it was Sean that broke the moment of contemplation.

"No smoking in the bars within two years. Who does he think he's kidding? What a load of FUCKING BOLLOCKS."

TO BE CONTINUED

SADLY, AND HEARTBREAKINGLY THIS BOOK IS DEDICATED TO THE MEMORY OF

SEAN 'FATTY' KEENAN. ROBERT MICHAEL TOMES, 'DOG'S NOB.' TERRY 'THE NICEST MAN IN BRADFORD' KEENAN, AND NIGEL 'THE JAM' 'DOYLEY' DOYLE. SELFISHLY, I CAN NOT FORGIVE YOU FOR DYING AND TAKING THE CRACK OUT OF MY LIFE. I MISS YOU MY BROTHERS BUT REST ASSURED THAT YOU WILL BE IN MY HEART AND THOUGHTS UNTIL THE DAY WE MEET AGAIN xx

The 7 P's

The 7 P's. An unusual title you may think, but its meaning will become as apparent to you as it did for four friends and comrades who, in a desperate move of self-preservation, escaped the troubles of 1980s Northern Ireland, and their home town of Belfast, only to find themselves just as deep, if not deeper, in trouble of a different kind on the treacherous streets of London.

The foursome are no strangers to danger, usually brought about for the other three by following the antics of their friend and leader, Michael Flynn, but this time young Flynn has opened a can of worms that will seem impossible to put the lid back on. London will now prove to be the toughest situation they have ever faced and to survive it they are going to have to do what they do best: stick together and fight for their lives.

The 7 P's is the first installment in a trilogy that will drag you into a sprawling story of violence, deceit, greed, and loyalty, where it becomes harder to distinguish the good guys from the bad. It is a white-knuckle ride of a read, based upon the author's real-life experiences, fictionalized to protect both the innocent and the guilty.

The 7 P's will appeal to fans of both fiction and true crime alike, but just when the reader may think he/she has an understanding of the world they have been drawn into, their preconceptions will be turned upside down by stinging twists that will leave them reeling for the continuing tale of Book Two and three?

Book Two of ZANI's Tales Trilogy

THE MAGNIFICENT SIX IN TALES OF AGGRO

Foreword by Drummer Steve White (The Style Council, Paul Weller, Trio Valore,)
'A vivid and enjoyable slice of London life in the 80s, with a wealth of detail and characters,'

'Tales of Aggro has got the feel of 'Green Street' and a touch of 'Lock Stock and Two Smoking Barrels'. This is fiction for realists.'
Vive Le Rock

'A real slice of life told in the vernacular of the streets'
Irvine Welsh

'Laugh out loud funny, exciting and above all, written with real warmth and passion for London and the Character's making their way through this tale and life itself.'
Gents of London

'It's A Treat to Read, Just Like A Crafty Cigarette'
John Cooper Clarke

'Tales of Aggro is lively and funny'
Phil Davis (British Actor - Quadrophenia, Silk, The Firm)

'Tales of Aggro is a kind of time machine that takes one back to the days of 'Scrubbers', 'Scum' and 'Get Carter'. Very redolent of those atmospherics.'
Jonathan Holloway – Theatre Director and Playwright

Meet Oscar De Paul, Eddie the Casual, Dino, Quicksilver, Jamie Joe and Honest Ron, collectively known around the streets of West London as The Magnificent Six. This gang of working-class lovable rogues have claimed Shepherds Bush and White City as their playground and are not going to let anyone spoil the fun.

Meet Stephanie, a wannabe pop star who is determined to knock spots off the Spice Girls, with her girl group. Above all though, meet West London and hear the stories of ordinary people getting up to extraordinary adventures.

Please note that Tales of Aggro is a work of fiction.

ISBN-13 : 978-1527235823

Book Three of ZANI's Tales Trilogy

TALES FROM THE FOXES OF FOXHAM

It is the late fifties and the Witches of Benevento are determined to plunge the world into darkness by kidnapping and sacrificing the jolly and young Neapolitan fox, Alberto Bandito, in a sinister ritual.

Yet, fortunately for Alberto, he is rescued, then guarded, by his loving mother Silvia and mob boss father Mario with his troops, a good witch Carlotta with an uncanny resemblance to Marilyn Monroe, the Bears of Campania, the boxing wolves' brothers Francesco and Leonardo, and other good folks of Naples and beyond.

However, their protection is not enough, for Alberto has been cursed. So, the young fox, along with his family, has to travel to the village of Foxham in Norfolk, the spiritual home of foxes across the world, to rid himself of this spell. The ritual has to be performed by a good fox witch, Trudi Milanese, but there is a problem, Trudi doesn't know she is a witch....

Tales from The Foxes of Foxham is a magical adventure story, packed with colourful characters and exciting situations, in a battle of good versus evil.

ISBN-13 : 978-1-8384624-0-6

PERFORMERS

Irvine Welsh and Dean Cavanagh revisit the dying days of the 1960s to reimagine what happened during the making of the first true British cult film.

They Don't Think They're Gonna Let You Stay in the Film Business.

Performers deals with masculinity at the point when the sexual revolution was saturating culture. For many working-class men, it was confusing and threatening. As secularism started to replace traditional Judaeo-Christian attitudes, a lot of men found themselves torn between embracing the liberation and clinging to the simpler, more morally binary past.

In the swinging and hallucinogenic London of 1968, visionary Scottish filmmaker Donald Cammell joined forces with cinematographer Nicolas Roeg to make "Performance". The film would star James Fox, Mick Jagger, and Anita Pallenberg, but the casting process was frustrating for Cammell because he insisted on bringing "real villains" into the roles that supported the lead character of South London gangster Chas Devlin.

What Welsh and Cavanagh identify is that strange cultural moment in 1960's London when bohemian intelligentsia flirted with the world of organised crime

VARIETY

MORE BOOKS FROM ZANI

www.zani.co.uk

Feltham Made Me – Paolo Sedazzari

Foreword by Mark Savage (Grange Hill)

The poet Richard F. Burton likened the truth to a large mirror, shattered into millions upon millions of pieces. Each of us owns a piece of that mirror, believing our one piece to be the whole truth. But you only get to see the whole truth when we put all the pieces together. This is the concept behind Feltham Made Me. It is the story of three lads growing up together in the suburbs of London, put together from the transcripts of many hours of interview.

ISBN-13 : 978-1527210608

The Secret Life Of The Novel: Faking Your Death is Illegal, Faking Your Life is Celebrated - Dean Cavanagh

"A unique metaphysical noir that reads like a map to the subconscious." **Irvine Welsh**

A militant atheist Scientist working at the CERN laboratory in Switzerland tries to make the flesh into Word whilst a Scotland Yard Detective is sent to Ibiza to investigate a ritual mass murder that never took place. Time is shown to be fragmenting before our very eyes as Unreliable Narrators, Homicidal Wannabe Authors, Metaphysical Tricksters & Lost Souls haunt the near life experiences of an Ampersand who is trying to collect memories to finish a novel nobody will ever read. Goat Killers, Apocalyptic Pirate Radio DJ's, Dead Pop Stars, Social Engineers and Cartoon Characters populate a twilight landscape that may or may not exist depending on who's narrating at the time.

ISBN-13 : 978-1527201538

7P'S Paperback – A.G.R

The 7 P's. An unusual title you may think, but its meaning will become as apparent to you as it did for four friends and comrades who, in a desperate move of self-preservation, escaped the troubles of 1980s Northern Ireland, and their hometown of Belfast, only to find themselves just as deep, if not deeper, in trouble of a different kind on the treacherous streets of London.

ISBN-13 : 978-1527258365

Printed in Great Britain
by Amazon

63891408R00393